PRAISE FOR

# RUTHLESS

"Smart, savvy, clever, and always entertaining. That's true of Riley Lawless, the hero in *Ruthless*, and likewise for his creator, Lexi Blake. Both are way ahead of the pack."

—*New York Times* bestselling author Steve Berry

## PRAISE FOR THE NOVELS OF LEXI BLAKE

"Explosive and intriguing."                           —Sultry Steamy Reading

"A satisfying snack of love, romance, and hot, steamy sex."

—Sizzling Hot Books

"Hot and emotional."                                —Two Lips Reviews

## PRAISE FOR THE PERFECT GENTLEMEN SERIES BY SHAYLA BLACK AND LEXI BLAKE

"Hot and edgy and laced with danger, the stories in the Perfect Gentlemen series are just that—perfect."

—*New York Times* bestselling author J. Kenner

"While there are certainly incendiary sex scenes at the top of this series opener, the strength is in the underlying murder and political mystery."                                —*RT Book Reviews*

*Titles by Lexi Blake*

*The Lawless Novels*

RUTHLESS

SATISFACTION

*The Perfect Gentlemen Novels*
(with Shayla Black)

SCANDAL NEVER SLEEPS

SEDUCTION IN SESSION

BIG EASY TEMPTATION

# Satisfaction

## LEXI BLAKE

BERKLEY
NEW YORK

BERKLEY
An imprint of Penguin Random House LLC
375 Hudson Street, New York, New York 10014

Library of Congress Cataloging-in-Publication Data

Names: Blake, Lexi, author.
Title: Satisfaction / Lexi Blake.
Description: First edition. | New York : Berkley, 2017. | Series: A Lawless
novel ; 2
Identifiers: LCCN 2016036493 (print) | LCCN 2016040795 (ebook) | ISBN
9780425283585 (softcover) | ISBN 9780698410312 (eBook)
Subjects: | BISAC: FICTION / Romance / Contemporary. | FICTION / Romance /
Suspense. | FICTION / Romance / General. | GSAFD: Romantic suspense
fiction. | Erotic fiction.
Classification: LCC PS3602.L3456 S28 2017 (print) | LCC PS3602.L3456 (ebook)
| DDC 813/.6—dc23
LC record available at https://lccn.loc.gov/2016036493

First Edition: January 2017

Printed in the United States of America
1   3   5   7   9   10   8   6   4   2

Photos: Traffic through downtown LA © Mikhail Tchkheidze/Shutterstock;
Man in shirt © Connor Evans/Shutterstock
Cover design by Sanny Chiu
Book design by Laura K. Corless

# *Acknowledgments*

Thanks to Berkley and the whole staff there. To my amazing editor, Kate Seaver, and agent, Merrilee Heifetz. Thanks to my girl Friday, Kim Guidroz, who never lets me down. Thanks to Inkslinger and my publicist, Danielle Sanchez. You're the best, Dani. And to my beta-readers, Stormy Pate, Riane Holt, and Kori Smith. You guys keep me honest and make me a better writer! Love to the awesome Liz Berry and Jillian Stein.

# *Prologue*

LOS ANGELES, CA

Carly sat back and took a deep breath. It was over. Almost. One last thing and then she could go home and figure out exactly what to do with the rest of her life.

She could sell the car. It was the only viable asset she had. The house would go back to the bank. That hurt. She'd turned that little townhouse into something beautiful. She would be lucky to find an apartment building that would rent to her. Very likely she would end up working retail or at some fast food restaurant. Everything she'd worked for was one big steaming pile of crap.

That's what happened when a girl fell for a slick con artist.

She'd lost her husband. She was about to lose her job, the domino that would send all the others falling—house, status, car. No more nice shoes for Carly. She would be lucky to have the money to buy secondhand, much less the Manolos and Prada she'd worn for the last few years because her boss insisted she look the part of Patricia Cain's right arm. She'd learned fast that Patricia Cain's right arm wore some expensive shit. But then so did her left arm, ankle, knee, and every other part of her.

She was about to lose a job millions of women would kill for.

Thank God.

She tidied up her desk and prepared for the confrontation. Ever since that moment when the police had hauled Roger off in handcuffs, she'd known this was coming. Carly glanced down the hallway. She wished it could have happened while they were in St. Augustine, where she wouldn't have to find a way back home, but Los Angeles was as good a place as any to make her final stand.

The door to the office opened and Emily's eyes flared as she took in the sight of Carly at her desk. "Fred from accounting said you were here. I didn't believe him. What are you doing?"

She was being brave for once. "I'm waiting to speak with Patricia."

"Because you're going to murder her?" Emily let the door slam behind her. "Oh God, you're going to do it, aren't you? Everyone's always said one day her assistant would strangle her. I knew you would be the one to do it. You're not an evil sheep like the rest of them."

"I'm not going to murder her." Though she'd often thought about it.

Emily shot her a sympathetic look. "She had your husband arrested. No one would blame you."

"The police would. Also the DA. Probably a jury of my peers, too. Roger embezzled a million dollars from Cain Corp. He deserves to go to jail." She believed every single accusation leveled at her soon-to-be ex-husband. She would throw in a couple more. Cheating. Lying. Gambling. Running up her credit cards, which she soon would have no way to pay for. And she'd bought it all for two years. She'd been the one to get him the job here where he'd managed to embezzle all that lovely money he'd spent on God knew what.

Now it was time to pay the piper. Or the righteous bitch, in this case. Patricia Cain would never pipe. Far below her dignity.

Emily worked on the magazine side of the business as a copyeditor. She was a nice girl, one Carly always had lunch with when they were in LA. "Seriously, you should walk out. She's going to be so mean to you."

And that was different how? "I'm going to give her my letter of resignation and leave with some dignity."

She had the cheapest ticket she could find online sitting in her purse waiting for her getaway. She left LAX for Jacksonville at eight tonight. She would find the cheapest wine she could and drown her sorrows.

And celebrate a little because she never had to see Patricia Cain's cosmetically enhanced face again. She never had to deal with another of that woman's issues. She was getting out right as the Queen of Domestic Bliss was planning her own wedding to a disgusting billionaire whose greatest talent seemed to be his ability to leer at women half his age and younger without a single ounce of shame.

Freedom. This was the one good thing Roger had done for her. She was going to be free.

What she'd never worked up the nerve to do was finally out of her hands. She'd worked for Patricia Cain for three hellish years, all the while telling herself it was only a matter of time before she was rewarded for all the ridiculously late nights and degrading tasks. She would do her time, make her connections, and then move on in the world. Everyone knew Patricia never kept an assistant for more than five years, and then she moved them out into the vast network of TV and publishing and home goods businesses that paid her considerable rent. A shiny new assistant would be brought in and the old one put out to happier pastures.

She couldn't hold out that long. Two more years of working for the ice queen would kill her no matter what was waiting at the end of the rainbow. Some things weren't worth the price she had to pay.

Now it was over and she could find a life free of Patricia Cain and Roger. She was going to be broke with zero prospects, and that suddenly seemed pretty damn fine to her.

The door opened again and Patricia entered. She was dressed in a Chanel business suit, her icy blond hair in a bun. When she filmed her highly rated television show, *Patricia's Paradise*, she wore denim and even T-shirts, her hair down and flowing, her makeup understated. She was the face of new American domesticity. Elegant but casual. Inviting.

This was the real Patricia. A shark in a designer suit. She turned her cold eyes Emily's way. "Out."

Without another word, Emily scurried away and Carly was left alone.

There was nothing to do but get this over with. She'd been terrified of this woman for long enough.

"Ms. Cain, I waited because I wanted to give this to you personally." She held up her well-thought-out resignation letter.

Patricia looked at it like it was something diseased. "No, thank you. I think we should have this discussion in my office. Where is my coffee?"

She started her day with a triple shot vanilla latte, no foam, no sugar. Every day without fail for the last three years, Carly had it waiting for her. Not today.

"This is my resignation letter, Ms. Cain. I'm no longer your assistant. You'll have to find someone else to get your coffee. I'll leave this here for you but I've also sent you an e-copy of the letter as well. Good luck finding someone new."

She wouldn't need it. There would be a line of applicants a mile long once word got out Carly had quit. After the news from last night, there might already be one forming. Roger's arrest had been all over the news, so there was no doubt people would be talking.

The never-ending backbiting and gossip—one more thing she wouldn't miss.

Patricia stared at her, cold snakelike eyes assessing. "I think you should come to my office, Carly. I have a few things I need to say to you. Legal things."

She thought about running out the door and not looking back. It would be easy since Patricia had turned and strode into her office, her heels thudding along the tasteful hardwood floors. Something about the way her boss had said the word *legal* made her follow.

She'd signed a contract when she'd first become Patricia's assistant. Carly's brain worked overtime thinking about what all she'd agreed to in exchange for a halfway decent salary, clothing allowance, and travel budget. All she'd had to sign away was her soul.

There had been a ton of nondisclosure stuff, which given some of her boss's proclivities was a damn fine idea. No tell-all books would be written about Patricia Cain by one of her assistants without a nice long legal battle. She'd been required to live within fifteen minutes of her boss's St. Augustine mansion. There had been a ton of blah-blah legal stuff, but she couldn't remember anything about a requirement that she stay for a certain length of time or there would be penalties. She was fairly certain that wasn't even legal. Patricia couldn't keep her here, so she followed along.

One last battle.

"Close the door behind you," Patricia said without turning around.

Carly shut it and faced Patricia as she lowered herself into her antique chair behind a desk Carly was fairly certain had once had a place at Versailles. "Did you need more than the resignation? I could give you a week or two, but after last night I thought you would want me gone."

Patricia settled back, crossing her long legs one over the other. "Last night was about your husband. Not you. I certainly don't think you were either smart enough or ballsy enough to try to steal from me."

Yes, there was the wit she'd come to love so much. "Still, I was dumb enough to marry him and bring him into the company. I think it's best we sever ties. I'm in the middle of divorcing him, but I'll still have to spend time dealing with the fallout of his arrest."

"Yes, timing is a problem, is it not? I've got the fall TV launch and there's the issue of my wedding to Kenneth. Having to break in a new assistant would be difficult."

Her stomach dropped. "I'm sure you can find one who will work."

"But I think you'll work nicely. You see there's something you don't know, dear. Something I've kept from my legal team and will continue to keep from them. Your husband stole two million dollars. Not one. He was quite intelligent but I'm smarter. Well, the people I pay for these types of things are smarter. Would you like to know whose name the second account was in?"

Her belly was now in complete free fall. "He wouldn't."

A laugh came from Patricia's mouth, but it was somehow sinister. "Not you, dear. That would have been far too easy. No. He asked your sweet sister to open an account. I believe he told her it was so he could buy you an anniversary present without you knowing about it."

Anger flared through her. She would kill Roger. She could actually see herself doing it. Meri was in college. She had her whole life ahead of her. There was nothing on the planet Carly loved more than her younger sister, and she could easily see Meri getting scammed into thinking she was doing something good. "My sister didn't have anything to do with this."

"Oh, but she did. That money is in her name. We caught Roger before he had a chance to withdraw it," Patricia said slowly. She sighed and sat back. "I've thought long and hard about this. You see, I realize I'm a difficult woman to work for. I like things certain ways, and you're quite good at following orders. I let the other assistants go because I needed them in other areas of the business. They form a network of sorts."

"They feed you information." What did any of this have to do with her sister? She would have to find a lawyer. She would fight this. There was no way she was letting her sister take the fall for Roger's greed.

"Yes, they spy for me. They tell me who's screwing who and who's meeting with my competitors. They take care of people I need taken care of. I realized about six months into your employment that you would never be good at that type of work. You have an air of innocence about you that's quite cloying."

No, she wouldn't spy on her fellow employees. It was easy to see she'd been incredibly naive. "All good reasons to let me go. But Meredith didn't touch that money, Ms. Cain."

"Yes, as I said, I know that. But it does make for very good leverage. I'm tired of training new assistants. I want one who is completely loyal to me. If I can't have that then I'll have one who is so afraid of what I can do to her that she'll fall in line. I decided long ago that it's better to be feared than loved. You've read Machiavelli, I presume."

It made complete sense to her that Patricia would quote Renaissance philosophy about how to rule the peasants to her. After all, this woman truly believed she was a queen, the type who took her crown by force. "Of course."

"Well then you understand where I'm coming from. I have plenty of spies. I need a mouse who'll do anything I say. I've got all the documentation, and your husband was more than willing to sign a statement saying your sister was involved. Eventually the statute of limitations on prosecution will run out, but I think until then, you and I will get along fine."

"What is this really about?" It couldn't be about having an employee who was certain to hate her.

The slightest smile curved her lips up. "You'll also go on public record as being deeply grateful to me for allowing you to keep your job after the horrible thing your husband did. I will pay for the lawyer and your divorce. You'll discuss how kind I am and how you were certain you would be out in the cold."

Shit. It all fell into place. Three weeks before, the *New York Times* had run a story on Cain Corp using Third World sweatshops to make cheap home goods. They'd found she'd paid pennies to young women who worked in the most terrible of conditions. "The network thinks your image is ruined and you're trying to rehab it."

"They think I could use a shine, and you're going to do it for me. Like I said, you have an air of innocence. It's what attracted that man to you in the first place. He knew he could use you. Now I'm going to use you. We're doing a special with one of the morning shows. We'll be flying to Cambodia and visiting the women who were horribly taken advantage of. Naturally I knew nothing about the conditions. It's certainly my responsibility, but I am horrified. After all, I do everything I can to lift other women up."

And drop them off the roof. "I won't do it. You knew exactly what was happening in those factories. You signed the papers authorizing a pay cut and longer hours."

"Did I? I doubt you'll be able to find that. No, I was foolish and taken advantage of as well. Now, you should decide if you're going to stay and do your job or if you would prefer for your sister to go to jail."

Her hands were shaking. Actually shaking. There was zero doubt in her mind that Patricia would do it. She never bluffed. The devil didn't have to. The devil always won. "I'll go get your coffee."

"And, Carly?"

She turned. "Yes, ma'am?"

"Drop some weight before we go to Cambodia. I can't have you looking like a cow on screen."

Carly walked out, wondering if she'd ever feel whole again.

# Chapter One

*Two years later*
St. Augustine, FL

Carly let the sunshine hit her face and sighed. A whole afternoon. One entire afternoon off and she was doing what with it? Meeting some ridiculously hot guy at a restaurant who would take one look at her, turn, and run. Drew. His name was Drew and the picture the matchmaking company had sent showed a blond man in his thirties who should probably be on the cover of a magazine. Had it been an online service, she might have felt more comfortable. People on those always used the absolutely most flattering picture they could. Sometimes they were years old and pounds of weight ago. Sometimes they were flat-out lies.

But the service she was using actually took the picture themselves. No lies. No hedging the truth. He was that hot.

She hesitated on the street outside the restaurant. It was a tiny Italian place in the middle of the old city. She loved this part of St. Augustine, with its cobblestone streets and tourists walking around. The sea was never far from here and she could feel a breeze from the Atlantic.

What was she doing? Why was she even trying?

Her cell rang, the sound emanating from her massive bag. It had to be massive because she was forced to carry around anything Patricia might need. That was her. She was a walking, talking convenience for the Antichrist.

Who was probably calling to revoke her afternoon off. Patricia rarely giveth, but she was awfully good at taking away.

This was one time it might come in handy. She grabbed her phone and frowned as the real reason she was standing in front of a restaurant wearing her finest Spanx and more makeup than normal was smiling from the screen. She flicked her hand across, accepting the call. "Hey, Meri. I thought you were finishing up class."

"I got out early and I wanted to make sure you're where you're supposed to be."

Sometimes her sister's instincts were scary good. "I'm at the restaurant, but only to tell him I changed my mind. This was a mistake."

Meri groaned. "No, it's not. Come on, Carly. I read the file on this guy. He's hot."

"How did you read the file?" Not that she should be surprised. Along with good instincts, Meri also had the tenacity of a pit bull with a particularly juicy bone.

"I took a peek last week when I was at your place."

"That's called invading my privacy." She tried her best big-sister voice.

It didn't faze Meri at all. "Yes, it's my favorite hobby! And that Drew guy is superhot. They should have the dudes take their shirts off."

"Hello, sexist much? What are they teaching you at that school?"

"That men have objectified women for thousands of years and we need to catch up. When he gets there ask him if he has those notches on his hips. That is so hot."

"I'm not asking him to strip down. I'm asking him to leave," she admitted. "I'm not ready for this. Even if I was ready for this, it wouldn't be with him. I want a nice, normal guy. One who isn't a felon. That's a hard line for me."

"Not every man in the world is Roger," Meri pointed out.

No, they weren't, but that one mistake wouldn't seem to go away. She thought about the message she'd gotten a few days before. Her husband owed money and they were coming after her for it. She'd tried telling them they were divorced and she wasn't responsible for some debt he'd taken on in prison, but apparently the mob wasn't big on divorce.

She put it out of her head. She would go to the cops. It would all go away. First she needed to deal with the problem of hot Drew and her sister's need to get her laid.

"I know that. But it was really bad and I need more me time."

Meri sighed over the line. "It's been two years. It's going to dry up. I learned that in my anatomy class. If you don't use it, a vagina turns to dust."

Her sister was so nasty sometimes, but Carly had to laugh. "Well, I will sweep that sucker up, then, because it's gotten me into a lot of trouble in the past." She sighed, missing her sister since she transferred to Duke. "I'll meet him and talk to him, but don't expect more than that."

"It's all I ask," Meri replied, sounding chipper. "Well, and that you give me all the dirty details. Tell me something. Have you thought about dumping Patricia the Terrible and moving up here with me? I found a job at the school you would love."

Yeah, she likely would. And then her sister might see the inside of a prison cell. Two more years. She had two more years until the statute of limitations ran out and her sister was free and clear. "You know I love my job."

There was a pause on the line. "I know you say that. I don't know how much I believe it. All right. I love you. Call me later and tell me everything and stop frowning."

The line clicked and she put her phone back in her bag. She wasn't frowning. Well, maybe a bit. The waitress showed her to a table on the patio overlooking the street.

She would smile, shake his hand, and they would both laugh about the mistake. They were horrifically mismatched.

She glanced down at the menu. Of course, he might not show at all. She might get to sit here in the sun and have a lovely meal that didn't include salad and she would pull out her tablet and read. That would be awesome. Lasagna and a book. Maybe a glass of pinot and some cheesecake. All alone.

She was sure that sounded pitiful to some people, but it was the perfect afternoon for her. Peace, quiet, solitude. No overbearing bosses or their lecherous husbands. If that man accidentally touched her ass one more time, she wasn't going to care that he was eighty-seven. He would get a colonoscopy the hard way. She would shove that cane of his right up his keister.

She glanced out and saw a man walking up the street. Whoa. Now, there was a man she could look at for days. With dark hair that curled around his ears, he looked like a movie star. She noticed two other women stopping to stare at him as he passed.

Was there a movie filming in town? No. Patricia always knew about those. She would try to get the stars to give her magazine an interview or get them on her show to talk about home decorating tips.

Of course, Patricia had been distracted lately. Ever since she'd come back from the funeral of an old business partner, she'd been distant, not quite her old evil self. Oh, she humiliated Carly at least twice a day, but she lacked the vigor and glee she used to have.

Carly had to wonder if Steven Castalano had been the one true love Patricia had talked about that night when she'd gotten too drunk, the day before her wedding when she'd acted almost human. That was the night she'd seen the devil cry.

Five more minutes and she would declare herself free and clear.

Maybe she would switch restaurants in case this Drew guy was the kind of man who showed up super late to a date. Columbia wasn't far away. She could get some sangria and Cuban food.

Anything to enjoy her one afternoon to herself. Soon they would go back to LA and the guesthouse she stayed in there. It was close to Patricia's Santa Monica mansion. Close enough that she could be at Patricia's side in less than a minute. She knew that because Patricia had timed her and told her not to go over that minute. The guesthouse was nice, but it had nothing of Carly in it. She would miss her townhouse.

Two more years. Just two more years.

She watched as the incredibly hot man walked her way. Not hers, of course, but in the general direction she was sitting in. Not general. Actual. He was walking right toward her, and that was when the grin hit his face.

When his lips curled up, he went from brooding god to an angel. The dark, fallen kind who could do all manner of dirty things because they weren't stuck up in heaven anymore.

When the hell had she gotten so creative?

He pulled out the chair across from Carly. "Hey, my name is Brandon Lawless."

She looked around. This was some kind of joke. It had to be. Or he was seriously mistaken. He didn't look drunk, but some guys hid it well. "Um, you have the wrong girl."

His grin moved to a full-out smile and she had to catch her breath. "Nope. I've got the right girl. Carly, your boss murdered my parents twenty years ago. What do you say you help me bring her to justice?"

"Are you insane?" She looked around again. There was definitely a camera hidden somewhere. She wouldn't put it past some network to talk Patricia into pranking her assistant. She would do it in a heartbeat if she thought it would help her image.

"Not at all. I'm quite serious."

So pretty and so crazy. "Look, I'm waiting for a date so I don't have time to talk." Something about what he'd said earlier clicked in her brain. "How did you know my name?"

He sat back, his eyes piercing into her. "I know everything about you."

A chill went through her as she realized exactly who this person could be. "Who sent you?"

He frowned, the expression marring his beauty not one bit. "Sent me? No one. You were supposed to meet with my brother, but he was going to confuse things and turn this whole operation into one big spy game. Our sister married a guy who's kind of a spy. He works for the CIA from time to time. I think Drew's jealous of Case. He's always thought he would make a good James Bond. But our last spy thing went horribly wrong and my new sister-in-law got arrested and almost walked out on Riley and . . . I should start at the beginning. First off, call me Bran. Everyone does. I'm not fond of Brandon."

He talked superfast. She didn't understand most of what he was saying, but she needed to get her point across. "Tell DiLuca that I don't care what Roger is doing in prison. His debts are no longer mine. Get with the damn twenty-first century. We're divorced. Shiv him or something. I don't care, but stop harassing me."

"What?"

She started to push her chair back. "You heard me. Tell your boss I'll go to the cops if he calls me again."

She stood to go, but he was faster. He got into her space, his hand shooting out to grasp her wrist. The touch sent a wave of heat through her. He didn't tighten his grip or try to force her to sit back down. The hand that wrapped around her was gentle and his eyes softened.

"Are you in trouble, sweetheart? Because I can help you."

She almost believed him. "You can let me go."

His hand dropped immediately but he was still in her space, his big body towering over her. She wasn't tiny but this man made her feel practically petite. "I can't. Please let me explain myself. I'll pay for lunch and everything. I'm not from this DiLuca person. He's not my boss. My brother would tell you he's the boss of me, but I protest. He'll probably try to fire me for fucking this up, but I don't think you can fire your little brother."

He was so close but somehow she didn't feel overwhelmed or threatened by him. His words were almost sweet. Still, she knew her instincts were a faulty thing. "I should go. I don't know what's going on with your brother, but it's none of my business."

"Let me make it your business. Carly, I've studied you and I think you're a good woman trapped in a nasty world. My parents were in your position twenty years ago and Patricia Cain murdered them. I don't want that to happen to you. Please let me make my case. If you can look at me and tell me the Patricia Cain you work for isn't capable of murder, then I will apologize for interrupting your afternoon and let you be. If you can't, please help me. I'm not looking for revenge. I'm looking for justice. For my parents."

There was absolutely nothing in his manner or demeanor that told her he was lying. This gorgeous man was asking her for help and she wanted to turn him away. Years of working under that woman and her marriage to Roger had turned her cold and uncaring of anyone but her sister. It was the only way to protect herself. She would do the smart thing and simply walk away.

Carly moved back, her hand on her chair as she began to sit down. He immediately moved in, holding the chair for her and easing her back to the table.

She was still the same idiot she'd been years ago, and suddenly there was something comforting about that knowledge. She wasn't as hard as she'd thought. The minute the chance to help someone else had come up, her dumb ass was sitting back down and trying to do the right thing.

"Hey, are you all right?" He was standing above her and his hand came down, thumb running over her cheek to catch the tear she hadn't realized she'd shed. "I don't want to hurt you."

She took a deep breath. "I'm fine. Please tell me your story because we both know that she's capable of anything."

It was a risk. He could have been sent here by Patricia herself to test Carly's loyalty, though Carly doubted it. Patricia was too self-centered to think Carly could hurt her.

Yes, it was a risk, but maybe it was a risk that would pay off.

He sat back down across from her and picked up his menu. "Lunch is on me. It's a long story. I think we'll need some wine."

She nodded. She could definitely use a drink.


She was so much more beautiful up close, where he could see her small expressions and the way her eyes lit up when the wine was placed in front of her. He'd watched her carefully, taking in all the tiny tics that made up who she was. Her lips had curled up as she'd taken a sip of the rich pinot noir she'd requested.

He'd asked her to order, realizing this was a woman who rarely got to be in charge.

"I think you'll like the lasagna here. Somehow they make it so it tastes almost light and fluffy," she said.

"I'm sure it's delicious."

"Not many men allow a woman to order for them."

"Not many men are as awesome as me." He said it with a grin that had her grinning back.

"What if you don't like it?"

He needed to put her at ease. From what he understood, her first marriage had been a bit of a nightmare. Her husband had been known for cheating on her, and his criminal activities likely hadn't endeared him, either. "I will. First of all, anyone who doesn't like lasagna has serious issues. Second, I will pretty much eat anything that's put in front of me, so we're cool. I learned a long time ago not to let a meal go by because I didn't like the food, which is funny because my older brothers tell me I was the world's pickiest eater when I was a kid."

"What changed?"

"I got shipped into the foster care system."

Her eyes went round with sympathy. He got that a lot, too. "After your parents were killed? You didn't have relatives who would take you in?"

"No. And we were split up because no one wanted four kids. My older brothers got shipped to a group home and me and little sis entered the system. We got split up after a couple of months and she got adopted. They attempted to get me into their home, but there were political issues." He always wondered what his life would have been like if the Danvers had been allowed to adopt him.

"That sounds horrible."

She didn't know the half of it and she never would. "Some foster parents were awesome. Some weren't so great. I survived, but I did learn to appreciate the food in front of me, so stop worrying that I won't like it. I suspect anyone who works for one of America's premiere cooks knows food."

She snorted, but somehow it was cute on her. "Oh, Patricia doesn't eat. She doesn't actually create those recipes, either. She's got a staff."

"That makes sense. I would hate to think that someone so evil could come up with her chocolate cake recipe. My sister made it before she realized what magazine it had come from. By then the damage was done, and I'm not one to waste cake." He'd had too little of it in his lifetime.

No birthday parties for him. He could vaguely remember one when his mother had lit the candle and put it in front of him. It had been some kind of superhero cake and he could still remember how she'd leaned in, her arm on his shoulder.

*Make a wish, my baby boy. Make a wish.*

He wished she hadn't died. He wished his father was still here. He wished he was meeting Carly Fisher because he'd swiped right on his phone and needed a date.

He wished he wasn't about to use her.

"So why do you believe Patricia killed your parents?"

He noted there wasn't a hint of suspicion in her voice. She wasn't sitting there thinking he was crazy now. She was calmly and coolly trying to figure out what was going on. Or she was attempting to gain information she could take back to her boss.

That last voice in his head had sounded an awful lot like big brother's. He was sure Drew was sitting in the background with Hatch somewhere, cursing his name and the fact that he'd tossed his earpiece and didn't have on a mike.

Let Drew know what it felt like to be helpless and left behind.

Shit. He wasn't going there. This wasn't some revenge on his brother. This was about playing Carly more fairly than they'd played Ellie, his now sister-in-law.

"My father was an engineer. He developed a cable that helped speed up the way we used the Internet way back when it was starting out. He formed a company with a couple of savvy investors. When they had the chance to sell the tech, my father balked because he thought he could use it better than some major corporation. My dad was a bit of a dreamer."

"The investors didn't like that, did they?"

"No, they did not."

Her eyes narrowed and a shrewd look came over her face. "Patricia made her initial money off tech investments. You think she had your father killed so the company could sell the product."

"Exactly. There was a fire in our house one night when I was eight. The doors were locked and barricaded so we couldn't get out. My oldest brother managed to break through and get us all into the backyard, where luckily a bunch of neighbors had gathered. I some-times wonder if someone was waiting in the shadows for us. I wonder what might have happened if those neighbors hadn't been there."

"You don't think the fire could have happened naturally? I'm not trying to be rude, but children often remember things differently than an adult would."

Yes, he remembered the fire as a monster threatening to eat him alive. Sometimes he still dreamed about it, dreamed of being dragged along by Drew as he looked back and saw a gaping mouth of flames coming for him. And then it always morphed into the real monster, the one he met when he was sixteen. Real monsters were always human.

"I understand your hesitance. If you read the police reports, which I expect you'll do, you'll find that they believe my father murdered my mother and then turned the gun on himself, but only after setting the fire that would ensure his whole family died."

She leaned forward, curiosity plain on her pretty face. "Why not shoot you, too?"

"Isn't that a good question? It's one they never really answered. They've never given a proper motive beyond the fact that he was probably mentally ill. And yet he passed many a background check and several psychological evaluations, one only a month before. He did some work for the government from time to time. Look, Carly, this is the truth. My father loved his family. There was nothing vio-lent about the man, despite what the reports will say. So my real evi-dence for you is that three days before the fire occurred, your boss sent fifty thousand dollars to a bank account in Switzerland that we've managed to associate with a contract killer. His going rate at the time was two hundred thousand dollars and two other major shareholders in the company also deposited fifty grand into the account. Have you ever heard the names Stratton and Castalano?"

Her eyes went wide, proving she had. "StratCast. Patricia was an investor in the beginning. She used the money from the IPO to start Cain Corp. Steven Castalano died recently."

Yes, that was a fact he knew quite well. "But only after he attempted to kill my brother and sister-in-law."

She'd gone a bit pale and he refilled her glass. "This sounds serious."

"It is."

"Why are you coming to me?"

"Because you're close to her. Because no one knows her the way you do." He noticed her hands were shaking slightly and he reached out, covering them with his own. "It's okay. If you don't want to help, it's all right. No one is going to make you do anything you don't want to do. I promise you that."

It was why he'd tossed his earpiece and made this play. He couldn't stand the thought of this woman going through what Ellie had, not when there was no chance of the end playing out the same. No white knight was going to carry Carly Fisher away the way Riley had with Ellie.

All Bran could offer her was honesty, maybe friendship.

Maybe sex if she wanted him. Definitely sex.

But he was getting ahead of himself.

She straightened up, though he noted she didn't move her hands. "I don't know what I can do to help. I don't even know that I should. What's your plan?"

He leaned back, breaking the contact, and was surprised at how much he didn't like that. She was warm, her hands fitting into his like they'd been made to nestle there. "I can't tell you the plan unless you're all in. I understand that might not happen. I'm only going to ask you not to talk to her about it if you decide to pass."

"Why do it this way? Why come at me through some dating service?" Carly asked.

"Like I said, my brother likes to play a deep game. His plan was to date you, charm you. He would have maneuvered his way into your life, maybe managed to get a job on the set of Cain's show and manipulated it from there."

Her lips firmed and she frowned. "Well, you can tell him it wouldn't have worked. I was planning on telling this Drew guy that I'd changed my mind."

Wasn't that interesting? "You didn't find him attractive?"

"No. I found him too attractive. It's ridiculous that he would be matched with me. I knew something was up the minute I saw his picture, but I thought it would be less rude if I explained in person that I was no longer interested in dating."

"Are you? Is it only Drew you object to or is it all men?"

She suddenly seemed to find her glass infinitely interesting. "It was a mistake for me to sign up for the matchmaking service in the first place. I only did it because my sister pushed me. I'm not ready to date. I might never be. My first marriage was pretty rough."

It was time to come back around to something she'd said in the beginning. He might be able to help her out, too. That would be so much better. Quid pro quo. He liked to have the scales balanced. "It sounds like he's still causing you trouble. Who's DiLuca?"

She shook her head. "It doesn't matter."

"It does if I can help. We might be able to help each other."

"What are you looking for? I seriously doubt she's got a journal detailing her plots and evil plans hidden somewhere. She's careful. I'm not sure what I can do for you."

This part was murky. He wished he could explain exactly what he needed, but they weren't entirely sure how the information had been kept. "She had something on Castalano, some kind of proof of what happened. All three of them did from what I can tell. Mutually assured destruction in case one of the others tried to flip on them."

Carly nodded. "That sounds like Patricia. She hoards information. She always says information is better than gold because gold won't buy everything. Information is leverage in her world. She keeps files on everyone. Including me."

"I want to look at those files, Carly."

"She keeps them private. I don't have access to them. They're not even here. She keeps them in LA."

"And you'll be going there in a few weeks."

She grimaced as though thinking about something unpleasant. "Yes, we've got a big fund-raiser and naturally it's all being filmed. But I'll have to be beside her when we're in LA."

"That fund-raiser is at her house, right?"

"Of course," she affirmed with a huff. "She has to show off how beautiful it is. But if you're thinking I can slip up to her office, you're high. She keeps me at her side all night because she can't remember names. I won't be out of her sight."

He had a plan for that. Or rather Drew had one. He'd simply substituted himself in. "But your boyfriend would likely go unnoticed. Especially if you got him a job in security. Or if you could convince her to hire a more friendly security firm. She likes to fire people. We could, perhaps, arrange it so her current firm is no longer useful to her and point her to one my brother-in-law works for."

"Somehow I don't think she'll go for that."

"I think she will when she realizes what a great story it could be. Have you heard of the film *Love After Death*?"

She rolled her eyes. "Who hasn't? And before you tell me it's crap, you should know I've seen it five times and it's awesome."

Touchy thing. "Do you know the story behind it?"

"I know the woman who wrote the book married a man who worked for a security firm and she got a lot of inspiration from them. I read an article about it. Mc-something."

"McKay-Taggart. My brother-in-law is Case Taggart. He's a former Navy SEAL, decorated for valor in combat. Imagine a real-life hero heading Patricia Cain's security. Imagine what we could do with all that access." It had been the plan all along. They intended to use the McKay-Taggart cache to tempt Cain into giving them access. Once they were in, the McKay-Taggart boys would do the job and do it well, and Drew would do his, too.

"That could work," Carly agreed. "She's always looking for publicity. So you're looking for some file that proves she hired an assassin to kill your parents."

"Yes. And beyond that, we're looking to find out who the fourth conspirator was. We don't know his name. He's remained hidden for the last twenty years."

"How do you know it's a he?"

He didn't. "It could be a woman, but men tend to be more vicious when it comes to money."

There was that cute snort again. "Spending time with Patricia will disabuse you of that notion. I don't know. I'm going to need to think about this."

At least she wasn't kicking him to the curb. "Think about it. Do some research. Now tell me about DiLuca and how I can help you."

"You can't and I don't even need it."

He sat silently, watching her because he'd already made his demand. He didn't need to make it a second time.

Sure enough, Carly squirmed under the silence. "Fine. He was someone my husband owed money to. Owes money to. You would think after he went to jail, he would stop gambling."

He wasn't so sure about that. From the files he'd read on her husband, Roger Fisher had been the kind of man who could rack up some serious debt. "Why don't you let me check into it? I can prove to be helpful to you, Carly."

"And if I decide not to play the spy for you?"

His brother would gleefully murder him and Bran wouldn't have to worry about the problem anymore. "I would still help you."

He was a sucker for a damsel in distress.

"All right. His name is Tommy DiLuca and he's been sending me nasty e-mails threatening me if I don't pay Roger's debt. He started texting me, too. I have no idea how he got my number."

He could easily find out everything about Tommy DiLuca in a matter of moments, but he would slow play this, allow her to think it took him days. "I'll see what I can find out. And you should get back out there. In the dating pool, I mean."

A single brow rose above her left eye. "Really? This happens and you think I should try again."

She was so cute when she was pissed. "I think you should never stop trying. You're a beautiful woman and someday you'll find a man who deserves you."

It wouldn't be him, but he might be able to make her happy for a while.

"You think you know me that well? Maybe I deserve to be alone."

"No, not you. Tell me something. I've been thinking about it for days. Why did you stay on with Patricia Cain? Did she threaten you after your husband's arrest?"

She stared at him for a moment. "How did you know that?"

"I'm good at what I do." Which was reading the reports he got from Drew and Case. And maybe reading between the lines a little.

There was a moment of silence as she obviously contemplated whether or not to talk. "She needed to have her image rehabbed after a magazine did a hatchet job on some of her business practices."

"No, hatchet job implies that the article is bent one way or another. I assure you everything in that article was true. I know because I did the research myself. I'm the one who handed the reporter that story." He and his brothers were always looking for ways to fuck with the men and woman who had killed their parents. Patricia Cain had made it easy and he'd been able to hurt her without a hint of his name getting out.

Now he wondered if he'd hurt Carly as well. He would do it again.

Patricia Cain really had been abusing those workers. It seemed like no matter what he did, the woman in front of him was collateral damage. He needed to figure out a way to minimize the pain.

"She came after my sister," Carly explained, her voice quiet.

She had a younger sibling who was in college. Bran understood the need to protect and be protected. "How could she do that?"

"Because my husband used her in his schemes. She was very naive and let him put some of the money in her name."

An excellent way to hide something he didn't want found. Unfortunately for Carly, Cain was smart. She likely saw an opportunity and took it. He'd seen the interview where Carly had tearfully told the nation about how kind her boss was, how supportive. That interview had gone a long way to repairing Cain's image. It had been a good play. This was what kept happening. He and his brothers would make a move and Cain would counter. It was time to end the game, time for checkmate.

"How much longer do you have to work for her?"

"At least two years, though I'm not entirely sure she won't have something else planned for me by then. Somehow I can't see her letting me walk. She uses people until they are utterly hollow and then she throws the shell away. I'm still useful to her."

"Not if she's in jail, you're not." He needed to make his plea as appealing as possible. "If you don't do it for justice, do it to get your sentence reduced. She's got you in prison. I can break you out."

"Not without my help you can't."

This was a woman who needed to be needed. She was probably invisible most of the time. The key to winning her over was to show her that he saw her. Which he did. He saw her beauty and her resilience, even if she did not. "You are the missing piece, Carly. We've been trying to take her down for years, but we can't do it without you. You're necessary, which is why I pray you'll think about becoming our partner in this."

The waitress chose that moment to return, bearing a tray full of what smelled like heaven. She set the plate in front of him and he breathed it in. It was a beautiful day and he was sitting with a gorgeous woman about to eat something delicious. It was a win. He didn't sweat the stuff to come. It would come whether he enjoyed this moment or not. He'd learned that long ago.

"For now, sit and talk with me and let's enjoy the afternoon. No more talk about the mission until you make your decision. Tell me about yourself."

She picked up her fork. "I don't know that there's much to tell."

"Oh, I think we can find something to talk about." He winked her way and proceeded to enjoy the day.

Carly Fisher would come around. She would say yes. He just knew it.

# Chapter Two

"Tell me you told her you were me." Drew's eyes were narrowed, his voice a low growl as Bran walked in the door two hours later.

He'd been a bit surprised that no one had been waiting for him in the lot where he'd parked his truck. He'd driven forty minutes from St. Augustine to the Palm Coast condo they were based at in complete silence, his mind working around the problem of Carly Fisher.

It was going to be difficult to keep his hands off her. She was too soft, too damaged. He liked that in a woman. It brought up his every instinct to cuddle her.

To fix her. Like he hadn't been able to fix Mandy.

He shoved that thought aside because while they'd left him behind before, it looked like Drew was ready, willing, and able to throw down now.

"I told her who I am. She doesn't need to be lied to. She needs to be one of the team."

Drew's head fell back with a sheer groan of frustration. "One of the team? Are you fucking kidding me? I thought you were one of the team."

"I am. I'm the last one with a conscience."

"You're the last one without a brain cell," Hatch said, stalking out of the kitchen, his face a nice shade of red. "What the hell were you thinking? Do you have any idea what you did?"

Staying calm was the key here. He had anger issues, but he was going to prove he didn't have to punch someone. He could be calm and rational. "I saved us a whole lot of time. She hates her boss. Everything's going to be fine. I'm going to solve a problem for her and she's going to help us."

"What kind of problem?" Drew asked.

"Apparently her ex-husband is in debt to some bad dudes. Probably the mafia."

Drew's eyes flared. "Are you fucking kidding me?"

"It's not a big deal. I'll handle it."

"What the hell do you know about handling the mob?" Hatch was on his game today. His pitch had reached the right spot where it threatened to make Bran's brain bleed. He was in full-on pissed-off-dad mode, like he'd caught his teenage son sneaking in after curfew.

Or playing around with the mob.

"It might not be the mob. It might be some sad sack bookie who wants some cash and thinks he can intimidate the ex-wife of a client into giving it to him. I don't know. I have to look into it." He strode past the dining area and turned into the kitchen. The condo was one large open space with a bank of windows giving a spectacular view of the Atlantic.

Well, it would if Drew ever opened the blinds.

Drew took a deep breath and placed both hands palms down on the bar overlooking the kitchen, as though he needed them there so he didn't use them improperly. His brother had some anger issues of his own. "Tell me why."

He'd thought a lot about this on the drive back. "She doesn't deserve to be used."

Hatch pointed Drew's way. "I told you so. I told you the minute he started walking her way that this was his knight-in-shining-armor syndrome." Hatch turned to Bran. "She's not a damsel in distress. She works for one of the evilest women I've ever met. Patricia Cain could give Satan a run for his money. Do you honestly think she's got some angel working for her?"

He already knew more about Carly than they did. Likely they wouldn't have even attempted to scratch her surface. This was why he'd done what he did. Because Drew and Hatch would have used her and not ever figured out if she deserved it. "I told you, she hates her boss."

"Then she should quit," Drew stated as though the world was a simple place where every choice was an easy one.

He should know better. "Cain's got leverage over her. I told you I thought she had something on the girl. Turns out that when Carly's ex-husband was caught with his hand in the cookie jar, he tried to drag her sister into it, too. He'd used her to hide some cash. Cain found out and used it as leverage to force Carly to do that interview."

Drew sighed and hopped up on the barstool. "Damn it. The interview she had to do because we'd outed her Asian operations. Get me a beer. It seems like I'm going to need it."

"Beer? We're going to need Scotch. I'm sure Taggart keeps the good stuff hidden somewhere." Hatch walked off in search of hooch.

Bran grabbed a couple of bottles of beer. "He might be disappointed. I know Taggart gave us the keys to this place, but it's owned by his partner. McKay's straighter an arrow than Big Tag. Speaking of Taggart, Carly thinks Cain will go for switching security companies under the right circumstances. She believes she'll choose McKay-Taggart because of the publicity from the film."

Bran flipped off the cap and handed it to Drew, keeping the other for himself. Although he'd ordered wine with Carly, he wasn't a wine guy. In the last decade he'd been exposed to some of the world's finest restaurants, but no one had managed to turn him into a foodie.

He'd loved watching Carly eat. He loved how her eyes had closed as though she savored every delicious bite. He wondered if she fucked the way she ate. With gusto, with purpose, with passion.

"You laid out the plan?" There was no way to miss the testy tone of Drew's voice.

He hadn't meant to, but she'd been interested. He shrugged as though it was no big deal. "I needed to let her know what she's getting into. I didn't go over everything, obviously. Just the general plan."

Drew's beer bottle hit the bar with a small crash. "And did it once occur to you that she might take what you said and walk back to her boss and inform her of our plans? Have you heard of the term *element of surprise*? Because we lost that."

"I don't think so." Bran stayed calm. He'd been there. He'd been the one to meet Carly and make the assessment. "Like I said, she's got zero love for Cain."

"Or she's a good actress."

"No, she's not at all." He would bet she was a horrible actress.

Drew leaned forward, his eyes lasering in. "Bran, you cannot rescue every woman you meet."

He was saved from having to answer that statement by Hatch walking back in, a bottle of amber liquid in his hand. Apparently McKay wasn't as sober as he seemed.

"Thank God. This Scotch can vote," Hatch said, striding to the cupboard and retrieving a glass. "We have to figure out what the hell we're going to do now that Bran has completely blown our plan."

He tightened his grip on his beer. "I didn't blow it. I saved it. She was planning on telling Drew she'd changed her mind. If I hadn't walked up to her, she would have been gone five minutes later."

Drew frowned. "Why would she turn me away? She agreed to the date. Was she going to turn me down because of the picture? But I looked good in that picture. Mia had a photographer friend take it. I was wearing perfectly respectable clothes. Ellie picked them out."

"I made him take the pocket protector out and everything," Hatch quipped with a smirk.

Drew held up his middle finger for his business partner before returning his attention to Bran. "Seriously, I looked good in that picture. My face was symmetrical. The lighting wasn't harsh. I smiled in a way that Riley said wasn't predatory."

Drew always looked like he was ready to take someone apart. There was a darkness about his brother that seemed to send many women running. Of course, it also brought in the more adventurous ones. From what Bran could tell, Drew's sex life involved a series of not-too-frequent one-night stands and a single long-term relationship that could only be called sexual for all its chilly practicality. He was a hot nerd who often lost himself in code and business.

Another reason it wouldn't have worked with Carly. She would have been able to sense his chill. Carly needed some warmth in her life.

"She thought you were too attractive for her." If he didn't put a stop to this they would end up discussing Drew's haircut or his posture. His brother would analyze the rejection to death and they wouldn't get to the real heart of the matter.

"That is disheartening. I don't usually lose a woman until I open my mouth." Drew made the statement with absolutely no irony. It was a simple fact in his brother's mind.

"Then you drop a whole lot of them," Hatch agreed.

Drew ignored him. "Why would she think I was too attractive?"

"She didn't think you were a good match."

Drew was quiet for a second as though trying to make sense of that statement. "Technically, I ensured that we were a match on every level. Actually, we were a fairly good match to begin with. We have practical notions about love and sex. I simply changed a few facts about myself. I said I was interested in architecture to suit her love for design. I wasn't lying. I do find architecture fascinating simply in terms of software architecture and not buildings. I also said I was interested in something called flea market finds. I don't really know what that means, but it was the thing that put me over the edge and paired us."

His brother always went for the logical explanation. "She thought she wasn't hot enough for you."

Drew frowned. "She's very appealing sexually. Her waist to hip ratio is almost perfect and she has a lovely set of breasts. I found her face quite symmetrical."

"This is why they run, brother." In Bran's opinion, Drew had spent way too much time in the pursuit of power and not nearly enough chasing women. Power meant nothing without women. "She's hot. She's sexy. Women don't like being called symmetrical."

Drew opened his mouth to argue.

Bran shut that shit down. "I don't want to hear a lecture on the biological imperatives that make us choose a mate. The truth is Carly has a hot body but she works in an industry where everyone worships unhealthy ideals. She's never going to be a stick and she's insecure about it, which is precisely why she was going to turn you down. How would you have handled that?"

"I don't know," Drew admitted. "I hadn't accounted for that possibility. This was why I sent Riley in the first time. Riley's the one with the charm. You don't suppose . . ."

Bran groaned. Only Drew would even suggest that. "No, I don't suppose Riley's wife wants him trolling chicks so we can have our revenge."

Drew wasn't giving up. "Ellie is quite reasonable. I have a meeting with her in a couple of hours. I could talk to her about it."

"No woman is that reasonable," Hatch pointed out. "Trust me. Bran's right on this. You ask Ellie if Riley can flirt with Cain's assistant to get close to her and she will twist your balls right off your body. And don't ask for Case, either. Mia's not letting her husband play around, not even in the name of revenge."

"See, this is why I don't get married. All of your options are taken away and apparently your balls get attached to your wife's handbag or something." Drew shook his head.

"We're not calling in anyone." Had they not been listening to him at all? This was how it always seemed to go. He was the invisible one. Drew was the genius. Riley was the charmer. Mia had the drive, and Bran . . . Bran was the fuckup everyone had to clean up after. Not this time. "I've got this handled. I'll deal with Carly. I've already got a relationship with her."

"A relationship?" Drew's eyes were suddenly hawkish and staring right through him.

"I meant I've made contact and she has my number."

Hatch shook his head. "Nah, that's not what you meant. You're already invested in this woman and we know next to nothing about her."

"We know a ton about her. We've got a fat file on her. She's not the bad guy."

"The fact that you can say that with a straight face is reason to send you back to Austin today," Drew said with a frown.

"I'm not going anywhere."

Drew's eyes narrowed. "You will if I tell you to."

Hatch put up a hand. "Stop it, both of you. Bran fucked up but he might have a point. You wouldn't have had any idea how to handle a woman rejecting you. You wouldn't have figured out the reason and you would have put her on her guard. Bran, do you honestly believe she's not going straight to Patricia and telling her everything?"

That was not the feeling he got. "I don't believe she'll do that."

Drew's blue eyes rolled. "This coming from the dude who always believes the strippers are really just innocent young women trying to put themselves through school."

"Hey," Hatch said. "Do I need to separate the two of you? You're acting like five-year-olds. We've got a change of situation and we need to adapt. Bran's the one with the relationship with the mark."

"She's not the mark." He didn't like hearing her talked about that way.

"See?" Drew said pointedly.

"Fine, she's a lovely woman who we're hoping will work with us," Hatch said before ruining the words with an eye roll. "There's nothing to do except wait. I take it you gave her some time to think it over."

"Yes, it's a big decision." It wasn't like he could force her to say yes then and there. She was a cautious woman after everything she'd been through.

"It's not her decision to make." Drew slammed the bottle down on the bar. "I would have kept her out of it. I'm not some kind of monster. And I would have figured a way to bring her back in. I've got half a brain. I would have done all of it and not gotten attached to her. You watch. He's going to pull his gallant routine and it'll all go to hell."

Before Bran could defend himself, Drew stalked off toward one of the back bedrooms. "Let him go," Hatch said. "And you know he's right about you. You don't think straight when it comes to women."

"Well, Drew doesn't feel anything for them at all." Sometimes his brother seemed to be more robot than man. "After what happened with Ellie, I couldn't stand there and let it happen all over again. It's wrong."

"I don't know about that, but I do understand your point. Now you see his. He already had to watch one brother be put in a dangerous situation. He wasn't going in himself because he didn't think you couldn't do the job. He did it because he didn't want you in harm's way."

"I doubt that." His brother often thought he was the weak link.

"That's your issue, not Drew's. He's given you a lot of responsibility in the company and he trusts you. You're the one who thinks you aren't good enough. He's trying to protect you. He couldn't do it when he was a kid and now he's overdoing it. It's how Drew deals with things. So he's worried and upset that you're going to be the one to walk into the lion's den. If she calls."

"She'll call." God, he hoped she called.

"How can you be sure?"

"She was interested. In more than my story." He knew damn well when a woman was interested in what he could do for her. There was something in the way she'd looked at him, leaned toward him. He'd spent years studying the way women responded both intimately and in their everyday lives. It told him how he could please them, what made them happy and what turned them chilly.

Carly Fisher might deny it, but she wanted a man who would be a true partner, who would help her. She was alone and the man who convinced her she didn't have to be would win her over. She would be loyal to that man, follow him wherever he went.

He couldn't be that man, but he could find a mutual satisfaction between them. He could help her. She could help him and then they would go their separate ways, better for having known each other.

At least that was the way it would work in theory. It was the way all his relationships worked. He usually fell into them. He'd find himself in bed with a lovely lady and then he would try to find a way to fix the things she needed help with. He'd gotten one out of a bad work situation by finding her a job at one of 4L's subsidiaries. He'd helped one deal with a customer who got a bit too obsessed with her work as an exotic dancer. He'd helped others in ways that ranged from loans to helping them move, but he always found a way to make them happy they'd been involved.

He would do the same with Carly. He would protect her. He would help her. If she let him, he would sleep with her and give her as much pleasure as she could handle. He would show her not all men were assholes, and when the time came to leave, she would be ready to find her *one*.

There was no *one* for Bran. He'd known that for a long time.

"You honestly think you can handle this and not get in too deep with that woman?" Hatch asked, sounding perfectly afraid of the answer.

"I know I can. Despite what everyone believes, I'm never too deep. I know the score."

Hatch nodded. "All right, then. I guess we wait."

Bran took a long swig of his beer and prayed Carly didn't make them wait too long.

Carly stared at the screen of her laptop, hating the way her heart clenched when she thought of that gorgeous man as a young child ripped from the only home he'd ever known. One day Brandon Lawless had been the beloved child, and the next he'd been alone and adrift in a world he couldn't have understood. She hadn't had the greatest childhood. Her dad had cheated on her mom and married his coworker. He'd done the weekend-dad thing for a while but then his new wife had a baby and the visits became rare. The last time she'd seen her father had been years before. But at least she'd had her sister. Brandon had no one.

Sure enough, it was all out there on the Internet for her to find. She'd even found an article where Patricia Cain had been interviewed about the loss of Benedict Lawless and his brilliant mind. The words had turned Carly's stomach because she could see her boss scripting them.

*The loss of Benedict will impact the tech world for years to come. His genius was only matched by his madness. We should have seen it. He had a variety of anger issues, but I'm afraid we chalked it up to having an artistic temperament. We never imagined he would kill his sweet wife and attempt to murder his own children. While I will mourn his lost genius, I can't help but be angry at what he did. I will never be able to forgive myself for not seeing what he was capable of.*

Bullshit. Patricia didn't care about people enough to truly mourn them. With a singular exception. And she'd never known the woman to feel a moment's guilt.

She'd spent the afternoon staring at her computer and wondering if she was actually going to call the number on that card Bran had left her with. How could she consider it? It was ridiculous. She wasn't some kind of spy.

Carly sat back, sighing. The smart play would be to do her time. She had two years left before her sister was safe. Why should she help some family she didn't know? From what she understood about Bran's family now, they didn't need a ton of help. They were wretchedly wealthy, having formed one of the world's largest software companies. Everyone used the 4L firewall.

She wondered what Patricia would think of the Lawless children growing up to be so powerful.

There was a reason they now went under different last names. Brandon Lang was Bran's legal name. They'd all taken the different surname. She was certain if anyone asked, Bran would say they'd done it to put their pasts behind them. She thought they'd done it for a completely different reason. They'd done it to hide in plain sight. They'd done it so their enemies wouldn't hear the Lawless name and put up their guards.

What was she supposed to do?

Her eyes caught on the sight of her cell phone, not the professional one that Patricia paid for. Naturally she was forced to have two. One for her personal calls and one strictly for Patricia. It was the newest, most technologically advanced phone on the market and it tended to ring incessantly. This was the one night out of the month that it was quiet because it was the evening Patricia spent with her husband. Their monthly dinners were sacred and not to be disturbed. One night of the whole month that she spent with her beloved. Yeah, that was how hot they were for each other.

Her own phone was fairly cheap since it didn't get a ton of use. Only two people ever called it. Carly was careful to leave it behind much of the time and it was safeguarded with a passcode.

Besides her sister, there was one person she talked to on a regular basis, and it wouldn't do to let Patricia know that tidbit of information.

Shelby Gates, journalist and activist and currently writing an unauthorized biography of one Patricia Cain.

Carly had refused to help her the first few times she'd called, and only gave her the barest of hints of where to look eventually because she happened to know Patricia was up to her old tricks exploiting the Third World manufacturing system, though more quietly this time. She had plausible deniability since she now worked through other companies for labor. The fact that she was still getting away with it had led her to answer Shelby's call and to give her the name of a particularly disgruntled employee of Cain Corp.

It also didn't hurt that Shelby intended to give all proceeds from the book to a fund she'd set up for the workers injured or killed because of conditions in manufacturing plants that spat out Cain Corp products. The book stood to make Shelby millions, but Carly rather believed she would do it. Shelby was the kind of woman who wasn't influenced by money or fame. Her mark on the world would be in making a difference.

Shelby Gates was the be-all, end-all of knowledge about Patricia Cain. She'd also become a close friend. Could she shed any light on the subject?

Carly picked up her phone and dialed the number. It wouldn't be late on the West Coast. Of course, Shelby was probably eating dinner at this time of day. She would give it three rings and then be done with it. She would take that as a sign to leave things well enough alone, and the next time she called Shelby they would talk about the latest fashion or what they were watching on TV.

Shelby picked up on the first ring. "Hey, Carly."

Well, she'd asked for a sign. "Please tell me you don't have my number in your phone."

"Nope. I've got it memorized. What's going on? It's so good to hear from you."

It had been a while and Carly felt guilty about that. "Sorry, it's been a crazy time for us here. I'm coming to LA in a few weeks though. I was hoping we could find some time to meet."

"I would adore that." Shelby sounded genuinely pleased. "I'll even find a suitable disguise. I think I would make a good pregnant blonde. It might be the closest I get to actual pregnancy. I need a date or two. Tell me how the date with Hottie McHotterston went. What was his name? Drew?"

And that was the last time she let Meri know who her friends were. "My sister got your name off this phone, didn't she?"

"She's a sweet one. And she's worried about you. She just thinks you should have some fun. So do I."

"I didn't call you to talk about my date. It was a little weird and I don't know if I want to see him again." That wasn't true. She knew damn well she wanted to see him, but she didn't know if she should. "I called about something else."

"Tell me you've left the witch and you want to do a public interview."

"I'm not leaving her."

Shelby sighed over the line. "Are you ever going to tell me what she's got on you? I have some suspicions, but I consider you a friend so I haven't looked too deep."

Thank the universe for small blessings. "Maybe one day. How did your interview with Lewis go?"

Lewis Smith had been a publicity rep for Patricia before she fired him for missing a red carpet event. His wife had been in labor at the time. One didn't put one's children before Patricia Cain and stay in her employ.

"He was a gold mine," Shelby said with a laugh. "Truly he made her sound like the Wicked Witch of the West. Do you have someone else for me? You need to be careful."

"No, I have a question. What do you know about how Patricia made her money in the beginning?"

"A lot. Why?"

"I'm curious."

"You're never curious, but you are cautious, so I'm going to assume you won't tell me. I owe you a massive favor and, like I said before, we're friends. So ask me anything."

Though she liked Shelby and believed she was one of the good ones, she didn't trust anyone at all when it came to Patricia. She trusted Shelby more than anyone else so she talked to her about the job. Over the year they'd known each other, she'd come to value her very much. "I want to know about her first company. It was about twenty years ago. There were only a few investors, right?"

Over the line she heard the sound of papers shuffling and she envisioned Shelby sitting at her desk, working through her dinner. This was one of the reasons Carly helped her out. They were a lot alike. "Yes, there were five investors, but one didn't actually put in a ton of money. He was the brains behind the company so he got sweat equity. Benedict Lawless. Genius of a man. There have been several magazine articles written about what happened with him. Apparently the pressure got to him and he snapped. He killed his wife and set his house on fire right before the company went public. He should have waited because, damn, that company made a shit-ton of money."

"Didn't he have kids?" She wasn't about to give away the fact that she'd talked to one of them today. She had questions that needed unbiased answers, but she wasn't going to out the Lawless siblings.

"Four kids. Three boys and a girl."

"Did they get a portion of the sale? After all, their parents would have had stock." It was the piece that didn't fit for her. Those kids should have been millionaires.

"Give me a sec. The kids got screwed, but I don't remember why offhand. I've got the research in here somewhere. I haven't done a ton of reading on the early businesses. I've been concentrating on the fun stuff first. You know, all her affairs and the fact that she got arrested for a drunken brawl as a teen. I've found some pictures of her looking super slutty, which I normally wouldn't use because I'm not into the whole shame game, but after her article on the decline of moral values in the country, a pic of her dressed in a miniskirt that doesn't quite cover her cootch is too much to pass up on. And let me tell you, younger Patty didn't believe in undies. Wait, here it is." There was a long pause over the line. "That explains it. Son of a bitch. What fucking bastards. There was a morality clause."

That sounded like Patricia. "So if Benedict violated the morality clause by committing a crime, his stock would revert to the other shareholders?"

"Yep, and last time I checked, murder was a crime. They stole the stock from those kids. They could do it because there was no family left to defend them. Wow. You know, I've never thought of interviewing them because I doubt they even remember her."

Oh, they remembered Patricia Cain. "I'm sure they've moved on with their lives."

"Well, if you consider becoming the world's youngest billionaire moving on, then yes, I suspect at least one of them has. I haven't paid any attention to Andrew Lawless because I honestly hadn't thought about what he'd been through. Think about it. He was left with nothing and he still found his way to the top. What kind of man does that? He's kind of an enigma. He doesn't do interviews, shies away from the press. There are only a few pictures of him. He's interesting. I don't know what happened to his brothers and the sister."

Andrew Lawless was apparently the only one who'd kept his name. "He does sound interesting. Who were the other investors?"

"Um, Stratton, Castalano, Cain, and Hatchard. You should know the first two. Bill Hatchard was a big deal at the time. He was brilliant when it came to investment strategy. Some people called him Midas because everything he touched turned to piles and piles of gold. He dropped out of public view a couple of months after the IPO. The rumor is he was deeply disturbed by what happened with Benedict Lawless, and the nastier rumor is he was having an affair with Iris

Lawless. So he drops out of the business world for years only to come roaring back as the COO of 4L Software. The way the story goes, when Drew Lawless wanted to form his company, he couldn't find investors. Now I get that since he didn't have cash backing him. Hatchard comes on and he manages to get them the money they need and the rest is history. He's an interesting story in and of himself. If I ever get this damn book done I'll take a look at him, too. I'd love to know what he was doing during those lost years."

Carly was certain it was a truly interesting story, but not the one she wanted to know more about. The Lawless siblings were specifically invested in Patricia Cain as one of the conspirators. "You don't know anything else?"

"I've got some notes. I took over this story from another reporter. His notes talk about the fact that he found some internal documents stating that Benedict Lawless was very much against selling any of his tech. According to these notes, there was a big fight among the board as to whether or not they would ever take the company public. Lawless and his wife wanted to keep it private so they could control how the tech was used. He was some kind of do-gooder."

"Doesn't it seem strange that a do-gooder turned out to be a killer?"

"The ways of men are strange, my friend. Of course, when you think about it, it was kind of neat and tidy that the argument got settled the way it did. And by tidy I mean bloody and awful, but the fight was over. There was no Lawless left who could fight the board. Hey, you don't think it was a setup, do you?"

This was why she'd tried to ask delicately. "I don't know about that."

"It's awfully convenient, don't you think?" Shelby's voice had gone soft, a sure sign that she was thinking.

"I don't understand why there would have been an argument in the first place. Not a real one. Couldn't the other investors have simply outvoted him? He only controlled twenty percent of the company." It was another thing she didn't understand.

"I'll have to look at his contract, but I think he controlled the entirety of anything produced outside of the company. That particular piece of tech was something he'd been working on since he was a teen playing around on his father's computer in the garage."

"Then the patent should have gone to the kids."

"Who had no lawyer to fight for them," Shelby pointed out. "Those kids immediately went into the system. They were just trying to survive. They didn't know a damn thing about contracts or patents. Lawless's contract was airtight, but someone thought it was fair. I doubt his wife would have let him sign it if she thought it wasn't. She was a lawyer. She hadn't practiced in years, but she would have known how to read a contract. Yuck. Now I have to go and read a bunch of contracts. I hate reading anything without a good love scene, you know what I mean?"

"I know you sound crazy sometimes." But Carly couldn't help but smile.

"You don't know the half of it, sister," Shelby agreed. "I think you're onto something. Lawless was ready for a fight. The other investors wanted their money, and this way they didn't even have to share it. Holy shit. This could be a way bigger story than I dreamed of."

"Put the brakes on the conspiracy theories. I was merely interested. I heard someone mentioning the old partners at one of the wakes Patricia attended for Steven Castalano." A total lie. She hadn't been there, but she needed an excuse for bringing the subject up. "I was curious about how she got started. When she talks about it, she was a businesswoman who got stuck in the rat race, and forming Cain Corp was how she got out of it. I wanted to know if that was true."

"Nothing that comes out of that woman's mouth has any grounding in fact. Cain Corp is about as rat race a corporation as you can get. I hadn't truly thought about going back and looking at her previous businesses. I've always focused on Cain Corp. Now I can see there might be a lot of potential. I'm coming at it all wrong. I was looking for the sexiest angle possible."

"Sexy?" There was nothing sexy about her boss.

"It's a word we use for a story that will bring a lot of publicity in. It's why I'm doing this unauthorized bio in the first place. Patricia Cain is a huge celebrity but she's also controversial. She's considered to be a helpful domestic diva by some and a bully trying to shove women back into domesticity by others. She's all about hearth and home, so proving she's actually a narcissist is a sexy idea. But what if she was something even worse. The business stuff requires thought. I can't sum it up in a photo or a couple of paragraphs, which is why I was avoiding it, but you might be onto something."

"I don't know about that."

"She stole a fortune from four homeless children who'd recently lost their parents. Those other investors worked together and yet not one of them stepped up to help out those kids? What kind of monsters were they? They made their futures from Benedict Lawless, and yet they couldn't put some of it in a trust for his children?"

There was something about the passion in Shelby's voice that made Carly ask the question she'd always wanted an answer to. "You know, I've never asked you why you decided to take on this project. Is it personal for you? Did she hurt you in some way?"

Shelby was quiet for a moment. "I can't stand a bully and she's a prime example. She sets women up to compete against one another and not over anything important. She sets us up to feel like shit because our homes aren't perfect or because we grab fast food one night a week because we're too tired to cook. She plays on our insecurities to build herself up. She's like every mean girl grew up and formed a single, massive tool. She's the mean girl equivalent of a Transformer, and I think it would be good to take her down."

It still felt like more than simple social justice, but Carly decided to let it go. "I don't suppose there's any way you would let me take a look at some of that business research you have?"

There was a pause on the line. "Do you have any idea how much trust I'm about to show in you? If Cain ever got word of what I'm doing, she would try to shut me down."

Thank God. She needed more than what she'd read. She needed to understand what had happened. It would be far easier to walk away and simply not call Bran back. In two years she could quit and everyone would go their own ways. "That's not going to happen."

So why couldn't she do it? Why was she sitting here looking at images of a dead couple and wondering if she had a responsibility to help them now that their children were adults?

What was it about Bran that made her want to be the woman she'd been before she'd gotten married, before she'd worked for Patricia Cain? That Carly wouldn't have hesitated. That Carly would have seen herself as a crusader, trying to right a wrong.

"All right, a copy of the file is being sent to your private e-mail," Shelby said after a moment. "You know, for a woman who claims to love her job, you do an awful lot to ensure your boss never finds out anything about your personal life."

Like she actually had one. "I'm erring on the side of caution. And thank you, Shelby. If I find anyone else you should talk to, I'll send them your way."

"And I will look into my new line of investigation. Thanks so much for making me read through contracts and patents. Boo."

She smiled again. Shelby would prefer the sexier stuff, but she would definitely be thorough in her investigation. "You're so welcome. Please let me know if you find anything. You know, I never asked why the first reporter dropped the story. He did all that research but then passed it on to you? That doesn't seem smart."

"John was the smartest man I ever met. He was brilliant and he didn't hand off the research to me. I inherited it. He was my brother and he died in a car accident."

"I'm so sorry." She didn't know what she would do if something happened to Meri.

"Yes, me, too," Shelby said quietly. "It was a single-vehicle accident that occurred shortly after he attempted to interview Patricia Cain. He'd been trying to get a one-on-one with her for months, but that day she deigned to talk to him. He died an hour later."

Holy shit. There was Shelby's reason. She'd always known it was there, an undercurrent in everything Shelby did. "You think Patricia had something to do with the accident."

"I can't prove it, but someday I will. Be careful, Carly. She's capable of anything."

The line went dead.

Carly took a deep breath and sat back, still wondering what she should do.

*Chapter Three*

Two hours later she was still wondering. It was almost eleven and she looked out over the balcony. From her apartment she could see the bay and the historic lighthouse that marked it. Once a year they did a reenactment of Sir Francis Drake's raid on old St. Augustine and everyone dressed in proper gowns and attire and did their part and then got rip-roaring drunk afterward. She'd only participated once. It had been a few months after she'd moved here for her job and she'd gone out with some friends and had the best time. Until morning and the humiliation only Patricia Cain could dish out.

She loved this town. Despite some of the crap that had happened here, it had become her home. It was pretty far from the small town in Alabama she'd grown up in. No one here knew her father had dumped her mom. No one knew she'd spent her teen years in a single-wide while her mom went through man after man. Here everything was clean and neat. Sometimes she thought that drab trailer where she'd shared a room with her sister was the reason she'd pursued the job with Patricia. At the time this world seemed so shiny, Patricia herself the queen of all things beautiful and welcoming.

It was all a facade. Just because a home looked lovely didn't mean she was welcome.

But she still loved this city with its cobblestone streets and horse-drawn tours. She simply hated the fact that if she squinted she could see Patricia's mansion off in the distance.

What was Bran doing tonight? Was he sitting in some hotel room plotting his revenge? Did he have a whiteboard with a checklist? Or had they tricked out some apartment somewhere to be their man cave/revenge den? He looked like a man who could brood with the best of them. But when he smiled, oh, when he smiled her heart nearly stopped.

It was time to recognize that his attractiveness was one of the barriers to her making the call she knew she should make.

When had her conscience fled? She might get out of this mess in two years, but what did any of it mean if she didn't come out even vaguely resembling the girl she'd been?

With a long sigh she turned and walked back into her apartment, closing the door behind her. She should get to bed and in the morning she would toss out the card Bran had given her and get on with her life. It was the smart play and she was a smart girl now. She wasn't the idiot who'd come from Alabama with a book of Southern recipes and the hope that Patricia Cain would be her fairy godmother.

She wasn't risking anything else. Let the Shelbys of the world take all the chances. She was done with that.

So why didn't she go and throw the card away right now?

She laid it on the nightstand beside her bed. She would sleep on it and it would be clearer in the morning. It was easy to blame her odd mood on the free time the day had given her. Usually she was constantly on the move, running from one errand to the next, always trying to please the queen. There was no real time to think about anything but the next task at hand. She woke up before the sun and hit the ground running, and sometime fourteen hours or so later she fell into bed completely exhausted and started the whole thing all over again the next day.

Two years had flown by and the next two would as well. She would be free of Patricia Cain and she would start over again.

What about the next girl? Or what if dear Patricia decided she liked having a slave and found another way to keep her locked in the cage? When had she started to wish her damn life away?

If she was going to get through the night she would need some tea. Chamomile. Something to help her get to sleep. She couldn't take sleeping pills. They made her too groggy the next day, and she'd had enough wine this afternoon.

She walked down the stairs toward her kitchen, her mind on the afternoon with Bran.

He'd been funny and charming. She'd loved watching him. Gallant. That was a good word for him. He'd pulled out her chair for her and poured the wine himself, but only after allowing her to make all the choices, even for him.

What would the day have been like if he'd merely been a man she'd been matched to on a dating site? Would they have walked through the old part of the city, talking the afternoon and evening away? They could have stopped somewhere and had coffee because they simply didn't want the date to end. She could have casually invited him back to her place.

How long had it been since she'd been kissed? Since a man had leaned over and pressed his mouth to hers and the world seemed to float away? Long before her marriage had been over. Roger had wooed her with kisses, but he hadn't had much time for them afterward. Even before, she could now see that every move he'd made had been calculated to manipulate her to the place he wanted her. He'd targeted her for her job. He'd known he could make serious cash off skimming from her boss. He'd gotten too greedy.

The Bran in her fantasy didn't want her for her job. He wasn't after revenge. He was after sex. In her head, he'd taken one look at her and decided he would have her. He would pursue her with no thought to anything she could give him beyond pure pleasure.

She'd read far too many romance novels. Sometimes she thought they were the only thing that kept her sane.

She tried to shake off those ridiculous fantasies as she turned on the light in her kitchen.

Then it was hard to think about anything but the scream that threatened to escape.

A man was sitting at her kitchen table, his big body encased in all black. There was even a black hat on his head that was likely pulled down over his face when he wanted to go unseen.

It was probably a bad sign that she could see his whole scarred and hardened face. And the gun he held in one hand. It was silvery and had one of those long noses attached to the muzzle. Silencer. Her heart rate tripled. She could actually hear it pounding in her chest.

"Don't scream, sweetheart. I don't want to have to use this on you. And don't run. I'm not the only one here."

She gasped as she felt someone move in behind her. Carly jumped in an effort to put some distance between them. This was what a rabbit had to feel like when it got caught between two wolves. Two immense and predatory wolves. She was so scared. What were they here for? She forced herself to speak because if she didn't she might start crying, and they didn't get that from her. "What are you doing in my house?"

Her hands were shaking and her voice was barely above a whisper.

The man at her kitchen table sat back as though this was nothing more than a friendly visit. He even holstered the gun. It wasn't like he needed it. Carly couldn't do anything. She was utterly helpless. "I've come on behalf of a mutual friend."

Her stomach threatened to revolt. She took a deep breath as she figured out who he was talking about. "That DiLuca guy?"

He smiled, though it wasn't a pleasant expression. It was more a baring of nasty, sharp teeth. "Yes, Mr. DiLuca sent me."

"He isn't my friend."

His head shook briefly. "Now, Mrs. Fisher, that's not true. Mr. DiLuca is a gentleman and he would greatly prefer to keep this friendly. You're the one who won't take his calls. You've been quite rude to him over the phone."

"I am not Mrs. Fisher." God she needed to change her last name. There simply never seemed to be time. "I divorced Roger a long time ago. Two years ago to be exact."

The man shook his head. "I'm afraid Mr. DiLuca is a traditional kind of man. He doesn't believe in divorce. When God brings a man and woman together, it's for life. That man and woman share everything, including their debts. Your husband's been a bad boy. Two years ago he stole some money from my boss and Mr. DiLuca would like it back."

"He went to prison two years ago." What the hell was going on? It felt surreal to be standing here and talking to this man.

The man with the gun didn't seem to find anything out of the ordinary about their conversation. "This was shortly before his unfortunate stay. He racked up quite a gambling debt under an assumed name. It took us a while to figure out exactly who he was. Your husband was a tricky one. The identification he presented was very believable."

"Tell me about it." She would hand it to Roger. He tended to be good at conning people out of money. She simply wished he'd been more careful about who he'd stolen from.

"By the time we tracked him down, he was incarcerated, so we've come to you, his lovely wife."

"How much did he owe?" She would write them a check right now if it got them out of her apartment. If it kept her alive. She wanted to argue, but unfortunately she wasn't the one with the gun. She needed to get them out of here and quickly. Then she could deal with the situation properly—by calling every police officer in the town.

"At the time it was ten thousand," the man explained. "He liked to bet on the ponies, you see. Unfortunately, he wasn't good at it."

She could actually manage ten grand. She might be able to come out of this alive. She prayed they didn't require cash. That would be way harder. She had a decent savings account. What did she have to spend money on? She had no free time and all her travel expenses were paid for by her job. "Ten thousand dollars."

"Ten K."

"I can get my hands on that." Her voice was still shaky, but she felt a bit more control come back to her. If money was all they wanted, she could work that out. All that mattered was getting them out of her apartment.

He sighed. "Oh, yes, but that was back then. You see, we do charge interest. It's a business, of course. It's been two years and three months, so while the principal was ten grand, I'm afraid with interest we're looking at a million now."

Her stomach dropped and that burgeoning feeling of control fled in an instant. "I don't have a million."

His shoulders moved in a negligent shrug. "I figured you didn't, but I thought you should understand the stakes. You're a smart lady and you work for someone who won't even miss it."

Oh, she would miss it. "Roger's in jail because my boss caught him skimming. He underestimated how closely she watches her money. I can't take anything from her or I'll end up exactly where he is."

"Better jail than a grave. Or something worse. Don't think there's nothing worse than death, sweetheart. There is and I've often been the tour guide. I don't particularly want that to happen to you." The criminal stood up, sliding his chair back in politely. "Look, maybe you can take a loan out or something, but my boss is firm in this. The debt has passed to you since there's nothing your husband can do for the next ten to fifteen years. It's a million dollars by the end of the week or something unfortunate will happen to you."

She would let him leave and then call the cops. This couldn't happen to her. The cops would handle it. It's what they did. They protected women like her from criminals.

He moved in, looming over her. When she tried to back up, she brushed against the other man and nearly jumped out of her skin.

"I can't steal from my boss. I won't do it and I seriously doubt I can get a million-dollar loan." Roger's theft was what had gotten her into this mess in the first place. She wasn't going to compound the mistake.

"I don't like hurting pretty women, but I'll do my job," he promised. "And my partner back there, he'll do his, too."

"Yeah, but I will like it," the other man said, his eyes steady on her. "I enjoy that part of the job very much, and you are exactly my type. In fact, I could give you some incentive right now."

She was deeply aware that she wasn't wearing anything but a thin tank top and a pair of pajama bottoms. She wasn't even wearing shoes. Once more she was utterly and completely vulnerable, and there was nothing she could do to save herself.

"Back off, Monty." Asshole number one sent his partner a dark look that made him move back a bit. "Do you understand what you're up against, Mrs. Fisher?"

She simply nodded because there wasn't anything else to do.

"I'm glad we understand each other. And don't call the cops. If you do, you won't ever see me coming, and I'll know because Mr. DiLuca keeps a good portion of them on retainer. He's a careful man. Maybe you'll get an honest cop who'll try to help you. Maybe you won't. I can promise you that all you'll do is buy yourself a couple of days and a much more painful outcome, because they can't hide you forever. They've got far too much to do, and after a few days of absolutely nothing happening to you and a logical explanation from Mr. DiLuca, they'll ease off and we'll be there. Waiting for you. Good night, Mrs. Fisher. You should see about getting a more secure lock."

He and his friend walked out, not bothering to look back. Why should they? What would she do to them? She was nothing to them.

Carly was left shaking as she heard the door close.

What would she do? She maybe could liquidate everything she owned and come up with a hundred grand. No more than that.

She could call the cops and pray he was lying.

Or she could bargain with a man who might be able to protect her. A man who had promised to work with her. A man who wouldn't miss a million dollars. She had one thing someone else needed.

With tears in her eyes she locked her door and went to do the only thing she could. She had a call to make.

The music blared through the club, but unfortunately nothing could quite drown out the sound of Hatch bitching at him.

"Do you have any idea what your brothers went through? They spent months putting this plan together and you blow it up in five seconds and now she hasn't called. If she hasn't called by now she's not going to, and we have to figure something else out. You and me, Bran. We have to make this right because Drew's got more on his plate than scrapping an entire multiyear plan for justice and having to start from scratch." Hatch took a long drink of the Scotch he'd ordered and then his shoulders shook, his face grimacing as he set the drink back down. "That tastes like swill after Taggart's. I think I'm getting too old for this shit. I never used to care what a damn drink tasted like as long as it worked."

Because Hatch had spent many years at the bottom of a bottle. Bran knew the story. Hatch had been his father's best friend, and after what had happened he'd lost his mind and roughly ten years of his life. After Drew had aged out of foster care, he'd gone searching for Hatch, forced the man to sober up, and they'd started the beginnings of 4L. A decade later and Hatch was once again the right-hand man to a Lawless genius. He was dedicated to playing the boozy, obnoxious but loving father Bran never had.

"I'm sure it was horrible for them," Bran replied as he looked out over the club. This particular club was one of the nicer ones he'd been to. It was still pretty trashy, but strip clubs were a hobby of his. He felt comfortable here. He'd spent the last couple of years in gorgeous mansions and the finest of hotels, but he could breathe here. He didn't think he stood out like a sore thumb. Like everyone could see straight through him and knew where he'd come from and why he didn't belong in their high-class worlds.

Of course, he would never admit why he truly liked them. It wasn't the women, though he definitely felt comfortable with them. It was because he could so often find a reason to fight, and that was what made him happy.

It was perverse that the only time he felt truly at peace was when he was punching some asshole who deserved it. It was the only time the rage that sat in his gut ever lessened. It was always there, boiling under the surface. Sometimes pounding on a deserving victim was the only thing that made him feel in control.

He let himself do it because he often worried if he didn't find a deserving victim, he might end up pounding on an innocent one.

It was bubbling up tonight, which was precisely why he'd come out here. He'd managed to stay perfectly calm while Drew railed at him. Now he needed a release or he might punch his own brother.

"It wasn't that bad." Riley put up his hand, a signal he was ready for his second and final beer of the evening. Bran had no illusions that his older brother was planning on sitting and drinking with him all night. Riley had something to go home to. Someone to go home to. He and his wife, Ellie, were in town to do some business with Drew, but Bran knew the truth. Riley wanted to make sure the next part of their plan got pulled off. Steven Castalano might have gotten what he deserved and Phillip Stratton had died before they could get to him, but neither death had served to clear their father's name. "And Bran had his own issues. I just wish I'd made it down in time to see the actual act. Did you really Inigo Montoya the Fisher chick?"

Ah, Inigo Montoya. He was the iconic character from the *The Princess Bride*, the one looking for the six-fingered man who'd killed his father. He'd dedicated his life to revenge and found peace once it was over.

Would Bran find any peace? He rather thought not since his sins might be as bad as those he sought revenge against.

Coward. Useless pathetic coward.

In his dreams, that was what she called him as he huddled behind the bed while she died.

"From what he told me, he walked right up to her and called Pat a murderer within the first minute of opening his damn mouth," Hatch complained. "I'm not kidding you, Ri. I thought Drew was going to have a heart attack when he realized Bran had gone rogue. I've never seen that boy turn that particular shade of red before. It was right on the edge of purple."

Riley took the beer from the blond waitress's hand and tipped her, but Bran noticed his eyes didn't move over the woman the way they used to. Riley had been the player of the group. There hadn't been a woman around who was safe from his charm before he'd met Ellie Stratton. "I've seen it happen. Do you remember the time I missed buying that stock he wanted because I was fooling around with his secretary? Yeah, he looked like an eggplant then."

At least he wasn't the only one who disappointed Drew. "It'll work out better this way."

The waitress leaned over, showing an enormous amount of cleavage. Her breasts were nice and round and looked to be soft. He liked soft, but somehow he couldn't get buttoned-up and a little prudey Carly Fisher out of his head. "Is there anything I can get for you, hon?"

He smiled back and fished a twenty out of his pocket. "How about a bottle of water? Keep the change."

It was a massive tip in a place like this, but then, he could see the fine lines on her belly from stretch marks. They didn't mar her loveliness, but they were likely why she was serving drinks instead of dancing. She wore a charm bracelet on her left wrist with small dangling soccer balls and ballet shoes. Her smiles were for cash, not because she was looking to find a date for the night. She had children to feed and probably no one to help her with it.

When she smiled his way this time, it seemed genuine. "Absolutely. I'll be right back."

Hatch's eyes rolled. "You tipped her like two hundred percent."

Riley shook his head. "Don't even bother. Overtipping strippers and down-on-their-luck servers is his reason for living. I'm glad he's slowing down tonight. He's usually halfway through a bottle of tequila."

It was something that made him feel better—the overtipping, not the tequila. The tequila simply dulled the pain for a while. The tipping made him feel better about life. He was pretty sure most women wouldn't work at a place like this unless they had no other way to get by.

Carly was in the same position, though she got to keep her clothes on. She was being forced to work for a woman who liked to humiliate her employees, from what he understood. He hated the thought of sweet Carly, who had made sure to praise their waitress and asked her to thank the chef for the meal, being in a position where she never got praise of her own. It was important to feel worthy, to know that you could do good. Tipping was a form of praise.

His brother leaned in, completely ignoring the show that was going on around them. "Are you sure this is going to work? Because I'm not certain what Drew will do if it doesn't."

"You think he'll finally lose it and kick me out?" He was well aware that he was the difficult brother. He was the one who'd barely made it through school. They'd pushed him and carried him through to get his MBA, and then shoved him in marketing, where he couldn't do too much damage. He was the one who got arrested from time to time when he didn't get away from a fight fast enough.

Riley shook his head and put a hand on Bran's shoulder. "He would never do that and you know it."

Because he felt guilty. They all did. Bran had gotten the short end of a shitty stick, and his siblings all felt bad about it. It was why they put up with him. He wasn't close to being the smartest or the smoothest. He didn't have Mia's never-ending light. He was the one who could take the most punches.

Maybe he had made a mistake today. Why should someone like Carly listen to a man like him? Maybe he'd played her the wrong way. Drew would have walked in and dominated the conversation. He would have proven how smart he was. Riley would have smoothed everything over, but he still would have been in control. By the end of the evening, Carly would have been eating out of the palm of his hand and there would have been no need to sit around and pray she called. Riley would have closed that particular deal. Hell, either one of his brothers would have gone home and gone to bed with her.

He hadn't wanted to sleep with her like that. Not under false pretenses. When he got in bed with her, he wanted to know it was because she wanted him, the real Bran.

He should have known that was a stupid idea.

What the hell had he been thinking?

Riley sighed and sat back. "It's not going to be so bad. We'll come up with another way."

Hatch frowned. "We have to scrap all our plans because there's no way of knowing what the girl told Pat. I know I haven't talked to that bitch in the last twenty years, but trust me. She hasn't changed. A woman like that never changes. She's just as hateful now as she was back then, and she rules her employees with an iron fist. Your girl probably called her boss the minute you walked away and they're sitting together right now making plans."

He didn't want to believe that. He wanted to believe Carly was exactly what she looked like. "I don't know. I think she would have told me."

"This is why you're in the marketing department and your brothers do the nasty jobs," Hatch pointed out.

Riley held up a hand Hatch's way. "Don't make this worse. And I happen to know she hasn't called Patricia. We're monitoring her phone lines, even the private one."

"Why does she need a private line?" a new voice asked. A feminine voice.

"I think she talks to her sister on that line. Her business line has to be kept open at all times for the grand dame to call." Bran looked up and his sister-in-law was behind him. Ellie was a lovely woman in her late twenties who looked utterly out of place in the dingy confines of the strip club. She was dressed for business even at this time of night, and in a city where her personal business had no offices. Which begged the question. "What are you doing here?"

She shrugged and sank down beside her husband, who immediately had an arm around her. "This is the only place you hang out, so we're all here. Well, everyone who's down here. Drew and I were working on the reports for the StratCast meeting next week. He was going to join me here but something apparently pinged. He seemed very worried about something pinging and so he dropped me off and he's sending a car out to get us later. Wow, this is a whole lotta naked people."

Women. There were no naked guys, and that was exactly how Bran liked it. He wouldn't even need the car tonight. He could safely drive the Jeep he'd picked up a few days before as Drew's "cover" car. Now it was Bran's, and since he wouldn't get trashed in front of his sister-in-law, he could drive it home. "What would have pinged?"

Riley frowned. "There's only one thing that would have him dropping off Ellie instead of seeing her inside. Someone pinged our personal data."

Hatch's finger immediately pointed Bran's way. "I told you so."

Shit. He'd fucked up.

"Hey, let's all chill. We have no idea who pinged what," Riley argued.

"If Carly looked up our personal data, it's only because I told her to. She should know what she's getting into." Bran felt his shoulders starting to tense, the rolling in his gut getting worse. He'd done it again. He'd screwed up something by thinking he was smarter than everyone else when he knew damn well he wasn't.

"Sure. Why don't you invite her back to our place? Let her look through our files. Just give her a damn key already." Hatch stood up. "I'm getting another drink."

Riley was hard on his heels. "I'll talk to him. Don't worry about it, Bran. It's going to be okay."

No, it wasn't. Eventually everyone would get sick of putting up with his shit and he would be on his own again. His hands fisted at his sides and all he could think about was finding some asshole and picking a fight. It usually wasn't hard. He could look out over a bar and select the man most likely to have a tiny penis and an overinflated ego. It was a dangerous combination but one he counted on to get his personal needs met.

Ellie leaned forward. They'd left him with Ellie. He couldn't lose his shit in front of his sister-in-law. "Hey, are you all right?"

When the waitress came back with the water, he'd order something strong. Tequila. A whole bottle. It didn't matter. Someone would give him a ride home. Sometimes he thought Drew and Riley lived for those moments when they could rescue their baby brother. "I'm fine."

Ellie's big brown eyes were steady on him. "No, you're not. Hatch is being too hard on you. And something crawled up Drew's backside and died. He was in a terrible mood. Was it all about the fact that you took charge?"

Took charge? He was fairly certain no one would use those words to describe what he'd done. "I screwed everything up."

Ellie leaned forward, her hand reaching across the table to cover his. "You did the one thing no one else could."

He laughed, though there was no humor in it. "What's that? Fucked it all up before the mission could even get off the ground? Managed to get everything exposed faster than the speed of light?"

"No, you did the right thing," she said. "You didn't use her. You didn't treat her like she meant nothing. You treated that woman like she had value and she had meaning beyond your own needs. You were a real man today and I'm proud of you."

He had to take a deep breath to ensure he didn't do anything foolish like cry in front of his sister-in-law and every stripper in St. Augustine. "I don't think my brothers agree."

"They have a different version of right than you do. Theirs is more selfish. Don't get me wrong. I love them all, but you're special. You didn't have to go through nearly losing someone you loved to make the right decision."

Oh, but he had. So long ago. "Riley thought he was doing the right thing."

Riley had gone undercover, much the way Drew had been planning to do with Carly. He'd taken a job at StratCast and begun romancing the boss. He'd fallen in love with Ellie, and his deception had nearly cost him in the end.

"It wasn't the choice you would have made. Tell me something. What did you think of the plan to get Castalano?"

He hated to disillusion her, but he wasn't about to throw his brothers under the bus to gain points with Ellie. "I thought it would hurt you. I also thought it was necessary. Don't make me out to be something I'm not. I was on board. It was watching you get hurt that made me do what I did today. I didn't want another woman to go through what you did. Now you tell me something. If I'd walked in and laid out my case, what would you have done?"

Her brow creased as she thought about it. "I don't know. I hope I would have looked into it and realized what was right, but I can't say. Would I have believed my father was capable of doing what he was accused of? Yes. There's no question in my mind I would have believed that, but would I have put myself and my company at risk for a family I just met? No idea. I only know that things will work out for the best.

I believe it deep down, Bran. You were meant to stop Drew today. You were meant to help that woman out. One way or another it will all end up okay."

"How can you know that?"

"Because no matter what happens, we're a family and as long as we're all okay, everything is right with the world. We can get through anything together. That's what real families do, and trust me, I've had the wrong kind in my life. Until I met you and your brothers I didn't truly understand what family meant."

Family. It was a confusing word in his head. He'd been a "part" of so many families. Family for Bran meant an ever-changing sea he couldn't quite learn to swim in. Years later and he was still expecting someone to show up and tell him it was time to shove all his shit in a trash bag and move on to the next place. "I think they're getting tired of dealing with my issues."

"No," Ellie said, her eyes soft. "They'll never get tired of you. They only want to see you happy. That's all. And Drew will get over this. You'll see." She patted his hand once more and then an unholy grin lit her face. "Now tell me where I'm supposed to shove the cash in. I've never been to a strip club before. Why do they call it stripping if they walk out and they're already naked? Come on. A girl needs a little time to get warmed up."

He couldn't help but grin because his sister-in-law was the sweetest shade of pink. A bleach-blonde with surgically enhanced breasts was currently making love to a pole in front of them. "She's got pasties on."

"Do I shove the five in her butt crack? That seems very personal to me."

"I think you can leave it on the stage. That's probably as close as you should get." It was odd but having his sister-in-law here made him really look around at how skeevy things were. He wasn't about to let her get too close to that stage where a bunch of drunken assholes were watching naked women. He wanted a fight, but he didn't want one that badly. "Actually, you don't go anywhere at all."

She frowned. "But I've never been in a strip club before. I'm embracing your world."

Yeah, his world seemed pretty damn nasty now that Ellie was here. "Maybe we should head home and see if the pinging stopped. I'm sure it was Carly. I'll explain that I told her to get out there and look. I didn't think she would actually get in that deep. Drew's only got alerts on certain things like someone trying to connect our legal last names with our birth names and some stuff that goes back to Dad. I expected her to look at the articles on the Internet. Anyone can find those."

Drew was going to have his ass. Carly had turned out to be pretty computer savvy if she set off Drew's alarms.

Riley and Hatch walked back up. Riley handed his wife a glass of wine.

Ellie smiled as she took it. "Pinot grigio?"

Riley grimaced. "Uh, they had white, red, or pink."

"Wine is not big with strip club crowds." Bran looked up and the waitress was making her way back with his water. She fought her way through the men who seemed to think it was their right to squeeze her ass as she walked by. She grimaced but kept walking, her shoulders back and head held high.

Yeah, the night might go his way. He might get to beat the holy shit out of some bastards.

"I think they're missing a valuable crowd," Ellie said. "Women are getting more and more adventurous these days. I think if they had a good wine selection, some artisanal cheeses, maybe they could bring in women with more exotic tastes."

"Dear God, don't let her start an upscale strip club," Hatch said with a frown. "Skanky is the only way to go in these places. It's an undeniable right of every strip club to look like the ass end of a junkyard."

Bran felt his phone vibrate in his pocket and sighed. Who could be calling him at this hour? It was almost certainly his brother, calling to let him know how Carly had wormed her way into data he didn't want her to see, and wasn't Bran happy he'd shown her the door and practically given her a key? He thought about not answering, but it was better to get it out of the way now.

Maybe he wouldn't need that water. The waitress handed it to him as he pulled his phone out.

"Thank you," he said.

She smiled and asked the table if there was anything else she could get them.

Bran didn't hear the answer because he got a glimpse of his phone and suddenly was scrambling to make sure he didn't miss the call. He swiped his finger across the screen. "Carly?"

"Hello? Is this Brandon?"

Damn. The music was so loud. He stood and started for the door. "This is Bran. Carly, are you all right? It's late. I didn't expect you to call."

He heard the distinct sound of sniffling as he made it out to the parking lot. It was quieter now, the sound of old hair metal mostly contained in the prefab walls. The gravel of the lot crunched under his feet.

"I had to call," Carly explained. "I made up my mind. I'm in. I'll help you with anything you need to bring her down, but I'm going to need something from you."

"What's that?"

Her voice was shaky as she replied, "A million dollars."

"I'll be at your place in five minutes." He disconnected the call and took a deep breath.

Either Carly wasn't the woman he'd thought she was or she'd managed to get into deep trouble at some point in time this evening.

Either way, he would figure out how to make it work for him.

*Chapter Four*

Carly jumped when she heard the knock on her door. Her hands were still shaking an hour later. She had to wonder if she would ever feel safe in her townhouse again.

*And what happens when Roger gets out of jail in a few years?* With prison overcrowding in California, it was entirely possible his ten to fifteen years could turn into five to seven with good behavior. He would be out and gambling his life away, and when he couldn't pay, would there be more of these people on her doorstep?

"Carly? It's me," a deep voice said. "Could you please let me in? I look pretty suspicious standing out here."

She forced herself to move across the living room. Why had he come here tonight? It was so late and the last thing she needed was to deal with another man. Still, he was the man who might be able to write a check and get her out of trouble, so he held all the cards at this stage.

God, she was so sick of this feeling, so sick of being helpless. She opened the door and stared at him for a second. Her memory didn't do him justice. Dark hair curled over the tops of his ears and tumbled down his forehead. His eyes were emerald green and he had the square jaw of an action hero. He filled up her doorway with his big, muscular body, but somehow he exuded security and safety. It took everything she had not to walk right into his arms and tell him everything and hand over all her problems to him.

He'd said he would take care of them for her. It was the exchange between them. He would take care of her problems and she would help him take down the worst human being she'd ever met.

And considering she'd dealt with the mob earlier in the evening and still thought Patricia was the worst, that was saying something.

Instead of hugging him, she stepped back and allowed him inside. "You didn't have to come over tonight."

He strode in, filling her frilly apartment with his uniquely masculine energy. "I think I did. While I was on my way over I was simply curious. Now I'm a little worried. Who broke in here tonight?"

"How did you know that?"

"There were distinct scratches on the lock of your door. Someone used a lock pick to try to get in here. They looked pretty fresh and there were the faintest scrapings of metal on the ground beneath. They were rough with it. Not a pro."

He was completely wrong about that. She could still see that man sitting at her table, a gun trained on her as she walked into her kitchen. "Oh, they were pros. Maybe not at picking locks, but they were definitely professionals."

"Tell me everything." His tone had gone deep, his eyes looking around her place as though assessing everywhere an attacker could hide. "Did they hurt you?"

For the first time since it had happened, she could take a deep breath. She wasn't alone. She got the feeling if they came back, they would have to go through Bran to get to her. Why? She had no idea, but there was something about the man that made her want to trust him.

"I'm fine. It was all threats for tonight."

"How did it start?"

"I'd been doing what you asked. I'd been doing some research into what happened with your dad."

His lips quirked up slightly. "Yes, you're more thorough than I thought you would be."

She wasn't sure what he meant by that. He started to move into the kitchen. "I'm very thorough. I'm quite competent. Anyway, I decided to call you in the morning. I came down to make some tea and when I got downstairs, there was a man at my kitchen table."

Bran kept moving. He glanced around the kitchen and then went straight for the back door. It led to the tiny yard where she kept her rosebushes and a bistro set. She barely got to use it, but some mornings she would sit outside and have her coffee before she went to work. Too often she was out of the place before dawn, but there were rare mornings when she got a little time.

"Why don't you have a dead bolt on the front door?"

She winced. "I haven't changed anything security-wise since I moved in here. My husband used to do all the home repair stuff. Not that he did much of it."

She'd married him so young. She'd learned how to cook and do some sewing and how to grow plants from the women in her trailer park, but she knew next to nothing about home repair. Their trailer had always been falling down around them.

"I'll have one installed tomorrow." Bran inspected the back door. "Keep talking. Who were they? Was it the DiLuca guy you mentioned this afternoon? I've already put in a request for a report on him."

It was good to know he worked fast. "They were his employees. Apparently Roger owed some money to the mob and they're finally getting around to trying to collect. I really know how to pick a husband."

"This door needs a dead bolt, too, and I'll have to secure the fences. You need an alarm system with video monitoring. And you're divorced," he said, turning back her way. "Do they need to see the divorce decree?"

"I'm afraid Mr. DiLuca is a traditional kind of guy."

"He's a greedy kind of guy." Bran slid out of the light jacket he'd been wearing and hooked it over the back of one of her chairs. The T-shirt he had on under it showed off how well toned his arms were.

"I think that goes without saying," she agreed. "Anyway, the man who broke in basically explained that I'm being held responsible for Roger's debt. He wasn't alone. There was a second man. I kind of think he's the one who does all the real dirty work."

Bran's jaw had gone tight. "I'm going to assume this million you suddenly need is to pay off the debt or they'll come back and hurt you."

She hated the way her eyes watered. "Yes, but if you don't think my services will be worth that much, then you should let me know now."

His whole demeanor softened and he stepped toward her, putting his hands on her shoulders and staring straight down at her. "I'll give you the million. It's not payment for anything."

"Why would you do that?"

"Because my brother set up a trust for me a few years back and he manages it. It's ridiculous but I'm worth a hundred million dollars. I won't miss it and you need it. So it's yours. I want you to work with me because you believe in the cause not because there's no other way out of your problems."

She couldn't stop the tears now because he was saying all the right things and she so wanted to believe him. She wanted to believe there was a man in the world who simply did good and wanted her to help him. "I don't know if I can trust you."

Suddenly she was wrapped up in his big arms, the heat of his body warming her in a way no blanket ever could. "It's all right. I'll prove myself to you, Carly. You go ahead and cry. I'm sure it was terrifying, but it's okay now. I'm not going to leave you alone again. Not tonight."

She knew she shouldn't but she couldn't help herself a second longer. The events of the day pressed down on her and she cried. Tears poured out and she let herself be surrounded by his warmth.

It was easy to let go with him. Stupid, yes, but so easy. She'd been alone for so long. Even when Roger had been with her, there'd been no comfort from him. There had been what passed for good sex and companionship, and the feeling that she had to be so smart to have married such an attractive, charming man. And there had been a deep need to please him. He'd done a good job of keeping her always on the edge. He would give her just enough praise and affection to keep her wanting more.

Bran gave her comfort. He gave her arms that wrapped around her, hugging her tight.

Finally she moved away, her tears drying. He'd smoothed her hair back, saying nothing while she wept. He'd just been there.

She wanted to turn her face up to him, to let him know how nice it would be if he kissed her.

*Stop. Don't go any farther down that road.*

She probably looked a mess and anything he gave her would be out of pity. She forced herself to step back.

"I'm sorry. I shouldn't have done that."

"Yes, you should have. You needed it and I liked being needed for a few minutes." He reached out and tucked a stray lock back. "You don't understand me yet, but that was meaningful to me. Now go sit down and we'll talk. You said you'd been coming down to make some tea. What kind do you want?"

Actually, some tea might settle her stomach. She wasn't as anxious now that he was here, but she still doubted she could get to sleep. "I'll get it."

He shook his head. "No, you sit. I'm perfectly capable of boiling water. We need to talk about how this is going to work. If it's going to work at all." He held out a chair for her. "I meant what I said. The money is yours whether you work with me or not."

"Why would you do that? Look, I get that you have plenty of cash, but it's a million dollars."

He grabbed her teakettle and quickly filled it. "I don't care about money. I care about bad shit happening to good people."

"How do you know I'm good?"

"Because you wouldn't let your sister go to jail. Hell, you wouldn't even allow her to be arrested. You do understand she could have gotten off with a good lawyer. I read up on your husband's case after I left you this afternoon. Your sister was very young. She likely knew nothing about the embezzlement. There's not a lot of chance a jury convicts her with a decent attorney."

"I couldn't take that chance." It hadn't even been a thought in her head. She couldn't let Meri come so close to danger.

"Does she know what you did for her?"

That was another thing she hadn't even considered. She never wanted Meri to know how poorly it could have gone. "No. Patricia allowed me to write her a check for the money in that account. Luckily Roger hadn't taken it yet. I explained to Meri that I needed it and she turned it all over without question. She was too involved in helping me hold everything together to ask too many questions. I didn't want her to feel bad about it. We didn't grow up in the best of circumstances. We had to watch out for each other. If she thought I was stuck in this job because of her, she would try to get me out of it any way she could. She's a great kid. She's worked hard and she deserves a bright future."

"But you don't?"

"Everything in my life that's messed up is because I made the wrong choices. Meri didn't. She made all the right ones. She's the smart one. She got a scholarship right out of high school. I barely made it through community college. I thought I was lucky to get the job with Cain Corp." She noticed him opening cabinet doors. "The tea is in the one on your left. I'll take the chamomile."

He found her tea box with its neatly organized bags and paraphernalia. He was smiling as he opened it. "You really like tea."

When he grinned like that she couldn't help but smile back. He was such a lovely man. "I do, but there's also wine in the fridge, and I think I have some brandy somewhere."

He settled a teacup in front of her and another across from her. "I can handle tea. Do I look like a man who only drinks alcohol?"

"Well, it sounded like you were in a bar when I called." The music had been so loud. She could envision him at a hot nightclub, dancing with all the ladies. He would be a hit with them.

"I was at a strip club," he said with a shrug. "It's a hobby. Now tell me how you did get the job at Cain Corp. You're right. You weren't qualified. All of her other assistants had degrees from prestigious schools."

They'd come from Harvard or Vassar. The one right before Carly had been a Brown graduate. They'd all gone on to bigger jobs in the corporation. "I was actually applying for another job but Patricia overheard me talking about a recipe my grandmother used to make. She'd been trying to put together a hometown Christmas theme for an episode of her show. I was trying to get a job at her magazine as a proofreader and I was talking about the fact that the recipe they were using wasn't truly Southern. It was too froufrou to be down-home. Patricia stopped and asked me to show her. We have these huge test kitchens in the offices. So I did. My grandma's sage corn bread dressing is now a staple in a lot of households and I suddenly became her assistant."

The kettle started to whistle and Bran made quick work of pouring the hot water. "Did she give you credit for the recipe?"

"That's not how it works."

"I would bet she claimed she'd found the recipe in her mother's attic or she invented it herself, right?"

Carly settled the tea bag in her cup. She preferred loose leaf, but her life ran at such a hectic pace that she didn't usually have time to let her tea steep properly, so she was left with this option. "She claimed she'd done all kinds of research with Southern cooks. All bullshit, naturally. But that's how one builds a brand. One lies through one's teeth."

"So she saw your potential and used it to prop herself up. How much have you given her over the years?"

"So much. It's a slippery slope. At first I shared with her because I thought if I did a good job, she would reward me. That never happened. I thought maybe she'd give me a byline in the magazine, or hell, maybe I can go on her lifestyle show and help out. That was when she explained I don't fit her image."

Bran slid into the seat across from her, selecting his own tea. A white tea with orange and passionflower. It was a vibrant tea with a bright finish. "Her image?"

"Celebrities and well-respected members of the community. She doesn't have assistants on."

"How much of her work do you do?"

"If Patricia gets stuck on something, she'll send me into the kitchens to figure it out. I'm the one who designed the Thanksgiving menu last year. She couldn't handle it so she shoved it off on me. She's getting worse about that. I think she likes the business part more than the actual core work. She would greatly prefer to be in a boardroom than the kitchens."

"Not you, though."

She felt a smile slide across her face. "Oh, I live for those days. You don't know what it's like. I have an unlimited budget and access to every tech aid I could ever want. I have top-of-the-line appliances, and no one cares what I do as long as it works. I grew up having to make do with whatever happened to be in the kitchen at the time, and mostly that was crap. I can actually do a lot with a can of Spam."

"There were days when I longed for Spam."

She'd forgotten. It was too easy to see only the wealth and privilege of his current state. "That's right. You were in the system for a long time. You know what it means to have to make do."

"I know what it means to not know if I'll make it through the night, but we were talking about you."

"I'm going to help you." She'd made up her mind before he'd come to her doorstep. He might be willing to write her a check and walk away, but she needed to pay him back in some small way. "I only ask that when you take her down, if you take her down, you try to leave me out of it. I don't think she'll come after me unless she figures out I was working with you. Actually, I don't care if she comes after me at all. I'm worried about Meri. The statute of limitations doesn't run out for another two years."

"I promise you no harm will come to your sister. She'll be protected by us. You don't have to worry about that, and you need to know this. We will take Patricia Cain down. We'll take her down and she won't be able to hurt anyone again."

"Do you promise?" She wasn't sure why she asked, wasn't exactly sure what she was asking him to promise her. It was more than simply taking down Patricia. She wanted to believe him.

He reached across the table, covering her hand with his. "I promise."

Somehow she got the feeling he, too, was thinking of more than the mission at hand.

"Are you absolutely sure you want to stay here?" Carly frowned as she brought out a blanket twenty minutes later. "The couch is pretty small. I'm not sure you'll be comfortable on it."

Bran was one hundred percent sure he wouldn't be, but that wasn't the point. He tugged his shirt over his head and folded it neatly. "I've slept in worse places. And I think it's best I stay here tonight. Unless you want to come home with me."

He knew she wasn't going to take that option, but it would be nice. If Drew and Riley and Hatch met her, got to know her, they wouldn't be so worried about her. All he'd had to do was spend a couple of hours with her to know that she was a deeply loyal woman. All he needed to do was prove he was worthy of that loyalty. She'd been bitten before and she was shy, but the man who gained her trust again would get everything from her.

She deserved to have someone who would watch her back, and that included ensuring that she could sleep the rest of the night. What little of it was left.

If someone showed up on her doorstep, he would take care of them. As viciously as he possibly could. He still intended to write her that check. He would do it because it would bring her peace of mind, but he was going to make sure none of them ever threatened her again. He would handle them in a way that would ensure her safety.

She shook her head. "You said your place is out in Palm Coast. That's forty minutes away. I have to be at work pretty early in the morning." She turned and started working on the couch, but not before he'd caught her staring at his chest. She smoothed out a sheet over the leather. "Why all the way out there? Why wouldn't you set up here in St. Augustine?"

He would have to thank his brother-in-law for all the workouts. It was how they'd bonded. Case Taggart liked to lift weights and he'd brought Bran into his daily routine the last time he was in town. It wasn't like Bran had been out of shape before, but Case's daily regime had taken his lanky frame and honed it to something strong and masculine. He wished he could tell her how soft and sexy she looked in her pj's. She had a robe wrapped around her, but every now and then it slipped open, revealing creamy skin and breasts he would love to get his hands on. He'd spent the majority of his evening watching women strip, but it was Carly in her pink tank top and perfectly respectable pajama bottoms that had his cock engaged. "We have some friends who have a condo out there and it's outfitted with the best tech possible both computer-wise and security. Also, we thought it would be best if we were close but not too close. Patricia knew our parents quite well. One new person in her life who reminds her of old enemies won't cause too much stress but if she were to see me and Drew, or worse, Hatch, she would definitely be suspicious. We're simply being careful."

"You have your mother's coloring, but you don't really look like her. You look more like your dad," Carly said as she worked a pillow into a soft-looking pillowcase.

"I'm taller than he was, a bit more built. I looked more like him when I was smaller. Take off about thirty pounds of muscle, cut my hair into a military buzz, and put some glasses on me, and I look quite like him. Of course I've been told my father had an air of unmistakable genius about him that I don't have." Not that Hatch had put it that way. He'd explained that most people didn't remember Benedict for his looks. They remembered his brilliant brain. "Drew is most like him. Another reason I thought it was better for me to go in instead of him. I think Drew would remind Patricia of our father."

"I don't know about that. She's not very observant. One of the things you need to know about her is that she's a narcissist. She doesn't care about anything but herself and her bottom line." She looked up at him. "Your brother is the man behind 4L?"

Naturally everyone was impressed with a thirty-four-year-old billionaire. "He is. I need you to understand that we have resources that we'll use to take care of you. You'll have a job at 4L if you want one. I'll promise you that right now."

"You need a personal assistant?" she said, her lips curling slightly.

He frowned because he hadn't thought she'd ask that question. "No. I don't really need one, but I promise I'll find something for you. You won't be left out in the cold. 4L is a big company and we own a lot of other companies. You would have your pick."

Actually, Ellie could use a new PA. That wouldn't be a bad fit. Ellie would be good to Carly and Bran spent a lot of time in New York. He could see her from time to time. He would have to think about it. He didn't mention it, though, because Ellie's last assistant had been brutally murdered in front of her. It wouldn't give Carly great faith in them as a group.

She settled the pillow down and smoothed out the blanket. "I don't know how I feel about a new job. Not that I'm not happy at the thought of keeping my house, but being a personal assistant wasn't exactly my life plan. I wanted to write cookbooks. Well, I wanted to start out by editing them and work my way up."

"It sounds like you want to be a chef."

Her head shook slightly. "No. It's different. I don't want my own restaurant or to be in charge of a kitchen. I want to work at a lifestyle magazine. I love looking at decorating trends and cooking trends. A chef tends to focus on one type of cuisine. I want to try them all, not necessarily be a master at them. I like making people comfortable. At my heart, I'm a homemaker."

Her home was lovely. The minute he'd walked in he'd felt a certain peace rush over him and not simply because the space was well decorated. Carly herself made a person feel at home.

Even when she was crying on his shoulder. She would probably run as fast as she could if she knew how much that had fed his soul. It wasn't that he liked watching her cry. He'd enjoyed knowing he was helping her. He'd loved the way she'd clung to him, her arms tight around his body.

He probably shouldn't tell her that, either. Best to stick to the plan. He sank down to the sofa, sitting beside her but giving her plenty of space. "We should talk about how you're going to integrate me into your life."

A fine blush crossed her cheeks. "Maybe we should say you're my cousin or something."

Little coward. "No. No one is going to believe I'm your cousin. And why would you take your cousin with you to LA?"

"Because we're family?"

"That won't work. I have to be your boyfriend. We have to be intimate. Your husband used to travel with you."

"He worked for Cain Corp, too." She frowned and he could tell there was some serious debating going on in her head. "There's a clause in my contract that states if I have to be gone for more than a month, I can bring a spouse or significant other with me as long as my work continues to be exemplary."

"I'm surprised she would allow that."

"A couple of years back she had an assistant who threatened to quit because she couldn't bring her girlfriend along. Patricia was all about the LGBT community at that point so she rewrote the contract. Let's just say after she put that clause in and was photographed with her assistant and the girlfriend, she suddenly had some of the world's best designers willing to design kitchen and barware for her lifestyle line. She made a hundred million dollars off that choice."

Luckily that choice now worked for him in more ways than one. "So she's narcissistic and savvy. Another reason why she'll never buy that I'm your cousin."

Carly frowned, obviously not convinced. "I don't know about that. I could say you recently got into town and you want to see what I do. She might buy that."

"Not for a second. A—she's probably got a fat file on you, including all of your relatives. B—it would be difficult for me to look at you like a cousin. I'm afraid we've got some chemistry between us that doesn't scream familial connection."

"We don't have chemistry," she replied quickly as though she couldn't get the words out of her mouth fast enough. "I don't have chemistry with anyone. Actually, I don't believe that chemistry thing exists."

So prim and so wrong. "Really? You're telling me you've never felt the pull of real sexual attraction? I'm not talking about being hard up and wanting to get laid. I'm talking about wanting one person so badly you think you might not be able to breathe unless you get to put a hand on her, have her touch you back. You think you might not want to live another second without kissing her."

The pink was back in her cheeks, but her eyes were steady on his. "This isn't going to work. Look, we should talk about this because I'm not that girl. You can't control me with sex because I'm not that into it. I did the marriage thing. I went into it a virgin and everything. According to him, he'd had a whole lot of lovers before me and while the sex was all right, it certainly wasn't worth what it cost me."

"You've had one lover your whole life?" That was a bit shocking. She was almost thirty years old. She should have had a couple of relationships, maybe a casual fling or two.

"I'm picky, I guess."

"Or you haven't met the right man."

She huffed a little. "I suppose that's you."

"I'm not going to say I'm the greatest lover in the world, but I do know how to take care of my partners. There's a difference between getting off and making love."

She stared at him like he'd grown an extra head. "Making love?"

"Most women prefer that term." He'd learned that the hard way.

She shook her head. "I'm not most women. I want up front and honest."

"All right. There's a difference between getting off and fucking someone you need for hours and hours on end because you can't quite seem to stop."

"You've had that?"

"I've had women I was attached to. I wouldn't say I've ever made love to a woman I was in love with." He forced the idea of Mandy out of his head. They'd been so young and he'd only kissed her a few times, fumbling attempts at showing her how much he cared. He could still remember the way she giggled the first time he'd pressed his lips to hers and how she'd squealed when he'd tried to use his tongue on her like the older kids had told him adults did.

Carly shook her head. "We've gotten off track. I'm trying to explain to you that the boyfriend route isn't something a lot of people at the company will buy. I haven't dated at all since the divorce and my lovely husband used to talk about how I was an ice queen. The last year of our marriage wasn't exactly warm between us. I caught him cheating a couple of times and was on the verge of kicking him out when the embezzlement charges came up. I'm afraid no one is going to believe I suddenly found a hottie and am getting my groove back. I didn't have a groove in the first place."

"They'll believe it because I'll sell it. They'll believe it because there is chemistry between us whether you want to acknowledge it or not. We sat there all afternoon talking and being perfectly comfortable together. How many strangers can do that? Unless you were pretending." He would bet everything he had that she was crap at pretending. It was precisely why he needed to get her comfortable with him. She wouldn't be able to fake it. They had a few weeks before they were supposed to go to California. If it was going to work, she needed to relax around him, to feel good about casually touching him, to look like a woman who regularly found herself in his bed.

Which meant he should make sure she did find herself there.

It wasn't a sacrifice. His dick would be perfectly happy going upstairs with her right now and climbing into her likely very luxurious bed.

"I wasn't pretending," she confirmed. "I had fun this afternoon. I enjoyed your company, but then I'm fairly lonely so it's not hard to entertain me. Be nice to me. Let me take the lead. Make me feel like the center of your attention. All good ways to manipulate me."

He was confused. "I was honest with you. I wasn't trying to manipulate you."

"Sure you weren't. That's why you would reach out and touch me every now and then."

"I did that because I wanted to. Carly, I wasn't lying. I'm not trying to seduce you so you'll work for me."

She frowned his way, her arms crossing over her chest. "Then why the seduction act?"

"Because I want to sleep with you."

That seemed to stop her in her tracks. She went silent and looked away. When she looked back, her jaw was square, her eyes steely. "I think you should leave."

"What?"

She stood up. "I'm not falling for this again. I'll deal with DiLuca on my own."

He needed to do some quick thinking. "Why are you pissed at me? What did I do?"

"I'm not buying the 'I want you' line of bullshit. It worked for Roger, but you're too late. I'm not falling for that again. You must have thought you hit the jackpot when you walked up to me today. You probably fist-pumped at the thought of how easy I would be to deal with. Plain girl, a little on the chubby side. She'll fall for the hot guy in a heartbeat. She'll do anything I want."

"Whoa, hold your horses there." He never lost his temper with a woman. Never. Carly was actually pushing his buttons. "I don't lie. I don't feel the need to do it to myself, so I don't bother to do it with other people. This situation is entirely different. I'm not your piece-of-shit ex-husband. I'm the man who's willing to write a big check to get you out of trouble. Watch the way the money flows, sweetheart, and then tell me who's manipulating whom."

Her eyes widened and her hands made fists at her sides. "There's the door. Feel free to use it."

He grabbed his shirt, pulled it over his head, and was glad he hadn't gotten around to kicking off his boots yet. It made for a more dignified retreat. She didn't want his help? That was fine with him. There were plenty of women out there who wouldn't accuse him of whatever the hell she was accusing him of. "And for the record, I do find you attractive. You're the one who seems to have a problem. I've done nothing but offer to help you."

"Yes, in exchange for betraying my boss."

She wanted to play this game? "I offered you the check without a single fucking string. I came over here in the middle of the night to make sure you were all right. And betraying your boss does nothing but make your life more livable."

She was silent for a moment and he grabbed his jacket.

Fuck. He'd totally fucked up again and he wasn't sure how he would handle it this time. The crazy thing was he wasn't this guy. He was always calm and patient with women, always on his best behavior. He knew when to keep his mouth closed and how to get back into a woman's good graces. He seemed incapable of doing either of those things tonight. Carly got him riled up.

It was a damn fine reason to go home and regroup. He would tell his brothers he'd screwed up. Hell, they were probably waiting for him to do just that. They'd been waiting for the news that she was walking away from the moment Bran strode up to her in the restaurant.

They would find a new way.

And he would be the idiot who still dealt with her mob problem because he couldn't stand the thought of her getting hurt.

He had his hand on the door when she reached out, touching his back.

"Please don't go."

He stood there for a moment, his back to her, his eyes on the door he should be walking through. "Maybe it's for the best. You don't seem to like me much. I've had my fill of people who don't think much of me. Enough to last a lifetime. If you're still interested in working with us, you can meet with Drew or we could send in a pro." There were trained bodyguards at McKay-Taggart and some men who'd served as CIA operatives. They would handle everything with cool professionalism. They wouldn't scare Carly away.

Could she sense how unworthy he was? Could she see past his outer mask and down to his cowardly soul?

"I'm sorry," she whispered. "You're right. This is my problem. I look at you and can't see a single way you would ever want me. I'm insecure and I've been taken for a ride before."

He let his head hit the door with a groan because he should have run. He was a sucker for a woman who didn't know how beautiful she was. He wanted to be the man to show her. "I'm not trying to take you for a ride. I swear. I'm not going to be anything but honest with you. I do want you. It's been a while since I wanted a woman the way I want you, but I'm not a long-term man. I'm the guy who can't offer you anything but a few weeks of my attention and a good time in bed. So I'll call in someone different tomorrow and maybe you can work the cousin angle with him."

"Or I can try not to let my asshole ex run my life any longer. You're right. You're not him. By our second date he was talking about how he could spend the rest of his life with me. And you're right when you say you've been nothing but helpful. I need to be honest with you, too. You scare me."

He didn't understand her. "I'm not trying to scare you."

"I know. And you're right about everything. No one will believe the cousin angle. Why the hell would my cousin spend so much time with me? And then there's the problem of me staring at my cousin's hot ass. And the fact that every woman in the company will be all over you if they think you're not taken. Some of them will still try. Some of those women had affairs with my husband."

He turned to her, realizing what the problem was. "I'm not going to make you look like a fool."

"I'm sorry. It's not easy for me. I've been the fool before. It's a hard role to play and it stripped me of every bit of confidence I had."

Finally she'd given him something he could work with. "Then let me give some of it back to you. Carly, I'm not lying. I think you're gorgeous. I thought it as I was walking up to you. I thought it as we sat and talked. I thought it as I ran here as fast as I possibly could after getting your phone call. I could have waited until morning. You were in. Think about it. I don't have to seduce you. You're in. So why would I do it?"

She shook her head, looking so damn young and vulnerable. "I don't know. That's why I'm scared."

"Don't be. Nothing happens that you don't choose." He held his hands up. "If you don't want to sleep with me, that's fine. I'll ease up. But that's why we might want to bring in someone different. You're going to have to show whoever plays your boyfriend some affection. If you don't think you can do that with me, let me find someone you'll feel comfortable with."

"Can we talk about this more in the morning? I need to sleep on this and I can't make a decision right now."

She looked so weary. It had been a rough day on them both, but for her it had been so much worse.

"Go to bed. I'll be here in the morning, and I meant what I said earlier. The check is yours. I'll handle it whether I'm your partner or not. This particular problem will be gone in a day or two, and I won't let you out of my sight until it's done."

She nodded and walked to the stairs before turning. "You see, that's why I'm scared. You're too good to be true."

He laughed, though there wasn't a lot of humor in it. "That's where you're wrong. Spend some time with me and you'll find out I'm nothing of the kind. I'm not joking or looking for sympathy, Carly. I'll disappoint you in the end. I disappoint everyone."

"Somehow I doubt that," she said with the faintest hint of a smile.

"I have to be at work early tomorrow. We'll talk about how we can make this work later. I'll start laying the groundwork. I'll tell everyone I've been quietly dating a man."

"I thought you wanted time to think."

"I don't need to think about the work," she explained. "I know I want to do that and I want to work with you. It's the other part I'm thinking about. I need some time to decide on whether that makes sense for me or not."

The other? His heart thudded a bit at the thought. She was thinking about sleeping with him? About making their ruse a reality? "All right. Take your time, because I'm not going anywhere."

"Good night, Bran."

"Good night, Carly." He pulled his shirt off again and got down to his boxers, a smile on his face. He had a shot. At the mission. He had a shot with her.

All in all, not a bad day.

## Chapter Five

Carly tried to focus on the computer screen in front of her, but somehow all the letters and pictures kept morphing into Bran. A full week after she'd met him and she still couldn't stop thinking about him. At some point his hotness had to become something she could ignore, right? She could still see him looking deliciously rumpled on the couch this morning before she'd left for work. She wasn't sure how he'd managed to force his body to sleep like that for a week, but he hadn't complained once. His long legs had hung off the side and his arms had been out over the blanket so she'd been able to see how cut they were. The man worked out. A lot. When he'd opened his eyes he'd reminded her of a sleepy panther, stretching his lean muscles. She'd left him yawning and pouring himself a cup of coffee.

He was still there, still at her townhouse. Or maybe he'd left by now. She'd given him her spare key because he was overseeing replacing the security at her place.

Was she a complete idiot? She was letting a man she barely knew deal with sensitive issues.

So why had it felt so right when she'd left him this morning and he'd told her not to worry, that he would handle everything?

So much temptation in one delicious body.

She'd lied to him when she'd said they didn't have chemistry. She felt it. Her breathing picked up when he entered a room, her skin warming. The physical reaction she had to that man smiling was completely unprecedented. She'd thought she'd been attracted to Roger. It was nothing compared to Bran.

Which was precisely why she should keep the relationship professional. She wanted him too much and that way lay danger.

Or she could grow up and have an actual real affair with a man she didn't intend to marry. She never planned on marrying again. Did she honestly think she would go the rest of her life without sex?

"There's a pretty girl," a tremulous voice said.

Yes, yes, she'd really thought she'd go the rest of her life without the touch of a man since all the ones she'd been surrounded by were complete assholes. She forced a smile on her face. "Good morning, Mr. Jones. I don't believe your wife has made it to the office yet. Is there anything I can do for you?"

Kenneth G. Jones had made his money the old-fashioned way. He'd inherited it. His father had been one of the railroad barons of old and the family had managed to weather the market crash of the twenties and the Great Depression. They'd come roaring back with real estate deals and network television stations that he'd finally merged into a media conglomerate. Now in his late eighties, Kenneth was one of the wealthiest men in America. He'd met Patricia a few years back and they'd married within six months.

Her boss had been waiting for Moneybags to die ever since.

On their wedding day, it had been announced that Patricia had become the head of her own network. That was why she'd married the lecherous geezer. She had what she wanted, but if she stayed with him until he died, she would also receive a nice portion of his assets according to their voluminous prenup. Of course it would likely be challenged in court by his two children, but Patricia didn't mind a fight and she usually won.

He leaned on his cane as he stared down at Carly. "There are many things you could do for me, but you haven't learned how to play ball yet, have you, honey? Your life would be so much easier if you did."

"I'm not sure what you mean, sir. Are you talking about baseball? I'm not into sports." She'd found that pretending to completely misunderstand his innuendo was the best way to handle things.

"Neither is Father," another voice said as Kenny Jr. joined them. He was in his fifties, dressed in a dapper suit. Unlike his father, he had some charm about him. "Unless you count cheating on that bat of a wife of his as a sport. He's managed to cheat on all five of his wives, so you are terribly smart to stay away from him."

He was also honest about his father's proclivities.

"Don't make me look bad in front of the girl, Kenny," his father said with a frown. "I'll wait in Patty's office. She should be here in a few moments. We need to talk about the art opening tonight."

She grimaced. Yep, she'd forgotten about it. There was a showing of a local artist who was being featured on *Patricia's Paradise*. They were filming for the show, but this was what Carly liked to call a "cuddly shoot," meaning it was to show Patricia with her family and as angelic and loving as possible. Maybe she wouldn't need her assistant there.

Maybe pigs would fly.

Kenneth walked off toward the office, his cane clacking against the floor, but Kenny stayed put. "You know at some point you should talk to Pat about how he treats you. Unless you would prefer I did it. I know she can be intimidating."

Carly was fairly certain Patricia couldn't care less that her octogenarian hubby felt free to sexually harass her on a regular basis. "It's fine. I'm sure he doesn't mean anything by it."

Kenny frowned, his handsome mouth turning down. "I think you underestimate him and that's a mistake. My father isn't a good man. Don't think for a second because he's old, he's frail. He uses that against a lot of people. I'm fairly certain his wife thought he'd be dead by now. I know when they were dating, he made a big deal out of how close to death he was."

Carly couldn't help but chuckle at that. "How very romantic."

"Well, there's not a lot of romance when there's that much money on the line. I should know. After being married for my money twice, I'm the dumbass who's always looking for number three. You would think after seeing how I grew up that I would prefer to be a bachelor."

"Yeah, well, I've only done the marriage thing once and I'm with you."

"He was a massive tool," Kenny said, not unkindly. "Not all men would treat you like that. You're the kind of woman who should be married. You would make someone an excellent wife. And I'm not simply talking about that egg thing you made in the kitchens the other day."

"Patricia's egg casserole?" It was going in a segment on best brunch recipes.

"Sure," he said with an eye roll. "Naturally she put her own name on it. Some of the crew was tasting it and I got a bite. I swear I want to come over to this side of the company. I do love real estate, but we don't get to eat all day like you guys."

"We have some fun. Hey, our jobs are to make entertaining easy. We're pretty good at it."

"You're pretty good at it." He glanced toward the door to Patricia's office. "Have you ever thought about doing your own thing? Everyone here knows you're the brains behind *Patricia's Paradise*. Have you ever thought about walking out of here and starting your own show?"

She dreamed about it, but there was the problem of leverage. Patricia had a ton of it. She would go ballistic if she thought Carly was going to become competition. "I'm not an on-camera personality."

Kenny's voice went low and he leaned over. "I disagree. I think you're exactly what the world needs to counterpoint my dear stepmother's chilly disdain for everyone. You're warm and funny, and you explain things in a simple way that brings people in rather than making them feel left out. Think about it. Despite what my father thinks, he won't live forever, and then I'll take over the media end of the company. I could work with you."

She would never get that shot. Patricia would see to it. "That's flattering."

He stood up again, his hands coming up as though conceding the issue for now. "Think about it. You've got plenty of time, but I would hate to see you waste your talents being my stepmother's flunky for too long. Learn everything you can from her and then get the hell out, because she'll turn on you in the end. It's how our world works. Hey, I had a thought."

She liked Kenny. He was a nice guy, it seemed. "What's that?"

"How about you come with me tonight to the showing? I know you have to work, but we could also hang out. Two confirmed single people providing cover for one another. You could help keep the gold diggers off me. I would view it as a huge favor."

"Are you that hard up, Kenny?" a frosty voice asked. Patricia stood in the doorway, her designer briefcase in hand. She focused on her stepson with a glacial glare. "I thought you were seeing that girl I set you up with."

There was no way to miss how tense Kenny got. His whole body seemed to stiffen. "I don't need you to set me up. And I definitely wouldn't go out with a woman you approved of, Patty."

"That's why your marriages failed. You chose the wrong women. My secretary would be another horrible choice," she said. "Not that you aren't perfectly nice, Carly dear. You simply aren't suited to be the wife of a powerful man. He needs someone who can move in our world, and you so often trip over your own two feet."

"I have zero interest in moving any further into society." She was still a little shocked Kenny had made the offer to escort her tonight.

He was often friendly, but in the years they'd known each other, he'd never once made a move on her. Maybe she was overthinking it and he really was trying to use her to keep other women away, but it seemed so odd for him to ask.

"I think you would do quite well," Kenny said. "You would be a refreshing change."

"Carly knows her place," Patricia replied. "It's one of the reasons she's such a good assistant. Why don't you go and wait in my office with your father? I assume you're here to discuss the event this evening."

"Fine." Kenny turned on his heels and strode away, every line of his body speaking to his anger.

Those two did not get along. The only reason they would be in the same room together was the company.

"Are the notes on tonight's filming schedule on my desk?"

"Yes." It was good to get back to focusing on work and not things she couldn't have. Oh, she didn't want Kenny. Not at all. Despite his handsomeness, she would never view him as more than a friend. There was no chemistry between them. Now that she knew what it really felt like, she could gauge her relationships properly. If the man didn't make her melt into her shoes with a simple look, she likely didn't need to worry about him. Since only one man seemed to have the ability to do that, she felt pretty confident she was safe. But the idea that she could have her own show, do her own thing? Yes, that was quite tempting. "The filming tonight is light. It won't be more than a ten-minute segment and I've ensured everyone is coming so we can maintain a family vibe. Jasmine's flight lands at three and I've got a car picking her up."

The minute her stepdaughter's name had been said, Patricia's nose had turned up. "Who's babysitting her? I don't want her drunk at the filming. The last time the editors had to cut out some excellent footage because Jasmine was dancing on a table in the background. And could someone please ensure the girl wears undergarments this time?"

"She's been assigned a bodyguard from the security firm. I've asked that he monitor her and give me a call if anything goes wrong. I'm actually hopeful he doesn't check her panties." Unlike Kenny, who headed the real estate division of his father's empire, Jasmine was more involved in playing the jet-setting heiress. She'd just filed for divorce number four from some Euro pseudo-royal and was now back in full-on party-like-a-Kardashian mode.

"Yes, she has a habit of sleeping with whatever bodyguard we send. I thought an unattractive one would be safe, but she didn't care. I also tried to send a female at one point. My stepdaughter doesn't discriminate in her promiscuity. Ah, well." Patricia turned but stopped, her eyes finding Carly again. "You would do well to stay away from my stepson. He's not as nice as he seems. That's simply his persona. And he wouldn't actually marry you. That doesn't mean he wouldn't use you."

"I'm not going to be dating Kenny anytime soon." It was time to start laying the groundwork for their cover. She'd been talking about Bran around the office with her co-workers, but she hadn't actually mentioned him to Patricia. "I'm actually seeing someone else. Someone new."

A single brow arced over Patricia's left eye. "You're dating? I heard some rumor about that but I discounted it."

She gave her boss a smile that wasn't one hundred percent fake. Bran kind of made her smile. And blush. "Yes, I met him online."

"That doesn't seem like a good decision."

"I don't have a ton of time to meet people, so I went with a matchmaking site." They'd talked about how to present themselves that first morning. They were going to keep it simple. She'd argued that they should have recently started dating while he'd pointed out if he was going to get an invite to the party in LA, it would be better if they'd been seeing each other for a while. "We met for coffee about six weeks ago and we've been seeing each other ever since."

"When on earth do you have time to date?"

She didn't. Not at all. The day she'd met Bran had been the first afternoon she'd had off in months. "Mostly late-night dinners. He's a night owl."

Patricia stared at her as though trying to assess how to handle the situation. "I rather thought you would be careful after your marriage. You know you deal with sensitive information about this business."

"Bran isn't interested in this business. He's not Roger." She had to keep telling herself that last part.

"He should have been properly vetted through our security team. All men are Rogers. Believe me, I know." Patricia glanced over at the glass doors that separated her suite of offices from the rest of the building. "Though some of them have their uses. Is that the new delivery boy? I haven't ordered lunch yet."

Carly followed her gaze and felt her eyes widen. What the hell? This was not what they'd planned. Bran was standing there with a bag in his hand. He was smiling down at the receptionist, who pointed their way. His head turned and he caught sight of her. His smile went from friendly down to hot and sensual as he began to make his way toward them.

"I ordered soup for you. Lemongrass, no salt. Your dress this evening will fit perfectly," Carly explained, standing. "I can get something else if you prefer, but it's what you normally eat for lunch before you go on camera. And he's not the delivery boy."

For the first and only time Carly could remember, Patricia looked surprised. Oh, on her overly Botoxed face it didn't register as much of an expression, but it was definitely there. "Is that the new boyfriend?"

Carly smoothed down her skirt. "Yes, though he could have called. I'm sorry. I'll tell him we don't normally accept visitors."

Patricia set her briefcase down, looking over Bran. "Not at all, dear. Visitors can be fun. I have to say, he isn't what I expected. That is a lovely young man."

He certainly was. He was stupidly gorgeous in jeans and a T-shirt and boots. With his pitch black hair and emerald eyes, he could have walked off the cover of a magazine. He opened the door and his eyes widened briefly when he recognized who was standing in the room with her.

*Don't give it away.* Just for the briefest of seconds, she was worried Bran would walk right up to Patricia and accuse her. He truly believed Patricia had killed his parents. For a second, she wondered if he hadn't been looking for justice at all, if he'd merely gotten close so he could have revenge.

And then the look was gone as though it had never been there at all. He looked back at Carly and smiled again. "Hey, I was in the neighborhood. I thought you might like some lunch. You said you usually eat at your desk."

"I do. Um, thanks." She was well aware of how awkward she sounded. Not at all like a woman who was used to seeing a man on a regular basis. She could blow this before they even got out of the gate. "Thanks so much. It's nice to see you, Bran."

Patricia cleared her throat, a subtle request for acknowledgment.

"Oh, this is Bran. Brandon Lowe. He's the man I was telling you about," she offered. "Bran, this is my boss, Patricia Cain."

Bran set the bag on her desk and held out a hand. "It's an honor to meet you. My mother is a huge fan. She never misses a show."

Patricia gave him her most gracious smile. "That's so nice. Well, if you're dating my Carly, we'll have to ensure your mother gets some autographed books or some swag. We can find some of that for a fan, can't we?"

What the hell? Patricia hated fans. She typically threw people out who asked for autographs at her office. Oh, she would smile and be gracious at an event, but she hated to be disrupted when the cameras weren't rolling. She certainly didn't offer to pass out swag to someone's mother. Carly managed to smile. "Of course. I'll put together a bag for her."

Bran shook Patricia's hand. "That's so kind of you. I was telling Carly how lucky she is to work at a place like this."

"And what do you do, Mr. Lowe?" Patricia stepped back, but she was still smiling.

"I'm pure muscle," he said with a grin. "I work with a company called McKay-Taggart. I'm in their personal security division. Right now, I'm out here for a couple of months working security for a writer. Apparently he pissed off a fan or something. No idea. It's historical stuff. I'm just around to take a bullet. Or maybe an arrow. Not sure."

This was their cover. Someone at McKay-Taggart was connected to a bunch of writers, one of whom lived in the St. Augustine area and wrote thrillers. He'd agreed to serve as Bran's cover employer in exchange for research. Writers, it turned out, would do a lot in the name of research.

Patricia laughed. "That sounds perfectly dreadful, though I do understand the need for a bodyguard from time to time."

"I spend a lot of time in bookstores right now. I've got a couple of days off, though. He's on a hard deadline and not doing any publicity." He winked Carly's way. "I was hoping to spend some time with that one."

Patricia glanced back as though remembering Carly existed. "Of course. Carly, why don't you show your friend around? I'll be in a meeting for at least an hour or two. If I need something, I'll text you."

"Really?" She was supposed to be at the grande dame's beck and call anytime the woman was in the office, and that meant sitting in on meetings so she could get people tea or coffee.

Patricia looked back at Bran, a faint smile on her lips. "Of course. I'm not a monster. You should take a nice long lunch. We'll have to work a bit tonight. Have you thought about bringing your friend to our little art show? Do you enjoy art, Bran?"

He had the most glowing smile. "I don't know much about it, Ms. Cain, but I do enjoy a party, and I know if you're in charge it's going to be an amazing one."

The woman actually blushed. "Well, then you should definitely come. I'll make sure there's an invitation waiting for you."

Bran nodded. "Thank you so much. Any excuse to spend some time with my girl."

The smile that lit Patricia's face dimmed a bit. "Of course. I'll expect you back in, say, an hour and a half, Carly. Brandon, it was lovely to meet you. You remind me of someone I knew. A long time ago."

Bran frowned. "Hopefully it was someone you liked."

"Yes," she said quietly, her eyes looking him up and down before she turned away. "Someone I liked quite a bit."

She walked away, her heels never making a sound against the hardwood.

Had Patricia-freaking-Cain hit on her boyfriend? Maybe there was some Alabama redneck still left in her, because she kind of wanted to throw down right now.

Bran's hand found hers, tangling their fingers together. "Let's go someplace quiet and have some lunch."

He squeezed her hand as though reminding her that they were in this together.

As partners. Not as boyfriend and girlfriend. This wasn't some grand romance and she didn't need to protect her man. He wasn't her man. As far as she knew, he might want Patricia's attention. It might make it easier for him to get what he needed if he was sleeping with the boss.

Was that why he'd really gotten close to her? Had she been a stepping-stone to the place he'd wanted to be?

That was when she realized he wasn't squeezing her hand. His hand was shaking.

She turned to him, moving close and taking his free hand in hers so she held them both. He hadn't enjoyed the attention. It had made him sick and scared and he needed her.

His face was perfectly blank, but he'd been shaken and she needed to do something to bring him back. He'd let her cry the first night they'd met. He'd held her then and eased her fears. He'd slept on her couch and dealt with the security stuff.

What could she do for him? She couldn't say anything, couldn't verbally give him any comfort while they were standing in her office. She could rush him out, but she needed him to know she was here with him.

"Kiss me."

He stared down at her, his eyes focusing for the first time since Patricia had walked away. "What?"

Yes, now she had his attention again. And it wasn't only his. Patricia had stopped at her door. Out of the corner of her eye, she could see her boss standing there with one elegantly manicured hand on the door. She was watching and Carly needed her to understand something.

"Kiss me," she whispered. "I'm so happy to see you. I need you to kiss me. I missed you."

His eyes flared and his lips curled up, and she was utterly mesmerized by the way he lit up. His hands moved from holding her own to coming up to her face, where his fingertips skimmed along her jawline before cradling her cheeks. He was gentle, but she could feel the strength in those hands.

His mouth descended and she expected a brushing of his lips over hers. There it was. A soft meeting of their lips. It was nice. She was about to pull away when his hands tightened ever so slightly and his mouth demanded more.

He drew her in, his body against hers as he settled in.

Her hands moved at first to balance herself against his body, and then she could feel him, feel his muscles through the thin cotton of his shirt, feel the heat his body gave off.

Suddenly it didn't matter that she'd begun this as a way to calm him down. All that mattered was the fact that his mouth moved on hers, tempting her, teasing her. Heat flashed through her system and she could feel her whole body softening under his kiss.

She followed him, opening for him and allowing his tongue to invade. She shivered against him as he took her mouth.

She'd been kissed before but not this way. Not in the sweetest, melt-against-him way that made the rest of the world seem to fade into the background.

He was calm and in control when he kissed her one last time and sighed as he pulled away. "Let's go find somewhere quiet to eat."

Yes, he was calm but her heart was pounding in her chest. And she could still feel Patricia's eyes on her. The door to her office closed with a thud and they were alone.

But she was never far away.

"I know just the place."

Bran stared at her over the small bistro table she'd walked him to at the back of the building. She'd put her hand in his and walked him through the office, stopping a couple of times to introduce him to some of her friends.

Somehow he'd thought she wouldn't have any. Not here. He'd seen her as completely alone since she was basically being forced to work for Cain Corp. He'd seen her as the princess in the tower, but the princess still had some friends.

And one nasty enemy.

He could still feel Patricia Cain's hand in his, the way she'd squeezed it ever so lightly and held it a fraction of a second too long. He could still feel the way she looked at him, like he was a nice piece of meat and she was suddenly hungry.

He'd been so aware in that moment of who she was. Of what she'd done.

"Are you all right?" Carly leaned forward. "We can talk out here. No one ever comes out here except when they're filming for the show.

Then it's supposed to look like a place where we all hang out because we're such a family."

"I'm good." He gave her what he hoped was a confident smile. "I'm sorry I didn't tell you I was coming in. The stuff at your place got wrapped up early, and I thought I should warn you that something's going down this evening. It's best you don't know what's happening, but I wanted to make sure I could be around just in case."

Her eyes widened. "Something's going down?"

"We've only got a couple of weeks to get her to fire her security team and hire on ours. I thought the best course of action was to get in here and start making myself a familiar figure. You've had a week to get them used to the idea of you dating. They needed to meet me before the party tonight." He hadn't liked the way some of those men had looked at her. When she'd introduced him to her friend in payroll, a man had come in and forced his way into the introduction, too. He'd openly gaped, as though the idea of Carly having a boyfriend was a revolutionary thing. And then he'd leered as though reconsidering something he'd dismissed before.

Asshole.

"Is it dangerous?"

"It will likely seem that way," he explained. "I don't know everything. They want me to react as naturally as anyone else would. Don't worry about it. I assure you my brother-in-law is a professional."

Case was an expert, and Case's big brother, Ian, had supposedly been an actual CIA operative. They were the best and brightest when it came to protection, hacking, or taking an asshole out, as Case would say. Bran was perfectly happy to leave everything in their hands. He would spend all of his time trying to get his own hands back on Carly's sweet ass.

Likely it would be something small, but embarrassing to Cain and her crew. It would be something that would anger the queen and get her current knights fired.

"All right," Carly said quietly, her eyes coming up. "But I wasn't talking about that. I was talking about you. Bran, your hands were shaking."

Damn it. She'd noticed. He'd tried so fucking hard to stay as calm as possible, even when his gut was rolling. "I guess I needed some protein more than I thought I did. If I'm going to stay at your place for much longer, we need to get some groceries. For a woman who loves to cook, you don't have a lot in the fridge."

"Because I have to eat out a lot," she said, her eyes steady on his. "Bran, she was flirting with you."

He didn't want to talk about this with her. He didn't want her to know how sick it had made him, how he'd almost broken down and screwed everything up. He needed to look stable and strong, so he gave her a smile and a wink. Arrogance was better than admitting how weak he'd been. "I get that a lot."

"Bran, she killed your mother and she was flirting with you and you flirted back."

He frowned. Was that really how she saw it? "It's an undercover op, sweetheart. That's part of the game. Should I have taken out a sword and dueled with her?"

She sat back up, all the softness gone from her bones. She was stiff as she started to unpack the lunch he'd bought. "I'm sorry. You know how to handle it, I suppose. Are the sandwiches the same?"

The idea that she thought he might welcome the attentions of the woman who'd killed his parents made him sick.

Why had she kissed him? Asked him to kiss her? He'd thought she was playing the part well, but why had she really done it?

There was only one reason a woman like Carly might do something like that.

He reached out and grasped her wrist. She set the sandwiches down and he tugged her to him.

Maybe she wouldn't see it as weakness. Maybe she wouldn't see him as something so broken he couldn't be fixed.

"Bran," she argued as she spilled onto his lap.

He wrapped an arm around her middle and drew her close, whispering in her ear. "It was horrible. I thought I was going to be sick for a moment. Please forgive me. I almost screwed everything up."

"It's all right." The minute he'd started whispering she'd relaxed in his arms, turning so she could hug him and fitting against him like a puzzle piece that had been missing. "You did good. She certainly didn't see anything."

He breathed her in, loving the smell of her shampoo. Strawberries and cream. She tasted like that, too. Sweet and rich. "I'm sorry I got defensive."

"It's okay," she whispered back. "I'm sorry I didn't explain well enough. I knew that hurt you."

This felt so much better than arrogance. "I didn't think I would react like that. It's not like I haven't seen her before."

"Being in the same room with her is different. You've seen her on TV. She doesn't interact on TV. She's a character there. This is the real woman and she had a hand in your parents' murder. You reacted, but you covered it up. There was no way she could tell. I could only tell because your hands were shaking. It's all right. Everything went well and now we've gotten the introduction out of the way so we don't have to do it at the party. I say we call it a win." She sat up and smiled down at him, the sun making her skin luminous.

She was a gorgeous woman. He had no idea why people seemed so shocked she had a boyfriend. Yes, she dressed a bit plain, but her beauty was in the generosity of her smile, in the glow she got in those brown eyes when she was excited.

The fact that she had a really round ass didn't hurt. Not at all. Of course, his chances for turning this impromptu meeting into a make-out session had gone way down since he'd figured out why she'd kissed him. "So that kiss was your way of getting me to chill out?"

She blushed and scrambled off his lap, straightening her khaki-colored skirt. "I thought it would help you focus. I also thought maybe if my boss saw you kiss me, she would keep her cougar paws off you."

Or maybe not. That was some sweet jealousy. It was all right. He'd felt some of that himself. "I'll make it plain to everyone I'm all about one girl."

"So the sandwiches?"

She wasn't ready to talk about chemistry yet, though he was pretty sure he'd proven his point with that kiss. "I bought two different kinds. Turkey on rye and a club. Your pick. You know me. I'll eat anything."

"You make things easy on a girl. And I like club sandwiches, but no pickles. Pickles are gross. I have a thing about them. I'm only telling you so we can make it look good."

Sure she was. She was also subtly telling him she liked lunch service.

He hoped she'd liked being kissed by him. He'd fucking loved it. He was still dealing with the aftermath. Maybe she'd only done it to help him calm down, but at the end she'd been with him. Her hands had been moving on his body, making their way from his waist down to his hips. He had to wonder if they'd had a bit longer, would she have been bold enough to cup his ass? He'd wanted to. For a moment he'd forgotten about everything but how she'd been in his arms, how good she'd smelled. It had been forever since he'd wanted one woman. Not *a* woman, but one woman.

"I'll make note of your preferences." He was already making a list of what she did and didn't like.

And how she liked to be kissed. She liked to be kissed wholeheartedly, and she offered back everything he gave her.

She sat down across from him. "So we're going to the art show tonight. I should probably prepare you for that."

He would rather she prepped him from the comfort of his lap, but it looked like that moment was done. The good news was she was still curious, and she definitely felt something for him. "Should I pick you up here?"

"I have to be there super early. I'll barely have time to go home and change."

"Is this an exhibit of Patricia's work?"

She shook her head. "No, it's an artist who did some work for the magazine. Well, and her father is a sixties rock icon. It's not like Patricia picks up starving artists. She only wants them hungry because they're so thin." She stopped. "She said you reminded her of someone. Should we be worried about that?"

"I don't think so. Hatch tells me I have my mom's eyes. From what I understand, my mom wasn't too involved in the business. She was a lawyer before she married my dad. She gave up her practice to raise us."

"Could Patricia have been friends with your mom?" Carly frowned. "*Friends* is the wrong word. Patricia doesn't have friends, but then, she might not have always been so cold."

"According to Hatch she was. I'm sure she knew my mother, but I can't imagine them being friends. Like I said, my mom wasn't involved in the business at all. I can't imagine she had a lot in common with Patricia."

"This Hatch person . . . Patricia would definitely know him. I read a bit on him after we met. I was wondering why you think you can trust him. He had a lot to gain from selling the technology. He even disappeared for a while after your parents died."

He didn't take offense to her question. Bill Hatchard had been like a father to him sometimes. A boozy, obnoxious, vulgar dad, but a dad. Still, it was easy to see why he would be a suspect on paper. "Hatch disappeared into a bottle for about eight years after my parents died. He did gain from their deaths, but he didn't use the money. He was my father's best friend. I trust him."

"If he was your father's best friend, why didn't he take you in?

Why didn't he fight the other partners to ensure you kids got your shares?"

All questions Bran had asked and had to shove down. "He wasn't the kind of man who could raise a bunch of kids."

"Anyone can raise kids if they care enough. I came from a mom who rarely paid attention to me and Meri, but at least we were together."

Together. One day he'd had a whole family around him and the next it had been him and Mia. After Riley and Drew had been taken to the youth home, he and Mia had been taken in by a woman in her forties who had three other foster kids. She'd been nice and taken good care of them, but when she'd been diagnosed with breast cancer she'd had to give them all up, and that meant splitting up him and Mia.

They'd run the night before. He'd shoved their pitiful belongings into a garbage bag and snuck out in the middle of the night to look for Riley and Drew.

When the police found them, they'd been separated and Bran given the lecture of a lifetime on how he'd nearly killed his sister and he wouldn't see her again.

He'd held on so tight but they'd broken them up and Bran had been alone.

Where had Hatch been that night?

"We did all right." He couldn't think about that. It was in the past and there was nothing to do but move forward. One foot in front of the other. That was the only way to get through. "After Drew aged out, he went to look for Hatch. He found him and cleaned him up and they managed to get Riley out of the youth home. Mia had been adopted by then and her parents welcomed us all to visit and spend time with them so they didn't worry about her."

"How long were you in foster care?"

About three months too long. "Eight years. Drew managed to get me out when I was sixteen. He had Hatch declared my legal guardian and then I was out. I moved from Dallas to Austin and they made sure I went to school and college and here I am today."

He wouldn't mention the scars he had or how he woke up screaming some nights because he was right back in that dingy bedroom where Mandy had died. He wouldn't mention how he'd cowered and hidden.

He'd survived, but sometimes he wondered if he would ever move past that moment.

"She still puts morality clauses in her contracts," Carly said. "Not for herself, of course, but for anyone who works with her or she invests with. I think it's a convenient way for her to get rid of someone if she needs to."

Somehow that didn't surprise him. "Hey, it worked once, right?"

"She fired one of her upper-level managers because she got a DUI. Naturally it was right before the manager's stock vested and she would have owned five percent of Cain Corp. I've always wondered if Patricia didn't set up that traffic stop. The people who were at the party that night swore Gayle had one glass of wine and ate a full meal. Needless to say, that's not what the reports said, and she found out her contract with Cain Corp was null and void and she was out several million dollars."

"Patricia has a history of underhanded business practices."

"So why bother with murder?" Carly queried. "Was your father such a Boy Scout that there was no way to catch him in a net like she did Gayle?"

"Did Gayle sue?"

"She tried, but the clause was pretty ironclad. It got tossed out. I know my boss. She rarely does anything that might bring bad press to her or one of her companies. The business with your father hurt the sale of that technology. According to the reports they should have gotten millions more."

He wasn't sure he liked her delving so deep, but at least she was interested. "You've been doing a lot of research."

"I read some stuff before the scary guy with the gun showed up, and then I was all about home security," she said with the cutest frown on her face. "Seriously though, I don't know everything about business, but if they could have caught your dad doing something immoral, they could have taken the stock right there. And why allow this Hatch guy to keep his?"

She was asking a lot of interesting questions, but none that meant anything now. "This was twenty years ago. She might not have perfected her methods back then. Like I said, my mom had been a lawyer. She would have kept them tied up in court for a long time. I think they did what was expedient. And afterward they lay low. They paid off Hatch so there wasn't more bad press. Maybe. I'm not sure. I only know that she was one of four people to pay for the assassin."

"And two of them are dead."

Castalano and Stratton. "Yes, both of natural causes."

"Are we sure about that? Patricia went to see Steven Castalano shortly before his heart attack. Maybe she put something in his IV."

He held a hand up. "Whoa, slow down, detective. I love your enthusiasm, but let's stick to the task at hand."

She shrugged. "I think she's capable of anything, although I do doubt she killed Castalano. I think she might have had an affair with him."

That thought sent a shudder through his system. "Really? Because that's pretty horrifying. What makes you think that? I know they hadn't seen each other for years. After Patricia sold off her shares of StratCast, they didn't spend much time together."

"She got drunk once, the only time I've ever seen her out of control. She got drunk and talked about someone she loved once. I got the feeling she was talking about a long time ago. She said they'd both been young and that she'd thought what they'd done would bring them closer together, but something happened to drive them apart. She said if she had to do it all over again, she would have found a way to keep her lover." Carly looked thoughtful for a moment. "It was odd. She didn't cry or anything. She said that maybe it wasn't worth it since she'd lost that chance."

"I have a hard time seeing anyone love Steven Castalano. He was married even back then. I can ask Hatch about it, but I think you and I should concentrate on tonight. At some point you're going to meet my brothers. Don't be scared of Drew. He's not as bad as he looks."

"He looks very attractive from the photo I got of him."

There was that nasty jealousy again. "When you meet him in real life, he might be a bit intimidating. He's also kind of pissed that you managed to find some information he didn't want you to find."

"Are you talking about the research on the business? That was easy to get my hands on."

"No, I'm talking about the deep stuff. I didn't realize you were so good with computers. According to Drew, you practically hacked into county records to get our files. He's spent the whole week trying to hunt down everything you looked into. That's why I'm saying he might be intimidating at first. He's been a little pissed at you all week."

She grimaced, her mouth turning down. "I didn't do that. Not even close. I had a friend send me some archived newspaper articles and some stuff on the business. I didn't look into anything personal. It seemed rude. I honestly wouldn't know how to hack into anything. I'm competent when it comes to a computer, but I'm not that good."

"I was sure it was you." Damn, if someone else was looking, this could get tricky. He hadn't talked to Drew in a few days. He'd intended to drive out to Palm Coast, but that had gone on hold when Carly had called. He'd spent the last week getting to know her, inserting himself into her world.

"It might have been my friend."

It was his turn to grimace. She'd told a friend? "Your friend? Sweetheart, please tell me you didn't bring someone else into this."

She waved him off. "Of course not. Not directly. I have a friend who's writing an unauthorized bio of Patricia. I haven't talked to her specifically about this and I won't, but I do send her the occasional disgruntled employee. I asked her about the business and how it had gotten started. She sent me some articles. I didn't realize she would go digging this soon."

"You brought a reporter in?" He could have sworn the air had taken on a chill. He wanted to look around and make sure there was no chance of Drew having listened in to that tidbit of information. This would be one of those times his big brother likely went purple.

She bit into her bottom lip, a gesture that made him want to tug her back into his lap and try the whole kissing thing again. "I don't think of her that way. She's a close friend of mine. I swear I didn't tell her anything about what's going on. I asked for some information. I couldn't go into this completely blind."

He understood. Whether his brother would understand was another story entirely. "Maybe you shouldn't meet Drew."

"I can handle him," she said with a confidence Bran wasn't sure she should have. "I handle Patricia Cain on a daily basis. How bad could he possibly be?"

So much worse. Drew likely thought she was some kind of hacker at this point. "Just stay close to me at all times when Drew's around. I'll explain the situation to him."

After all, what was the worst that could happen? He picked up his sandwich and started to eat. If Drew was going to murder them both, they might as well enjoy the day.

## Chapter Six

"What do you mean she brought in a reporter? Are you telling me the person I've been tangling with online all week is a damn reporter?"

Bran winced. Yeah, there was murder in his brother's tone. "Carly didn't bring anyone in. She asked a friend of hers who happens to be a reporter for some articles on the company Dad started. She was doing some research that I told her to do before she made up her mind. I don't know what her friend is doing. She was supposedly working on a story about Patricia. Not us."

His brother stood in Carly's pretty living room and stared at him. Bran was fairly certain it was the way a cobra stared at a bunny rabbit before striking. This was precisely why he'd decided to get all this horrible predatory shit over before Carly came home. He'd called and asked Drew to bring him something to wear to tonight's art show and waited to tell him in person that Carly wasn't the mystery pinger. Maybe he would be able to put his brother in a calmer mood and he wouldn't scare her off.

Or he would murder Bran and then it would all be over anyway.

"I find this utterly fascinating," Case said from his place on Carly's couch. His massive linebacker-sized brother-in-law didn't fit any better on her tiny couch than Bran had all week long. "See, my big brother would have been screaming by now. Or offering to show me my own entrails. He likes to talk about entrails a lot. Drew just stares like he's going to do something really bad."

He and Case had something in common. They both had to face big brother. "He won't. At least he never has in the past."

"Perhaps I should take a page out of the eldest Taggart's handbook and explain what I intend to do to your new girlfriend once I get hold of her." Each word out of Drew's mouth was clipped and nasty.

Bran felt every muscle in his body go taut. "You're going to stay away from Carly. If you can't speak civilly to her then you won't speak at all."

Drew's eyes closed. "Shit."

"I told you," Case said.

"What?" Somehow he'd fallen into some kind of trap.

Drew's eyes opened, narrowing on him. "You've spent one week with her and now you're defending the fact that she brought a reporter in. Do you have any idea what kind of chaos she's going to cause? She came damn close to putting Drew Lawless and Andrew Lang together. None of this works if national news starts running stories about how four homeless orphans became billionaires. If they get even a hint of the story, everything we've worked for gets blown out of the water."

He hadn't thought that much about it. He'd been too busy with Carly. "You stopped the reporter, right?"

Drew sighed and sank into the lounge chair across from the sofa. "Yes, for now. And I'm working on hiding all the records that link us to who we used to be, but it's not easy. I can bribe the right people, but you know as well as I do that there's always a trace left."

"Maybe we could talk to the reporter." If she was friends with Carly, she might be helpful.

"I'm not talking to her," Drew said with an irritated snort. "I'm going to destroy her. What do we know about her?"

"Her name is Shelby. I don't know if I should give you her last name if you're planning on annihilating her." It was a real risk with Drew.

"She's a snarky little thing. I was actually coming here to pull you out because that woman is dangerous. I thought she was Carly. I'm happy to discover that Whovian639 isn't Carly."

"Whovian? Like the Whos in Whoville?" Someone had read him that story a long time ago. The Grinch. Sometimes that dude and Drew had a lot in common. Drew was known for working through Christmas dinner.

"I think she's a *Doctor Who* fan. Which is ridiculous because everyone knows that there is zero scientific basis in that show," Drew said with a frown. "*Star Trek* is much more reality based."

God, sometimes he forgot how much of a nerd his brother was. If he ever got his revenge, he would likely bury himself in playing geeky board games and arguing about *Game of Thrones*. "Yeah, her choice of sci-fi is not a reason for murder. Maybe we should figure out if she can help us."

Wasn't there always room for more allies? Case Taggart sat on the couch like a big old sign for how allies had helped them out. They'd started on opposite sides of the fence, and now Case and Mia did it like five times a day and everyone was happier for it.

Drew didn't seem to take the same lesson from his sibling's marriage that Bran did. "No. We are not bringing anyone outside of family into this. I don't like that this Fisher girl knows our plan."

How many times did they have to go over this? "Hey, she's fine, and let's face facts. I don't even know the whole plan. Unless you want to let me know what you're doing tonight."

"It's going to be fun," Case said with a grin.

Drew held a hand out. "Don't. He'll probably go on social media and make it his freaking status. He'll definitely tell his new girlfriend."

"She's not my girlfriend. She's my partner." That kiss hadn't been real. Oh, it had felt real and he definitely wanted to kiss her again, but he didn't do the girlfriend thing. He didn't deserve it.

Drew's eyes narrowed. "Tell me you didn't sleep with her. You haven't been home all week. I assume you spent it in Carly's bed."

Bran pointed to the couch. "As for last night and every night before, my ass slept right there, brother. Well, it hung off there because I'm way too tall for that sucker, but I absolutely have not slept with her."

"But you stayed here."

"She had a scare and she didn't want to be alone." He wasn't sure if he was ready to go into an explanation on that one. Soon enough he would have to write that check, and there was no way that didn't get back to Drew.

"Is this why you wanted the report on Tommy DiLuca?" Case asked, suddenly getting serious. "Because I had a friend run up some information on him and he's a serious dude, Bran. If she's involved with DiLuca, she's got mob connections."

Bran was fairly certain Drew was going to blow an artery or something. His eldest brother turned a lovely shade of purple while Bran turned on Case. "Dude, I thought we were on the same page. There are things big brother doesn't need to know. I swear the next time I get something on you, I'm running straight to Big Tag."

Case put up his hands in a conciliatory fashion. "Sorry. I thought he knew." The big guy sat back. "DiLuca has serious mob connections."

"Mob? Like the Italian mafia? Carly Fisher has ties to the fucking mafia?" Drew spat the questions out in rapid fire. "Is there anything else you want to tell me? Maybe she's pregnant with an alien love child and we'll have to stave off an invasion in order for this operation to work."

He could totally handle his brother's sarcasm. "Good news. She's one hundred percent alien-free. It's just the mob ties and the reporter."

The best way to deal with Drew was straight on. Well, his preferred method was to hide all fuckups until he absolutely had to tell, but Case had made that impossible.

"Why do I find myself on the set of *The Godfather*?"

At least his brother sounded more reasonable now. "Carly's ex was a gambling man. They want her to pay off his debts, and last week they broke in and had a talk with her. Hence all the new security equipment I had installed."

"They broke in?" Case asked, his tone going low.

"They scared the shit out of her," Bran explained. "It's why I spent the week here and I'll probably spend more until I can get her out of this."

"How do you plan to get her out of this?" Drew asked.

Shit. "I'm going to write them a check and they'll go away. It's not a big deal."

*Don't ask how much. Don't ask how much.*

"How large is this check you're writing?"

Double shit. He couldn't lie to his brother. He could be a bit negligent with the truth, but he wasn't going to outright lie. "It's a million. It's not a big deal."

Drew's eyes widened. "A million dollars is not a big deal?"

"Yeah, I'm never going to get used to that," Case admitted. "My brothers have money but not shrug-off-a-million money."

"I'm using my own money." He hated this feeling. He hated the way Drew was looking at him. Like he was a kid, and not a particularly smart one at that. "I'm not asking you for a dime."

"I gave you that money."

He wanted to play it that way? "Then take it all back and I'll figure out another way to help her."

Drew sighed. "No, it's yours to do whatever you want. It's your part of the company. I'm sorry. I don't like to see you being taken advantage of."

"She's not that way." How could he make Drew understand? Drew was the most cynical person Bran knew. He always saw the worst in people. "She's kind."

"Yes, she's kindly asking you for a million dollars. Case, you need to see if this is some sort of scam. Perhaps she's working with this DiLuca person."

Case shook his head. "There's zero chance of that. It would have come up in our initial reports about her. I've had the best investigators in the world working on this. They would have figured out if she was a con artist looking to take out billionaires who came around asking for help with their revenge plots. Do you understand how paranoid you sound right now?"

"Yeah, well, I'm the son of a man who wasn't paranoid enough," Drew shot back. "And my brother is far too optimistic for his own good. He's known her for a week and he's already paying off her debts?"

"I'm smoothing the way for your plan to work, Drew. If she's grateful to me, she'll be a better partner. I would think a million is a drop in the bucket compared to what you're willing to pay. Hell, you've already paid in years of your life."

"I didn't come here to fight," Drew said quietly. "You're right. If a million will smooth the way then I'll pay for it myself, but be careful. If they figure out she's an easy mark, they'll come back for more and you won't be around to protect her again."

He intended to make certain DiLuca understood Carly was off-limits after this. "Don't worry about it. We've got other things to worry about. I'm fairly certain Patricia Cain is attracted to me."

"Whoa, are you all right with that?" Case asked.

Drew suddenly looked like he gave a shit. "Of course he's not. What happened? Did she try something with you?"

Well, at least he got some sympathy on that front. "No, it was more of a feeling. I know when a woman is interested and she definitely was. It made me sick, Drew. Touching her made me want to puke. I didn't think I would have that reaction. Carly saved it, though. I'm worried about what will happen if . . . What if she makes a move on me?"

"You'll handle it," Drew said, leaning forward. "Bran, you have this. It's all right that you had that reaction."

"It occurs to me that getting close to Patricia might be a good way to get where we need to go." He hated to admit it, but maybe his brother had been right all along. Maybe Drew would have been the better choice.

"If you think for one second I would sleep with that woman to get revenge, you need to think again. And if you think I'll allow you to do it, you don't know me, brother."

"Riley slept with Ellie."

Drew rolled his eyes. "Riley wanted Ellie the minute he laid eyes on her. I offered to switch with him and he damn near took my head off. The truth of the matter was it was always Riley's choice how he got close. He had no qualms about spending time in her bed even before he'd met her. Riley really was a manwhore. You're different, but I don't think your reaction to Carly is different."

"I want to sleep with her because she's attractive." That wasn't the whole story. "I like her."

"And that's why she scares me."

Before he could say anything else, there was the sound of the alarm chiming as the door came open and the woman in question stood in the doorway, her eyes wide, and carrying way too much for only two arms. She had her purse, her laptop bag, some sort of grocery bag, and what looked like a dress from the dry cleaners.

"I don't remember the code. I know I should. I'm so sorry." She looked at the other men in the room as the alarm kept chiming. "Wow. Your parents had seriously good genes, Bran."

He hopped up, happy to see her. The conversation with Drew had taken a turn for the way-too-real, and Carly was like a breath of fresh air. He quickly inputted the security code and eased the grocery bag and dry cleaner bag out of her hands. "I'll go over all the new security stuff, but this is my brother Drew, and my brother-in-law, Case Taggart."

Case stood and offered his hand. "I don't share any genes with this lot. Their sister just has amazing taste in men."

Drew shook his head. "You praise the day she even thought to look your way, Taggart." He glanced back at Carly. "And I rather thought you didn't like my family genes since you intended to send me away."

Carly blushed. "I kind of thought you were too attractive. And honestly, I think it worked out better this way. Bran is sweet. That's more my speed. Did you get the notes I sent you on arrival times and where the security will be placed?"

Carly had been hard at work this afternoon, and not only for Cain Corp. She'd sent over notes that would help them all tonight. His brother now knew when and where Patricia would be every step of the evening.

"I did and they will work quite nicely," Drew said, shaking her hand. "I think after this evening she'll be desperate to find a new security company. Don't worry about anything. We'll handle all of it. I would, however, stay a few feet away from your boss this evening."

Case was grinning again. "It's going to be fun. Juvenile but fun."

Bran didn't even want to know. "We should get ready. Thanks for the suit. I'll be in touch after Carly and I get home."

Drew nodded. "See that you do. And remember what I said about the other stuff. Be careful. Take someone with you when you make the payment. And not her. Someone who can watch your back."

"I watched his back earlier today," she said with a nod, and then she blushed as though realizing what she'd said. "Only because he was walking away and I couldn't see his front."

Drew shook his head and led Case out.

"Watched my back, huh?"

She was still the sweetest shade of pink. "I can't believe I said that in front of your brother. What's wrong with me? I think being a spy has made me too sassy."

He kind of thought being a spy was making her more confident.

It could happen to a person. Carly was finally doing something that might change her situation. She was becoming more aware of her own power. It looked good on her. "I think you're exactly as sassy as you should be. Now, what's this?"

"My dress for tonight and our dinner."

"I thought we would eat at the art show."

She shook her head. "Oh, people do not eat at art shows. People show off how thin they are at art shows. So I thought we would have a nice meal and then I'll pour myself into some Spanx and we'll deal with all the skinny, hungry people who think painting a daisy on an old washing machine is art."

"Seriously?" He'd tried to avoid the art world as much as possible. Drew often brought in designers to redo offices and Ellie firmly believed in hanging stuff on walls, but Bran was happy with nothing more than a nice bed, a TV, and an Xbox. That was enough decoration for him.

He often thought he was the worst multimillionaire in the whole world.

It didn't seem to bother Carly. She simply gave him a breezy smile. "I think she would say it's a statement on the uselessness of our modern society in juxtaposition with the power of nature. Or something like that. We might need a drink or two before we get there."

He followed her into the kitchen. Yes, he would definitely need that drink.


Carly thanked the caterer and looked out over the spread. Despite what she'd told Bran, there were always appetizers at anything Patricia hosted. All *Patricia's Paradise*–approved recipes. Unfortunately, they were all tiny bite-sized things, and a man Bran's size wouldn't fill up on mini goat cheese crostini.

"All of this stuff is weird." Bran looked over the selection and grabbed a tiny tart. "Why is there a carburetor sitting in the middle of the floor?"

He'd been walking around the exhibit since they'd gotten here. Carly had to come in an hour ahead of time to ensure everything was perfect, from the catering to the champagne service to the lighting. Ten percent dimmer than normal and nothing in a harsh white or Patricia would walk out. While she'd ensured that no harsh light cast itself on her employer, Bran had walked around, frowning mostly. Apparently this wasn't his style of art.

"This is what folks in the art world call reclaimed art. It's done with stuff the artist found in a junkyard. This particular artist is extremely earth friendly. She's designing a line of recycled home goods for the online store. That's what we're pushing tonight."

Bran looked around, taking in the venue. "So the family vibe is all for show. I know it shouldn't surprise me."

"Patricia doesn't have any close family. She was an only child and never speaks to her parents. As for her stepchildren, they're only dragged out for events like this. She goes skiing during the holidays. They are not invited."

"I don't get that. I spend every holiday with my family. If I don't, let's just say my sister is good with the guilt. We do holidays big in my family. I think it'll be worse now since one of my brothers got married last year. I guess it's because we spent so much time apart," Bran said.

Because of the actions of Patricia Cain and her partners. "I don't spend much time with my family. Not after my grandma died. Mom's still around but she moved to Nevada a couple of years ago and she got married. She said it might be weird for us to come out and see her for Christmas since the new husband's family is so big." That had hurt more than she'd imagined. Even though she hadn't been close to her mom, knowing how little she cared had kicked her in the gut. "So it's only me and my sister, but we have fun."

"I bet you do. I bet you cook a lot."

"Always." Food was the language of her love. She'd enjoyed making him lemon chicken with asparagus and quinoa earlier. They were simple recipes, but he'd dug in like he was eating at the finest restaurant in the world. It had been a long time since she cooked for someone who didn't take the recipe apart and question every single ingredient. Bran simply enjoyed it, and that had done something for her.

Out of the corner of her eye she noticed the doors had been opened and there was now a crowd milling around the exhibit space. It was time to get to work. "Okay, to your left is her stepson. His name is Kenny Jr. He seems to have gotten the majority of common sense in the family. He runs the real estate arm of his father's company, but I think he'll have a serious fight with Patricia after his dad passes. If his dad passes. I sometimes think he's drinking the blood of virgins to stay alive."

"That bad?"

"He's positively vile, which is why it's a surprise Kenny's such a nice guy. The woman he's talking to is our artist. She'll give the family a tour of the show for the cameras. There are only two tonight because it's kind of a tight space. They're good at staying in the background, but we'll have to deal with them once Patricia arrives." How would that work? Did he want to be on camera? "Maybe you should stay away from the cameras."

"I'll try, but if they catch me, it's all right," he said with a smile. Was he really thinking about this? "People might know you."

"When will this air?"

Now she saw his point. "Six months from now, likely. You're right."

Six months from now this mission would be over. Six months from now he would be out of her life, and if everything worked, she would have moved on as well.

But she had the next month with him. Was she going to waste it?

She'd thought about him all afternoon. Since that moment when he'd pulled her down into his lap and wrapped his arms around her, she couldn't get him out of her head. That moment had affected her even more than the kiss, which had been incendiary. It had proven once and for all that there was a sexual being hiding under her prim skirts. She'd thought she'd buried the sexual part of her after the divorce, but Bran brought it out.

Still, it was realizing he needed more from her than sex that got her thinking. Bran had been scared and he'd allowed her to comfort him. Most men wouldn't ever admit their fear. They would have laughed off the episode, but Bran had taken her kindness and it seemed to settle him.

He needed her. She needed him. Even if it was only for a while.

"Are you all right?" Bran asked.

She was nervous as hell and she wasn't sure how to ask for what she wanted. Now probably wasn't the time to have a conversation about moving their mutually beneficial relationship into the bedroom.

There wasn't a Miss Manners for hooking up.

Bran reached out and cupped her shoulder. "It's going to be okay. I promise. As soon as tonight's over, if everything goes well, the world goes back to normal until we head to California."

"Normal? So I won't see you?" She hadn't considered that.

His lips curved up in the sexiest smile. "I meant normal as in new normal. I think we should be seen together as much as possible. On that note, I want you to think about letting me stay over for a little while longer. Just until I manage to get the other situation handled."

Until he managed to pay off the million-dollar debt she found herself with. It had seemed so easy in the beginning. Now all she could think about was the fact that he was going to write a check for a million dollars to get her out of trouble.

"I've been thinking about that." She couldn't let him do it. Could she?

He leaned over. "Don't think. Let me take care of it. Let me take care of you."

When he said those words in that oh-so-deep voice of his, she wanted to melt and follow his every instruction. "Bran, it's too much. I don't know that I'll ever be able to pay you back."

His lips hovered over hers. "I am thinking so many non-PC things right now."

She laughed because of all the men she'd met, he was the last one she could think of who would demand sex for cash. He was all white knight in shining armor. "I bet you are."

It hit her that she was in way too deep with this guy. She'd known him for so little time and here she was trusting him. He was too good to be true, and too good to be true often landed her in hot water.

"Carly? What the hell?"

Carly winced. She knew that slightly too-loud voice. She straightened up and forced herself to smile. "Hi, Jas."

Jasmine wasn't bad, exactly. She was, however, very loud at times, and it looked like her bodyguard hadn't done his job. She had a glass of champagne in her hand, but it looked like it wasn't her first. Or second. "Hey, girl. Come here and give me a hug. I just got rid of Enrique. That's the last time I'm shopping in Spain, if you know what I mean. It's also the last time I settle for a second cousin. If I get married again, it's going to be a king or nothing at all."

Carly found herself enveloped in some kind of floral scent that couldn't quite mask the herbal fragrance underneath. Damn it. She was smoking pot again. This was what Jasmine did when a relationship ended. She sank herself into pot and alcohol and shocking amounts of retail therapy. "Welcome back to the States."

Jas stepped back. "I'm so happy to be home. Well, I'm not happy that the minute I get off a plane I'm forced to perform, but hey, at least I look good. The stepmonster sent this pretty Cavalli along with a bodyguard. Do I have you to thank for that? He was lovely. All of twenty-five, and with the stamina of a rutting bull. It made the flight go quickly."

She caught Bran's brief grin. Yes, she knew who to thank for that since Carly had requested a senior agent. Both experience and age. "I'm glad you enjoyed it. Where is he? Shouldn't he be here with you?"

Jas waved that off. "We had a fight this afternoon so I fired him. It was good while it lasted. I'm so glad I ran into you. I wanted some advice. You know, I've been thinking about trying to get my own reality show. I have a proposal I want to take to Daddy."

Ah, yes, she also tried to talk her father into funding her reality show every time she got a divorce. At least it might keep Ken Sr. occupied for a few days. "I think that's a wonderful idea."

Jas's eyes flared as she realized Carly wasn't alone. "Hello, hottie. How are you? Are you one of the cameramen tonight? I take back everything I said about having to be here."

Was she going to have to defend Bran from every member of her boss's family? "His name is Brandon. Bran, this is Jasmine Jones. She's Patricia's stepdaughter. Jas, Bran is my guest tonight."

"I'm her boyfriend." He put out his hand. "It's nice to meet you."

"Seriously?" For once Jas seemed too shocked to speak. Naturally it was because she couldn't believe Carly could get a guy like Bran. Yes, that was kind of how it seemed to be going today. Everyone she'd introduced Bran to had been all wide-eyed and disbelieving. Like she could never get a date.

Though it wasn't like he was truly her date. He was here for different reasons. And yet she couldn't help but think about what she'd overheard earlier today. Apparently Bran and his brothers hadn't figured out that the window near the door was super thin and sound carried pretty easily out of it. She'd heard them talking as she walked up to open the door. She'd stopped because she'd heard an unfamiliar deep voice. For a second she'd frozen, certain her would-be attackers had come back. Then she'd realized she was listening to something entirely different.

*He had no qualms about spending time in her bed even before he'd met her.*

*Riley really was a manwhore. You're different, but I don't think your reaction to Carly is different.*

*I want to sleep with her because she's attractive. I like her.* Her heart had seized when she realized that was Bran and he was talking about her.

*And that's why she scares me.*

She'd opened the door, unwilling to eavesdrop further on a private conversation, but she'd wondered about it. He had zero reason to lie. He hadn't known she could hear him. It obviously would have put his brother at ease if Bran had said something different.

So the logical conclusion was he wasn't lying when he said he wanted her.

She slid her hand into his and felt him lean against her. "I think we're pretty serious. He's staying with me while he's here."

Bran's fingers tightened briefly around hers. "Staying with Carly is so much nicer than a nasty hotel. Who knows? I might stay for a good long while." He leaned over and briefly brushed his lips against hers. "Why don't you show me the rest of the exhibit? I know you have to get back to work soon."

There he was again. Saving her from an awkward situation.

She gave Jas a smile. "I'll see you later on. You look gorgeous, by the way. Once your father is reminded of how lovely you are on camera, he'll certainly have to think about producing that show."

Jas preened. "Thanks, doll. I'll get myself some more champagne. Having to deal with the stepmonster always makes me thirsty."

Bran steered her away. "Wow, she's already a couple of sheets to the wind."

Carly waved that off. "Not really. That's kind of how she is. It will definitely be enough to completely irritate the boss. I'll be honest, I'm kind of anxious about what your brother has in store for us tonight. I'm not looking forward to the drama."

He gave her the wickedest grin, and then she found herself being hauled down a short hallway and into a room right off the gallery floor. "I am looking forward to this."

She didn't get a chance to look around because Bran was suddenly kissing her. His head swooped down and his lips brushed hers, and she couldn't think about anything but how overwhelmingly sexy he was.

His hands came up, fingers twisting lightly in her hair, drawing her back so he had a better angle.

He wasn't particularly gentle this time. He seemed even hungrier than he'd been before. His tongue licked along her bottom lip and she didn't even try to hold out. She opened her mouth, welcoming him in.

"Now see, that's what I meant by chemistry, Carly," he whispered before kissing her again.

She could do this all damn day. Kissing Brandon Lawless was more erotic than all the sex she'd ever had with her husband.

"Excuse me?"

She nearly jumped back and fell on her ass, but Bran's hands were there, holding her upright. Dear God, she'd forgotten where she was. The lead cameraman was standing there with a grin on his face.

"Sorry, Ms. Fisher, but I need to set up for the entrance. Ms. Cain's limo is almost here." Mike Davis gave her a wink. "I also need to make sure the lighting in here is all right. I'll have the new guy set that up. Apparently this is the showcase room." He sighed as he looked around. "I don't understand art. What the hell is that thing?"

"I'm with you," Bran said, apparently not at all embarrassed that they'd been caught making out by the camera guy. "I greatly prefer that painting of the dogs playing poker."

Carly looked over. That must have been one of the artist's signature pieces. It was an old antique stove with a fire flowing through the grate. Yes, now Carly remembered because she'd had to pay for the gas for this particular piece. Patricia had insisted the collection couldn't be shown without it. She'd said something about living art.

The gallery hadn't loved running a gas line into the room to feed the stove that supposedly represented global warming and the collusion of big business to heat up the world. Yeah, it was definitely one of those shows. And now that Bran wasn't all over her, she could feel the heat. That was the purpose of having it in a small room where the door closed. The observers were supposed to feel "the heat."

Mike shook his head. "Does it have to be this hot in here? It could steam up the lenses."

Yet another thing she would have to deal with. "I believe the artist would say yes. I'll try to convince her global warming can be a bit cooler than this."

She glanced up at Brandon and wished they could have had a little longer. Her evening was just beginning, and the rest, she was sure, would be a lot less pleasurable.

## Chapter Seven

"So I hear you're dating our Carly."

Bran turned slightly and noticed there was a man in a fashionable suit standing next to him looking up at the trash can that had been affixed to the wall. It was nothing more than a plastic garbage can that had been torn in places, its smelly contents peeking out from the slashes and threatening to tumble into the space. He'd seen that this particular piece was called *Waste Land Suburbia*. Apparently *Waste Land Suburbia* needed an HOA.

"I'm Carly's boyfriend. Name's Brandon." He held out a hand.

Which the new guy did not take. He looked down at it and then back up at the trash can.

So much for friendly conversation. He recognized the man. Carly had pointed him out. Kenny Jones, the head of the real estate division. So this was Patricia Cain's stepson.

"I'm Ken Jones. My father is married to Carly's boss. I thought we should talk, if you're determined to go through with this," he said, his voice low.

For a second Bran went on the defensive. How the hell could this man know what he was planning? "Go through with what?"

"With dating Carly. Or whatever you choose to call it." He sniffed, his face pinching. "I think it would be best if you understood that

Carly's had a rough time of it. I'm rather surprised to hear she's attempting to date again."

He managed to not sigh with relief. The stepson didn't know anything. This was interesting. Was he going to get the protective-big-brother lecture? Or the pissed-off-potential-lover, get-the-fuck-out-of-my-way talk? Either way, it would be far more interesting than the art exhibit. He'd recently met the artist, who despite her hatred of materialism had shown up in a designer dress that likely had cost thousands of dollars. He would bet those shoes she was wearing weren't earth friendly, either. They looked deadly.

He greatly preferred Carly's kitten heels. That's what she was. A pretty kitten in his arms when he kissed her. She melted against him and he felt about ten feet tall.

Nothing, it seemed, had ever felt as good as kissing Carly Fisher.

"I know her last marriage was a disaster. The good news is I'm not a con artist looking to make a quick buck." He would give Kenny the benefit of the doubt for the time being. He could understand a guy being protective of Carly.

"Well, that remains to be seen. How did the two of you meet?"

"On the Internet. A dating site matched us up. I was hesitant in the beginning, but it turned out they were good at what they do. Carly and I are quite well matched." He actually wondered what a dating site would say about them. Maybe they looked like opposites on paper, but sometimes opposites worked. His brother and Ellie didn't have a ton in common, but they somehow completed each other.

"I doubt that," Kenny said without ever looking his way. "You're nothing like her. You work security. Or at least you have for the past five years. You barely made it out of college with an undergraduate degree. You have no upward mobility at all and no family to speak of. Just a mother who isn't at all interesting."

Okay, his optimism was fading rapidly. "And how do you know any of this?"

"I have my sources, and if you think you'll be allowed anywhere near the evil queen without a proper background check, you're obviously out of your league. I assure you the small check I did on you is nothing compared to what Patricia will do once she realizes how close you seem to be to her assistant. She's not about to let Carly go without a fight, and I don't think you'll like how she fights."

Which brought up a question he'd had since he started researching for this mission. "And why is that? Carly's a personal assistant but from what I understand your stepmother has had plenty of those. She used to go through several a year. Why fight so hard to keep this one?"

Kenny finally turned to look at him, his eyes narrow with suspicion. "And how would you know that?"

"Like you said, I work security. When I started dating Carly, I had her vetted. I have a sensitive job as well, and if you think your stepmother is paranoid then I don't even know what to call Ian Taggart. He's my boss and he vets everyone his employees date because our firm often works for the government. So yes, I know a great deal about your stepmother, though I will tell you I don't know a lot about you, a fact I intend to correct shortly." If he hadn't even gotten a call about the trace on him then it had to have been light. All his cover information had been approved by his brother-in-law, and Bran was sure it had been guarded by the best hackers on the planet.

According to everything on the official records, he was who he said he was—a hardworking blue-collar guy with a mother back in Dallas who watched far too much home-and-garden television. He was sure if they needed to, an actress would be provided to play that role. He could look at Kenny Jones Jr. with absolute certainty that this man couldn't crack his cover.

So it was all about getting him to talk. Everything Case had taught him came roaring back. While his brother-in-law had worked out with him, he'd also given Bran tips on how to work as an operative. Not that he thought Bran would ever play the part, but Bran had found the conversations useful. Any piece of information, no matter how small or how odd the source might seem, could help the operation. Information was everything.

"If you want the real truth, I'll tell you," Kenny offered, his chest puffing out. "It's because Carly has what none of those other assistants had. True talent. The rest of them were nothing but window dressing with decent organizational skills. They didn't have a tenth of Carly's instinct for what works."

"What works?"

"In the kitchen. In the household. My stepmother is excellent at branding herself and making money, but she's always relied on someone else to give her ideas. She was a halfway decent cook who got a shot at a lifestyle show. None of those recipes were hers. They belonged to her first producer, a woman she formed a partnership with. A woman who refused to be on air or even come to the set. I think she was probably elderly, and Patricia took advantage of her. From what I can tell, she died a few years ago or she was hospitalized or something. I don't know, but right before Carly came on, Patricia was on her own for the first time."

That was quite interesting. He'd known Patricia had stepped on a whole lot of people on her way to the top, but the fact that there had been such a private source behind her in the beginning was definitely intriguing. "So she couldn't hack it without a partner?"

"She was failing miserably. She could smile for the cameras, but she couldn't come up with the concepts that fuel the show." Kenny straightened his tie, looking around as though ensuring that they were alone. "And then Carly shows up and she's not at all what Patricia would want in an assistant. My stepmother prefers her assistants to be something like a reflection of her. They all look like younger versions of herself and she trains them to dress like her, act like her. Carly doesn't fit in at all. But it turns out she's even better than old Francine Wells. Patricia doesn't have to go meet Carly. She's got Carly right here. She can hide her in plain sight."

"So Carly does the work and Patricia takes the credit." Francine Wells. He would be looking her up soon.

"And very little pay. I'm fairly certain that my stepmother strong-armed her into staying in this job. She's got dirt on everyone."

"Dirt? There's nothing dirty about Carly."

Kenny shook his head, a dismissive gesture. "Everyone has something to hide. My stepmother has made an art of finding those secrets and making them work for her. She doesn't care who she hurts. The woman keeps files on everyone in her life."

That was the rumor. He would love to get into those files. "Somehow I can't see Carly's file having anything big in it."

"Patricia will use anything. Hell, she'll make it up if she has to. She'll do anything to stay on top and that includes hurting anyone she has to. She'll do it without a moment's remorse."

It was too bad he couldn't simply ask where those damn files were. "I still don't understand what any of this has to do with my relationship with Carly."

A determined look came into Kenny's eyes. "I intend to develop a show around Carly, a show that will make *Patricia's Paradise* look as cold as it is. So don't screw this up for Carly."

She hadn't mentioned anything about this. "I have no intention of screwing anything up for her. I told you. I'm interested in Carly. If she wants her own show, I don't see how I would stop that."

"I need her to keep her eyes on the prize," he said fervently. "You're a distraction. How much to make you go away? You can't possibly be interested in her. You're playing some kind of angle, and I won't allow it to happen. I'm betting a lot on her and I won't let some two-bit gigolo fuck everything up."

"I'm here for her. Nothing else," Bran said, his voice going hard.

"Don't feed me that line of bullshit. Look, if anyone's going to get close to her it's going to be me. I'm the one who stands to gain the most from her. I've been planning this for years. So give me a number so I can pay you off."

There it was—that nasty feeling in his gut that made his fists tighten. It was like his vision narrowed and all he could see was Kenny Boy's face. If he let his fist go, let those instincts flow, he would feel so good. That's what the voice of rage always whispered to him. Once the blood started flowing, it would be like a release valve had been set loose and he could breathe again.

"Kenny? Are you bothering the new boy?"

He turned, his rage finding a new focus. Patricia Cain stepped up, her manicured fingers finding Kenny's shoulder.

"Do be a dear and get me a glass of champagne," she ordered.

Kenny stiffened but turned and walked away.

"Was he being annoying?"

Annoying but not evil. It might be pure imagination, but Bran could practically feel the evil rolling off her. Still, he found some strength. He remembered how tightly Carly had held on to him before they'd been interrupted. She was ready. She wanted him and not for anything more than the affection and pleasure he could give her. "He was being enlightening."

That seemed to confuse her, which was a serious plus. She frowned his way. "I often find him obnoxious."

"I think he's got a crush on my girlfriend."

Her lips curled up in something resembling a smile. "I think he believes your girlfriend can dethrone me, but he's wrong."

So she wasn't so oblivious. "If it's any consolation, I happen to know she doesn't want to dethrone anyone. She enjoys her job. She doesn't like attention."

It was the plain truth. No matter what Kenny Jr. thought, Carly would never want the attention of a TV show. She was the kind of woman who would deeply enjoy writing cookbooks, and perhaps a column in a newspaper or a magazine or a daily blog. She wasn't ever going to want the kind of attention Patricia Cain needed to get by.

"I think you're right, but that doesn't mean Kenny won't attempt to play Mephistopheles," she mused. "What did he offer you?"

He wasn't about to lie to the woman. Not when he didn't have to. It was important to build some trust with her. "Oh, we hadn't actually gotten around to a real number. He was offering to buy me off. Something about writing a check for me to walk out of Carly's life."

Patricia laughed, sounding truly amused for once. "He's watched far too many films. He's also not a good judge of character. You're not the type of man who can be purchased. Did he call you a gigolo?"

"That was one of the words he used to describe me." He followed at her side as she began walking slowly around the gallery.

"You'll have to forgive him. He considers anyone younger and more attractive than he is to be some form of gold digger. Believe me, he's called me every name in the book. He even got drunk at my wedding to his father and toasted my status as a social climber. And I brought a forty-million-dollar empire into the family. The Jones family doesn't understand the real world. In their estimation, even someone like me obviously wants their money."

"Well, I don't understand that world at all." No lies there. He often thought he would be happier if he had an ordinary job, lived a regular life. He was so out of place in his brother's world. He felt out of place here tonight. All around him everyone was oohing and ahhing and discussing the "art" and gossiping about one another, and all he wanted to do was take Carly home and finally get her in bed. "Or this one, really."

"You don't like the work?" She sighed, a sound of eternal disdain. "Well, I don't, either, but her father is very influential. The things we do for business. I think I rather like having you around to influence Carly. You seem like a genuine young man."

"I don't know how to be anything else."

"I think you might be exactly the kind of man Carly needs. You're right. She's not like so many in my employ. They live on the hopes of finding their way on screen or of doing their own things, but Carly understands the value of what she does. I think we should talk further. Perhaps we could have lunch at some point. I do feel the need to get to know anyone who's close to my most valued employee." She waved to someone ahead of her and then frowned. "Tell me something. What do you think of the security here tonight? I'm unimpressed. First they apparently screwed up with my stepdaughter since she's here without a handler and has already doused herself in champagne, and now I see no sign of them."

Likely because his brothers were distracting them with silly pranks they still felt forced to check out. "I saw someone on the door, but I'll be honest, he wasn't particularly professional. He didn't even require tickets."

The guy had kind of yawned and waved them through the way most people would in this sleepy, wealthy part of town.

"I'll have to talk to you about that, too, then," Patricia said. "I've been thinking of firing this firm for a while now."

Right on schedule. She hadn't kept a security firm for more than eighteen months. She was rapidly going through them. It wouldn't take much to convince her to hire on McKay-Taggart. "Anytime, Ms. Cain. I would love to do anything that could possibly help out Carly."

She turned and studied him for a moment. "What do you see in the girl?"

"Carly's got a light that not a lot of people have. It's dimmed right now, but I think when she's truly happy, she can bring that light out into the world and warm all the people around her. She's kinder than almost anyone I've met and she's not afraid to show affection. She gives me the things I need, the things I can't provide for myself."

"Yes, I've seen a bit of her glow. I'll be honest. I don't understand it at all, but I do know it attracts people to her. I have to go and smile for the camera and pretend to love my hideous family now. Appearances are everything, you know. We'll talk again. And please let Carly know that once the filming is over, she's free to leave. I've been thinking lately that the girl works too hard. She needs an assistant of her own. I'll see to it." A brilliant smile crossed her face, though Bran noted it still didn't reach her eyes. "Hello, Thierry, dear. Are you enjoying the show?"

What the hell had that been about? The woman sounded almost human. She wasn't supposed to be. She was supposed to be the evil queen who held Carly down. Bran watched her move through the crowd, playing the gracious hostess, and wondered what she had planned.

Unfortunately, he was fairly certain none of it was good.

He turned away and started looking for Carly.

Carly nearly growled her frustration. It was all going to hell in a handbasket. Jas had way too much champagne and had kicked off her shoes and was dancing around until one of the wayward security guards had finally shoved her into a limo and sent her on her way. Kenny was sulking and refusing to go on camera. The gallery director was on her ass because the heat from the showcase room was causing patrons to avoid it and the entire back end of the gallery, including the small desk they'd placed to drive gallery membership.

And now the junior cameraman needed to finish the setup for the family shot in the showcase room before they closed the whole thing down. She wasn't sure why they were closing it, but she knew she needed to get that shot. It looked like it would be a small shot, but maybe she could get Patricia and the artist in there, with the artist explaining her work. It had to be good or rock star dad might pull out of his deal with Cain Corp, and then all hell would break loose.

"Hey, do you need any help?" Bran moved to her side. It looked like he'd been standing by the bar, staying fully out of the way of the crowd. He was as smart as he was sexy.

"I'm trying to round up the gang, so to speak. This is not going as well as I'd hoped. What put Kenny in such a bad mood? He's usually the one I can count on to be reasonable."

"Oh, I think that's me," Bran said with a wince. "He's not particularly happy about our new relationship."

"Why would he care?"

"I believe he thinks you're his way out of real estate."

She rolled her eyes. "Not that again. He's high if he thinks he can pull that off. There's zero way his father allows anyone to compete with Patricia, and I can't even leave this job."

"Not for another two years, but then you'll be free." He looked out over the crowd. "Unless she finds some other way to keep you tethered to her."

It was her worst nightmare. "I don't know how she can. I'm not intending to give her anything else to hold over my head."

"I think she's counting on me to do that. We had a private conversation. She approves of me, by the way. It was odd. She wants to have lunch and I was supposed to let you know that as soon as the on-camera work is done, you can go. She'll have someone else oversee the cleanup."

"What?" A cold chill went down her spine because that was not the way the world worked. "She never lets me go home before everything is done. I'm accountable for every last napkin and bottle of champagne."

"Apparently not now."

"What is she up to?"

"No idea, but I got the distinct feeling she's planning something. And she knows about Kenny's plans to turn you into the next home-guru idol or whatever. He's right that you would be good at that, but wrong about how and where you should do it."

She didn't have time to worry about that now. She needed to get everything together and then she would worry about family politics and who was going to get their asses kicked. Because if Patricia knew that Kenny was plotting behind her back, she would be plotting behind his, too.

It could all turn into World War III, and she did not want to get caught in the cross fire.

"Hey, it's going to be all right." Bran stepped in front of her, taking both of her hands in his.

"You don't know how nasty they can get." She wanted to get through these last two years calmly and peacefully. She didn't want to have to pick sides in a family war because any way she went, she would be the one who got hurt. They would be left standing at the end and all the little people would bear the burden.

"Like I said, it's going to be okay. I'm going to make sure of it. Let me handle Patricia. I'll try to figure out what's going on and then we can plan your best move. You have to hold on for a few more weeks, and then Patricia will hopefully be so involved in saving her own ass that she won't have time to worry about you."

In a few weeks he might be gone, and she was under no illusions that he would hang around to ensure her comfort then. Still, he was sweet and he was here with her now.

She went up on her toes and brushed her lips across his. "Let me finish up here and we can talk more at home. This is the last shot of the night. I should be done in about twenty minutes, but don't hold me to it. I have to convince everyone to stand in a room together. The room is unfortunately way too hot for comfort and it's not going to get any cooler."

"I would think Patricia's very presence would ensure a temperature drop of twenty degrees," Bran said with a grin.

If only it worked that way. She gave him a wink and looked around the room. There she was. Her boss was talking to a group of people, all of whom were watching her with rapt attention as she shamelessly name-dropped.

Carly stood on the outside of the crowd.

Patricia looked up, but it was obvious she was happy where she was. Holding court. With a small tilt of her head, she informed Carly it was fine to come forward.

Carly eased her way around and finally got to her boss, whispering in her ear, "We need one last shot. I'll have everything set up in the showcase room in five minutes and then you're free."

"Don't forget to move Kenneth's cane. He'll need it to stand, but he's far too vain to walk with it around all these people. And grab my cape from the cloakroom. I promised the designer I would show it off," Patricia ordered.

"It's hot in . . ." At the look Patricia sent her, Carly decided not to argue. "Absolutely. It will be there when you are."

Patricia went back to her conversation like she'd never stopped.

Carly made her way to the cloakroom and grabbed the ridiculously overdone silver capelet that went perfectly with the designer gown Patricia was wearing but not great with the Florida heat. It was far too heavy, meant for a place with a true winter, but designers were willing to pay to have Patricia feature their clothes on her show, so weather be damned.

The material was stupidly delicate. The woman working the counter passed it to her without a hanger. If she carried it in her hands it might wrinkle.

Wrinkling wouldn't go with the Cain brand. She slipped it over her shoulders to keep the lines fresh. It wouldn't matter once the filming was over. It would be one more thing tossed in the back of Patricia's closet, but for the next few minutes it was super important.

She strode down the hall after locating the cane, the ornate capelet on her shoulders. It was already stupid hot but the truth was Patricia wouldn't complain. Not once. She would simply toss the damn thing Carly's way when it all was done. The one thing she could say about her boss was she was a pro.

"I'm set up in there," Mike said as she turned down the hall that led to the signature room and the back of the gallery. "But it's so hot it's giving me a damn headache. I sent Tim in. I need some water or something. I'll be ready in a few minutes."

"If you're not . . ." Carly began.

Mike shook his head. "I've been working for that woman long enough. I'll keep an eye on her. The minute she starts heading that way I'll be there. After I find some damn aspirin. Who thought this was a good idea?"

Absolutely no one with half a brain. She watched Mike walk away. This was going to be so much fun. She glanced back at Bran. He was frowning at a TV with nothing but static.

It would be nice to walk out of here with him, to know that she wouldn't be alone tonight.

Live in the moment. She wasn't going to think about the inevitable future or mourn the past tonight. She would take pleasure in today because it was all she really had.

Well, she would have it after this damn shoot was through.

She needed to go and make sure everything ran as smoothly as possible so they could get the shot and be in and out in a few minutes. She would take her boss on her word and flee at the first available opportunity.

The hall was still. Up ahead she could hear some people talking in the back room, but otherwise all was quiet. All the better to film. There wouldn't be ambient noise to screw up the dialogue. Of course it would also be a tight fit, so maybe it was best that Jas had been sent back to the house. They'd already gotten several shots that made it look like the family was together. Mike was excellent at managing to get the right camera angle to shrink distance between them and make them look like they actually enjoyed being near one another.

Not that they did. She had zero desire to sit down to dinner with that family.

She let the cane clack on the marbled floor. One day she would need a cane. She would be old and gray, and she didn't want to live the way Kenneth Sr. did. Yes, he had all the money in the world, but everyone hated him.

A whole lot of people had hated her mother, too. Her mother had a lot in common with the elder Jones, now that she thought about it. He'd spent his life in pursuit of more wealth and Carly's mom had chased after comfort for herself. She'd bore two children in the hopes of snagging a husband and when she finally had, she shut her daughters out, unwilling to risk any of her happiness for her children.

What did Bran want out of life? That was what it came down to. Carly had always thought what she wanted was independence, but now she wondered. She hadn't realized how lonely she'd been before Bran walked into her life.

He was in pursuit of revenge. She was setting herself up for a nasty fall.

With a long sigh she opened the door to the signature room and was assaulted with hot air.

The little stove was definitely doing its job. The small room was thick with heat. The door closed behind her and Carly glanced around. The artist had plastered pictures of ecological disasters on murals around the room. She did not believe in subtlety.

Mike was right. It was too hot. Something was wrong. There was no way she'd meant for it to get this bad. Carly set the cane down. They would have to prop the door open and turn down the heat. Otherwise Patricia's carefully prepared hair was going to wilt and turn into frizzy waves, and everything would be ruined because she would bury that footage deep.

It looked like her night wasn't quite over yet.

With a long sigh, she turned back to the door and went to open it.

The knob turned, but the door wouldn't open. It was stuck. She tried again but got nothing.

She had to stop for a moment, her head spinning. What was going on? Carly leaned against the door for support because it suddenly felt like the world was moving. Her stomach turned and she tried pushing the door open.

She glanced down because if there was a lock, it had to be on the inside of the door. Why would it be on the outside?

Nothing. The knob was smooth with no way to turn and lock the door.

Someone had locked her in from the outside. She pounded on the door, her palm slapping against the wood.

"Hey! I'm stuck in here."

That was when it hit her. A wave of nausea. She was going to be sick. Carly couldn't stand anymore. She slid to her knees.

Heat alone wouldn't do that. No way. She'd lived through Alabama summers and it wasn't like Florida was a bastion of cool weather.

Something else. Something was going on.

Carly reached into her pocket, dragging her phone out. She tried to make her fingers work. Her vision was getting blurry. She managed to pull up the last person she'd texted and got out two letters.

CO

Carbon monoxide. She prayed Bran knew a little something about chemistry. Real chemistry.

They had chemistry.

It was her last thought before the darkness took her.

*Chapter Eight*

Bran was ready to be done. Spy work was boring. No one had told him that. No, when Case started telling stories of his spy days, it was all about the lovely women and bullets flying and that time he'd gotten blown up. According to Case, it had been in a heroic blaze of glory that had cost him a broken leg and one truck he still mourned to this day.

Not once had Case mentioned hours spent in avant-garde galleries listening in on the conversations of the rich and clueless.

He'd heard more about aesthetics and clean lines and statement-making opportunities to last a lifetime. His brother needed to throw in his chaos so he and Carly could get the hell out of here and maybe he could seduce her. That would be a good way to spend the rest of the evening.

Where was she? He slipped past where Patricia was posing for pictures, hoping she didn't see him. She seemed to be playing the grande dame of the show. She stood with the artist as someone from the press took pictures of them.

She was different from what he'd imagined. Cold, yes, but she seemed to like Carly. When they'd spoken earlier, she'd seemed to actually give a damn whether Carly was happy or not. Was that an act? He wasn't sure.

Once again he had to wonder if he was the right man for this job. He so often took people at face value, not wanting to look deeper.

He walked up to one of the few people he'd met tonight that he felt comfortable talking to. Mike was the cameraman and they'd talked some football before he'd had to go and set up for his shots. He also might know where Carly was and how long this was going to take.

Because his brother was totally right about a few things. He would rather spend his time seducing the girl than following around after Patricia Cain and her band of creepy hangers-on.

He was starting to think he might want the girl more than anything he'd wanted in his life. "Hey, Mike. Have you seen Carly?"

Mike nodded, his expression pained. "Yeah, I talked to her about a minute ago. She's setting things up with the family for the last shot of the night. She was going to talk to Patricia and then go back and help Tim finish. I got a horrible headache all of a sudden."

"Yeah, I can buy that. This whole place gives me a headache."

"I thought I'd try some caffeine." Mike flipped open a red can of soda. "Sometimes that helps. It's already clearing up. I think that room is way too hot. I'll be glad to get back to filming in studio. I hate these on-location shoots. It's always in cramped quarters inside."

No one expected Patricia to shoot outdoors. He and Carly had eaten dinner al fresco. They'd sat at a pretty bistro table, their knees brushing from time to time. Her small backyard was a mini oasis of peace and calm.

Something about her seemed to settle him.

Where was the chaos his brother had talked about? He almost dreaded it now because it could cause Carly discomfort. Hopefully switching out Jasmine's bodyguard for a wild asshole had done the trick. Patricia had seemed perfectly annoyed that her stepdaughter had caused a scene.

"Any idea how long it's going to take?" Maybe he should pull the car around and get her out of here before the chaos started. While she would have to deal with the fallout, she wouldn't be directly in the line of fire.

"I can get them in and out in about fifteen minutes. Twenty, tops, if the old man gives us trouble. He likes to be the center of attention so he sometimes causes some drama with his wife."

"How long have you been working for them?"

Mike took a long swallow before answering. "Too long, if you ask me. I started out filming a couple of reality shows for Kenneth's network. When he and Patricia got hitched, I filmed it for *Patricia's Paradise*. Apparently I'm good at finding her best angles and here I am. It's not too bad if you ignore the hideous infighting. I'm mostly ignored and that's how I like it. As long as I'm getting paid, I'll keep my head down. Carly's the one who bears the brunt of it."

"I don't know. She seems to be pretty well treated to me." All night long Patricia had seemed on her best behavior. She hadn't once raised her voice or asked anything overly taxing of Carly.

Mike rolled his eyes. "Shit. I should have known. That is all for you. You need to watch yourself or you'll fall into her trap."

"Trap?"

"She likes to play around with young men," Mike explained. "Those flirtations are the only time she's ever easy to be around. She's courting you in her own weird way, and part of that means looking like an actual human being around you."

"You have to be wrong about that. I explained that I'm one hundred percent involved with Carly."

"Another reason for her to go after you, buddy. That might be the best reason of all. She can't stand the fact that Carly is better than she is at everything that truly counts. Oh, she wouldn't put it that way. I'm sure she would say making money and collecting power counts more than anything, but she hates how much she relies on Carly. She hates that everyone loves Carly. She definitely hates that Carly's Cinderella to her wicked stepmother. Despite the fact that she won't ever change her behavior, she wants to be loved."

"She's a narcissist."

"A classic one," Mike agreed. "I'm sure in her head she's the hard worker and Carly is only along for the ride. Look, I shouldn't talk about the boss this way and I hope you can keep this between us, but you seem like a nice guy. You should know to take anything she says with a grain of salt. And watch your back."

Bran knew good advice when he heard it. "I will. I have no interest in anyone but Carly, though I will admit I find the entire thing fascinating. Like a train wreck, but fascinating."

Mike's lips quirked up. "It's a fucked-up soap opera around here."

He was about to gently steer the conversation toward Francine Wells when his cell vibrated. He pulled it out. One text message from Carly.

Maybe she'd finished up. Or more likely she was telling him she needed more time. Damn. He wanted to leave.

"I'm feeling so much better," Mike said.

Bran pulled up the text.

CO

What did that mean? He texted her back.

Do you need me? Is CO a riddle? What do I get if I figure it out?

Maybe she was planning a surprise. He could get into that. The night wouldn't be a waste if he could get her somewhere private.

"Is there a room in this place that might go with the letters CO?" Bran asked. Mike knew the place way better than he did. "Carly texted me. CO. All I can come up with is commanding officer."

It didn't seem like a fantasy Carly would have.

Mike frowned. "I don't know what she meant, but it makes me think. I'm feeling so much better since getting out of that room. I think we need to go check for a gas leak."

"Carbon monoxide? CO is the chemical symbol for carbon monoxide and you sent Carly back to that room where the gas heater is. Call 911 right now." Bran didn't stop to ask more questions. He took off running down the hall.

That room was small. If the door was shut, it would fill with colorless, odorless gas quickly and it would overwhelm anyone who was in there. It might even incapacitate them so quickly all a person could do was get out one quick text.

"Get everyone out of here now!" He shouted because if he was right, then it would affect the entire place eventually. And it posed the risk of igniting. "Get these people out right now."

He could hear the chaos that started behind him, but his only thought was to get to Carly.

Maybe it was all a mistake and he would find out she really did have commanding officer fantasies. He would be completely embarrassed when the cops showed up and all he had to show them was one horny girl and his overreaction.

That was all this was. An overreaction.

She probably hadn't meant anything at all. The text had likely been a mistake. He was going to run in and scare the hell out of her and then they would laugh and he would have screwed up the entire mission and you know what, he was okay with that.

Anything as long as she was okay.

Anything so she wasn't a broken doll on the floor. So she wasn't limp and dead and cold by the time he got to her, by the time he found the courage to reach for her. Anything so he didn't have to look at another dead girl and know he was the reason she wouldn't breathe again.

"Carly!" He shouted because he could already see that someone had closed the door.

He didn't hear a thing except the sound of people leaving the gallery en masse. Behind him it sounded like Mike was ordering everyone out, getting them all through the front doors and out onto the street.

He reached for the door, but it didn't budge. Fear gripped him. She was in there. He knew she was. She was stuck in there and how long did she have? Not enough time for him to deal with the situation rationally. He needed to go a little crazy.

"Baby, if you can hear me, back up. I'm coming in." When he heard nothing, he prayed he wasn't about to make a bad situation worse. He backed up and then tossed his body at the door. Pain flared through him, but the door gave way.

Heat blasted out of the room but he saw her.

She was crumpled up on the floor, her cell phone in one hand. He pulled his shirt up over his mouth because he couldn't get sick now. He had to be strong for her, had to get her out of the building. Already he could feel some of the effects of the gas. His stomach churned and he could feel the beginnings of a headache start.

None of that mattered. Only Carly mattered.

He knelt down and picked her up, hauling her high against his chest. There wasn't time to figure out where the leak was or to turn it off. There was only time to run like hell and pray nothing worse happened.

Carly was dead weight in his arms. He made his way back out to the hall and into the gallery.

*Please. Please don't let her die. Don't let me be too late this time.*

Bran ran out the doors, the night air hitting him. That smell of salt air was the sweetest thing.

"What is going on?" Patricia demanded.

He ignored her, carrying Carly out and onto the patch of grass as he heard the sirens start up. He laid her down gently and put a hand to her head. "Breathe. I need you to breathe."

"I asked you what was happening, young man," Patricia said again. "And what is wrong with my assistant? Why on earth is she wearing my cape? Did she get drunk and ruin this entire evening? I want some answers."

"And I'm telling you to back off if you want to live," he practically snarled. The only reason he responded at all was the movement of Carly's chest. She was breathing. She was alive. Now he had to hope she hadn't been down long enough to cause real damage. "There was a gas leak in your precious gallery that damn near killed two of your employees, so you need to back off or I swear I'll go to the television cameras that will inevitably show up and explain to them that all you gave a damn about was your clothing. Do you understand me?"

Her eyes flared, but she backed off.

"Was trying to not get it wrinkled," Carly said, her voice a bit shaky. "Fabric like this wrinkles in the heat and you wouldn't have liked that." Her eyes fluttered open and she gave him the sweetest half smile. "You knew chemistry."

Relief swept through him and he held her to him. "I suck at chemistry but luckily Mike doesn't. You gave me a scare."

"We should move everyone farther away," Patricia muttered, seeming to finally give a damn about something. "There could be a fire. We should all get to a safe distance until the fire department can sort it out. Carly, you should go to the hospital."

"I'll take care of her," Bran vowed. If anyone thought they were separating him from her, they needed to think again.

Patricia nodded, though she wasn't looking at them anymore. Her eyes were wandering, as though looking for something she couldn't find. "All right. I'll see to getting everyone out of here. Brandon, I believe we should have a talk when things are calmer. Perhaps you could put me in touch with your employer."

He simply nodded, but a sick feeling had started in his gut again, and this time it had nothing to do with the gas.

This was the chaos his brother had promised.

He and Drew were about to have a long, maybe bloody talk.

Bran tucked her into bed hours later. It wasn't long before dawn, but he thought it would be a miracle if he got any sleep at all. He hadn't talked to his brother. Even as he'd carried her in, he hadn't said a word to his brother.

"Where am I?" Her eyes opened, but he didn't see any fear in them. Merely curiosity. "This is not my bedroom, Brandon Lawless." Her eyes widened in obvious panic. "Oh, God. I called you by your name."

"Hush, it's all right." He sat down beside her and smoothed back her hair. "We're safe and you're fine and everything is all right. I brought you home with me. We're at the condo in Palm Coast, where you will be recovering for a few days while I ensure that everything is safe and sound at your place."

"You think this was DiLuca? I thought you paid him this afternoon. God, I still feel so bad about that."

He thought it was something else entirely, but he wasn't sure he would ever tell Carly what he thought had really happened. "He has been paid off. I wired him the money before dinner. I got confirmation that he has it and he's cleared the debt so he's got no reason to come after you. And I doubt this would be his style. I think I'm going to find out what's going on before I let you out in the open again. I already have someone working on it. Now, you rest and relax and I'll handle everything."

"I'm the world's worst spy partner," she said with a frown. "I cause more problems than I solve."

"Nonsense. I already learned more at that single party than we could have in a year's worth of research. Now go to sleep."

She sighed as she laid back. He'd managed to get her into scrubs at the hospital, and they would have to serve as pajamas this evening. She looked soft and sweet all cuddled up in the bed. "Where are you going to be?"

"I've got some issues to clear up and then I'll be right outside on the couch." The way he had been for a solid week. His back ached at the thought but at least the couch here was bigger than the one at her place.

She reached out, her hand finding his arm. "Don't sleep out there. When you're done, come to bed with me. Just to sleep. I won't attack you. I'm feeling a little weak so you're safe from me. I can't stand the thought of you on the couch. Please sleep with me."

After what she'd been through, could he tell her no? Could he explain that sleeping next to her and not taking her would be way more uncomfortable than the couch? Naturally not. He would do whatever it took to make her feel safe again. Especially since it had been his own brother's fucked-up-all-to-hell plan that had nearly killed her. "I'll be back in a while. You get some sleep. The doctor said you would be fine, but you're supposed to rest for a few days. I've already told Patricia you won't be back until Monday."

"I can't miss work." She shook her head. "You can't tell Patricia stuff like that. She doesn't take orders."

He leaned over and kissed her forehead. "Yes, I can. It's all arranged. Like I said, you rest and leave everything else to me."

He stood and walked to the door.

"Bran?"

"Yes?"

"Did it work?"

He closed his eyes for a second, the question threatening to make him lose it. She didn't ask it in an angry fashion. She was merely checking to see if they'd done their job. "It worked. She wants a meeting with Taggart. I think it scared her for some reason. It definitely threw her off balance."

"Good." Her eyes closed again.

He stalked out of the room, managing to close the door behind him quietly when what he wanted to do was slam it as hard as he could. He strode down the hall, searching for his brother. It was time to have it out. Naturally his brother was waiting for him.

"Why don't you explain what happened and why you haven't answered my calls or texts for the last five hours, Bran. All I got was one snippy text explaining that you were coming out here and I should vacate the master bedroom. Did you think that was acceptable?" Drew was standing in the living room. Only Hatch was present at this late-night meeting. Ellie and Riley had flown back to New York the previous morning and Case and Mia had left for Dallas hours before. "Do you have any idea what you put us through?"

Bran had known this was a conversation best had in person. And with a minimum of words. Drew was worried about what he'd been put through?

He walked right up to his asshole brother and popped him in the face. His hand felt like it cracked with pain, but that was just one more ache the night had brought. "You're a fucking asshole, Drew, and I swear if you ever put her in that kind of danger again, I will walk right into Patricia Cain's office and I'll give her everything. Do you understand me?"

Drew backed off, his hand going to his face, eyes flaring. "What the fuck are you talking about, Bran?"

Hatch got right in the middle, his hands coming out to keep them apart. "Everyone calm down. There has obviously been a misunderstanding here."

Naturally Hatch would take Drew's side. "There's no misunderstanding. Carly nearly died tonight. I had to break down that door, Drew. How could you? How could you possibly think that was all right? You didn't tell me because you wanted me to have an honest reaction? Here it is, brother. I'm taking her out of this and if you try to stop me, I'll make good on my threat."

Drew stared at him as if trying to process. "You think I did that? You think I started a gas leak in a building where my brother was?

Where you could have gotten hurt? Do you even know me? Do you know what I went through to make sure you were safe?"

Safe? Drew thought he'd been safe? The impulse to hit his brother again rose like a giant hammer, straightening his spine, making his fists pulse. His mind raced with images of some of the *safety* he'd been given in his childhood.

Hiding in a dirty closet for two days because his foster father was drunk and threatened to beat him to death. Two days without food or water. Two days without a bathroom.

Safe? He'd never once been fucking safe. Not since the night Riley had awakened him and the monster had started his chase.

Hatch stepped in front of him. "Bran, don't do this right now. You look at me. You're here with me. Do you understand?"

Only the feel of Hatch's hands on his face, his voice calling him back, made him stand down. He hated this weakness, hated that it welled up so unexpectedly at times. He wasn't a child anymore, but he seemed forever stuck in that nasty house. No matter how much money Drew tossed his way, he would always be the kid no one wanted. He shoved it all aside. This wasn't a therapy session. This was about Carly. "I understand my brother is a ruthless bastard who doesn't care about anyone but himself."

Hatch stepped back, all tenderness gone from his expression. "You stop right now and explain yourself. Are you trying to say you think Drew had anything to do with that gas leak?"

"How do you know there was a gas leak if you didn't do it? You wanted to cause some chaos. You got it." But even as he said the words, he was coming down from his volcanic rage.

"I was there, Bran. I was across the street waiting to send in the agent I hired to protest against Cain Corp's history of animal abuse. She was going to rush Patricia and scare the crap out of her and make a scene. I wanted to wait until the end of the night for Carly's sake. I thought it would be easier on her. That was the chaos I was going to cause," Drew said, striding into the kitchen and opening the freezer. "Instead I had to stay away and flip the hell out when I realized that building could explode and my baby brother was still in it."

"I had to hold him back," Hatch said with a shake of his head.

"If you ever do that to me again, I swear I'll cut you off from everything," Drew vowed, pointing at Hatch.

"Yeah, I've heard that all night long." A long huff issued from Hatch and he stalked over to the bar and poured himself a drink. "What the hell were you going to do besides screw up everything? Did you honestly think he would have left with you? He wasn't going to do anything until he got that girl out."

"I wasn't planning on giving him a choice," Drew shot back.

Shit. Ever since that moment that he'd realized Carly was in danger, all he could think about was making someone pay. He'd meant every word he'd said. He'd intended to pull Carly out and damn the consequences. Not that he'd talked to her about the decision, and she'd probably want to have a say.

"I'm sorry." Why had he gone to the worst possible place? Was he always going to do that? It seemed to be his way. The minute something bad happened he went to the darkest explanation possible. "I thought it was you. Hell, Carly asked me if it worked. Which it did. Patricia requested a meeting with my boss."

"Carly thinks I put her in that kind of danger?" Drew asked, his voice tight.

"No." He wasn't going to let Drew think that. Carly had been smarter than him, it seemed. Or perhaps she simply had less history and a more optimistic outlook. "She thinks it has something to do with her mob debt, but she was smart enough to know that it could have sent Patricia right over the edge."

Drew slapped an ice pack over the left side of his face. "At least one of you has faith in me."

"Again with the sorry. It's been a rough night."

Hatch slumped down on the couch, Scotch in hand. "Is she really all right? How was she the only one who had to go to the hospital? I don't think we understand what happened."

"I would have understood a hell of a lot more if you'd let me go in," Drew complained.

That would have been real chaos. "Hatch was right to hold you back. We needed people out of the building, not rushing in. And she wasn't the only one who felt the effects. The cameraman had been in there for a few minutes and he came out complaining about a headache."

"Go back to the beginning." Drew sat down beside Hatch. "Why on earth was the gas on? It's not cold at all."

Bran quickly described the art exhibit and the signature piece. He managed to get through it with a minimum of snark, which he thought was very professional of him. "At some point in time, a leak must have started. Carly and I had been in the room earlier in the evening and we didn't have any trouble. Then later Mike went in to set up his camera and that was when he walked out complaining of a headache. Carly had gone in to make all the final preparations with Tim."

Who he hadn't seen at all. If Tim had been in that room, why had he found Carly in there alone? Why hadn't he seen Tim running down the hall or milling around afterward? He'd talked to Mike and several of the other employees, but he hadn't seen hide nor hair of Tim.

"So this was some kind of accident?" Hatch asked. "Do you think they screwed something up with the stove thing when they were messing with all those cameras?"

No, he was starting to think something much more sinister was going on. It made some sense when he'd thought it was his brother. Though even in that case he hadn't been thinking clearly. Now that he was out of the situation, he had a few questions. "She was locked in."

Drew sat up, his jaw tightening. "Locked in the room with the gas leak?"

He could still remember the terror he'd felt when he couldn't get that door open. "Yes, it was locked, but I didn't have time to figure out how. I broke it open and got her out of there. She was locked in from the outside. I can assure you she tried to get out. When she came to she told me she'd tried to get the door open and then she'd gotten too dizzy to walk. She barely managed to text me a message."

If she hadn't, he would have stood there talking to Mike while she was breathing in poison. She would have died while he joked about football or something else inane. He would have found her on the floor. Another girl he couldn't save.

"Hey, she did and she's fine," Drew said. "Are you sure the door couldn't have simply been stuck? That gallery is in one of the older buildings in the city. Sometimes doors stick."

He thought back, trying to remember every detail. "I tried the doorknob. It turned, but the door wouldn't open. So I threw my body at it and managed to get through. The question is why was the door closed at all? The camera was still set up, but Carly was the only one in the room. Tim, the junior cameraman, was supposed to be there waiting for the last shot, but he was nowhere to be found."

"All right. We need more than a first name." Hatch pulled out his phone and started typing. "I'll fill in Case on everything that went down. Would this Tim person be an employee?"

"I think so. Carly will know more." He wasn't going to wake her up now, but in the morning they could all sit down and go over the events of the evening. "Tell Case we need a meeting with his brother. I don't think Patricia will accept talking to anyone but Ian. And I want to see all the reports on the gas leak as soon as they're available."

"I've already got a friend working that angle. The fire department will be investigating. As soon as they know anything, we should have some information, too." Drew looked back at the bedroom. "Is she really all right? She didn't look good when you carried her out."

"The EMTs got her oxygen. She wasn't in there for more than a few minutes." His brain was whirling. "What if someone screwed up? What if that was meant to be a slow leak? Carbon monoxide is odorless, colorless. Carly survived because it got to her fast and she hit the floor."

"With a slow leak, sometimes no one even realizes they're being poisoned." Hatch took up his thinking. "If they'd closed the door during that filming, it could have gone poorly. Especially if it was locked from the outside. They would have done their work and then found themselves getting sick but with no explanation or real capacity to understand. And with more people in the room there would be less oxygen."

"The filming was supposed to be private. No one would have gone back there for twenty or thirty minutes." Now that he was thinking about it, all kinds of dark theories made sense. "It's more than enough time to kill a bunch of people. All our friend Tim would have to do was open the door again and the whole thing would be viewed as a horrible accident."

"That's pure supposition," Drew replied. "You can't know that. It was very likely an accident. Otherwise, why would Carly have been the one locked inside? Who would want to hurt her?"

There was something about the way Patricia had acted afterward that made Bran think. "I don't think it was Carly. She was wearing something of Patricia's. A distinct cape that everyone saw her wearing in and that was supposed to be featured in the final shot of the night. Carly had talked about it on our way there. I was asking her about what she had to do tonight and one of the things she joked about was making sure the lighting worked to take ten years off her boss's face and that the silly designer cape looked white and not cream on film. The cameramen would have known about it."

"You think this Tim person was trying to kill Patricia?" Hatch asked with a whistle. "Well, I wouldn't blame him. I wanted to kill her several times over the years."

"We also need to look into a woman named Francine Wells." The night hadn't been a complete clusterfuck. He had found a few things out. "Do you know that name, Hatch?"

Hatch nodded after a moment. "She worked for the company back in the day. Is she involved with Patty?"

Well, that answered one question. "According to Patricia's stepson, Francine was Patricia's first Carly."

Hatch nodded. "Yeah, I always wondered about that. The Patty I knew could barely boil water. Oh, she was always interested in making everything as fancy as possible, but she wasn't what I would call a homemaker. She hired decorators and caterers. I'm not surprised to hear there was someone else behind her."

"Apparently Francine died a few years back or they had some kind of falling out," Bran explained. "Since then she's used Carly to prop her up idea-wise. It's why she went to such careful lengths to force Carly to keep working for her, and it's why I fear if we don't do something, in a couple of years, she'll do something worse to maintain the status quo."

"The Patty I knew wouldn't let a good thing go," Hatch agreed. "Not if there was any way she could manage it. She'll find something else to hold over Carly's head once she can't threaten her sister anymore. I can promise you that. She's planning it right now. It's why she's got so damn many enemies."

"Enemies who are willing to hurt a lot of people to get to her. I think this Tim person was hired to do this job. I think Patricia was the target and he thought he had her when Carly walked in. Maybe he was supposed to wait until everyone got there or maybe he simply panicked, but I definitely don't think this was an accident."

"We can't know anything until we get those reports back in." Drew winced as he took the ice pack off. "Damn, Bran, when did you learn to hit so hard?"

Sometime after he figured out no one was coming to save him. "I'm sorry. I wasn't thinking. If I had I would have known it wasn't you."

"I would never put you in that kind of danger. I hate the fact that you're involved in this at all," Drew admitted.

"They were my parents, too." He could say the words all he wanted, but he knew it wouldn't change his brother's mind. In Drew's head he was now the head of the family and the rest of them were all still kids. It was best to stay on task. "I'll want those reports, and let me know when Patricia can meet with Taggart. Once that's set, we hold on until we get to California. We get the information we need and we get out."

And then he wouldn't have a reason to be close to Carly anymore. He would go back to Austin and resume his usual round of work and strippers and booze, and not giving a shit if he woke up the next day.

But she would be out of danger. Now that he was fairly certain someone was after her boss, he wanted her to be safe.

"I should probably get to bed," Drew said with a long sigh. "If Big Tag is going to be here soon, I need all the rest I can get. I swear that is the single most sarcastic bastard I've ever met. Why Mia had to pick a family of mercenaries to attach herself to I will never understand."

He was pretty sure it had something to do with the way his sister smiled whenever her own personal Taggart walked in a room. "I'll go to bed, too."

Hatch stared at him. "Has it progressed that far? The last I heard you were sleeping on the couch."

"I still am." Why did he feel a blush creep across his skin? He was a man. He didn't need to explain where he was sleeping or with whom. Hell, he never did. He'd slept his way through a couple of strip clubs in his time. So why did it feel different with Carly? Why did he find himself fumbling and trying to explain? "She's scared. She was hurt tonight and she's in foreign surroundings and she doesn't want to be alone. It's not like that."

Oh, it was so like that, but he wasn't going to follow his instincts.

He cared about her too much to put her through what would inevitably happen. He would walk away in the end because he wasn't good for anyone over the long haul.

Hell, the truth was he was afraid of sleeping with her. He had terrible dreams, but he would get into bed with her and hold her. He would nap tomorrow sometime.

"You're seriously not sleeping with her?" Drew asked, a frown on his face.

"I thought you would be thrilled." He didn't understand why his brother wasn't fist-pumping at the news. "I told you. I like the girl. I want to protect the girl."

"You also want the girl," Drew argued.

"That's precisely why he's not sleeping with her." Hatch knocked back the last of his Scotch.

"He sleeps with everyone else. Is this another one of those emotional things I don't understand?"

Sometimes his genius brother was a little out of touch. "There's nothing to understand."

Hatch obviously wasn't going to let it go. "I told you this about Bran. He's got it in his head he's damaged goods. He sleeps with a woman if he's sure he's giving her something she needs."

"He gave her a million dollars," Drew pointed out in that oh-so-logical way of his.

Hatch groaned. "She's not a prostitute. Not everything is transactional, you robot. He likes her and that means he thinks he doesn't deserve her. He thinks he doesn't deserve any of this and I'm not exactly sure why because he's a shutdown motherfucker who doesn't talk to anyone."

"He talks in his sleep." Drew's eyes came up to meet his. "He talks about Mandy. I haven't interfered because I want you to trust me enough to tell me, but I'm beginning to think I'll have to."

"Stay out of it, Andrew. You weren't there then and you don't get to play at fixing me now. If you don't like who I am, then tell me to walk out." He hated having his back against a wall, and he certainly wasn't going to have a therapy session with his brother. No one needed to know about it. It was his burden to bear. It was his secret to keep. His.

He turned and started toward the bedroom door. He felt toxic. He didn't want to go in there. He wanted to get in a car, find a bar, and do what he did best. Obliterate himself.

"She'll need a new job," Drew said, his voice even, as though he didn't want to spark another argument. "It would be quite easy to find her one. You like her. There's no reason for you not to have a relationship with her."

"Dating much, big brother?" He could be such a hypocrite. It wasn't like Drew was out there searching for his one true love, either. "It seems to me you spend all your time plotting and planning. Leave me out of those plans. If you don't want me to walk out, you'll let me handle Carly the way I see fit."

Before his brother could say another word, Bran opened the door and strode inside. He closed it and stopped, taking a deep breath. Fuck. What would he do if she came to Austin? He was barely managing to keep his hands off her here.

She'd left the light on. To his right was the darkened bathroom and to his left a short hall with two closets on either side. The smaller closet held men's clothes, the larger one a mass of pretty female outfits and accessories. Case's friends stayed here on vacation. He couldn't remember their names but their happy marriage and family were stamped across the place. Pictures of their wedding day were framed in the hall alongside snapshots of the couple and their small boy playing on the beach.

Happy, normal people. People who had probably never been through a single shitty thing in their lives. People who hadn't had to fight to survive. They lived in pretty places and had pretty lives. Like Carly deserved.

He shouldn't walk in there, shouldn't crawl into bed with her. It would lead to the inevitable because his brother was right. He'd wanted Carly the minute he'd seen her. He wanted her warmth and all that sweet affection she had inside her waiting to get out. She would lavish it on the right man.

He wasn't the right man.

He was a toxic mess waiting to explode and he would do it all over her world.

"Bran?"

He tried to let go of the fight, of the tension of the night, and walked into the bedroom. He couldn't walk out on her. Not after what she'd been through. "I'm here. You're supposed to be asleep."

She sat up. "It was a little hot and I couldn't stand the scrubs another second. I found a T-shirt in the closet. Do you think it's okay for me to borrow it?"

It wasn't a T-shirt. It was a freaking tank top and it clung to her every curve. "I'm sure it's fine. Are you sure you want me to stay with you?"

"Unless you don't want to." Her voice went low. "I thought it would be okay. If it bothers you . . ."

He kicked off his shoes and pulled his shirt over his head. If she was comfortable, he could be the same. He shoved his slacks off and got down to his boxers. And just for good measure turned on the ceiling fan. Cold. Cold was his friend. "It's fine, sweetheart. I assure you there's nothing about sleeping with you that bothers me."

Except the part where he didn't cover her with his body, spread her legs, and slide inside her like he was coming home. Only that part bothered him.

Damn it. He was getting a hard-on. He flipped the lights off.

"Are you sure?" She sounded very small and that killed him.

Who had made her feel that way? Her husband? People in her past?

"Am I sure I would rather sleep with a gorgeous woman in a comfortable bed than suffering on a couch? I'm pretty positive about that." He slid in on the side opposite from her. "Besides, we're practically living together for the next month or so. We should get used to it."

She turned on her side. Despite the fact that he'd turned off the light, he could still see the outline of her form in the shadows. "Good, because it seems silly for you to sleep on the couch when you would be happier here. I would fit on the couch better."

That was so never happening. He would never let her sleep on a couch or suffer any discomfort when he could do it for her. He rolled to his side, enjoying the intimate feel of being alone with her. "Let's be practical and sleep together. I'm going to warn you, though. I don't sleep with anyone. I have some bad dreams."

Her hand came out, brushing along his cheek. "I can handle some bad dreams. Bran, I've been alone for so long. Tonight kind of sucked. I would love to sleep in your arms. I know it doesn't mean anything."

This was the moment that he should say something, but he moved so damn quickly there wasn't time for the logical and rational words to come out. He shifted and found his arms wrapped around her, her head nestling against his chest. "It's okay now. I promise I won't let anything happen to you. I can get you away from all of this if you want."

Her arm moved over the skin of his chest as she cuddled close. "I'm fine. What happened tonight was horrible, but I'll be more careful. I want to see this through. I need to. I need to do something good. I've been a dreadful coward the last few years."

She'd protected herself and her sister. There was nothing cowardly about that, but he wasn't going to force her out. It would hurt her in a way he couldn't. He would have to be more careful with her. There was so little left that she would have to do. All they needed her for was to distract Patricia during the party in California while they searched for the hard drive. Then she would be free. She had something to gain from this, too.

She could go to Kenny Jones and he would do anything it took to make her a star. She would have a good life, and somewhere along the way she would meet a man who could love her the way she deserved to be loved.

He wrapped his arms around her and drew her close, loving how warm he suddenly felt. He was always so cold, but being close to her settled him somehow. "We'll do it together."

She moved even closer, her head rubbing against his chest. "Together. That sounds nice. You were great tonight, Bran. Did I tell you that?"

Her breathing evened out and she was asleep.

She'd waited for him. She'd been scared and had the crappiest of nights and she'd waited for him to come to bed so she could sleep.

He held her close and for the first time in years found some peace.

## Chapter Nine

Carly stirred but didn't open her eyes, not wanting to leave the happy warmth she found herself in.

Bran.

She was cuddled up close to Bran, his arms wrapped around her. She was warm and happy and safe. She could hear his heart beating under her ear. He'd gotten into bed with her and he hadn't let her go.

Yesterday had been horrible but this morning she'd woken up safer than she'd felt in years. Maybe ever.

She could still remember how scared she'd been when she'd passed out, how she'd felt the moment she'd opened her eyes and Bran had been there and she'd known he wouldn't let her die. He'd gotten her out of that building. He'd come for her and he hadn't left her alone. Patricia had been her usual nasty self, but Bran had defended her from that, too. Somehow her words hadn't seemed so hurtful because he'd been there like a wall holding everything else out.

His arm tightened around her and she knew he was awake.

"Morning, sunshine," he said with a yawn. "How did you sleep? Are you feeling better?"

She felt a little desperate. It was so silly, but she wanted him to kiss her, to roll her over and cover her body with his. She didn't want another day to go by without knowing what it meant to be with Brandon Lawless. So much time had gone by. She knew it wasn't that much, but it seemed like he'd been in her life for a while and she hadn't had more than kisses. He kissed her but hadn't taken it past that. They'd talked for days, gotten to know each other, but they hadn't been physically intimate. Wasn't that the next step?

She cuddled closer. "I feel perfect."

She'd been so adamant in the beginning that he likely needed something more than a physical cue to tell him she was ready to move this past the friend zone.

He wanted that, right?

He'd been so careful with her, so gallant. Didn't that mean he wanted her? When he kissed her it felt like he wanted her. He kissed her a lot. He kissed her whenever it was right.

Did that mean he only kissed her when he should for their cover?

"I slept pretty well myself," he said, his voice deliciously husky.

"That's surprising. I usually sleep like shit." He shifted, turning onto his side but pulling her against him. It was so intimate in the dim light of morning, their bodies snuggled close together. "Are you really all right? The doctor said you could be tired for a day or two. It's why I brought you out here, far away from the temptations of work."

She definitely wasn't feeling tired. Her body felt electric. She turned her face up. He was shadowy since the blinds were closed and he'd turned off the light, but she could tell where his lips were. "I'm good, Bran. I feel great."

His hand smoothed back her hair. "I'm glad, but you're resting. No phone calls. No work. The most I want you to do today is sit by the pool, or maybe if you're feeling up to it, take a walk along the beach. But I'll do that with you."

He was treating her like an invalid. That wasn't the impression she wanted to give. It was time to make a move. She pushed up and brushed her lips against his. "I'm feeling quite energized. Though I could stay in bed for a few hours."

He jumped back like she'd touched him with fire. He rolled out of bed, his back straightening. "That's not a good idea. I mean it is for you. You should rest. I've got a bunch of things to do."

Well, that answered that question. Maybe he hadn't played the gentleman for her sake alone. He'd spent a whole week staying at her place and being the best houseguest ever. She'd thought he was giving her space, letting her set the pace.

Maybe it had been a convenient way to control her. Now that they had the in with Cain Corp's security, they didn't need to control her so much anymore.

"Do you want some coffee?" Bran asked as he stood up and reached for his slacks. "I can bring you some. Unless you were thinking about going back to sleep. You had a long night."

Thank God it was fairly dark in the room or he might see how flushed with embarrassment she'd gotten. She pulled the covers up to her neck. The night before she'd felt a little naughty going to bed in nothing but her undies and a too-tight tank top. She'd thought she would do some seducing of her own.

Now she realized she probably looked ridiculous and was deeply grateful he couldn't see the whole of it. "No. I'm fine."

"Some water or juice? I'm not sure what we have, but I'll find something and then I'll see about breakfast." He zipped up his pants, not looking back at her.

"I said I'm fine. What I would like is to go home. I can rest at home as easily as I can here. Probably more so since I would prefer some privacy." And some time to deal with this new development. Had he thought she wouldn't give in? That he was safe to flirt all he liked because she wouldn't ever take him seriously? Some guys were like that with her. They viewed her as almost nonsexual and therefore safe.

Of course those guys usually relegated their flirting to the non-physical. They didn't kiss her like they needed her to breathe. They didn't haul her into private rooms so they could get their hands on her.

But that appeared to all be an act and now that she was playing the game, he was obviously out. It was time to take an all-important step back and reevaluate the whole live-for-today plan.

Bran turned. "I told you, you're staying here for a couple of days. You'll be more inclined to rest if you can't easily get to the office."

She sat up, pulling the sheets with her. "I'm going home. I don't know anyone here. I don't want to be here."

"You were fine with it last night."

Last night she'd thought she'd had a shot at him. He'd made it plain that she had a shot at him. Today she felt used. "As you've pointed out, I was out of it last night. This morning I'm much more present and I'm going home. I don't even have any clothes here. Now if you would please give me some privacy, I'll take a shower and then I'll call a cab. You have your meeting with Patricia. You can take a few days off from babysitting duty."

He stopped, his body going completely still. "Babysitting duty?"

How else was she supposed to think of it? "Look, last night was obviously some kind of accident. I've thought about it and DiLuca doesn't have a reason to come after me anymore. You saw to that and I thank you. I'm not scared of him so there's zero reason for you to stay at my place now. I'm sorry I dragged it out."

He strode over to the wall and the lights suddenly blinked on. "What the hell is this about?"

He stood at the end of the bed they'd shared the night before, his jaw tense and his eyes staring right through her. He looked . . . angry. Why? Because she was being defiant? Well, he needed to deal with that right now.

"I want to go home. I don't intend to spend three days in a place I don't know anything about. Where I don't know anyone."

"You know me."

Did she? She knew the sweet Bran who sat at her table and ate anything she put in front of him. She knew the guy who kissed her and said she was beautiful. She wasn't sure about the Bran who was standing in front of her now. He looked like a gorgeous, angry bull, but she wasn't about to back down from him. "You got what you wanted. You're in with my boss. Now you can back off. We'll go to California soon and you'll get your job done and I'll do mine. I don't need to sit here for three days."

"I thought we agreed I would stay with you until this was over."

Frustration welled. She was trying to be reasonable and logical and he was pushing her buttons. "We agreed you would stay with me while it made sense. You dealt with the DiLuca situation. I'm not in danger anymore."

"I'm not sure about that," he replied, stubbornness stamped on his features.

She was through with this argument. It was time to get dressed. She would feel better once she had some armor on. In this case armor would have to be hospital scrubs, but anything was better than her failed attempt at seduction. "Well, I'm a big girl and I can handle it. Why don't you leave so I can get dressed?"

His eyes flared. "Why don't you stop pretending to be some prissy historical character? I've seen most of it, Carly. You don't have to cover yourself up like I'll attack you the first chance I get."

And now she'd had enough of him. Her insecurities got tossed aside because being mad felt better than being ashamed. He'd led her here. She hadn't mistaken him or gotten the wrong idea. He'd led her to believe he wanted her and now he seemed to get off pretending like he didn't know what happened.

It turned out he wasn't too good to be true. He was better at hiding it than most men. If she'd been true to her normal mousy self, he would have been able to play her right until the end. He would have used her desire against her.

She threw the covers off. "No, I suppose we both know you're not going to do that, don't we?"

He huffed and shook that gorgeous head of his. "What does that mean? Carly, I don't know why you're so pissed at me."

She needed to make a few things clear to him about how this partnership would work from now on. It was actually freeing to have it out in the open. She'd taken him at his word, but like most men, his words had more than one meaning, more than one purpose. "I'm pissed because you didn't have to play me the way you did. I would have been perfectly comfortable working with you without all the acting on your part."

"Acting?"

She rolled her eyes and got out of bed. "Yes, acting like you wanted me. I believe I gave you several perfectly reasonable scenarios in the beginning that didn't involve you playing me for a fool."

"How did I play you for a fool?"

"Why are you still pretending? I get it. I don't have to be told twice. I won't bug you for sex again. We can play the part in front of an audience, but if we're not on stage I would greatly prefer you weren't around. Now please leave this bedroom and let me get cleaned up. If you need something from me, use your phone or send me an e-mail." She stalked past him toward the gorgeously done bathroom down the hall of the suite.

Another reason to not stay here. The whole place was stunning and obviously owned by people who had a charmed life. She'd learned that staying someplace nice could often make her feel like her life was nice, too. It could delude a person into believing they could have a life like that.

She'd almost made it to the bathroom when a rough hand reached out and grabbed her. She was hauled around and pushed up against the wall.

"I've done nothing to deserve you treating me this way."

Anger bubbled up inside her. "Really? I suppose you do see it that way. Did you think flirting with the fat chick was a public service? Is that how you view it? Because let me tell you something, Brandon. I didn't see it quite that way. A real public service would have been if you could have gone through with it, but you weren't man enough for that, were you?"

His hand tightened around her wrist.

"Let me go. What are you going to do, Bran? Are you mad that the fat chick saw through your plan?"

She glared up at him and then stopped. Right above his left eye she could see a vein ticking. He seemed to be staring at her, but his eyes were vacant. His whole body shook with a fine tremble.

What the hell was she doing? Why was she pushing him like this? Tears pierced her eyes. Maybe what he'd done hadn't been the nicest thing in the world, but what she was doing was even worse. She wasn't this woman.

Whatever he'd done, he likely thought he was doing it for the right reasons. He'd never told her he would be her boyfriend. He'd never told her any untruth, except he'd kissed her when he obviously hadn't wanted to. Maybe he'd thought he needed that kind of control but he hadn't been able to go through with it.

He'd saved her twice already and she was ready to turn on him because he wouldn't sleep with her. And he was obviously going through something of his own. There were times when he seemed so distant, like he was stuck somewhere and needed her to bring him out of whatever world was in his head.

She reached out with her free hand. She should have accepted his rejection with some grace. A man couldn't help what he wanted. He couldn't change the fact that he didn't find her attractive any more than she could change the fact that she was half in love with him. She ran her fingers over his left brow, trying to ease the tension.

"Bran, I'm sorry. I shouldn't have said those things. It was mean and beneath me. Please calm down. We don't have to fight. I won't be cruel anymore."

The hand around her wrist eased slightly, but he still didn't say anything.

"It's okay. We're all right if you'll forgive me. I was hurt and I lashed out."

"How did I hurt you?" The words came out on a guttural growl. "I didn't mean to hurt you."

Did he not understand? A few minutes ago she would have thought he was torturing her further, but now she had to wonder. Maybe he didn't get what she was upset about. It was humiliating, but then, she'd said some awful things to him. "I tried to get you to make love to me and I got hurt when you pretty much jumped away as soon as you could. It's all right. The kissing stuff was just to get me comfortable around you. I wish you had explained that to me because I thought it meant something more, but I shouldn't have been so nasty."

"You kissed me." He was looking at her again, into her eyes and not through her.

"I'm sorry."

His other hand caught her free one and suddenly she found her hands caged in his and high above her head. "You kissed me. You meant to do that?"

Was she that bad at it? Had he not even known she was kissing him? "I did, but I can see that it was a mistake."

She felt so flipping vulnerable. She thought she'd been vulnerable before, but now he was holding her tight and his eyes wandered down. His tongue came out, raking over that full lower lip of his like the Big Bad Wolf getting ready to take a juicy bite.

"I jumped out of bed so you wouldn't know."

Had the temperature gone up ten degrees in the last few seconds?

Her whole body had gone hot and she wasn't sure she could handle whatever he was about to say. Still, like a moth to the flame, she couldn't stop herself from asking. "Know what?"

His hair was messy from sleep, tumbling down over his eyes. They focused in on hers as he pressed his body in. She was caught between the wall and a ridiculously healthy male body. A very aroused male body.

"I thought it was cold and you were trying to get warmer. I thought if you felt how hard my cock was you might be a little scared. I didn't want to scare you." He didn't seem to have the same issues now. He rubbed his hips against hers, letting her feel exactly how hard he was. "In the future, when you want to ask for sex, a polite 'Bran, could we please have sex?' will do. Or we could set up a code word for times when we're in public and you want to let me know you need me. Something innocuous like 'I'm hungry.' Then I'll know to get you somewhere private as quickly as possible."

"And what if I'm really hungry?"

"Then I'll feed you after I fuck you." His mouth hovered above hers. "I thought it would be best if we avoided this. Best for you. I'm not the man you think I am. That's why I jumped out of bed. I wanted to protect you."

"You don't want to protect me now?"

"Can't. Not now. Like I said, I'm not the man you think I am. I learned a long time ago to take my pleasure when and where I can. I learned to be selfish, and I'm about to be very selfish with you, Carly. I'm going to give you one last chance to run. I'm going to let go of your hands and you can walk out and give me a minute to compose myself and then we'll go right back to where we were before. We'll be friends and I'll treat you like a lady because I really like you."

"And if I don't run away?" She'd already made her choice. There was no way she could walk out that door.

"Then you'll be mine until this is done. Carly, think about this. I want you, but I'm not good for anyone. I've stayed away from you because I think I could hurt you."

At least he was honest. Hurt would be better than the horrible numbness of the last few years. Anything was better than the aching loneliness she felt. It might only be for a few weeks, but at least she would feel alive.

His hands released hers and he stepped back. Gone was the sweet Bran she knew so well and in his place was a hungry panther. A gorgeous predator and she wanted nothing more than for him to make a meal of her. She was no longer worrying about her weight or how her boobs weren't perfect anymore. All that mattered was the moment and showing this man that she wasn't going to run from him.

And maybe this time she would get it right.

She moved up to Bran, happy that he was the one pressed against the wall. She reached out and grabbed those big wrists and held them up, giving as good as she'd gotten. "I need to make something plain to you, Lawless. I'm a big girl and I can make my own decisions about things like this. You've been honest with me. That's all I ask." She crowded him, rubbing her belly against that erection of his. "I want to spend the next few weeks with you. I'm not asking beyond those few weeks and some kindness when our relationship is done. Can you give me that?"

"I won't ever be unkind to you, Carly. I can't stay in a relationship long-term. I'm not built for it. I want it. I do, but it won't work."

Honesty. It's what she wanted. It didn't matter because she wasn't walking away from him. She was going in with her eyes open, and she would handle the fallout when he left. But for now, she was going to enjoy him. "Let's see if you understand me better this time."

She went up on her toes and brushed her lips against his, dragging her tongue across his bottom lip. She let her body nestle against his, feeling all that strength and power. Her man was all muscle and that did something for her.

"Don't say I didn't warn you," he growled before breaking her hold.

His hands moved, running down her back and cupping the cheeks of her ass. She barely managed to take a breath before she found herself being lifted up against his chest. Her legs moved as though on pure instinct, wrapping around Bran's lean waist as her heart rate tripled. She held on as Bran took over, his mouth taking hers.

He was moving but she no longer cared about anything but the way his mouth felt, how his tongue slid inside and danced with her own. His big hands squeezed her cheeks as he moved them back to the bed.

He eased her down, covering her with his body. He kept his mouth on hers while his hands roamed. So long. It had been so long since she'd had the solace of another body against hers. All through the night, she'd felt connected and safe in a way she'd never felt before. Somehow she hadn't stayed awake for worry she'd snore or move the wrong way and wake him up. She'd curled up and it had been right to sleep by his side.

Kissing him felt right, too. His hand sliding under her tank top and moving toward her breast felt like joy. She gasped when he cupped her there. His callused palm moved over her nipple and she could feel the electricity spark between them.

"How long has it been for you?" The question rumbled over her skin because he was kissing her neck when he asked it.

"Too long. A couple of years. I haven't done this since before I got divorced." Even then it hadn't felt like this. Roger had been charming and attractive and apparently he'd used all his good bedroom moves on women who weren't her because she felt more for Bran in the few seconds he'd been on top of her than all the times she'd slept with Roger. Her whole body was active. With Roger, she hadn't known what she was doing so she'd pretty much let him control everything.

She still didn't know what she was doing, but her hands wouldn't stop moving. She couldn't seem to stay still.

His thumb circled her nipple as he kissed along her jawline. "I want to fuck you right now, Carly. I want to shove my cock in deep, but I suspect you're going to need some time to heat up."

Nope. That sounded like a fine idea to her. "I'm good. Let's go."

He rolled her nipple between his thumb and forefinger, tweaking her lightly. It hurt the tiniest bit and then heat flashed through her system. "Not until I'm sure you're ready. You're practically a virgin. I want to make this good for you. I know about your previous history. You should know something about mine."

Why was he talking so much? Roger never talked this damn much. Of course, she'd also never needed Roger like she needed Bran. If he didn't keep touching her she might die. "Just send me a list of your previous lovers and we'll call it done. Now can you please kiss me again?"

He chuckled and laid the sweetest kiss on the tip of her nose. "So impatient. You know, it kind of makes me want to slow down. I'm going to do this right. After we've been together for a while, you'll come to associate me with pleasure and your body will respond properly. I'll be able to touch you exactly the right way and you'll get soft and wet for me. I worry that you're not ready yet and I want this to be good for you, so how about we make a deal? As a man who's been completely dedicated to bringing women pleasure since he was a far-too-young teen, why don't you let me lead you in this. You control the cooking and the house and hell, if you want to dress me, I'll let you. But I'm in control here."

He was the only one. She felt completely out of control. Every word seemed to take her higher and he wasn't inside her yet. "Bran, I'm ready. I've never felt like this before. I want you."

He kept that perfect control of his. "Not the way you will in twenty minutes or so. Hush and let me show you how well and thoroughly I can worship you." His mouth came down on hers again and she couldn't fight him.

He was going to kill her, but it was also apparent that he was going to have his way. And he was right. She wasn't very experienced sexually and he did let her take the lead in almost everything else. He always let her watch what she wanted on TV. He sat beside her and watched with her as though simply being around her was enough to keep him entertained. The one time they'd slipped out to see a movie, he'd made sure it was something she would enjoy.

The man knew how to take care of a lady.

"Have I told you how beautiful you are?" He nipped at her ear, the tiny pain sending her squirming because it seemed to go straight to her core.

"You always do." He never failed to compliment her when she walked down dressed for the day. It made her look at herself in a different way. "I thought you were flattering me so I would get close to you. That's not how you work, is it, Bran?"

He kissed along her jaw. "No. I will always say what I mean, baby. I won't play games with you. I don't ever want you to feel insecure with me."

She let her hands run through that silky black hair of his. She'd never met a man quite like him and he seemed way too good to be true, but she was going to stop overthinking. Overthinking and being insecure had almost ruined everything a few minutes ago. She should have told him how his actions made her feel and then they would probably be way further along in this process by now. No more wasted moments. Not when they likely had so little time together. "You make me feel beautiful, Bran. I need you to know how much I want you. Have I told you how handsome you are?"

His head came up and the grin on his face was piercingly sweet. "You're not upset you got me and not Drew?"

He knew the answer to that, arrogant man. "You're the most beautiful man I've ever met and I can't wait until you're inside me."

Maybe she could speed things up with some dirty talk.

"Sweet," he conceded. "Still not going to make me rush. I'm going to take my time because I want to know every single inch of you."

He moved down her body. Apparently Bran's version of knowing really meant kissing. His lips seemed to touch every inch of her skin while his hand cupped her breast. The only moment he stopped his slow exploration was to drag the tank over her head and toss it away.

"Now, those are some gorgeous breasts. I've wanted my hands on them since the moment I saw you." He lowered himself down again.

Carly couldn't help the gasp that came when he brushed his lips over her nipple and sucked it inside.

Her legs seemed to spread of their own accord, making a place for him, trying to tempt him inside. Every tug of his lips seemed to heat her up further.

This was why he'd slowed things down. Sex before had been hurried, and while she'd had some satisfying outcomes with Roger, she'd never been so devoted to being in the moment. There had always been stray thoughts invading the time with her ex-husband. Here with Bran, no other thoughts intruded, no worries or insecurities. He built a world where only the two of them existed. He built it with every slow kiss and caress of his hands over her flesh.

She relaxed, finally understanding that he was going to have his way and nothing would change his mind. He wanted this long and slow and he knew what he was doing. Worshipping. That was the word he'd used. He was slowly ensuring that she understood how much he wanted her, every inch of her.

"These need to go." He pressed kisses down her belly to the top of the panties she was wearing.

He dragged them down her legs, moving off the bed as he did it. She felt raw and exposed, but something about the way he stared down at her made all of it okay. In the past she would have wanted the lights out or to be under the covers, but the heat in Bran's eyes did make her feel sexy. She was more when she was with him. More than someone's assistant. More than someone's sister. She was Carly and this choice she made to be with him was all about her. Her selfish choice.

She didn't have to be someone's assistant here. She didn't have to look out for anyone else. Here someone took care of her.

"Are you going to leave me like this? The only one of us naked? Because I've been waiting days to see what you look like without all those clothes on."

Again his grin nearly lit up the room. She loved that about Bran. He didn't play. If he felt something, she could see it. When she made him happy, he smiled. She didn't have to worry about what he was thinking. It was all right there on his gorgeous face.

He unbuttoned the top of his slacks and slowly pushed them down, revealing the deliciously toned abs and hips and legs that went perfectly with his cut chest. He spent a lot of time in the gym. A lot. He was perfectly masculine. Really masculine.

He had a really big dick. Big and gorgeous and perfect, like the rest of him.

"Now, that is a look I'm going to remember forever," he said as his hands came out and circled her ankles. "You like the way I look."

"Every woman with eyes likes the way you look, Bran." Who wouldn't be attracted to him? With pitch-black hair and emerald eyes, he was every woman's fantasy.

"I only care about you," he said quietly. "I want you to think I'm hot."

*Hot* didn't begin to describe him. He was hot and sweet and sometimes he was such a mystery to her that she was sure she could spend a lifetime trying to figure him out. "I'm crazy about you."

His expression softened. "I'm crazy about you, too, Carly."

It was enough. For now.

He dragged her down the bed, getting to his knees in front of her. Her heart pounded in her chest at the thought of what he was going to do. He was going to make a meal of her and she knew damn well that Bran loved a good meal.

Again, this was where she would usually get self-conscious, but there wasn't a place for it with him. She wanted to be with him more than anything. More than her own fears. She wanted to feel alive in the way she only did when she was with Bran.

"See, this is what I want to see. Look at that. You're getting wet and ready for me. That's what I wanted." His mouth hovered above her, his words heating her skin. His hands pressed on her inner thighs, spreading her wide, leaving her vulnerable, and that did something for her. It wouldn't with anyone else, but she was safe with him. It was all right to spread her legs and open for this one man.

She could feel her core practically pulsing for him. "Please, Bran. You're going to drive me crazy."

"You have no idea how true that is, baby." He brought his mouth down, covering her sex. His eyes remained on her, dark hair tumbling over his forehead. She watched as he dragged his tongue over the delicate flesh of her sex.

Pure pleasure quaked through her. Soft and hot, her whole world narrowed to the feel of his mouth on her. Nothing else mattered but his mouth. His tongue dragged over her, drawing out her cream. Her pussy was getting hot and desperate with every second of his attention.

He parted the petals of her sex, giving himself access to her. He lavished her with affection, groaning against her as he sucked on first one half of her labia and then drawing the other in.

His left hand moved up, thumb running over her clitoris.

She damn near came off the bed.

"Relax. You'll get there." Every word out of his mouth vibrated over her. "And then we'll get there together. Let me do this my way and I promise the next time you want a quickie, I'm your guy." His eyes turned up and there was a frown on his face. "I'm your only guy. We should make that clear."

Seriously? He wanted to have a relationship discussion now? He was the most infuriating man. "I did not wait two years so I could take a lover and then go trolling for five more. While we're together, you're my only man."

She was worried he would be with her forever whether they were together or not.

"I don't want anyone but you, either." He pressed his thumb down lightly but with just enough pressure to make her squirm. "You like that?"

A whimper came out of her mouth and she fisted her hands around the bedsheets to keep from pressing herself up against his hand again. "Yes."

"How about this?" He removed his thumb, lowering his head down and dragging that seriously talented tongue over her clitoris.

"Yes." She managed to breathe out the word. Barely.

"And if I do this?"

She couldn't see what he was doing, but she felt it. One long finger penetrated her, curling up inside her. It wasn't enough. Not nearly enough. She wanted more, but she clenched around him. "Please, Bran. You're killing me."

"Well, I wouldn't want to kill you. Not when I worked so hard to save you." His mouth lowered again and he sucked her clit between his lips as his finger began to move in and out.

Her body tightened, every nerve readying itself for what he'd primed her for. This was why he'd gone so slowly. He'd wanted her completely on the edge, unable to think about anything but how good it felt, how hot she was.

He pressed up and found some magical place that no one had found before. She'd had some orgasms, but nothing that made her entire body bow. She bit back a cry as her whole body went taut and the pleasure seemed to course through her entire system. It pounded through her, making time seem to slow as she watched Bran's head move over her, his hands tighten on her hips.

So close. She felt so close to him. So intimate and connected. She pressed up against him, trying to get the last second of pleasure she could.

She let her whole body sag, blood pounding pleasantly through her as Bran got to his feet.

"Tell me I can have you."

She had to force her eyes open. What was it about this man? He was different from anyone she'd ever met. Any other man would have fallen on her, certain they'd played their part and now it was their time. Not Bran. He stood over her, needing her acknowledgment. He wouldn't touch her without a verbal response. She stared up at him. His cock was stiff against his rock-hard abs. He was so rigid, so ready, and yet this man was waiting for her to tell him it was all right.

"Bran, please," she whispered. She didn't move. She didn't want to give any indication that she had a single hesitation. She didn't. She needed him inside her. He was the right man at the right time and she wanted nothing more than to give him the pleasure he'd given her. "Please come here and be with me."

He reached over and pulled up his slacks, his hands going to the pocket. He fished out his wallet and she watched as he produced a condom.

"I'm on the pill." She hadn't changed her habits. She knew she likely should have, but she'd taken that little pill for years, and though she hadn't needed it for a long time, now it could come in handy.

He shook his head as he ripped the packet open. "Not on your life. I'll go to the doctor and get tested but I won't touch you without a condom until then. Do you know what I want?"

She did. "You want you and me until this is over."

"But I don't want to hurt you."

She lifted her hands up. "Please, Bran. I need you."

He stroked himself as he looked down at her, his hand sliding over his big cock. She watched, her whole body languid and sated, and yet she could feel the need starting to rise again. He was getting ready for her. He was going to spread her wide and take her.

And it felt more right than anything before.

Bran eased the condom over his cock and moved over her. She sighed as she felt the heat of his skin against hers. He made a place for himself at her core. He pressed in, stretching her, but she was more than ready for him. This was what he'd wanted. No pain. Only pleasure and an amazing sense of being filled with him. She let her hands run over his back as she got used to how big he was inside her.

"You feel so good," Bran whispered as he pressed in.

Like everything else the man did, he was slow and methodical and in perfect control. He held himself still, allowing her to relax. He kissed her long and slow, his tongue sliding against hers over and over. It was one more seduction, lighting the fires deep inside her once more. She'd wanted him, wanted to give back to him, but now she was starting to want more again.

He was so big, overwhelming her with his masculine body, making her feel soft and feminine and desperate for him.

"Stay with me," he said when she started to close her eyes. "Stay with me."

She looked up and watched the way his expression changed as he began to move. His eyes flared and his jaw hardened, but he watched her as though trying to pick up on the tiniest fluctuations.

This was about more than her body feeling good. Bran was trying to connect. Her experiences before had been physical, with none of the talking Bran seemed to need. Talking to him, connecting with him, that was what made this more than sex, more than a bodily function.

"You feel good," she whispered. "I love how you feel on top of me."

"You're so beautiful, Carly. You should know how beautiful you are to me. I thought I lost you last night."

She pressed up, forcing him deeper. He filled every inch of her, stretching her deliciously wide. "I knew you would find me."

Even as she'd given in to the darkness, she'd been thinking about him.

His hips pumped, harder and faster. He angled up and Carly gasped as she felt him grind against her clitoris. Fire flashed through her and she gripped Bran's backside. Her body moved with his, finding the rhythm that would take her where she needed to go. He thrust in and pulled out, his face turning fierce.

She could feel him touching her everywhere. It seemed there wasn't an inch of her that wasn't caressed by him. She held on, legs tight around his waist, nails digging in. He didn't seem to mind that. He kissed her again, dominating her mouth as his cock plunged in and out.

"Come for me. I want to hear you, Carly. None of this silent bullshit. Let me hear how you feel. You're too quiet and there's no place for that here with me."

He wanted more than her orgasm. She could feel that coming from him. He wanted something she'd never given anyone before. It should have made her feel vulnerable, but his savage words opened Carly up, freeing something that had been buried deep inside her.

When the orgasm bloomed, she screamed out his name.

Bran groaned and pumped himself into her, his whole body tight before he finally fell on top of her.

He was breathless as he kissed her neck, cuddling them close. He seemed in no hurry to move off her and she liked it. She liked how he pressed her down and her whole world seemed filled with him.

"That's what I wanted," he murmured.

She held him close. It was what she wanted, too.

# Chapter Ten

**B**ran slid the door closed and watched her for a moment as she stood on the balcony, staring out at the ocean. The sun hit her hair, bringing out the threads of gold and red. Her face was turned up to the sky and he had to catch his breath because she was so fucking beautiful to him.

He'd thought she was pretty when they'd first met, but now he thought she was the most stunning woman on the planet.

"Is everything all right?" Carly asked, not turning around. Her voice was husky and her hair was still a bit damp from the shower she'd taken. "They didn't give you too much hell?"

He moved in behind her because it was his right to cuddle her close now. She leaned back against him, sighing as he put his lips to her ears. "They were merciless. My brother is an asshole and Hatch isn't any better. How did you know?"

"Because I have a sister and she would totally give me hell about having raucous sex where everyone could hear me. They heard us, didn't they?"

He was relieved by the way she chuckled and let her head fall back against his shoulder. She wasn't upset if she was so casual. He'd worried she would feel self-conscious once she realized they weren't alone in the condo and her very vocal appreciation had likely been heard by all.

She'd been everything he'd thought she would be. She hadn't held back. She'd given him all of her and it had been the single most intimate encounter of his life.

He wasn't sure he would be able to let her go. As he'd lain there with her in his arms, he'd started bargaining. There was no reason why he shouldn't try with her. She wouldn't have anywhere to go after they'd taken down Cain Corp. Why couldn't she have a future with 4L? She could move to Austin and there was zero reason why he couldn't see her. They would be working together. It would be natural to date.

He was more peaceful when he was around her. She brought it out in him and that meant she never had to know about his dark places. If he could always hold it together around her, she didn't have to see that part of his soul.

"Oh, they heard you, baby. I'm a fairly quiet lover. You, on the other hand, can't help yourself, and that means Drew and Hatch know how we spent our morning. Of course if they didn't they likely would have known because that was my last condom and I had to ask for more."

"Oh my God." But she didn't try to break away from him. "You couldn't sneak out and pick some up?"

He'd been kind of hoping for a second round until he'd heard the news that Taggart was on his way to the condo. "I don't want to hide it. I want them to know. I have no intention of pretending we're not together. They won't tease you. Just me. But we need to talk about someone who will. My sister's brother-in-law is on his way in. He's a lot to handle."

"Am I going to have to handle him?"

"He's got some information. You don't have to go to the meeting, though." He'd thought she would want to be in the middle of everything. It would be far easier on him if she let him handle the situation.

He could keep her out of all the bad stuff. Shelter her. He would like that. She'd done her part. She didn't have to sit in on the meetings or hear about their plans for revenge. His background was bloody and nasty and the further he could keep her from it the better.

Besides, Ian Taggart could be a lot to take.

She moved away from him, turning and shaking her head. Her eyes sparkled as she pointed at him. "Not on your life, babe. I'm so going to that meeting. I'm the one who almost died, so I want to hear everything. You're not cutting me out."

And there was the girl he knew so well. It had been wishful thinking that she would sit out. "I would never cut you out. But you do have to understand that Big Tag has an extremely dark wit."

She'd changed into some clothes Mia had left behind. She was wearing a T-shirt and jeans that never quite fit his sister that way. They clung to her curves and made his mouth water, and he wanted nothing more than to get his hands on her again.

"I can handle it," she said with a smile. She seemed somehow more confident than she'd been before.

But he had to remember that she'd been through something terrible not so many hours ago. He reached for her, not quite able to keep his hands off her. "Are you sure you're up to this? I kind of think you should go back to bed and rest. You haven't even eaten yet."

"Is there something to eat?" She had a teasing tone to her voice as she moved into his arms again. "Does your super-genius, revenge-seeking brother have a secret talent as a chef?"

"There's Pop-Tarts." He hadn't even thought about the sad state of food in this household when he'd brought her here the night before. He'd only been thinking of getting his fist in Drew's face.

She shuddered. "Tell me there are ingredients here."

He hadn't exactly checked the pantry. "I have no idea. I'll go out and get us something."

"Or I can go and figure out if there's anything decent in the kitchen. You said this Taggart person is on his way? How far out is he?" She looked up at him, her chin resting on his chest.

If he'd thought she might be self-conscious after a morning of raw and rough sex, he'd been completely wrong. She was a sweet kitten purring in his arms, and didn't that make him feel about ten feet tall? "He'll be here in twenty minutes."

In twenty minutes he could totally give her the quickie she'd demanded earlier today. He could get back inside her and make her scream and then maybe she would be okay with sleeping through the meeting.

He wasn't sure he wanted her sitting at the war room table. Oh, they weren't allowed to call it that anymore, but any time he, his brothers, and Hatch sat around a table plotting it felt like a war room table.

She sighed. "Then I should get to work. I bet he's been on a morning flight, and even if he came in first-class the food was likely terrible."

"Ian Taggart doesn't fly commercial, baby. We sent the jet for him."

She went up on her toes and brushed her lips against his. "Well la-di-da. I happen to fly private all the time and you can't get a real kitchen at thirty thousand feet. I'll be better." She broke off from him, moving back to the sliding door that led to their bedroom. "Am I alone in a sea of vengeful men?"

"You are indeed." He thought she would have been more worried about that than she obviously was. "Though I think Mia and Case are coming back with Taggart. Ellie and Riley are in New York for a couple of days."

She walked through the room and to the door that led to the main rooms of the condo, her bare feet shuffling along the floor. He couldn't help but stare because her hips swayed so sweetly in those jeans. She strode through the door and stopped as she came upon Drew and Hatch sitting at the dining room table.

"You two should be ashamed of yourselves."

Drew's eyes went wide but Hatch grinned.

"For what? You're going to have to be more specific because I have a lot to be ashamed of, darlin'," Hatch said, obviously amused.

Carly wagged a finger Hatch's way. "You shouldn't tease him. You might make him self-conscious and I happen to think he's an excellent lover. He's absolutely the best I've ever had and he should be proud that he managed to make someone as delicate and ladylike as me scream that way. I won't have you shaming him into a lesser performance. Am I understood?"

What his brother hadn't managed to do Carly did with a few prim words out of her mouth. He felt himself flush. Where the hell had that come from? Sex had made her way more take-charge than she'd been before.

Or had that tigress merely been napping for a few years? Had happiness made her spine straighter, her Southern accent a little deeper? He'd made her happy and that brought out her sassy side.

It also made Drew's jaw drop. While Hatch laughed, Drew stared at Carly and then slowly nodded.

"I won't make fun of my brother again. He's obviously an amazing lover," Drew said slowly.

Carly nodded as though satisfied and then turned on her heels and set off for the kitchen. "Excellent."

"I love her already," Hatch said in a whisper everyone could hear.

Drew finally chuckled. "Well, at least she's not easily intimidated. She's going to need that."

"I've had to work with some of the nastiest people in the world for years," Carly said as she opened the fridge. "Just because I sometimes act like a mouse because it's the best way to get through a day doesn't mean I'm actually a mouse. Someone stocked this kitchen. Nice. How about muffins?"

Drew stood up and closed his laptop. "How about you tell me what you know about Shelby Gates?"

"Drew, I thought I explained we were going to leave her out of this." Bran had already had the conversation once this morning.

Carly started getting out ingredients and placing them on the island with the efficiency of a professional chef. "What is the evil one doing to Shelby?"

"When did I get to be evil?" Drew asked with a deep frown.

"When you decided to set me up," Carly replied. "I was looking for a date and you came in and decided your revenge was more important than my love life."

"It is more important," Drew replied.

"See?" Carly pointed out. "Evil."

Drew stood his ground. "I do believe that getting justice for the deaths of my parents is more important than your social life. Besides, as you've already pointed out, your social life was very lively this morning."

Carly winked Bran's way. "Ah, but that was thanks to him. Not you. Tell me something, Dr. Evil. Would you have been the one in bed with me if Bran hadn't foiled your plans?"

Drew turned to him. "I don't know how to answer that question and now she has a knife. If I say yes she could get mad because that means I would have followed through on my plan to seduce her. If I say no, she might think I don't find her attractive. Her personality profile didn't come off as reckless and unstable. Are you sure she's the same woman?"

Bran had to laugh. And fall even harder for Carly because so few people managed to throw Drew off. His brother looked seriously worried that the hot brunette might come at him with a knife if he got the answer to her question wrong.

"I would definitely have been in bed with you, darlin'," Hatch offered. "And it wouldn't have been for some mission."

She ignored him, preferring to stare at Drew.

"I think she'll probably accept a simple apology." It was time to let his brother off the hook.

"I'm sorry I was going to use you to further my plans for justice,"

Drew offered. "Bran was obviously smarter than me on this one occasion. He thought you would be a better partner than a pawn. Turns out he was right."

"Forgiven," Carly said with a smile.

Drew turned his way. "She's more trouble than Ellie. She might be more trouble than Mia."

The door came open and the devil they were speaking of strode in. "No one is more trouble than me! Bran!"

Mia crossed the room quickly, throwing herself into his arms. One of the drawbacks of spending so much time with Carly was having to skip the time he would spend with his baby sister. He hugged Mia tight. Of all his siblings, she was the one he was closest to. Perhaps it was because they were nearest in age or the fact that he could still remember how she'd clung to him when they'd separated them. How he'd told her she had to be brave and he would come for her.

How he'd failed.

"She's right, you know." Mia's husband followed her in. "I can't think of a single person who causes more chaos than my wife."

"Shelby Gates is giving her a damn run for her money," Drew complained.

"Well until you've had a wife die in front of your eyes, come back from the grave to insist on taking fifty percent of your company, and then proceed to die again only to be revived and give you twin hellions, you can't talk around me," a deep voice said.

At one point in time, Bran had thought Case Taggart had to be the biggest dude he'd ever seen. Not even close. Case's big brother was six foot five and at least two hundred and forty pounds of pure Viking muscle.

Hatch got up and shook hands with the big guy. Drew came forward as well, while Mia was looking into the kitchen.

"I heard she was here," Mia whispered. "Is everything all right with her?"

Bran couldn't help but smile. "Everything's awesome. Carly, come and meet my baby sister."

Mia's eyebrow arched as she looked between the two of them. He could see the silent question in her eyes but he'd done enough talking about his romantic life in front of people who didn't need to know what kind of a lover he was.

"Carly, this is my sister, Mia. You've met Case Taggart, and the even bigger dude is his brother Ian Taggart, who runs the security company we'll be working with." He couldn't help the way he ran his arm around her shoulder or how he stood a little taller because her arm wound around his waist.

Taggart nodded Carly's way. "Nice to meet you, but I'm a get-to-the-heart-of-the-matter kind of guy. Would someone like to explain to me why I'm trying to take down the woman who invented luscious lemon cookies? They're my favorite. I have a moral problem with taking out a woman who can bring something like that into the world. I don't care about your revenge, Lawless. Those cookies bring joy to the world."

Carly raised her hand. "I actually perfected that recipe. It's a slightly different take on Mrs. Miller's lemon shortbread. She used to bring it to potlucks in our trailer park. I made it lighter and added the powdered sugar."

"Patricia Cain is just a figurehead, Ian," Case said with a sigh.

Ian ignored him and nodded Carly's way. "Then we're protecting the girl. I'm going to need you to talk to the Pie Maker."

"Don't even let him get started. He says he'll protect you, but what he'll really do is collect you. His brother runs a restaurant in Dallas and Ian's set on gathering all the best cooks to work there and personally feed him," Mia said with a groan. "You can't take her back to Dallas. I think my brother would have an issue with that."

Bran tightened his arm around her. Big Tag was definitely not collecting his girl. It didn't matter that he would only use her for her cooking skills. Those belonged to Bran, too.

"You're all weirdos," Carly said with a grin. "Now I'm going to make some muffins. Why don't y'all have your meeting at the dining room table and I'll listen in. I'll also double the recipe and maybe cook some eggs because I know how this one eats. I'm going to assume the rest of you do, too."

Mia shook her head and took Carly's hand. "You have no idea. I'll help. Talk loud, guys. Just because we're cooking doesn't mean we're not here."

He watched as his sister and his girl walked off and started whispering to each other.

"That's trouble right there, brother," Case said with a shake of his head.

Trouble looked pretty good to him.

"So I've already made contact with the fire department and you're not going to like what I found out," Taggart said an hour later.

"It wasn't an accident." Bran had been thinking about it ever since the incident. Well, he'd been thinking about it when he hadn't been accusing his brother or making love to Carly. It was too convenient. He didn't believe in coincidences.

And then there had been the haunted look in Patricia's eyes as she'd stared back at the building. She'd changed when he'd told her that there had been a gas leak. She'd lost her angry-diva ways and gotten quiet, contemplative even.

He hadn't talked to Carly about it. He wasn't even sure she'd noticed the change in Patricia's attitude. They'd gone to the hospital and not seen or heard from Patricia again with the single exception of an e-mail agreeing to meet with Ian Taggart and requesting that Bran attend the meeting.

It was set for two p.m. later in the day, and he was so glad Carly wouldn't be there.

"The initial report is that someone tinkered with the gas line," Taggart explained. "They weren't even subtle about it. Someone took a small knife and cut the line. The investigator was adamant that the whole thing was a piece of shit anyway and he's looking at the art gallery because they were violating several safety codes, but it was obvious someone had cut the line."

"The cameramen usually carry one of those small tool kits with them." Carly placed the plate of muffins on the table. "You know, like a Swiss army knife."

"A Leatherman tool," Hatch corrected. "It would contain a knife. But wasn't the cameraman one of the people who got sick?"

"We're not looking at Mike Davis. He's been with the crew for a long time," Bran said.

"Mike's a solid guy." Carly slid into the seat beside him, her leg brushing his and making his whole body come alive. Simply being around her seemed to make him more aware of everything. "I can't imagine he would do anything like this. He's got a wife and three kids. Now, the other guy hired on recently. His name was Tim something."

Taggart was on top of it. He slapped a file down on the table. "Tim Connors. He hired on with Cain Corp two months ago and according to passport records fled the country for South America at ten p.m. last night before anyone could stop him. He barely made his flight, but it touched down before the authorities could find him. He's in the wind now."

A chill went through Bran's system. "He must have gotten desperate. His time was ticking away. More than likely he thought he'd get through the job faster than he did."

Carly shook her head. "I don't understand what's going on. Are you saying the camera guy was trying to kill me?"

"I don't think it was you," Bran murmured.

"Give me a rundown of the night, Bran." Taggart leaned back after grabbing a muffin.

It made more sense now that he was looking at it from a logical perspective. "That last shot of the night was late. It was scheduled to be done an hour and a half before they finally called in the family. Some of that was our doing. We made sure the stepdaughter showed up drunk and out of control because we switched the bodyguards around."

"Was he trying to get the whole family?" Mia asked.

Carly's hand reached for Bran's. That felt right, her palm sliding along his and nestling there for comfort. "He only got me."

"But you were wearing Patricia's cape. No one else was wearing anything like it." Bran squeezed her hand, trying to give her some of his strength. He wasn't going to let anyone hurt her again. "What if he ran out of time and decided that his main target was better than nothing at all? I don't think he was after you. I think he was after Patricia."

"But I'll beat him the hell up when we find him anyway," Taggart said. "Because he could have killed you and these muffins are incredible."

Taggart often thought with his stomach. "You're looking for the guy?"

Taggart shrugged as though it was no big deal to be able to get a man on the ground in South America within twenty-four hours. "He's our best bet to know exactly what's going on. I have a team in Cartagena right now. They'll find him and figure out who hired him, because there's no way there wasn't some money on the line with this job. However, I know this guy wasn't a pro. I think he really did hire on for the business, but then one week in there was a deposit of ten grand into his bank account from an account in Switzerland."

Drew sat up straighter. "That's the system they used to pay the assassin who killed my parents."

"Yes, it's not the same account, but it's from the same bank," Taggart agreed. "I have someone looking into that as well. Tim Connors received another payment yesterday of five grand. He was hired to make this look like an accident. I'm with Bran. He panicked when the timeline didn't go his way and he overcompensated. He should have nicked the line. That would have been easier. Or he could have loosened it. The gas would have discharged during the shoot, but slowly. He could have shut the door for sound purposes and suddenly that small room becomes a casket for a whole group of people."

"But we created enough chaos that the shoot ran late," Drew pointed out.

"He panicked, and when he thought he saw Patricia Cain walk into the room, he pounced and prayed for the best," Taggart concluded. "I've got him on CCTV running down the road toward his car two minutes after Carly was locked in. He didn't stay to ensure the job was done. He ran as fast as he could and he prayed, and that is precisely why I think when my guys catch up to him he'll likely be a corpse."

"He took the money but didn't do the job. Why are you so certain it's Patricia they were after?" Carly asked.

Everyone stared at her like she was the slow one in the room.

"Fine," she conceded. "My boss is a horrible human being and there are lots of people who want her dead. But that whole family is awful. I think you should look into them first. They all stand to gain if Patricia's out of the way."

"Particularly Kenny Jr." He'd been thinking about this a lot, too. He'd watched the man all night long. Kenny's eyes often strayed to Carly. He'd made sure he got close to her several times. "He thinks Carly is his stepping-stone away from real estate and into TV production. He wants to take over after his father dies."

Taggart nodded. "I'll see what I can find out about any wills that might be on record. And I'm definitely looking into the money angles. I find it interesting that it's the same bank from twenty years ago. I also worked up a profile on your girl Gates. Interesting lady. She's an investigative reporter. She worked for a couple of newspapers until her brother died a while back and then she took over his project, which was an exposé book of our fair queen of mean."

"You're investigating Shelby?" Carly's eyes had widened.

Bran squeezed her hand. "It's not a big deal."

"Not a big deal?" Drew's question came out on an icy huff. "You've been out of touch, brother. She's becoming an annoyance I might have to deal with. She's been investigating every single one of us. I've had to hustle to keep her from putting the Lang family and 4L Software together. She came damn close to figuring it out. I had to work hard to keep her out of those records. I sicced the feds on her and that woman still managed to talk her way out of it."

"What? You tried to have her arrested?" Carly gasped. "She's not trying to hurt anyone."

He needed to do some serious damage control. "Baby, it's important that we keep our covers or this whole thing falls apart. We can't have a reporter out there asking questions and possibly printing something that would give us away. I assure you that if Patricia Cain hears the name Lawless, she'll be on her guard and we won't get a second chance."

"I'll talk to her," Carly offered. "She started this because I needed some information. I didn't tell her anything, but she's got a good instinct for a story. We're close friends and she's a good person at heart. If I tell her to back off, she will."

"I doubt that," Drew shot back. "Did you know she's requested our parents' autopsy reports?"

"Why the hell would she do that?" Hatch was getting red in the face.

"I have no idea," Drew replied. "But I will find out. If she's planning on doing some kind of a hatchet job on my parents, I'll do more than sic the feds on her. I'll bury her."

Carly's eyes had a sheen to them. "She wouldn't do that."

Drew stared at her. "And you know her so well, Carly? You're conspiring against your boss to help that woman tear her apart in print."

Bran stood, moving slightly so he was in front of Carly. His brother could be intimidating and he wasn't about to have Carly feel threatened. "Back off, Drew."

Drew started to say something, but Hatch reached out and put a hand on his arm.

"Take a deep breath. None of this is Carly's fault," Hatch said in a reasonable tone. "Shelby Gates was looking into Patty long before she met Carly, and God knows there isn't a woman on the planet who deserves a takedown more than Patricia Cain."

"Can I give you some advice, Drew?" Taggart was the only one who looked completely unemotional.

"You'll do it even if I say no."

"Talk to this Shelby woman. Bring her in," Taggart said. "Otherwise you'll have to deal with her in a way you don't want on your conscience. She's curious and a woman like that won't let a little thing like some feds investigating her for hacking stop her if she thinks she's found a truly juicy story."

"I'm not talking to her." Drew's face went stubborn, his jaw locking.

"You're already talking to her," Taggart said with a shake of his head, as though he was speaking but he already knew he'd be ignored. "You're her new online friend."

"How the hell did you know that?" Drew turned to stare at Taggart, his eyes wide.

"Because big brother knows everything," Case said with a laugh. "You've had Adam tailing him, haven't you?"

"He's reckless and he makes decisions based on emotion and not logic," Taggart said quietly. "He's got you involved in his plans, so yes, I do keep an eye on him. If you think for a second I'll let you go running around unwatched, you don't know me at all, brother."

This was where Drew should acknowledge that he understood. He was the head of the family and he watched out for his brothers and sister the same way Taggart watched over his family. Bran wished that was true, but he wasn't surprised at all at Drew's reaction.

His big brother stood up, Drew's face implacable because when he got pissed, Drew didn't go hot. He went arctic cold. "Mr. Taggart, please feel free to turn around and take yourself back to Texas. We'll handle things from here."

Hatch shook his head and Mia's eyes went wide. Bran knew he had to deal with that shit now. Drew didn't handle anyone questioning his authority, but they needed Taggart. He was their in. If they didn't have McKay-Taggart, they would have to start at the beginning. And they would really piss off Case, and that meant upsetting Mia.

Bran stood and reached his hand out. "Don't mind him. You're right. He's not thinking logically. We've got a meeting with Cain Corp in a couple of hours. Why don't you go and clean up and we'll have some lunch before we have to head into St. Augustine?"

Taggart stood and shook his hand, but his eyes went right to Carly. "Is she making lunch?"

Carly didn't miss a beat. Despite what Drew had said about her friend, she stood beside Bran like they were a team. "I've got the ingredients to make a lovely tomato bisque and grilled cheese sandwiches."

That was his girl. She knew when to stand by his side.

Taggart nodded. "I'm going to take a shower and get ready. I'll be back in an hour. Deal with your brother. I'm not going to lose mine because your brother can't keep his head on straight. And when we get to Cain Corp, you're going to let me do all the talking. After all, I'm putting my company on the line here." Without another word he turned to Carly, his expression softening and his whole demeanor changing. "Thank you for the muffins. They were delicious. If you ever need a job, my brother and I own a chain of restaurants in Dallas. There's a job for you there no matter what happens with this crazy revenge plan."

Carly practically glowed. "Thank you."

Taggart nodded his brother's way and turned and walked toward the small office that served as the fourth bedroom of the condo. Mia and Case would take over the room Drew had been sleeping in and

Drew and Hatch would double up until Bran and Carly went back to her place.

Drew stared Bran's way. "I think it might be time to cut our losses with McKay-Taggart."

Case's head fell back with a groan.

Mia leaned in. "Don't you dare. He's been nothing but helpful. Do you have any idea what he's been through? He's not willing to lose another brother. His whole company is on the line for you."

"And I don't need him if he's not all in," Drew shot back.

Hatch stared at Drew. "He's right and you know it. You're thinking emotionally with this Shelby girl. You need to figure out what she knows and move on. But no, you're playing games with her. You're spending all your time poking this woman and trying to get her attention."

"I'm trying to get her to give up the story," Drew practically snarled.

But Bran saw through that. "You would have talked to her and tried to bribe her if you wanted her to give up the story. She's hit a nerve and you're playing with her. Let Carly talk to her."

"It won't work," Drew shot back. "She's got it under her skin. She's not simply asking for autopsy reports and the police reports. She's trying to find all the records CPS had on us."

"Are you kidding?" It sent a shiver through Bran. No one needed to know about those days. "Why would she need that?"

He heard the door close down the hall and they were alone. Not that it meant anything. They still needed Taggart. They needed him and his firm.

Drew's tone was icy cold. "I don't know why she wants to see pictures of our dead parents, but I intend to stop her from publishing them. Your girl started this. Tell her to finish it or I'll do it myself, and you watch every single thing that man does. We have to get out of this whole."

Case frowned. "It won't be my brother's fault if you don't."

Drew strode out, walking back to his bedroom.

Mia put a hand on her husband's shoulder. "We know that. Drew's worried. It's been hard to keep the Lang identities separate from Lawless. He's on edge because there's a reporter looking into us now. We all know what Ian's doing for us but this kind of thing is hard on Drew."

Hatch sighed and stood up. "I'll go talk to him. Bran, take care of Taggart this afternoon. Mia's right. We need him. And maybe Carly should figure out what's going on with her reporter friend."

Bran didn't want Carly more involved in this than she needed to be. "I'll deal with it."

"I can talk to her," Carly said, ignoring him.

He wasn't going to argue in front of everyone. They'd done enough of that already. He simply squeezed her hand and started to lead her back toward the bedroom. "We'll talk about how to handle it but for now, someone calm Drew down."

He closed the door behind them as Carly turned.

"I can help, Bran."

"You are helping, but I want you to think about what we learned from last night. Someone is trying to kill your boss and they won't mind taking you out if you get in the way. It might be time to get you out of the line of fire."

"I can't quit and you know why."

"I can hire the very best lawyer for your sister."

"That's not happening."

Why wasn't she listening to him? "Sweetheart, I can do this job without you. Hell, it doesn't even have to be me. We can send in a McKay-Taggart operative and they can get the job done."

"You do whatever you like, but I'm not leaving my job. I made that plain. You can have a partner or you can walk away, but I'll still be at Cain Corp no matter what you decide." She stared up at him, pure will in her eyes.

He wanted to growl at her and put her on a plane with Taggart when he left. In the past they hadn't been above a little kidnapping when it came to keeping loved ones safe.

Shit. Had he thought that word? He couldn't think that word.

Bran took a deep breath. Why the fuck couldn't he think it? He wanted her. She wanted him. He could control himself. Maybe if he wasn't out prowling around every night looking for a fight he would find himself more in control of the volcanic rage that always seemed to simmer under his surface.

It was bubbling up right now, but he quashed it. He wasn't going to get angry. Not with Carly.

"All right." They could talk about something else. He'd told his brother he would figure out how to handle the reporter. "How well do you know this Shelby woman?"

She stopped for a moment as though trying to decide if she wanted to continue the conversation. He gave her some space, striding into the bedroom and hoping she would follow.

Her eyes were cautious as she watched him pull his shirt over his head. If he was going to meet with Patricia, he would need to clean up a bit.

"Like I told you before, she contacted me when she took over the book from her brother. I decided to help her and we became friends. I know her and she doesn't publish stories that would hurt innocent people. She actually has a lot in common with you. She firmly believes Patricia killed her brother. I think the big blond guy is right. I think she could make a valuable ally."

The trouble was Drew didn't believe in allies who weren't family. "Why does your friend think Patricia killed her brother?"

Carly was still watching him, her back to the wall while he slid out of his slacks. "Because he died in a single-vehicle accident the same day he met her for an interview."

He couldn't miss the fact that while the room wasn't chilly at all,

Carly's nipples were suddenly visible against the shirt she was wearing. Drew's overreaction might have made her wary, but Bran thought he might be able to warm her up. He needed to tempt her, coax her back into intimacy.

"That does seem convenient." He turned, unbothered by his nudity. She seemed to like his body well enough. He wished he could drag the clothes off her and haul her back to bed, but he wanted her to come to him again. "I suppose the police called it an accident."

She suddenly seemed to find the carpet endlessly fascinating. "Are you going to walk around naked?"

Did she think they were going to go back to being polite after the day they'd had?

"I'm going to take a shower. I usually do that naked."

"Bran, you're all . . . aroused and stuff."

Yes, he was. He'd gotten hard the minute he realized her nipples were rigid, and he envisioned getting those sweet berries in his mouth again. "I get that way around you."

Her face was flushed when she looked back up at him. "Your brother doesn't like me."

He knew her wall had something to do with Drew. She'd been a perfect partner, though. She hadn't shown a single sign of being upset until they'd gotten into private. He moved into her space. She had to get used to him being naked around her. He intended to do it a lot. "My brother doesn't matter. Not when it comes to us."

She shook her head, but her hands came up, grazing along his chest. "He does. Your family is everything to you. You won't hang around a woman for long if your brother doesn't approve."

"I think you don't know me as well as you think you do." He tilted her chin up. "Carly, I do what I want. I learned a long time ago that tomorrow's not guaranteed for any of us. I'm not about to walk away from you because my brother threw a fit. He's incredibly smart, but he's not that great when it comes to people. You have to be direct with

Drew. He often misses subtleties. You handled him fine. And if you want me to deal with him, I will. I'm not going to let him make you feel uncomfortable."

"Why are you trying to get rid of me?"

"What?" They were having trouble communicating today. "I'm not trying to get rid of you. Not at all. I'm worried about you. Someone tried to kill you last night."

Her hands moved over his skin. "They tried to kill Patricia. I think you're right. I think he wasn't a pro and he panicked. He saw the cape and thought it was her. I got caught in the cross fire, but I'll be more careful from now on. I thought that was your way of getting rid of me."

"Why the hell would I get rid of you?"

"I thought maybe the sex hadn't been as good as you hoped."

Oh, it was time to disabuse her of that notion. "The sex was the best I've ever had."

Her lips curled up. "Really?"

He lowered his mouth, hovering above hers. "Really."

The sound of a chime nearly made him growl in frustration.

Carly sighed. "I've got to see who it is."

"Or you can ignore it."

"It could be my sister." She ducked out from under his arms and grabbed her phone. "It's Shelby. I should take this."

And his playtime was done. He kissed her forehead. "I'll be in the shower if you need anything. Find out what you can about how deep she's gotten into our business."

He kissed her again and walked off to take a cold shower. It looked like his afternoon wasn't going to start as well as his morning had.

# *Chapter Eleven*

Carly watched as Bran strode off, his incredibly toned backside making her catch her breath. That was one beautiful man and apparently he trusted her. He wasn't standing around waiting to listen in on her conversation. She'd been honest about who was calling, and Bran had rewarded her with his trust.

Not so much his brother, though. Despite Bran's sweet talk, she knew Drew could cause serious problems between them if he chose to.

Why was she even thinking that way? It wasn't like they had long-term plans. And yet she'd sat there and her heart had ached when she realized Drew didn't trust her.

And maybe he had good reason.

"Hello?"

"Hey, I wanted to call and make sure you're all right," Shelby said, her words rushing out. "I saw on the news that something happened at the art gallery you were supposed to be in last night. The grande dame was caught looking not so perfect. She's got to be pissed about that."

Carly hadn't turned on the TV all day. She also hadn't looked at her phone like she usually would. Normally she would have spent the entire day making sure any and all press concerning the night before was positive. She would have been on the line with the promotions department and Patricia's personal publicist. She likely would have been called into Patricia's office and had her head nearly taken off if even a single unflattering photograph had surfaced.

And yet her phone had been silent all day. Her boss should have called or texted a hundred times today no matter what Bran had said. She could be on her deathbed and Patricia would still be texting.

What was going on?

"How is the media covering it?"

"They said it was an accident. Something about a gas leak from an art piece," Shelby said. "Is there something they're not saying?"

How far would Shelby go to avenge her brother?

"All I know at this point is I'm never going to love modern art." She heard the shower turn on. She glanced back and caught sight of the most magnificent male backside she'd ever seen.

"Well, the press got pictures of Patricia looking very harried. In one of them she's obviously yelling and her makeup . . . It looks like she was crying, Carly. What the hell happened at an art show that made the ice queen cry?"

Carly took a deep breath because Patricia had to be furious. Maybe the reason she hadn't gotten a call or a text was that she no longer had a job. Would they arrest Meri? Another deep breath. She had a few questions for her friend first, and then she would figure out what was happening at the office. "I don't know. I was at the hospital. I happened to be in the room with the gas leak."

There was a moment of silence on the other end of the line and when Shelby spoke again, her voice had gone low and serious. "I think you should leave. Now. Come out here to LA and stay with me."

"Why would I do that?"

"Because I think someone powerful wants Patricia Cain dead."

"Why would you think that?"

"I've been looking into some notes my brother left and I started thinking about what you said to me last week. It made me look into the first company Cain made money off of. I don't think Benedict Lawless killed his wife. I think he was assassinated along with her and it was paid for by the other investors in the business. Do you know who the man behind 4L Software is?"

So Shelby had been connecting dots. "I do."

"What if Andrew Lawless is clearing up his debts? I want you to think about this. Phillip Stratton died before 4L was stratospheric. He couldn't get to Stratton. But someone got to Castalano and now they're trying to get to Cain."

"Steven Castalano had a heart attack."

"Did he? He died about two hours after Patricia went to see him. It was also the day before he was set to talk to the police. I think that is interesting timing. I looked at CCTV of the hospital. Here's the crazy thing. I've got a woman going into Castalano's room ten minutes before his heart attack. The police officer steps away and then mysteriously returns after the woman slips back out."

"Was it a nurse?" Sometimes Shelby could get carried away with her theories.

"She was dressed in scrubs, but they were in the middle of a shift change. He wasn't scheduled for another check for at least an hour. And this so-called nurse manages to never look directly at a camera. I think she killed Castalano and now she's coming after Cain. What if the Lawless siblings are out for revenge? They're all alive. They're rarely photographed. Why would they try to keep their faces out of the press if they weren't planning something?"

"Maybe they like their privacy. Maybe they've had enough press to last a lifetime." It wasn't the reason, but she could imagine it.

"No. That man has plans and I don't want you caught in the middle," Shelby pleaded.

"I'm already in the middle. And you need to back off. Let me look into things from this end, but if Drew Lawless is as dangerous as you say he is, you need to leave him be. The man could hurt you. He's likely more dangerous than Patricia ever thought about being."

"He's already tried. I say bring it," Shelby said, rebellion plain in her tone. "I'm not going to let some one percenter shove me around. Keep in touch and be careful, Carly. Call me if you need help. I'm going to figure this out. I can't help myself now."

The line went dead and Carly had to sit for a minute. Shelby knew too much. Or she thought she did.

Where did her loyalties truly lie? If she marched in and told Bran, he would immediately tell Drew. What would Drew do? Would he go after Shelby?

She'd just asked herself how far Shelby would go to avenge her brother. How far would Drew Lawless go? He'd already proven he would have used her to his own ends.

What should she say to him? If she told Bran, he'd tell Drew, and Shelby would likely get hurt. She didn't think Drew would kill her, but he could do other things. Carly knew there were other ways to ruin a life.

Her gut knotted. She knew Drew was stalking Shelby online and she hadn't said a thing. She knew Shelby was putting together pieces that could hurt Drew's plans.

Where did her loyalties lie? With a woman who'd been her friend over the years? Or a man she barely knew. A man she knew she had limited time with?

A man she might be falling in love with.

Carly banished the thought for a moment. She had another problem. With shaking hands, she pressed the button that would take her to her boss. Patricia answered on the second ring.

"Carly? I expected you would be half dead by now. According to your boy toy, you're far too precious to get up today and do your job. Is there a reason you're bothering me?"

Well, the bitch was back. She might have been crying the night before, but Patricia Cain was in full force today. "I'm fine now. The doctors wanted me to rest for a day or two. That's all. If you need me at the office, I can be there in an hour."

A long sigh came over the line. "Work from home. I'm afraid I find myself in actual need of your boyfriend's services. Apparently he works for one of the world's premiere security teams. I spoke with some colleagues earlier and they claim this Taggart person is the best, but he has odd notions about how to treat the help."

Carly could only imagine. Having met the man and understanding the fact that all of his brothers at one time had worked for him, he likely thought of his employees as actual human beings. That would definitely throw Patricia off. "You fired the security team?"

"Of course. They did a terrible job of dealing with Jasmine and then the utter debacle at the art show. The whole evening was ruined. And the cape Giovanni designed for me is a complete loss. There are grass stains on it. Do you know how furious he was?"

"I can imagine." The grass stains got there because Carly had been dying at the time. "The next time I nearly die, I'll make sure to do it so nothing needs dry cleaning."

An icy chill came over the line. "Watch it, dear. I'm willing to give you the time off your boyfriend requested, but don't you forget for an instant who holds the power here. I expect you back in the office on Monday. In the meantime, work on the fall issue and ensure that the menu for the LA party is exquisite. I expect the launch for the season will go without incident. Everyone will be there. If it fails, I'll have your head. Or rather your sister's."

The line went dead. Sometimes she could practically hear Patricia cackling like the Wicked Witch of the West. All she needed was a line about "and your little dog, too."

Patricia Cain was never going to let her go. There was no magic exit door at the end of the next two years. She would find another way to keep Carly in her clutches because Carly kept right on giving her what she needed. She gave that woman all her ideas and her energy and her talent and took no credit, was given no real compensation.

The rest of her life played out like a pathetic reality show. She would always be in the background, always unappreciated. It wasn't that she needed fame. It was only that she needed something, anything, that was hers.

All of her life it seemed had been spent serving everyone around her, from taking care of her mother to protecting her sister to attempting to be the best wife she could be.

When would she simply get to be Carly? Not someone's useful thing.

She could hear Bran humming in the bathroom as the shower kept flowing.

Bran might want her help, but he wanted something else from her, too. When Bran was inside her she felt more than she had in years. When he kissed her the numbness faded and she could feel a spark of the girl she used to be.

Who was she fooling? She'd never been that girl. She felt a tiny spark of the woman she wanted to be. A woman who didn't grovel and beg for the smallest crumbs of fairness. A woman who fought for herself.

Carly stood up and let the phone drop to the bed. Couldn't she have a few more moments of that feeling before she had to decide which way to go? In the end she would be alone, but for a few days she could be with him.

Bran would always side with his family. He would always go where Drew wanted him to go, but just until the job was over maybe she could pretend that he was with her.

Then they could take down Patricia Cain and she wouldn't have to deal with the dangerous world of the Lawless clan again. She could move on to the next job and try to find some peace.

For now, she didn't want peace. She wanted him.

Carly let her hands drift to the bottom of her shirt. By the time she entered the bathroom she was naked and ready to feel again.

Bran thought seriously about masturbating. He wasn't going to get what he wanted. He would get clean and then spend the rest of the day with the most sarcastic bastard he'd ever met and creepy Patricia Cain, who he hoped wouldn't hit on him again.

And Carly would be here.

Maybe they should go back to her place. Drew was being an ass. The last thing he wanted was Carly to feel insecure because his big brother was completely paranoid.

Maybe then he could get what he wanted, which was back inside Carly's tight body with her arms wrapped around him. Tonight he could cuddle with her. He could sleep with her body snuggled up to his and wake up and do it all over again.

He really should masturbate. The damn thing wasn't going down and all the cold water in the world wasn't going to help at this point. Every time he closed his eyes, all he could see was Carly's face staring up at him when he penetrated her. Those gorgeous eyes had widened and her hands had tightened on him like she wasn't ever going to let him go.

And then Drew had practically screamed at her over the reporter. Shelby Gates was driving his brother insane, but Bran wasn't about to allow that to hurt Carly.

He flipped the dial over to hot. It didn't matter. He was going to be hard until the next time he fucked her. Then he would have a blissful few moments of peace before he needed her again.

She'd been so sweet. She'd told him he didn't need a condom because she was on the pill. He never rode a woman bareback, but he would with her. When he was absolutely sure he was safe for her, he would take her without anything between them. Never before, but she was special. He would ensure her safety and then for the entire time they were together he wouldn't touch another woman.

Of course, after how intimidating his brother had been, she might not want to touch him again.

He reached for the soap and felt a draft at his backside. He turned and then there was zero question of his dick getting soft again.

Carly stood there in the shower doorway, her curvy body soft and naked. Her hair was a halo around her head, her breasts pert and nipples tight. She looked like a fucking goddess standing there. She was so perfect with her curvy hips and soft lips.

He knew exactly what he wanted those lips to do. Need rose up, hard and fast, and he knew in an instant that he wouldn't be able to be soft and patient with her. Not after the way the meeting had gone. Not after the worry of someone looking into their pasts and trying to make connections none of them wanted made.

He wanted her on her knees. He wanted her serving him, her lips worshipping his cock. His hand hard in all that soft hair so she knew who her lover was.

"Maybe this isn't the best time, sweetheart." The last thing he wanted was to scare her. He could be . . . intense. He'd managed to hold off this morning. He was on edge now. He had to go back into the belly of the beast. He had to face Patricia Cain and it bugged him. It made him want to feel like he was in control, and that could frighten someone as sweet and innocent as Carly.

She'd had one freaking lover. She didn't need to move on to his kinkier needs. She needed a patient, tender lover, and he wasn't sure he could be that right now.

Her eyes weren't on his face. "It looks like the perfect time, Bran."

He nearly growled his frustration. "Sweetheart, I'm a little on edge. I was thinking we could head back to your place. Why don't you get ready and you can drive into St. Augustine with me and Taggart? We'll spend the weekend there."

Anything so she wouldn't see how dirty he wanted to get with her. So she wouldn't see how he could use her to take away his pain.

"That sounds wonderful," Carly replied as she stepped into the oversized shower.

It was beautifully done in sandy tile. He was sure Carly would have all kinds of designer words for the large shower with its bench seating and multiple showerheads. He just thought it was nice.

What was even nicer was Carly herself. Her skin practically glowed. She sighed as the water hit her and ran her hands back through her hair. Her body bowed, breasts upthrust toward him.

His cock jerked as though mere proximity to her was like a magnet, drawing him closer. He had to force his hands not to reach out for her. The instinct to reach out and pull her close was damn near impossible to resist.

"But I think we have some time before we need to head back." She reached out for him, her hand going straight to his chest. She placed her palm right over his heart and seemed completely unselfconscious of her nudity. "I can get the lunch ready in no time at all. We've got at least an hour and a half before we need to leave here. I can think of some ways to spend it."

Damn it. His cock pulsed. He gritted his teeth. The hot water beat down on him. "Carly, I can't be tender right now. I think I should go and let you get cleaned up."

Her lips tugged up in the sexiest smile. "I already took a shower. I'm not here to get clean, Bran. I thought it might be fun to get dirty again."

Her soft palm worked its way down, brushing over his abs all the way down to his pelvis. She stopped right before she reached his dick.

He reached down and gripped her wrist. She needed to understand what she was getting into because he was rapidly approaching the point of no return. She was too close, too sweet, too much for him to turn away. "Carly, this isn't a good idea."

She turned her face up to him. "Why?"

"I'm not in control." That wasn't exactly the problem. "Or rather, I want to be in control."

"You're always in control, Bran." She made it sound like a bad thing.

She had no idea how wrong she was. He took a deep breath and tried to find his patience. "I want to be in control of you, Carly. I want you to get on your knees and I'll teach you how I like to have my cock sucked. I'll put my hands in your hair and I'll force my dick to the back of your throat, and at some point I'll come. I'll make you drink it down and I'll want you to thank me for it when I'm done. That kind of control. I don't want to be tender with you."

Her hand moved lower, fingertips brushing his cock. She moved in and her nipples touched his chest. "You think you should always be tender?"

He hadn't been for so much of his life, but he wanted her to have what she deserved. It was precisely why he couldn't stay with her. There was too much of him that was dirty and undeserving. "I think I should with you."

She frowned up at him. "I want you, Bran. I want all of you, and that means I want the rough side, too. I don't want to be some doll you gently make love to and then treat me like I'm made of porcelain. I'm not. I'm strong. I want to be your lover, not some sympathy lay."

His right hand found her hair and twisted lightly because she needed to understand that was not acceptable. He would take a lot from her, but never that. "Don't talk about yourself like that. You're no one's sympathy lay."

Her lips curled up, and he realized he'd fallen into her trap. "Then show me the Bran who wants to control me. I can handle you. I want to handle you."

She dropped down to her knees, his hand coming out of her hair. Her palms ran up his thighs, her eyes tilted up and on him.

And he couldn't stop himself another second. "You want to know me? You might not like all of me."

"I think you'll be surprised at what I can handle." Her tongue licked over her bottom lip.

Fuck. She was going to make him insane.

He stared down at her, his whole system threatening to go on overload. This was a part of himself he wrestled with, the need to overpower and overwhelm. Not in a bad way, but in a way that would end in her pleasure. He was always about a woman's pleasure. There had been times in his life he'd taken none for himself. He'd started eating pussy at a young age, finding he enjoyed making women happy, watching them come. Sometimes he hadn't needed more than that.

He wanted to be selfish with her. He wanted more than the mere knowledge she'd enjoyed her time with him.

He wanted her to crave him and what he could give her, and to need to give back to him.

"How do you like having your cock sucked, Bran?" Her voice was low, but every word went right to the body part in question.

He bit back a growl and resigned being gentle to hell. Maybe he could show her a little of the beast inside him. Maybe if he started to feed it the smallest of meals it wouldn't come out, it wouldn't need blood. Maybe he could hide that nasty side of himself from her.

He reached out and touched her hair, threading his fingers through. "I told you how I want it, though I was serious about the testing. I won't come down your throat. Not until I'm sure it's safe. I don't have sex without condoms, but I've been to some unsavory places and nothing's a hundred percent effective. That particular lesson is going to have to wait, but that doesn't mean we can't play a few games. Stay on your knees, but move to the bench. Spread your legs wide."

He'd been careful about sex, but there were nights he didn't remember, nights when he tried to obliterate himself with alcohol only to wake up in some random woman's bed. He had a yearly checkup, but he wasn't putting her at risk. He stepped out into the bathroom and opened the drawer where he'd stashed the condoms Drew had given him when he'd asked for some. Drew had rolled his eyes, shaken his head, and muttered some sort of lecture about not falling for the girl.

Bran hadn't mentioned that he'd already done that.

"Did you really get condoms from your brother?" She was turned and looking at him. Not at all in the place he'd left her in.

"Yes, I did. Get to the bench, Carly, or we can clean up and I'll gently make love to you and put this whole idea of play out of our heads."

She turned quickly, her legs moving apart. She likely didn't realize it, but it gave him a spectacular view of her ass. Pretty heart-shaped ass. She was built for a man to fuck, with curves and hips and breasts that made his mouth water.

He got to his knees and ran a hand down her spine. "Don't move. If you move I'll stop what I'm doing."

"What kind of game is this, Bran? One of those kinky games where I call you Sir?"

"No. It's one of those games where you do as I say and then I give you an orgasm. No Sirs needed, though if you ever want a spanking, I'm your guy." He would love to see her over his knee, the globes of her round ass waiting for the smack of his hand.

"You would spank me?"

He gave her ass a smack. Nothing too rough, though he bet the heat of the water made it sting.

She gasped but managed not to move.

"That wasn't so bad, was it?" Bran asked, running his hand over the spot he'd smacked. He didn't need it. If she hated it, he would never do it again. He could fantasize about it, but he didn't really want to hurt her.

"No, it wasn't bad." The breathless sound of her voice let him know she was telling the truth.

"Lovers should be able to play games. Sex should be fun." Or at least he'd always thought it should be. Not that he'd had many women he would call lovers. Only two had stayed with him for more than a few nights, but those two he'd definitely had fun with. Light sessions where they role-played, talking through their fantasies.

No. Talking through her fantasies. He'd always catered to his lover. Carly was offering to give to him.

What was his real fantasy? A woman who explored with him, who let him find what he needed and then gave it to him.

He needed her to trust him. He needed her to need him.

He smacked her again, watching the way her skin went pink. The squeal that came out of her mouth went straight to his dick, making it pulse and demand attention.

It could wait. His fantasy couldn't.

"You need to tell me if you don't like something." He leaned over and pushed her now-wet hair to one side before kissing the back of her neck. Such a soft, vulnerable spot. He let his tongue play there for a moment.

"I will. I swear I will. I wouldn't have told you I would ever like that, but I did. It hurt, but then it made me hot. Do you want me to turn around so I can kiss you, too?"

He liked her like this. On her knees, her body open to him. He let his hands run down to her breasts, cupping them. He gently bit her neck, just a nip. "You don't move until I move you. You said you didn't want to be treated like a porcelain doll. How about my sex toy? My pretty little sex toy. This is all for me and I can do anything I want with you. I ordered you. They asked what I wanted and I said I wanted breasts that fit my hand, pretty pink nipples I can twist and play with."

Her chest moved against his hands as though she couldn't quite help herself. Her backside moved, too. A subtle arch of her back, but it brought her ass into contact with his cock. She liked the dirty stuff.

He could give her more. So much more. His sweet homemaker needed some dirty talk to get her hot and ready? He could do that all day long. It was easy because she inspired him to think some really filthy thoughts.

"I would have told them to make my toy sweet and sassy and smart." He licked the back of her neck, running his tongue down her spine. "I would have told them to make her skin taste like sunshine and to give her curves I could hold on to when I sink my dick deep inside her."

With his hands on her, his body pressed to hers, he could feel her reactions. Every dirty word he whispered to her seemed to send her heart racing, her body squirming slightly against his as though begging him to do what he was promising.

"I would be specific about what I needed from my own personal sex toy." He moved down again, his hands finding her hips as he placed a kiss on the small of her back. "I would need her to have beautiful brown and red and gold hair and lovely skin. She would have to be strong enough to stand up to my family and sweet enough to know when to stand beside me. Did I thank you for that, by the way? Don't move your hands or I'll stop what I'm doing."

What he was doing was inching his right hand toward her clitoris. She stopped and seemed to hold her breath for a moment.

"I won't move."

That's what he wanted to hear. He wanted that whine in her voice that begged for him to continue on. He was grateful for whoever had decided they needed a shower built for like ten people because it gave him plenty of room to move. He slid back up, his left hand on her breast, his right so close to her clitoris. His cock nestled against the cheeks of her ass. He pumped his hips slightly, enjoying the skin-to-skin contact.

"I would make sure my sex toy loved my attention because she would get a whole lot of it." He slid the pad of his middle finger over her clit. It was wet and ripe and all he'd had to do was touch her a little, give her some dirty talk. She responded to him so quickly. "Do you like my attention, Carly?"

She whimpered. "Yes. Please, Bran. It's so hard to stay still."

"But you'll do it for me. Won't you?" He licked the shell of her ear, palming her breast with his free hand.

She nodded her head, the rest of her body still beneath him. "Yes."

"Why are you so wet? Is this from the shower?" He slid his finger over her again, sliding through her arousal. This time he pressed in, giving her a bit more pressure.

She gasped but managed to stay still. "No. It's not from the water. It's because of you."

"Me? This is for me?" He circled her again and again. Her pussy was soaking wet, her arousal coating his hand.

"Yes. All for you."

"What do you want me to do with this?" He let his thumb rub her clit while his middle finger dipped into her pussy. So much sweet juice there and it was all his.

"Anything you want."

"What would you say if I wanted to lick it? Would you let me taste you?"

"Yes."

"Would you spread your legs right here and now and let me put my mouth on you? I should warn you, my tongue would be all over this sweet flesh. There wouldn't be a single spot I wouldn't lick and suck."

She gasped before she managed to get her answer out. "I would spread my legs."

"Would you let me spear my tongue as deep as it can go before I settled in and suckled that pearl of a clit? I'll suck hard and you'll come all over my mouth and I'll love it. And then do you know what I'll do to you?"

"Please fuck me, Bran. I can't stand it. I want you to fuck me. Hard and long. Any way you want it."

He pinched her clit lightly, forcing her attention to him. "Not it. I don't want it. I want you. I want to fuck you, Carly Fisher. You need to understand that I might be playing a game, but the only woman I see is you. So tell me again."

"Any way you want me," she said. "I want you, Bran. I want your cock and your lips and tongue. Only yours."

That was what he wanted to hear. "Up on the bench. Put your heels up, legs spread. I want access."

She twisted, moving as fast as she could. He helped her up. She wasn't thinking about anything but the pleasure he could give her.

Neither was he. It struck him that everything else fell away when he was with her. He wasn't thinking or planning or doing anything but concentrating on the time with her. All the reasons he couldn't stay with her fell away and he wanted nothing more than to make the moment last. Maybe that was his true fantasy, that he wouldn't have to leave her, wouldn't need to be a better man. Here he could be enough for her. Here he deserved her.

This bench was the perfect height. There was zero chance he was the first person who had fucked a lover in this shower. Apparently the married couple who vacationed here kept things hot. He silently thanked Alex McKay for being around the same height. On his knees he was in the perfect position to do all the things he'd told her he would.

She was so beautiful. He was certain she felt awkward with her legs spread but she'd never looked more gorgeous to him. She was a passionate woman making no excuses for what she wanted. And she wanted him.

"My toy is the single sexiest thing I've ever seen. She's perfectly made for me," he said. "You're perfect for me, Carly."

Even if they were playing, he didn't ever want her to forget that.

"You bring out things in me I never thought existed. I'm not this woman, Bran. Not for anyone but you. And I swear I'll scream soon if you don't touch me again."

He would have to teach her later that he liked to look at her. He would stare at her for hours if she would allow him to. She was a fucking work of art. But he was in agreement with her. He couldn't wait to touch her again, to taste her again.

Her pussy was perfect and creamy, the jewel of her clit primed and ready.

"I do believe I promised I would taste you again. I have to say that if your skin tastes like sunshine, then your pussy is pure sin." He ran his tongue over her, reveling in the way she tasted, how good her arousal smelled.

A possessive instinct like nothing he'd ever felt before raced through him. He licked her, spearing his tongue deep so he wouldn't miss a drop. She was his. She fucking belonged to him. She never responded this way to another man because she belonged to him. Her husband hadn't been able to make her scream because she'd needed Bran.

He spread her labia gently, his tongue fucking her in a blatant imitation of what he would do with his cock. Soon. He would fuck her every way a man could fuck his woman. He wanted her in every single way he could have her so there wasn't an inch of her without his mark.

He replaced his tongue with his fingers, sending two deep inside her pussy. He looked up and caught her eyes looking down. She watched him, her pupils dark and wide with hot desire.

"Please."

He leaned over and sucked her clit as he curled his fingers deep inside her.

Her shout echoed through the room and sent his heart pounding.

He licked and sucked until she stilled. His cock pulsed. It was his time. It was fucking his time and he wanted it. He wanted that orgasm more than he wanted the knowledge that he'd made her happy. He wanted to be inside her, to know she opened herself and submitted her body to him.

"Hands and knees. Right now." The words ground out of him as he reached for the condom he'd stashed before they'd started playing.

He wanted to play with her forever. This was the right woman.

Was it the right time?

He shoved the thought aside as she didn't miss a beat. Her face was flushed as she slid down and got to her hands and knees before him. She offered herself with no questions. She went down in front of him and made herself vulnerable.

It was the best high he'd ever had, and in his fucked-up youth he'd tried them all.

He stroked himself though he didn't really need to. He was hard as a rock. He rolled the condom on and tossed the wrapper aside. He moved in behind her. He liked the rough feel of the tile on his knees. It contrasted with how soft her skin was beneath his hands and how damn hot her flesh was when he pressed up and shoved his cock against her pussy.

Soft and warm and wet. He gripped her hips and pressed in. Tight. Her pussy clenched around him. This was what he needed. He needed her tight and drenched and clenched around him. He forced his dick in, loving the way she pressed back against him.

"Do that again, baby. You can move all you like now." He wanted her passion, her heat. The play was done and he was ready to get down to the real pleasure of the day.

He thrust into her, giving up any thought of being gentle. He didn't need to be now. She was wet and open and he could do whatever he wanted with her. She would have nothing but pleasure from the encounter.

Over and over he thrust in and pulled out as she pumped back against him. He loved the fact that she fought for her pleasure. She didn't hold back. She moved, groans filling the small space until his whole world seemed to consist of nothing but the sounds and sights of his Carly.

His.

He reached around and found the button of her clitoris again. This time she would last longer since he'd made her come all over his tongue before. He could still taste her, and the sweet tang made him swell inside. He gave over to the beast that always seemed so close to the surface. He pounded inside her.

She came again, the muscles of her pussy clenching around him and sending him over the edge.

He held her tight as he came down from the high. Held her tight and thought about never letting her go again.

*Chapter Twelve*

Three hours later Bran wished he was back at Carly's townhouse instead of sitting here in the far too elegant room of Patricia Cain's house. It was in a nice part of St. Augustine with a lovely view of the bay and the historic lighthouse in the distance. The entire room was done in shades of white and the furniture was some form of tiny. He was sure Carly would call it delicate, but it seemed fragile to Bran. He wasn't certain the chair he was sitting in wouldn't disintegrate at some point.

Taggart shifted in the seat he'd been shown to. He looked like a hulking beast perched on a teeny tiny throne. "Is there a reason we moved the meeting from your office?"

Patricia nodded to the servant who'd brought tea on a silver platter. She set it down on the table and silently began to pour. "I thought this was a much more civilized place to meet, Mr. Taggart. The office is less personal, and I find security to be a very personal thing indeed. How do you like your tea?"

"With a healthy splash of Scotch, and by healthy I mean skip the tea and bring a Scotch or a beer. Seriously, I don't drink tea, and this show of wealth, while impressive, doesn't answer my question," Taggart replied.

Case's brother was the single coolest human being Bran had met.

He'd patiently, albeit with a level of sarcasm Bran hadn't known existed, described how they would work with Cain today. Taggart had explained that they wouldn't go in looking to kiss Cain's ass. They would go in expecting her to explain why they should work for her.

Bran really liked that plan.

Taggart had seemed slightly surprised at the change of plans when they'd been redirected to Cain's house, but he'd said their own intentions didn't change.

Patricia lowered herself to the settee. She wore a casually elegant pantsuit, her hair back. If it weren't for the pinched expression on her face, she might have been somewhat attractive. Though Bran knew he was a bit prejudiced because of the whole murderer thing.

"Is this the way you treat your clients, Mr. Taggart?"

And now it was Bran's turn. He was the good cop. He rather envied Big Tag's role. "I'm sorry. My boss can be a bit harsh at times. It's a leftover from years in Special Ops. He's also not good with niceties, but then, you have to ask yourself if you want a security team led by a man who knows security or who plays the social game well."

"I can't have both?" She turned her attention back to Bran.

"Not if you want to deal with Ian Taggart," Bran replied. "I will take some tea. Two sugars, please. Unless you're going to ask us to leave."

"She's not going to ask us to leave, Brandon. She's got bigger issues than she's willing to talk about," Taggart said with a sigh.

Cain frowned, crossing one long leg over the other as she sat back. "And what issues are those? You seem to be completely in control of the situation. What have you learned about me?"

"Tell her what we've learned, Brandon," Taggart said with a smirk on his face.

He was good at playing the arrogant asshole. It was a way to ensure that Bran was the one who would be "handling" Patricia Cain. "The gas leak wasn't an accident."

Her eyes flared slightly. "The fire department hasn't released their report yet."

"They haven't released it to the public, but there are ways around their protocols." He reached into his briefcase and handed her the manila folder containing the report the fire department would almost certainly send her in a week or so when they'd crossed all their t's.

He couldn't help but notice that her hands trembled slightly as she took the folder. She drew the reading glasses that were held by a chain around her neck and perched them on the end of her nose.

"Your tea, sir." The middle-aged woman in a black-and-white uniform held out the china cup and saucer. She turned to Taggart, her lips quirking up slightly as she took him in. "Would you like your Scotch on the rocks or neat?"

"I like my Scotch able to drink itself and don't let any ice near it." Taggart smiled and winked at the woman, who blushed.

"I wouldn't think of it, sir." There was a spring to her step as she walked out.

Cain set the file down. "They believe this was deliberate, but they don't talk about a motive. Shouldn't you be looking into the gallery owner? Perhaps he has debts and was seeking to pay them off with the insurance he would receive."

Taggart stared at her, his demeanor as icy with Cain as it was warm with the servant. "Naturally I looked into everyone who could have gained from the crime. Money is the first motive I take into account, but given that the gallery owner was standing not more than ten feet away from the scene, I sincerely doubt that insurance was the motive. Unless he was going to cash that check from the grave."

"What my boss is trying to say is we believe there was a specific target. We don't think there was any reason to believe the intent was for the gallery to be destroyed. Otherwise the fire department would have found some type of incendiary device that would have allowed the suspect to spark a flame once he'd exited the building. There was nothing like that."

"What they did find was a small device that had been mounted to the door," Taggart explained. "It was cleverly done. The doorframe was white, and the latching system matched it. If no one was inspecting it closely, it would have been easy to miss."

"Latching system?" Patricia opened the folder again, turning to the pictures.

"Yes." Bran pointed to the item in question. "It's a simple thing. That particular door actually opens into the hallway instead of into the room. The gallery owner explained it was designed that way to maximize space in the private showing rooms. They can open those doors and not lose square footage on the inside. Our would-be killer used that to his advantage. He placed a flip lock here on the upper part of the door. Once it's locked, it's difficult to open and, given the color and where it was placed, hard to see and therefore undo."

"You're the one who got her out." Cain closed the folder again. "How did you do it?"

"Pure adrenaline." He could still feel it, that bolt of energy that had come with knowing Carly was on the other side of the door.

Cain sighed and shook her head. "Well, if they were attempting to make it look like an accident, how on earth did they expect to get away with it?"

Taggart took over. "I believe our man panicked. He was out of time. He'd set everything up properly, but the shoot didn't go as expected. The latch was attached with an industrial glue and not properly installed. That was smart on his part. If he'd installed it with nails, even taking it away would raise questions because he wouldn't have time to repair the door and frame to its original state."

They'd gone over this in the car on the way over. Carly had seemed fascinated with the ins and outs of the attempt on her life. It had made Bran sick. "There's a simple solvent that would dissolve the glue and then Tim could have pocketed the latch, wiped off the door, and no one would be the wiser."

"But that's not what happened." Cain rolled her eyes. "Obviously he wasn't very professional."

"He was exactly what he claimed to be. Thank you so much." Taggart took the drink from the servant's hand before turning back to Cain. "Tim Connors really was a cameraman. From what I can tell, he had zero connections to you or your family before he was hired. I believe he was hired specifically to assassinate you and make it look like an accident, if possible. He fled the country a few hours after the attempt before the police could figure out it hadn't been an accident. His financial records show large sums of money deposited into his account after he hired on. I don't suppose that was some sort of hiring bonus."

Despite the fact that her expression never wavered, there was a slight flush to her cheeks that didn't come from makeup. That news had upset her.

"That seems a rather far leap, Mr. Taggart. And no. I don't give out bonuses to employees of his stature. Why exactly do you believe it was me he was after?" Her tone was perfect, only that slight flush giving away her emotional state.

Taggart took a sip of the Scotch and sat back. "Now that is damn fine Scotch."

"It should be. It's about to reach retirement age," Cain replied. "You were going to explain your logic. Please proceed."

"My logic," Taggart shot back, "is that you have many, many people who would love to see you dead. My logic is that of all the people in that room, only you were truly targeted. And my last bit of logic is that we're here and not in your office because you know damn well this is all about you and you don't want anyone to hear what you're going to tell me. You better tell me. I already know and I make it a habit to not deal with clients who lie to me or hide the truth."

For a fraction of a second Bran was thrilled. Taggart had definitely overplayed their hand and Patricia Cain would show them the door. Bran would be free to get Carly out of here and Drew could deal with the cleanup. He knew it made him a bad brother, but he wanted something for once in his fucking miserable life. He wanted her. He wanted her safe and happy and he thought maybe he could give that to her.

But then Cain's eyes closed as though defeated and Bran knew Taggart had her.

"I believe it could be one of a couple of people, including my stepson," she said, her voice low. "But I also need you to look into some of my ex-employees."

"Your stepson is obvious." Bran shoved his disappointment aside. He had a job to do and the quicker it got done, the faster he could find out if a relationship with Carly would work. "Though I would think you signed a prenup before you married his father. Is he worried you'll fight it?"

"He knows I've already won that battle," Patricia conceded. "When Ken passes on, I'll receive ownership of the media portion of the empire. As part of our prenup, that came to me when I agreed to move *Patricia's Paradise* to the network Jones Unlimited owns. They were in trouble and it was dragging the rest of the company down. If my show and management of the network brought the division out of the red, I was to receive a majority share stock in the division after Ken's death. Though my stepson won't believe it, I saved the entire company. He would be penniless without me and he still gains eighty percent of the company on his father's death."

"What about the daughter?" Taggart asked. "She could be angry she's not involved in the company."

Cain waved that thought off. "Jasmine has zero interest in business. When her father dies her brother controls her stock and she receives a nice income, including a hundred million in a trust fund. She's not hurting and despite her obnoxious drinking, we actually get along fairly well. I've gotten her in contact with several designers who give her free couture in exchange for my featuring them. All of that dries up, along with appearances on my show, if I die. I do not suspect Jas at all."

For a moment she'd sounded almost affectionate, as though not despising someone was close to love in Patricia Cain's world.

"Who do you suspect?" Bran asked, wary of the answer.

Cain stood and walked to the window, her slender figure illuminated by the afternoon light. "There is one specific person beyond my stepson and a few disgruntled workers I believe you should look into, and I don't believe you'll want to deal with him."

"You would be surprised," Taggart replied. "I tend to like a challenge."

"Do you know who Andrew Lawless is?"

Bran's heart clenched but Taggart didn't miss a beat.

"He's the owner of 4L Software and he's the son of a man you used to do business with. I do believe you screwed him over royally. Yes, I would definitely look into him if you hired me."

Everything they'd worked for came down to this test. Did she know? Drew had kept his face out of the public, allowing others to handle the media. Bran and Riley had changed their names to Lang and their stock in 4L was hidden under layers and layers of holding companies. Mia had taken her adoptive parents' name. Once she'd married Case, McKay-Taggart had ensured their covers would hold and that Riley and Bran Lawless couldn't be connected to their new names. The paperwork had been buried in classified files. Working closely with the CIA had brought many blessings to Taggart and then to them.

Patricia didn't blink as she turned back. "I did nothing that wasn't in the contract Benedict himself signed. He was a prissy sort of man. He was all about the rules. I simply followed them to the letter."

"I'm sure his children would have a different view," Taggart said.

She shrugged. "I'm sure they would, which is precisely why you should look into them for me. My last firm kept an eye on the oldest. It seems the family lost touch after their years in foster care. Andrew is the only one who made something of himself. The others are scattered around. Unless you can find something different. My last company did prove to be useless it seems."

"I read the files on the situation." Bran was happy with how even his voice sounded. "I have to ask how long you've been following the children? What made you think to do it? Was it another incident? According to everything I've found, the police reports are fairly clear about what happened that night."

"I didn't think anything of it until recently," Patricia admitted. "The boy has money enough of his own and his father did attempt to kill him and the others. I should think he wouldn't want revenge. If he did, he could have gone to the press and trashed us for employing the contract clause that kept the money from him. He didn't. He's played everything well. He's a much better businessman than his father ever was."

Bran took a deep breath and forced about a hundred nasty thoughts to the back of his head. Cold. He had to be cold instead of hot. It was hard for him because his rage had always been like lava spewing forth. He could feel his blood pressure tick up, but Taggart took over. The big Texan's steady voice grounded Bran.

"What made you worry about the Lawless kid if you hadn't before?"

"It was something Steven told me the last time I saw him," Patricia said, her heels moving across the floor as she paced.

"Steven Castalano? Your old business partner?" Taggart sat up, his eyes on Patricia as though ready to take her out if he had to. Taggart knew Castalano had made them. He'd recognized Riley. Had he warned his old friend before he'd died?

She shuddered. "Yes, that piece of offal. I hated that man. Phillip was always the gentleman of the two and he was horrible as well. I heard that daughter of his is an idiot, though. It doesn't matter now. I got what Steven owed me but he told me I would get what's coming. I wasn't sure what he meant by that, but now I have to wonder if he meant that Benedict's children had finally made a move."

So they were definitely not friends. Bran sipped the damn tea because it gave him something to do, but he wished he'd been able to have the Scotch instead. Being in the same room with Patricia Cain put him on edge.

That nasty feeling in his gut—the one that went away when he was with Carly—was back in full force. He wanted a drink. He wanted a whole night of it. Anything to forget that he was sitting in the same room with the woman who'd casually ordered the killings of his parents and then hadn't batted an eye about taking their childhoods away.

"I had similar thoughts," Taggart said, his voice as cool as a cucumber. "If you like, I can have an operative watch him. He seems to value his privacy above everything else. I can certainly look into his financials."

She shook her head. "I don't know. I would think a man like that would hire a better assassin. He can afford it."

"I'll put Bran on it and I'll take a look at the disgruntled employees. I take it you agree to our fees." Taggart stood up, a signal he was ready to be done. "I've already got a crew in California who can ensure the security of your house there. I'll have another team out here by tomorrow to do an assessment."

"I want Brandon to be my bodyguard."

His stomach turned.

Taggart shook his head. "You'll need three and they'll work shifts. More than eight hours and the attention span and focus suffers. He'll be your day shift and I'll bring two more in for the rest of the time."

At least he would usually be in the same building as Carly. "When

I'm not on duty, I'll look into your stepson and the rest of the names on your list."

Patricia nodded and her focus shifted back. "I agree to your terms. Mr. Taggart, could I have a moment alone with Brandon?"

Taggart looked his way.

What the hell was he supposed to do? He couldn't exactly explain that there was zero chance he would be alone with that bitch since he'd just been hired as her bodyguard. "Of course."

Taggart swallowed the last of his Scotch and started for the door. "I'll be in the car. Your two secondary guards will be here in the morning. Until then you should set your alarm."

He strode out, leaving Bran alone with Cain.

"How is Carly?" She sounded almost like she cared.

"She's recovering."

"Excellent." Patricia moved closer, her expression softening. "She's quite good at her job. I would prefer not to lose her."

Yes, she'd done a lot to ensure that. "She'll be back at work on Monday. I'll start then, too. You've got a bodyguard until then. I'll start first thing Monday morning and I'll accompany her out to California. She goes out two days before you."

Patricia frowned. "And if I prefer you remain with me?"

"Then you'll need another bodyguard." He wasn't going to give on that. He wouldn't send Carly out on her own.

Patricia moved in, sitting down in front of him, their knees nearly touching. "All right. I can understand that. You want to do some of the advance work. The party is important."

"And Carly is important to me. She's my primary concern. I want to do my job, but she comes first."

Patricia leaned forward, her hand coming out to touch his knee. "I find your loyalty impressive. Not many men are so willing to care about a woman who can't give them much."

"I don't know what kind of men you've been around, Ms. Cain, but

I assure you I'm not interested in a woman taking care of me. It's quite the other way around. I'm happy with Carly."

She sat back, looking him over. "I'm afraid I don't see what a virile young man like yourself sees in my assistant."

"Perhaps because you're not interested in women." The whole conversation made him uneasy.

"You would be surprised what I'm interested in. Would it shock you to know the love of my life was a woman?"

The fact that she used the word "love" in an unironic fashion was what truly shocked him. "Not at all. To each his own, as I like to say."

"Yes, your generation seems to be very open about your sexuality. *Fluid* is the term, I believe. I want you to spend the next few weeks truly seeing what wealth can bring to you. A smart man knows when to think with his head and not his . . . other parts. I like to keep a companion with me. My last companion was let go a few days ago. I think we would get along quite well, Brandon."

He wasn't going to pretend to misunderstand her. "I would think you would be more careful about doing something that could cause your assistant to quit. I hear she's important to the company. Companions, I assume, aren't as valuable as an assistant who truly knows the business."

A low chuckle came from her mouth. "I assure you Carly won't go anywhere until I am ready to allow her to leave. And she's not so important. Like I said, I don't believe you fully understand what I'm offering you. When we get to California, you'll see. Until then I would like complete reports on the people I mentioned."

He stood up because that seemed like an out and he was going to take it. Maybe his brother had been right and he'd been all wrong for this job. Drew likely would have played it cool, flirting a bit and leaving the discussion open.

Bran wanted out. He wanted to get out before he did something he shouldn't.

Being trapped, put in a corner, it was a trigger. Someone looking at him like he was a piece of meat. He could practically smell cigarette smoke and see that manicured hand on his chest. *Come to my room tonight. The husband won't be around. We can have fun you and I.* Trigger. Feeling helpless. Yep. He was definitely feeling that old need to put his fist through something. *It's okay, Bran. We'll get out of here tonight. You don't have to do that nasty woman. We'll leave and never look back.* All the peace Carly had brought him seemed to get buried under the panic and rage that he'd fought his whole life.

"I'll get those to you as soon as possible. I'll see you on Monday."

"Yes, you will," she practically purred.

He walked out, his hands fisting at his sides.

Carly closed the door to her townhouse and glanced at the clock. She didn't bother with the alarm. Bran would be back soon. While he'd been meeting with Patricia, she'd gone to the store. It was something she found soothing, walking the aisles and deciding on meals she could make.

It gave her time to think. She needed to tell Bran what she'd discovered. It might be absolutely nothing, but he should have a chance to look into it. If someone had murdered Patricia's former business partner, that could explain the recent attempt on her life. She would give the information to Bran and he could do what he pleased with it. In a week or so they would either find what they were looking for at Patricia's place in California or . . .

She wasn't actually sure how to complete that sentence. What would they do if they didn't find this missing file they were looking for? Would he stay on as Patricia's bodyguard? Would they work together until they found what they needed?

"I was wondering when you would get here."

She screamed and the grocery bag started falling to the floor.

Drew Lawless reached out and caught it with ease, hefting it up and setting it on her counter.

"You nearly gave me a heart attack." She had to drag air into her lungs.

Drew turned, his handsome face frowning. "I'm sorry. I thought about waiting outside but I got bored and hacking into your security system seemed like a fun way to pass the time. I'm going to have to talk to Taggart about that system. It's one his company recommends. I got through it with my tablet and an app I wrote. It's sketchy."

"So you broke in to my house for fun?"

"No. I busted through your security system for fun. The house part was because I really had to use the bathroom. After that it seemed silly to go wait in my car again."

He was too literal. "Well, now that I've had my adrenaline rush for the day, I'll go and start dinner. You can wait wherever. Bran should be home soon."

He got to the grocery bag before she could, lifting it up and heading for her kitchen. "I didn't really come to see Bran. I came to see you."

Why did that thought send a shiver down her spine? "You don't have to worry. I know the score. Bran and I are having fun with our . . . what would you call it? Cover? We're having a good time and I will graciously let him go back to his family when the job is over. You'll get your file. I'll get my freedom. Everyone wins."

"I don't think Bran will call that winning." He put the bag on her kitchen table.

She turned because she hadn't expected that from him. "What are you trying to say, Mr. Lawless?"

"Drew, please. Mr. Lawless makes me sound like my father, and I've been reminded all too often that I'm not my dad."

She softened slightly because there was definite melancholy in his voice. "All right, why are you truly here, Drew?"

He was a stunning man despite his slightly nerdy clothes. "Apparently I acted like . . . what was the word my sister used? An asshat. I'm not honestly sure what that means, but it sounds bad. I came here to say I'm very sorry."

Wow. She got the feeling Drew Lawless wasn't a man who apologized lightly. "It's all right. I know you got some upsetting news." She had more for him, but she intended to give it to Bran and let him figure out what to do with it. "I know you don't like Shelby looking into your business, but she's one of the good guys."

"I'll have to take your word for it, but I've discovered that sometimes the good guys and the bad guys are hard to tell apart." He leaned against her counter, a predatory cat lazing around her sunny kitchen. "I'm also here to talk to you about Bran."

Ah, here came the stay-away-from-my-brother speech. "No need. Like I told you, I understand the parameters of my relationship with Bran. It's casual."

Drew stared at her as though sizing her up. "Is it? You don't seem like a casual woman."

"How would you know?"

One broad shoulder shrugged. "Because despite what my brother would have you believe, I did make a study of you. I was supposed to be the one dating you."

"I don't think that would have worked out the way you think it would."

"I can be quite charming when I want to be. I simply rarely want to be. I prefer honesty. The honest truth is you're not the kind of woman who can sleep with a man and not have an emotional connection to him. Why else would you wait so long to sleep with my brother?"

"It was a whole week. Trust me, it wasn't that long." She'd put off Roger until a week before they decided to get married. Three months of dating before she made the decision to go to bed with him. She'd been thoughtful and made sure it was the right decision. It had been totally wrong, of course, but a lot of thought had gone into it.

She'd wanted Bran the minute she'd seen him. Putting him off for a week had seemed like forever and roughly three hours after they'd made love the first time, she'd been chucking her clothes and going after him again.

"You can fool yourself all you like, but you're not a woman who takes sex lightly. You haven't had a single lover since your divorce."

"Well, since he went to jail, I decided to be pickier than I'd been before." Where was he going with this?

"But you were so picky before. He was your first lover and Bran is your second."

She felt her cheeks heat with embarrassment. "And how would you know that? I didn't exactly fill that out on the dating website."

"I might have a file on you," Drew admitted. "I might have sent someone to discreetly talk to some people who know you. Not in any way they would understand as investigative. My sister has a way of making women comfortable around her. She likes Meri, by the way."

"How dare you." Anger flared through her. He was bringing her sister in this?

"I dare a lot and I thought it was important. Your sister's been used to force you to do something you didn't want to do before. I can't allow her to be used again. She's got someone watching over her. I believe you'll also find that the banking records showing she took those deposits for your husband have mysteriously disappeared. It's amazing what you can do with a couple of billion dollars and a working knowledge of how to hack a system."

She stared at him and finally understood what he'd meant before. She couldn't tell if he was a good guy or a bad guy. Sometimes good men did bad things. Sometimes good things were done by bad men to serve their purposes. "What are you trying to tell me, Drew?"

"I'm trying to explain that no matter how this plays out, your sister is in the clear. You don't have to worry about her being arrested. She's out of the game, and you can be, too, if you like. There's no longer anything keeping you at Cain Corp. I would like to offer you a job with 4L. We're looking to buy a media company. If you want your own show, we can talk about development."

She felt her jaw drop. "Why would you do that?"

"Because I think my brother is in love with you and I want you to save him. You love your sister. You would do anything for her. I would do anything for Bran. If that means buying him a wife, I'll do it. I wouldn't consider it if I wasn't sure of the type of woman you are. You care about him."

She was half in love with him, but she certainly hadn't expected to basically be offered cash for . . . what? "You want me to marry Bran? This is not how I thought the conversation would go."

He smiled slightly, the expression giving him a little levity. "I like to surprise people from time to time. And obviously you wouldn't be marrying him right away. I want you to stay close and let nature take its course."

There was a problem with the scenario. "Bran was clear. This relationship is only going to last as long as we're working together."

"Yes, he would be the 4L executive you would deal with."

Ah, so Drew assumed proximity would solve their issues. "I don't think he wants something long-term. Even if I would consider your inappropriate proposal."

He groaned. "I don't care about appropriate or inappropriate. It's the best course of action for Bran. Did he give you the speech about how he's not good for anyone?"

Embarrassment flared again. "Yes. Does he use it on all women? He's perfected it, by the way. He's got the wounded-warrior thing down."

"He believes it with his whole heart," Drew replied. "He truly thinks he's too damaged for anyone to love and I did that to him,

Carly. You're the first woman he lights up around. You're the first he's fought me over. My brother doesn't fight me over much. When I asked him to get an MBA he did it, though I knew it wasn't his passion. When I asked him to work for 4L he did it, though I'm pretty sure he hates his job. I asked him to change his name so no one would realize we were related. He signed the paperwork without a blink."

"That's why his last name is Lang? Why would you ask him . . . The revenge thing. Of course. Why did you keep it? You're the only one, right?"

Drew nodded shortly. "Yes. I'm the last legal Lawless. It's protection on several fronts. The story of my parents' death wasn't a major event. Unfortunately, domestic violence wasn't such an odd thing back then. The same as now. The company hadn't taken off. It was a minor blip on the news, but my status now drags it back into the press every now and then. I've taken to not commenting on it or my family. I've also taken to using my influence to persuade any reporter who wants to write a story about that time to change their mind and refocus."

"So you bully them." She wasn't so sure Shelby could be bullied. She could be awfully stubborn when it came to a good story.

"Only when I have to. I prefer persuasion of a positive nature. Grateful people tend be more useful than angry ones."

"Why keep the name at all?" Carly asked.

"Because I can't let my father's name die completely. When everything is done, my brothers can come back if they choose. The point is Bran doesn't care about much. He cares about you. I think he needs you."

"I'm not going to be bought, Drew, and I don't know if you're right about Bran. He's never given me any indication that he wants more than what we have right now. And honestly, it's been a week. I've basically lived with the man for a week and we just started sleeping together."

Drew didn't seem willing to back off. "And you're already emo-tionally involved. Tell me you aren't."

She wished she could. He was right about that. She hadn't been able to hold herself back. Bran made her feel alive. "He's special. He's sweet and I also feel safe with him. But I've been wrong before."

"You're not wrong about him. Look, I know he wants you out of this. I think it would be better for you to stay on at Cain Corp until we've reached the goal, but I owe Bran. He wants you out and I've made it possible. If you choose to quit, there won't be anything Patri-cia can do about it. I can provide you with a lawyer just in case, and she won't ever know it's come from me. I can have you packed up and moved to Austin in a few hours. I can do the same for Meri if you're worried about her. There's a slot for her at UT in their medical pro-gram. You never have to see Patricia Cain again."

She wasn't sure the man wasn't the devil. How much could she trust him? He was offering her almost everything she'd ever wanted. Unless she truly thought Bran was telling her the truth about their relationship being done the minute they weren't working together to bring down Patricia. This could all be a clever plan to separate her from Bran early on so his brother didn't get in too deep.

"Why? Why do you think you owe Bran?" She needed to look this man in the eye and figure out what his motivations were. He could play a long game. That was apparent. The question was, could he truly love his brother?

Drew's jaw tightened. "I left him there. I got Riley out when he was eighteen, but I left Bran there for two years while I set up the infrastructure of 4L. I told myself that he would be fine. It was only another year and we'd been apart for so long. I visited him when I could."

"How old were you at the time?"

"Twenty-one. I found Hatch and I started working toward build-ing 4L. When Riley aged out of the system, I forced him to go to college. I worked two jobs to put him through and every spare moment was spent on the original software that we built the company on. Hatch worked, too, but honestly in those early years he worked on staying sober more than anything else. It was easier to leave Bran in the system than to deal with a fifteen-year-old while I was juggling everything else."

"I can understand that."

"It was fine until I got a call one day and he'd been taken to the hospital. The official story was he and another girl from his foster care home had snuck out and were doing drugs at a local crack house when they were attacked by unknown assailants. The girl died. Bran lived, barely. I don't know how much he remembers."

Her heart ached for them all. "That wasn't your fault. You weren't exactly out partying. I understand. Not completely but I understand feeling responsible for a sibling. My mother wasn't exactly invested in our welfare. I had to raise myself and Meri for the most part. You were trying to build something for him."

"Do you know why I started 4L?"

"To build something for your family."

"Sweet, naive girl. Don't think we're so alike. I built it so I could do what I'm doing today. So I could take down the people who killed my parents. I was thinking about revenge every single night as I stayed up and formulated my code and tested it. I wanted the money and the power not for my family. I wanted it for revenge. I chose it over Bran back then and he paid the price. He's never been the same since that day. Bran was a light. That light went out and I didn't see it again until this morning when he walked out and demanded I get him a box of condoms and a doctor's appointment."

Tears pierced her eyes. "I think that means he enjoyed the . . ." Why was she trying to make less of this than she felt? Was she so afraid she couldn't admit it? "It was meaningful to me, too. You're right. I have feelings for him, but it's too soon, Drew."

"Which is why you should take the job with me and stay close and see where it goes." His voice had softened. "That's all I'm asking. You don't have to commit to anything today."

"Except to change my whole life."

"Well, it's not that great, is it? You can't say you love your boss. Bran would be your boss. You can say you kind of like him."

She shook her head. "I need a few days to think about this. I don't think it's a good idea to leave my job before we go to California. Have you thought about the fact that she might fire Bran in the wake of my walking away?"

"Of course I have. I think there's a high probability of that outcome, but I've thought a lot lately about what my father would have wanted. I think I'm getting old. Or it's the fact that all my siblings are getting married despite me. My actions and stubbornness could have cost both Mia and Riley their spouses. I don't want that to happen with Bran. I owe him too great a debt to do that to him. If she fires him, he's out and I do the rest of this alone, as it should be."

She stared at him for a moment, really seeing him for the first time. He might love his family, but he didn't know how to reach them. He was trying, trying to fix Bran's life, trying to give Bran what he thought Bran wanted. How lonely was he to bear the burden all by himself? How hard was it to watch his siblings as they let go of the one thing that seemed to propel him forward? And yet he was willing to help them leave him behind.

"I will think about your offer, but I'm not leaving Bran alone with her." She'd seen how Patricia looked at Bran. She'd only asked the question to see how Drew would answer. Patricia wouldn't fire him. She'd likely draw him in closer.

While Patricia didn't do it often, she did take a lover every now and then. Usually a lovely young man. They never lasted long and she was extremely discreet, but she seemed to enjoy them.

There was no way she was letting Patricia enjoy Bran.

Drew stared at her, his lips curling up slightly. "I thought that would be your answer. Do you know how many women would jump at the chance to have everything they dreamed of? But you want to take care of Bran."

"I told you I like him." That was all she would give this man. She got the feeling that when Drew decided he wanted something, he would go after it and use any tools his opponent was foolish enough to give him.

She moved to the table and started unloading the groceries she'd bought. She was making chicken piccata. It was simple, but she could make enough to satisfy Bran's seemingly never-ending appetite.

"Do you think you can forgive me for being mean to your reporter friend?" Drew asked.

"Probably." If he was willing to soften a little, she could do the same. "But you should know that she has no idea I know any of you."

"That's likely for the best. She's tenacious." Drew crossed his arms over his muscular chest. "And resourceful. What's she like as a friend?"

Carly held a hand up. "Not going there with you because she is a friend. If you decide to bring her in on this, you can find out for yourself." A sudden thought struck her. "Unless you're asking for personal reasons."

She could have sworn his face flushed slightly.

"No. Strictly professional."

She couldn't help but smile. It was kind of awesome to see the hot nerd king blush over a girl. "You like her."

Drew frowned. "I do not like her. She's annoying and she thinks way too much of herself. That being said, she is highly intelligent and it's always best to get to know one's enemies."

"It doesn't hurt that she's got the body of a swimsuit model and all that glorious red hair, does it?" She had him.

He cleared his throat and suddenly looked ready to change the topic. "I might have seen some pictures of her. I rather thought they were fakes. You know not everyone is honest on social media."

"She's even prettier in person," Carly said with a grin. She had a vision of Drew sitting at his computer screen staring at pictures of her sunny friend. They would be like Beauty and the Beast. Well, if the beast was a gorgeous tech billionaire. "I've watched grown men act like fumbling teenage boys just to get her to smile at them."

"Well, that explains the arrogance, doesn't it?" Drew suddenly sounded oddly prim. "She's probably never had anyone tell her no."

It was time to let him off the hook. "I left a bag in the car. Can you run out and grab it for me? The keys are on the desk by the door. I assume I'm feeding you."

"I wouldn't turn down dinner," Drew said, flashing a smile. "Otherwise I'll end up eating alone with Taggart, and he goes on and on about his old days in the CIA. He can really tell a torture story. I often think it's his roundabout way of intimidating me. If we eat here with you, he might tone it down. Might."

She could handle Ian Taggart. She'd already figured him out. He loved to talk about his family. She'd learned he had two baby girls and a wife with an entertaining past. She would ask about them. She'd heard the wife was pregnant again. "Then I should have bought more chicken. Luckily I can fill in the gaps with some pasta."

Drew nodded. "I'll go get your bag. And think about what I said. I think Bran needs you. He can get dark at times, but he seems lighter around you. I think you bring him out of it."

Drew turned and walked out.

She wasn't sure that was true. She'd never seen real darkness in Bran. Drew was shoving some of his own guilt out and seeing something that wasn't there. Still, at times she felt an aching sadness from Bran. And fear.

Drew's offer was definitely intriguing, but he was being impatient.

She and Bran had only recently started their relationship. They needed time.

Even though she was pretty sure she was already in love with him.

She glanced out the back window. From here she could see where she'd parked. There were two spaces, though she'd only needed the one for the last few years. Now she watched as Bran's car pulled in and Drew held a hand up, greeting his brother.

Bran put the car in park and she could practically read his lips.

*What are you doing here?*

Taggart got out of the passenger side of Bran's Jeep.

Yeah, she was going to need a whole lot of pasta.

Behind her she heard the front door open. It was a creaking sound that Bran swore he could fix with some WD-40.

Everyone was outside. Her heart nearly stopped as she realized she was no longer alone.

She turned and recognized the man from that night. Not the one who had talked. It was the big one who'd threatened her.

"Hello, I'm afraid I had to come back to see you," he said with a nasty smile. He raised the gun. "I'm going to have to have some more money. Or maybe we can have some fun together now that I've got you alone. Don't scream or I'll have to shoot. I wouldn't want this to be over so quickly."

She tried to reach for one of her knives, but he was on her in an instant.

*Chapter Thirteen*

Bran frowned his brother's way as he put the car in park.

"Does puppy need a leash?" Taggart asked from behind his mirrored aviators. His head was back and Bran had thought he'd fallen asleep.

"Puppy?" What was Drew doing here? If he'd come to upset Carly, they were about to have a serious fight.

He wanted it. Spending time with Patricia had gotten him tense and angry all over again.

"Yep, you're one of those puppies who looks all soft and sweet on the outside and then you go rabid and bite everyone around you. So I'll ask again. You need a leash or can you handle big brother without biting the shit out of him?"

He didn't need Taggart's sarcasm. "I'll be fine."

He pulled the keys and shot out of the car as Drew held up a hand. He was standing beside Carly's car with a bag in his other hand. "What the hell are you doing here?"

Drew cocked an eyebrow, the expression telling Bran he was unhappy with his tone. "I came to tell Carly that I've ensured her sister can't ever be prosecuted for the embezzlement her ex-husband had her involved in. And I offered her a job."

Somewhere in the back of his head, he knew that was exactly what he wanted for Carly, but in the moment, all he heard was Carly could walk away. Walk away from Cain Corp. Walk away from him. Drew was going to get exactly what he wanted. He would hire Carly and shove her somewhere far away from Austin.

"What the hell right do you have to make that decision? Wait, I get it. You make all the decisions. Whatever the mighty fucking Drew wants, he gets. You want Carly gone, you'll find a way to do it." The pressure had been building for days and he felt it so purely now.

"Hey, I don't deserve that," Drew replied with a frown. "I thought you wanted Carly out of this. I'm trying to give you what you want."

"Do you know how sick I am of your interference?" He couldn't quite stop the words from coming out of his mouth. They seemed to flow with all the anger and vitriol that had been building up. "Stay away from her. I decide when and how she gets out of this. Do you understand me? She's mine. I decide."

"What the hell has gotten into you?" Drew asked.

"Puppy needs to bite someone," Taggart said, though he sounded far more serious now. "I think he's chosen you. I would treat him with extreme caution until you get him to calm down. He had a rough time with Cain. I had to leave him in there alone with her and it seems to have triggered an episode."

"Stay out of it," Bran practically growled. There they were, the two big brothers minimizing him all over again. Bran was the weak one. He was the one who couldn't do much so they gave him the easy jobs. Bran was so fragile.

He could show them how solid he was. He didn't stay on the floor anymore. He got up time and time again. Yeah, he didn't stay down and let himself get kicked.

"Hey, why don't we go and get a drink somewhere?" Drew sounded altogether too calm. His tone had deepened to a soothing timbre.

Like he would use on a dog that was growling at him.

"Why don't you head back to the condo and leave me and Carly alone. I can handle her. If I find out you're trying to interfere with my relationship with her again, I swear I'll walk away, Drew."

He turned and started up toward the townhouse. There was a row of them with Carly's in the middle. He needed to calm down. Patricia Cain had made him feel vulnerable, small, like he was that dumbass teenager again and no one could save him. He made all the wrong moves. He wasn't going to do the same this time.

"You don't want Carly to see you like this," Drew said, coming up behind him. "Bran, we need to sit down and talk. You don't understand how crazy you look right now."

That was his perfect brother. Drew was always in control. Drew never lost it and nearly bashed a dude's head in. Drew had it easy. Need some cash? Drew could build a software program that made billions. Need advice? Drew always knew what to do. Everyone looked up to him.

They pitied Bran. They always would.

He banged through the door and stopped, taking a deep breath. Some of Drew's words managed to filter in. Carly. Carly didn't need to see him like this. Carly was sweet and lovely and she deserved to not have to deal with a rabid dog.

He wasn't sure he could control himself, so Drew was right. He should walk away. He should go and have a drink and try to bury this shit deep again. He could shove it down under a shit-ton of alcohol and tomorrow he would be a better man.

His hands were shaking as he turned. Drew was behind him. Had Carly heard him come in?

"Come on, let's go sit and talk and Carly will have dinner ready by the time we come back," Drew said reasonably.

That was when he heard it. It was a low moan, as though someone was in pain.

Taggart must have heard it, too, because the usually lazy-looking dude was suddenly stark and hawklike. He put a hand up as though to silence them.

Bran wasn't about to be silenced. If she was in trouble, he was going to help her. He took off for the kitchen, paying no mind to the sounds he heard behind him. They didn't matter. It sounded like it had come from the kitchen. He strode through the door and the sight made him stop.

Carly was pressed against the refrigerator. She was being held there by a man who had his hand wrapped around her throat. His back was to Bran and it was easy to see the asshole wasn't very observant since he obviously hadn't heard Bran come through the door.

"The way I see it, whoever gave you that million the first time will pay up again. This time to me. So we're going to head back to my place and when the asshole with the checkbook forks over another million, he can have you back. You're going to walk out of here with me or I'll kill you. Do you understand?"

Bran only understood one thing—the red mist that swamped his vision. He didn't think, didn't stop and reason his way through the problem. Carly's safety didn't even really reach his brain. All that mattered was killing the bastard who would hurt her. Who'd hurt him. In that moment it was difficult to differentiate the then and the now.

He was sixteen again, hiding in that dilapidated house, and the monster had found them. The monster had tracked them even as they ran. He'd shown up and wrapped his hand around Bran's throat and hauled him up.

No. He wasn't taking that again. Never again.

The red tinge seemed to coat everything, but Bran was far past thinking. He reached out and grabbed the man, whirling him around. He didn't see his face. Rather he saw another face. So clear. It was clear to him that this time he couldn't let anything stop him. This time he wouldn't stop. He wouldn't listen to anyone.

He wasn't sure how many times he'd hit the man. Every thud of his fist against the man's flesh was satisfying. The sight of blood welling, the sound of his strangled moan as Bran almost certainly broke his nose brought him peace. Though he continued, it was like the world slowed down and he understood it. This was a place where he was comfortable, where the rage poured out of him and he could breathe.

It made him never want to stop. Never. Not until the monster was dead and gone.

He would protect them all. He would save Mia and Mandy. He would make sure no one could hurt them again.

In his rage-addled brain, all things coalesced into one long nightmare, the shifting parts drifting over him. He could feel the heat of the fire and know his parents were burning. He could feel Mia's arms around him, begging him not to leave her. He could see Mandy's eyes, once so lovely, now vacant and dull.

He felt something warm splash on his face and somewhere in the background he heard a soft voice.

"Bran. Bran, please."

He turned, his fist raised and then he was flat on his back, his brother standing over him.

"Stop it now," Drew shouted, placing himself in front of Carly.

Taggart was busy examining the guy on the floor. "Told you puppy needed a leash. Luckily, this one's going to live. Should I call the cops?"

"Let me figure out what the hell is happening," Drew replied.

"You got time," Taggart assured him. "He won't be conscious for a while. This the mob guy?"

Bran stared up, his vision clearing and the world refocusing. What had happened? He'd known what he was doing while he was doing it, but now it seemed so far away. He'd walked in and found someone hurting Carly. He'd beaten the man and hadn't wanted to stop.

God, he'd almost hit her. She'd tried to stop him and he'd turned on her.

"Carly?"

Her face was white as a sheet, tears running down her face and making a mess of her mascara. "I'm fine. I'm good. I have to . . . I'll be back."

She disappeared out the kitchen door and he had to wonder if he had lost her forever.

Carly took a deep breath. What the hell had happened? Her blood pressure was sky-high and her hands were shaking like crazy as she buttoned up her shirt. She'd changed because she'd gotten blood on the first one. Not hers. Or Bran's. The other guy's. It had flown around while Bran was busy beating on the man.

She wasn't sure what had frightened her more—the mob guy or the look in Bran's eyes as he'd raised a fist her way.

He hadn't seen her. He couldn't have. There had been a wild look in his eyes that told her he'd been far away from her in that moment.

There was a knock on the bedroom door and then a deep voice.

"Are you all right, Carly?"

She wasn't sure she was ready to see him, but at least he sounded like Bran again. "I'm fine. I'll be out in a second."

"You've been in there for an hour. Are you sure you're all right? Should I call an ambulance?"

Had she been in here for that long? She'd closed the door and sat for a moment before deciding to clean up. She'd gone to her private bathroom, run water, and washed her face before changing clothes. And apparently time had passed quickly. She glanced at herself in the mirror. She looked pale but at least the mascara was gone.

She opened the door.

Bran looked like Bran, but she could still see him punching that man over and over. She'd begged him, pleaded with him to stop.

"Did he hurt you?" Bran didn't move closer to her.

She could still feel her attacker's hand around her neck, squeezing lightly as he'd told her how it was going to go. He would get his money or he would kill her. She'd been an easy mark. He wasn't about to let that go. "Nothing that won't heal."

Bran nodded and couldn't quite meet her eyes. "I would feel better if you had someone look you over. I could take you to the ER."

She started toward the stairs, Bran hard on her heels.

"It's not necessary and I get the feeling you haven't called the police. They would ask questions in the ER that might bring the police in. Can I ask why you chose not to call?" She walked into the living room. They seemed to be alone. The house was so quiet, almost eerily so.

"Taggart is going to take care of the situation. Apparently our guy woke up and admitted DiLuca hadn't sent him. He thought you were an easy target. I'm pretty sure he doesn't anymore."

Yes, she would be shocked if that asshole ever thought about walking into her place again. "I still think we should call the cops."

Bran frowned. "And explain that we already paid the mob a million dollars? I assure you that will likely come out."

They would also have to explain the extreme state of their intruder. While it was a clear case of defense of her person, the cops might still have questions. And reporters might get hold of the story, splashing Bran's name and face across the Internet.

Drew was busy protecting his brother and himself.

The Lawless clan would always protect their secrets. For the first time since Bran had sat down across from her at that restaurant, she realized how deep those secrets truly went. She'd understood it in intellectual terms, but these were people who'd changed their names, hid their alliances, stuck to the shadows.

"How can we be sure he won't be back?" Maybe she should move. Bran wouldn't always be here to go all Hulk-smash on the guy. If word had gotten around that she was an easy mark, why couldn't another visitor come by looking for a quick payday?

"I don't think that's going to be a problem," Bran said quietly. "I'm fairly certain Taggart is explaining the situation to Mr. DiLuca even as we speak. You won't see the man again or any of his brethren."

"Why? I would think he would simply wait until I was alone again."

"Sweetheart, DiLuca will make an example for the others to follow. The way I understand there's honor among mobsters. He wasn't coming after you for more than the debt. That guy went rogue and now he's being taken care of."

She wasn't sure she wanted to know what that meant. "I thought Roger had done something wrong again."

"I don't think so. I think he knew someone would always pay a lot of money to make sure you were safe." Bran walked over to the small bar she kept and poured out a measure of brandy.

She rarely drank anything more than wine and the occasional vodka tonic, but she had a small selection of liquor. One she'd featured as one of Patricia's entertaining tips. He turned and held out the glass. He'd used a highball glass, but she thought it wasn't the right time to explain proper barware usage.

She took the glass and a healthy swig as she realized what he was really saying. "You think DiLuca will have him killed."

Bran poured himself a nice dose of her Scotch. "I think that his employer will deal with the situation and then we don't have to involve the cops. We're supposed to leave for California in a few days. Do you want that derailed because we're dealing with the police? Calling them in would open a whole lot of inquiries we don't want to have to answer. You would have to deal with your ex-husband again."

"No, I would have to deal with the police. They would have to deal with Roger." For some reason the idea of covering it all up didn't sit well with her. She understood what he was saying, but it seemed like one more way they were protecting themselves and not her.

"It would be a mess, Carly, and we've got a lot to deal with soon." He sounded so calm and reasonable now.

Her hands were still shaking. "Don't you think this is more important?"

He sighed and leaned against the couch, looking so much like the stunning man she'd gone to bed with this morning. "No. I think this was inconsequential. It's over. I won't let anyone hurt you."

They were tiptoeing around the subject, skirting it like the coward she was. She couldn't quite bring herself to ask the question.

He set his drink down and moved toward her. Before she had a chance to step back, she found herself wrapped up in his arms.

"I know you were scared. I'm sorry. I'm so sorry that happened to you. It won't happen again because that man will never come close again. I promise."

She didn't push him away. It felt too good. The whole time she'd been alone with that man all she'd wanted was Bran's arms around her. She'd silently screamed for him to find her, save her.

She didn't really know who he was. How could she tell him that she'd been far more frightened by the man he'd become in those moments than she'd been of the one who attacked her?

She had to ask him about it. She had to. She couldn't let that go.

"Do you want me to call in some dinner? I think Taggart and Drew are planning on coming back to update us. We should have something for them to eat. We can sit down and have dinner and maybe that will make you feel more normal."

"I'm not hungry, Bran."

He kissed the top of her forehead, his lips brushing her there, and despite the fact that she'd nearly watched him kill a man, her body responded.

That was what finally made her push him away.

"We have to talk about it." She strode back to the bar and poured herself another drink.

"No, we don't. It's over. There's nothing to talk about. You're safe now."

Was she? "I begged you to stop."

He sighed, an impatient sound. "That man tried to hurt you. I'm not going to apologize for hurting him back."

"I begged you to stop, Bran. I cried and begged and you wouldn't."

"Are you seriously angry at me for beating up the asshole who wanted to kidnap you and trade you for cash?"

She took a deep breath. The truth was she was half in love with this man and maybe she was lying to herself about that percentage. She cared about him. She needed to get to the heart of what was happening with him. "Bran, you scared me."

His face softened marginally. "I'm sorry. You haven't been around a lot of violence. I'm sure it did scare you."

"Bran, *you* scared me."

Bran's hands came up, his frustration apparent. "Fine, next time someone tries to attack you I'll make sure to disable him with puppies or rainbows or something."

"Don't make light of this. I'm trying to figure out what happened." Why couldn't he understand?

"You got attacked," he shot back. "I dealt with it. That's what happened, Carly. Don't try to psychoanalyze it or make it into more than it needs to be. I got pissed off that some asshole was trying to hurt my woman."

"You almost hit me."

He rolled his eyes. "Now who's overreacting?"

She would never be able to forget that moment. "I'm not. You did. I don't know how much you remember, but at the end when I tried to get you off him, you turned and almost hit me. Drew got in the way."

His jaw went tight, his face mulish. "I wouldn't hurt you."

"You might if you thought I was someone else. Bran, where were you?"

"I was here, trying to protect you."

"I know that, but you took it too far and I think it's because of something that happened to you." She'd seen PTSD before. She'd grown up with a girl whose father had been in the Gulf War, and even decades later the man would jump every time a car backfired. His wife had left him and after a while CPS had taken her friend away because her father couldn't stay sober. When he was drunk he talked about what he'd seen, sometimes like he was living it in the moment.

He'd killed himself shortly after losing his daughter. She could still remember standing outside with Meri while everyone shook their heads and claimed they'd always known it would happen.

Bran's eyes narrowed. "You want to delve into my childhood, Carly? Want to take a look into it so you can see if I'm the kind of man you deserve? I suppose you don't want anyone nasty screwing up your perfect life, do you?"

"What is that supposed to mean?"

"I mean you're a woman who seeks perfection. You want everything to be pretty and neat and clean, and maybe I'm not that man. Maybe I'm good to go to bed with but not for anything else."

"Bran, don't be ridiculous. We're talking about what happened in that kitchen. You went crazy. You weren't really here with me."

"I suppose your white knight would have defused the situation without violence," he grumbled. "Your dream man would have been smart enough to talk the man down."

"That's not what I'm saying."

He shrugged as if it was no big deal. "Hey, baby, if you think I'm going to lay down on your couch and open my soul to you, you've got the wrong guy."

"I want you to talk to me." She watched the way his hands fisted at his sides.

This wasn't the Bran she knew, but then she had to wonder if she knew him at all. She'd fooled herself into thinking that the way a man acted correlated to who he was deep inside. A stupid mistake. One she seemed to make time and again.

"No, you want me to tell you some deep dark secret. Do you think I don't know this game, Carly? You want me to open up and let you in, and then anything I say can and will be used against me forever and ever amen."

She couldn't stand the way he was looking at her. "It's obvious something went wrong today. Can't we talk about it?"

"I don't want to talk about it. I want to move on, but you're not going to let us, are you?"

"Why are you being this way?" She couldn't help the tears that welled. She stared at him through glassy eyes.

He started to pace, like a tiger in a cage. "I had a rough day. I know you had one, too. I'm not saying you didn't. But I tried to comfort you and all you can give me is a bunch of psychological crap that leads to one thing and one thing only—you deciding I'm not good enough."

"Why would you say that?"

He stopped and put out a hand. "You know what? It doesn't matter. I made a mistake. I should have called the cops and let them handle it. Would you be standing here looking at me like I'm some kind of fucking monster if I'd done that? If I'd waited for the pros to come and save you?"

"Of course not. I'm glad you saved me, but you were so brutal."

"That's who I am." He turned and faced her, all expression gone from his handsome face. "You want the real me? That's him. Do you know why I wouldn't touch you without a condom, Carly?"

She shook her head. Maybe he was right and they were both too emotional to have this conversation. "It doesn't matter."

"I thought it didn't, but it does. You saw the man with a massive trust fund, the one who smiles and seems so easygoing. The one who holds the door open for you and tries to treat you like a princess. But that's not who I was, who I still can be. I thought you would see past that, but the first time I don't behave the way you think I should, you look at me like I'm the scum of the earth."

"That's not what I'm doing." He was being so sensitive. She needed a few answers. Didn't she deserve those?

"Oh, yes, you are. You think I don't know the look of a sanctimonious woman when I see one? Strippers. Hookers. That's why I wouldn't touch you without a condom. Do you have any idea how many hookers I've gone through?" Every word that came out of his mouth seemed laced with venom.

Or toxin. Venom was something a predator was born with, but toxins leached into a person's system. They moved slowly so the victim often didn't know they were being poisoned.

"No, I don't know," she replied quietly. "Why don't you tell me?"

"I can't, sweetheart. I lost count so long ago. It has to be at least a hundred. That's right. I've slept with a hundred women and you let me touch your near-virginal body. I'm good at that at least. I'm good at making a woman come. I didn't—" He stopped as though he'd been about to go somewhere he didn't want to go.

But toxins could be pulled from a system. They could be released. She moved toward him. "Go on. You didn't what, Bran?"

His eyes went cold. "I told you I'm not doing this."

"But if we don't talk about it, it's always there. You can't get rid of it if you don't talk about it. Please, Bran. I won't think less of you. I promise. I want to be here for you. If we're going to have any kind of a future, we have to discuss this. Drew says something happened to you."

"Drew has no right to talk about me to anyone outside my family. I told you this thing between us would last as long as we're working together. I don't intend to open my past to a woman who won't be around in a few weeks. Do I make myself plain?"

He was so cold. Bran was never cold. Bran was always warm. She nodded. "Yes, I understand. I thought . . ."

"I know what you thought. You thought I'd change my mind. You thought if you slept with me that I would change my mind about ending the relationship when the job was done." He shrugged. "I was never anything but honest with you. I told you what our boundaries were."

He had been honest with her, but she was fairly certain he wasn't being honest with himself. Not at all. He was being cruel and that wasn't who this man was.

Or was it? Had she seen only his beauty and not the harsh truth underneath? Or was he putting walls up to protect himself because that was what he'd learned to do all those years ago?

"Maybe we don't need boundaries."

Bran shook his head. "Don't make more of this than it is. Be smarter than that, Carly. You were right to be afraid of me. The only thing I love more than spending time with hookers is beating the shit out of people. I like it. I crave it. I go out and look for it. Drew's done a good job in the last couple of years covering it up, but I've spent a lot of time cooling my heels in jail. How do you like that? You seem to have a type. Maybe I was wrong and you do want me. You seem to enjoy getting down in the mud, don't you?"

There was a knock on the door or she was sure Bran would have continued spewing his bile and vitriol. Drew and Taggart stood there in the doorway.

"Hey," Drew said quietly. "Are we interrupting something?"

Bran's expression went blank again. "Nothing. Nothing at all. I'll be back late, Carly. Leave the blankets on the couch for me and set the damn alarm."

He strode out the door without another word.

Drew turned to her. "What the hell happened?"

She stared at the door where Bran had disappeared. She wasn't entirely sure what had happened, but it felt bad. It felt like the end. "I wanted him to tell me why he'd done that."

Drew's eyes closed briefly. "I told you he won't talk about it. You can't push him. He's not dangerous. He needs time to come down. I'll go and talk to him. He'll be okay. You sit tight and don't judge him harshly."

He ran out after his brother.

And she was left alone with a massive hulk of Viking man.

"Yeah, they pretty much did that. Uncomfortable, huh?" Taggart locked the door. "You know what makes everything better? Dinner. I've had to deal with mafia assholes and that creepy fucking chick and rabid puppies, and did anyone offer me a French fry? Nope. This evening is going to go so much more quickly if you cook and I eat. And you don't cry. Because I don't deal well with that. Should I get my wife on the phone? Or maybe you have some girlfriend you call when your boy toy goes all shitty on you. Could you ask her to bring some burgers or something?"

Her heart ached and she wanted to sit down and cry, but what the hell was she supposed to do? She turned toward the kitchen and began to do the only thing that made sense. She started to cook. She would find solace in it. Cooking made sense to her. She put the right ingredients in and they made something new, something that was more than the sum of its parts. Something that fed and nourished. She could do that.

The door to the kitchen swung open.

"You know he won't bother you anymore," Taggart said quietly.

"Yes, I heard you had him murdered."

Taggart leaned against the counter, seemingly unworried about her accusation. "I didn't have anyone killed. I merely presented his boss with the situation at hand. I happen to know a couple of mafia guys. Mine are all Russian but they tend to have the same mentality. The boss has to maintain a level of trust or people will turn him in to the cops. Mafia dons are not your typical blackmailers. They take what they believe they're owed and walk away. He promised me he's done with you. He now understands you're no longer connected to your ex-husband."

She filled a pot with water and set it on the stove to boil. "That's nice to know."

He was silent for a moment and it didn't do her any good. It made her sink into her own misery. What had gone wrong? She'd been scared. She should have been able to talk to him about it. How could they have anything real if he couldn't talk to her?

She stared at the pot. The water shimmered as the heat started to reach it. According to Bran, they didn't have anything at all. They ended the minute the job did, and it actually sounded like they'd ended the moment she'd questioned him.

There wasn't anything she could do if he wouldn't admit something was wrong. She would be beating her head against a concrete wall.

"He likely doesn't want to be a rabid puppy."

She clenched her teeth and then forced herself to relax. "Don't call him that."

"Why?" Taggart asked quietly. "It's what he is. I don't mean any disrespect by it. I've known a lot of men like Bran. They're good men, but they saw too much, experienced something horrible. Sometimes many horrible things. Things they don't think they can come back from. So they smile. They're happy puppies most of the time. They want to fit in. They want to be petted and adored. And then something happens and they bite the hand that feeds them."

"It's not important. It was only a fling. I made too much of it." She found the pasta and set it to boil. Normally she would prefer to make her own, but she rarely had time for it. She found the lemon juice she kept on hand and butter and started her sauce.

"If that's true, then it's good you know who he is now." Taggart sat down at the kitchen table and started playing with his phone.

"He's not a bad man." She couldn't handle the silence. Even talking to someone she didn't know was better than thinking about what Bran had said to her.

"I didn't say he was but he's also not as harmless as Drew would have you believe. He would have killed that man tonight."

Her stomach sank. "You can't be sure."

"Like I said, I've dealt with guys like Bran. They're good men, but they've got something inside them that won't let them find peace. They hold what happened to them inside. They'll tell you it's their burden, but they hoard it like it's gold. I'm sure my shrink friend would tell you it's a way to not admit what happened to themselves. But I think they're scared. We don't always see things logically. We place blame where there is none to be had and refuse to call out the truly guilty parties even when just saying it out loud would make things so much easier."

He was far deeper than he looked on the surface. Maybe all men were. She'd lived in a world of the superficial for so long she'd forgotten what it meant to look past the surface.

"What happened to your rabid puppy?" She kept stirring even though the world was seen through a wall of tears. She couldn't seem to help them.

"Which one?" Taggart chuckled. He sobered quickly. "Some of them are still out there. Still smiling when it means nothing and snarling and attacking anyone who gets close. My brother was one of the happiest people I've ever known. Then something happened. Something awful and it damn near killed him. I think he would be one of those puppies today if not for one thing."

"What was that?"

"The right woman."

"I can't fix him," Carly said quietly.

"No, you can't. But you can make him want to fix himself. You can give him a reason to change if you want. Or you can walk away and protect yourself. It's your choice. He won't make it easy for you. He'll bite and scratch and he'll do it with words, and those hurt so much fucking more than claws and fangs."

Her choice. It should be simple. She should walk away. She'd been hurt too many times. The last few years she'd been so numb, and there had been a certain peace in that.

Suddenly Taggart was behind her, offering her a tissue. "I can stir that if you like. My brother's a chef. I've learned a few things."

She stepped away and tried to dry her eyes.

The big guy worked the wooden spoon like he knew what he was doing. "Think about it. I know from your files that you haven't had an easy time."

"I should walk away." Even though it made her heart hurt to think about it.

"What would you tell your sister to do?" Taggart asked. "Sometimes that's an easier way to look at it. You practically raised her. When I think about things now, I ask myself what I would want for my girls. If they came to me and asked what to do, what would I want for them? Not the outcome. You can't predict the outcome. So all you can really do is ask how you would want them to behave. Would you tell your sister to be smart and cut her losses?"

"It would depend on whether she loved the man or not." On whether the man might be the love of her life.

"And if she loved him? Would you tell her to be safe?"

If Meri was standing in front of her, tears in her eyes, what would she say? "I would tell her to be brave."

"Then you have your answer."

Had Bran meant what he'd said? Or had it all been a way to distance himself, to hoard that pain so he didn't have to face it?

Was she the woman who could make him want to fix himself?

The idea of him always being alone made her heart ache and she realized she was in love with him. Truly and fully, and there was no going back. She realized it because she became so certain that his happiness was more important to her than her own.

It didn't matter that he might not love her back. It was all right. Her love was meaningful. If she turned away, she made it less.

Carly took a deep breath, her decision made. "I'll take over again. Why don't you grab the salad from the fridge?"

He frowned. "Salad?"

Men. "Yes, there's also a lemon tart in there."

He groaned. "Women. You always draw us in with the good stuff and then make us eat salad. Have I told you the story of how I got a terrorist to talk just by feeding him kale?"

It was going to be a long night. She stirred her sauce and hoped Bran was safe out there.

# Chapter Fourteen

Bran finished his . . . he wasn't sure how many it was anymore. He finished the shot and slammed it down, nodding to the bartender to pour him another. His anger flared when he noticed the bartender's eyes drift to the left as though waiting for permission to fill the request.

"Hey, I'm a damn adult and if I want another shot, I'll take one. Do you understand?"

The bartender sighed and poured another measure of what had to be the nastiest rotgut whiskey in Central Florida. It burned down Bran's throat, but that was kind of what he wanted.

He needed to be reminded that while his brother might afford him the finer things, he was still rotgut whiskey waiting to wreck someone's life.

"I believe he's trying to ensure you don't kill yourself with alcohol poisoning right here at his bar, brother," Drew said. "They tend to frown on that sort of thing."

Naturally he couldn't be left alone to drink himself to death in peace. He had big brother watching out for him. Drew had slid into the car beside him before Bran had thought to lock him out. Now he was fairly certain Drew had stolen the keys to the Jeep and he would be driven home by his perfect, sober brother. Drew would be able to sleep well knowing he'd taken care of his idiot sibling.

Self-hatred welled inside him.

Why had he said that shit to Carly? Who the hell had been talking? The words had flowed out of his mouth like noxious gas. He'd stood there and spewed a total load of bullshit her way because he would rather be the bad guy than the pathetic asshole who couldn't handle his own rage.

She wanted to talk. He didn't do that. If she knew . . . Well, it didn't matter now. She didn't ever have to know what a piece of shit he was, and that was the way he wanted it.

He'd made her cry, made her afraid. God, that hurt like nothing he'd felt before. Seeing her cry and knowing he was the reason for it left him hollow.

"What time is it?" Not that he cared, but he had to go back to her place and he didn't want to wake her.

Would he even remember the damn code?

"Late," Drew said quietly, a mug of coffee in front of him. "But it's all right. Taggart's with her."

Shit. He'd left her with that snarky dude. Another thing she likely wouldn't forgive him for.

"Want to tell me why you chose this place instead of your usual?" It was the most words Drew had said since he'd gotten in the car.

Drew tended to know when he didn't want to talk. Unlike Carly.

"It was close." A lie, but then he was good at those tonight.

"Nope. The closest place was the strip club we went to the night after you met her. You always go to strip clubs. Sometimes I think it's because you need to feel as seedy and dirty as possible."

"Maybe I like to look at naked women. Did you think of that, Mr. Psychiatrist?"

"I think you didn't go to a strip club because you knew that would hurt Carly."

He chuckled, though there was no humor in the sound. "I told Carly how many strippers I've slept with earlier tonight. I think she knows."

Drew cursed under his breath. "Why would you do that?"

He shrugged. "She should know. She thinks I'm something I'm not."

"What do you want to do, Bran? What do you want me to do?" Drew sounded past tired. "I thought I was doing what you wanted when I offered her a job. I thought you wanted her out. I thought if I gave her a position at 4L, then maybe she would hang around and you two could see if it would work."

That was where Drew was wrong. "It can't."

"Why?"

"I'm not the kind of man she needs. You saw what happened to-night. She freaked out because of that little fight? What happens when I lose it? It's better to let it go now. I would disappoint her in the end." He got to his feet and motioned for the check.

"Already taken care of," the bartender replied with a sigh of what sounded like relief.

"Of course it is." He couldn't even take care of his drunken stupor. Naturally Drew had to arrange that for him. He turned and started toward the door.

His brother followed after him. "Let's go back to the condo. I'll text Taggart and we'll pick him up on our way out."

And leave Carly alone? He was drunk, but he wasn't stupid. "I'm going back ho— To her place."

He would sleep on the couch. It was his punishment for fucking everything up. He could have had another couple of weeks. It wouldn't have lasted much longer than that, but he wished like hell he'd had those weeks with her.

"She tastes like sunshine."

A hand steadied him. "I'm sure she does, which is a good reason to not let her see you like this. She's seen enough for one night."

But then she would be alone. Despite the fact that they'd taken care of one of her problems, he couldn't stand the thought of leaving her alone. "Someone tried to kill her last night."

"No, someone tried to kill Patricia."

"We don't know that for sure. Carly is the one who walked through that door," he said stubbornly. The ground seemed uneven beneath his feet, but then, wasn't it always? When had he ever had sure and steady ground to walk on?

Whiskey made him way too melancholy. Or then, maybe it was the fact that Carly had broken up with him.

Not in so many words, but all he'd needed was the look on her face to know it was over before it had really begun.

"What went on between the two of you tonight?" Drew asked, opening the passenger side of the car.

Bran didn't argue. He couldn't drive. He'd been stupid to take the car out at all, and if Drew wasn't here he would have to have called a cab. He definitely wouldn't have called Carly. No way. He was going to sneak in quietly and try to act like they were nothing but partners again in the morning.

Try to pretend like he'd never had his mouth on her, never ran his tongue over her skin down to her feminine flesh. Never watched her as she came, her whole body tightening under his.

Yeah, he was going to make that happen. He would have to pretend because he wouldn't ever forget her.

"She decided she didn't know me well enough. She thought she did, but the events of the evening changed her mind." At least he wasn't slurring. He'd managed to stop before he did. He could sort of walk. All he had to do was make it from the car to the couch.

"I think you should come home, Bran."

"No. I have a job to do." He wasn't going to let this get the best of him. He could be better. He wasn't going to let everyone down. He'd lost Carly. He wasn't going to go back to Austin with his stinking tail between his legs. "Patricia Cain hired me. Not you. She wants me."

That was part of the problem. He shuddered thinking about it.

The door slammed and then Drew was sliding in beside him, turning the key and moving them toward Carly's pretty townhouse with its yellow curtains and soft pillows. Everything about the woman was inviting.

Tired. He was so damn tired of fighting and yet he couldn't seem to stop.

"Give me one good reason not to pull the plug on all of this," Drew muttered. "I think I made a horrible mistake. Riley was right. This isn't what our father would have wanted. Not if it means losing you."

"You can't make me come home."

"I can have you kidnapped and taken to that same freaking island where we stuffed Ellie's sister," Drew said under his breath.

"I don't want to go home." He wanted to be with Carly. Even if he wasn't *with* Carly. Even if she looked at him like he was the scum of the earth. He wanted to see this thing through. If Drew called the mission off, he wouldn't see her again. She would take a job somewhere or that fucker Kenny Jr. would find a way to build a network around her and she would probably get married to someone who didn't carry around a monster inside him. The next time he saw her she would be on TV talking about her perfect fucking husband and all the kids they had.

He would go on the way he always had. He would laugh and pretend he wasn't decaying on the inside until he couldn't stand it a second longer and then he would take his rage out on some asshole. He'd managed to make sure whoever it was deserved it so far. He placed himself in the perfect position to find men who abused women and then he let his fists fly.

What if one day he wasn't so careful? What if one day he hurt someone who didn't deserve it? Or he went too far and Drew's money and power couldn't get him out of it?

Would he wind up in jail like Carly's first husband?

It was enough of a reason to stay away from her.

Before he knew it, Drew was pulling into the small parking lot outside her row of townhomes. He could see the light was still on downstairs. Taggart was probably sitting up, pissed as hell that he'd been kept waiting.

He managed to make his way out of the car and up the steps to the street.

"You're going to kill me, Bran."

He stared at her door. "Not if you don't let me. Have you thought that maybe you should let me go? I wonder about it a lot. I know you put up with my shit because you feel guilty, but this was never about you, Drew. This was always about me. Maybe if Mom and Dad hadn't died I wouldn't have had to know myself so well. I wouldn't have seen who I am deep down, but it wouldn't change it. It would just hide it. I'm not like you and Riley and Mia."

"What the hell is that supposed to mean?"

He shook his head. He didn't want to talk about this shit. He hadn't talked about it with Carly. He sure as fuck wasn't going into it with Drew. Years and years had gone by and Drew didn't know the full extent of how fucked up he was, and Bran wasn't about to tell him now. He'd already had one person he cared about look at him like he was a monster. He wasn't going for the double play.

How long would it be before he got her out of his head? He'd lied to Drew about the strip club. He hadn't gone because none of those women were Carly. He'd slept with them because they'd typically seen the darker side of life and accepted him for what he could give them—a good time, some cash to help them out, violence against the men who'd done them wrong.

Carly would want more. She would want all of him, and he'd proven it wasn't enough.

He made his decision. He would walk in and get his things and let her alone. He would do what Drew wanted him to do. He would go home to Austin and not look back. He would let whatever happened happen.

"If I leave with you will you look out for her?" He felt a little dead on the inside in a way that had nothing to do with the liquor.

"Yes," Drew said quietly. "I'll make sure she's safe."

Bran nodded and opened the door.

The house was as welcoming as ever, the soft light illuminating the living room. She hadn't set up the couch. There was no blanket or pillows laid out for him. No welcome for him here anymore.

"I think you cheat," a deep voice said.

"No, I'm better at this than you," a bright, familiar one replied. "I should have taken your bet. I would have all your money at this point, Tag."

Drew turned off the alarm as the kitchen door swung open and Taggart walked through, shaking his head.

"Well, I'm glad you didn't because I would have to explain to my wife how I lost at poker to a decorator." He nodded Bran's way. "You okay to stay here or should I?"

He was about to explain what was going to happen when Carly walked in. She'd changed into pajama bottoms and a T-shirt, her hair up in a bun and slippers on her feet. She looked so soft he wanted to hold her, but he'd given up that right when he'd been so vicious with her.

"He's fine," Carly said before shaking her head. "All right, he smells like a bar, but he'll be fine tomorrow, in the strictest sense of the word. Y'all head back. We have an early morning and I need to get him to bed."

What? How much had he had? Had he passed out?

Carly's hand slipped into his. "Can you make it up the stairs?"

"The couch is down here."

"Adults sleep in beds, Bran. Let's go to bed. I think you're the one who's going to have to rest all day tomorrow. We have to be at work bright and shiny Monday morning, and you can't look like you drank your way through a liquor store. Or a strip club."

"No strip club," he said quickly. "No. Just a bar. There weren't even women there."

Drew nodded beside him. "I'm pretty sure it was a gay bar. You know I've always thought I would do well in one. I was right. I got hit on three times." He looked Carly's way. "So you can handle this one?"

"I can," Carly assured him.

Something wasn't right. "We were fighting."

"Yes," she agreed. "Now we're not. Now we're going to bed."

"What about tomorrow?" Was she planning to hit him with questions all over again tomorrow?

"We'll deal with that as it comes. For now, come to bed with me." Her hand squeezed his.

And he forgot all about what he'd promised Drew. He consigned Austin to memory because there was no way he would go there when Carly was offering him something else. He let her say good-bye to his brother and Taggart, managed to remain upright while she locked the door and set the alarm. She got him upstairs and out of his clothes, tucking him in before turning out the lights and climbing in beside him.

A warm hand brushed over his chest. "Everything's going to be all right, Bran."

He reached up and put his hand over hers, holding it close to his heart as her warmth started to seep into his skin. "Stay with me."

She didn't reply, but the press of her body against his was answer enough. For now. He would take what he could get.

Bran gave in and let himself sleep.

Carly looked up from the stove as Bran walked in. She gave him a smile, remembering how he'd held on to her the night before. His arms had wound around her and he'd whispered to her.

*Stay with me.*

She hadn't answered him, but emotion had welled deep inside her.

*You can make him want to fix himself.* Taggart's words had floated into her brain in that instance. She'd thought about them all night. She couldn't fix Bran. No person could fix another one. But she might be able to help him see he could get better.

"Good morning." His words sounded gravelly, as though his throat was sore.

"Did you take the aspirin I left for you?" She'd set the beginnings of her hangover cure by his side of the bed.

He settled himself in the chair. "I drank the entire bottle of water, too."

She turned and poured the second part of the treatment. Good Colombian coffee. "Drink this while I get your breakfast ready."

His eyes were hooded, wary as he watched her. "Why are you doing this?"

She'd thought about it all night long. Once she'd made her decision it had been easy to justify it. "Because you're worth the trouble, Bran."

"I'm not. I really did all those things I told you I did. I wasn't playing around with you."

She turned back to her bacon. The bacon was rational. Bran was not because he was a bit of a nut job. That might have scared her off the day before, but she'd decided. She'd decided on which future was worse—a future where she was safe and hadn't tried with him, or one where she knew she'd done everything she could to make it work with a man she loved.

She was being brave.

"You were a manwhore," she replied. "How many girls did you sleep with last night?"

He sighed. "None, Carly. I went out and I got drunk because we had a fight."

And that had rocked his world. She'd been startled and frightened by his behavior. His pessimist brain had gone to the worst possible place.

Something deep and dark had happened to Bran. Something that made him think he wasn't worthy of being loved. It made him wary of conflict and always looking to be the one who got pushed away.

"Then drink your coffee and we'll deal with it."

"It doesn't change anything," he said, sorrow in his voice. "I'm still not willing to give you what you want."

"I'm not asking you to bare your soul. I'm asking you to love yourself enough to work through some issues, but if you can't, I won't toss you aside." She did need to know one thing. How far was he willing to push this? If she backed off slightly, would he take that? Or was he going to be stubborn? "Unless you meant everything you said last night."

He moved fast for a man with what had to be a hell of a hangover. "I didn't. Baby, I didn't mean any of it. Please forgive me."

That was what she wanted. He was standing behind her, his front pressed to her back, his arms winding around her waist. "I forgive you. I hope you can be kinder to me in the future."

His head tilted forward, nestling in the crook of her neck. "I'm so sorry I scared you."

Puppy needed affection. She frowned. She had to stop thinking of him like that. "I'm all right, but you know we're going to have to talk about it at some point."

He stiffened. "And if I can't?"

"I don't know." She wasn't sure she could stay long-term with a man who wouldn't talk to her about the important things. She would always have to be wary, always worried that he could explode again.

He moved back and she heard the chair scuff against the floor. "I thought about going back to Austin last night. I don't think I can do this. It bothers me being around her."

Hey, he was talking about something. It wasn't what she wanted to talk about, but it suddenly felt like a breakthrough. She pulled the bacon out and left it to rest for a few minutes. "Are you talking about being near Patricia? That's what bothers you?"

"Yes."

One word. She would have to pull it out of him. She set a plate in front of him. What she'd decided the night before when Bran had gone to sleep had been that he needed normalcy. He needed routine. He found comfort and affection in knowing what happened next. She was certain that even in his adult life there had been an enormous amount of chaos. Drew had spent his time building a company and then Bran had worked there. Long hours. He needed domesticity. Her puppy needed to be domesticated.

One day she was going to tell Ian Taggart what a bastard he was for planting that idea in her head. She couldn't seem to make it go away.

"Do you want toast?"

He looked up at her with wary eyes, as though she was going to kick him at any moment. "Sure."

"I've got some apricot jam."

"I like grape." He said it sullenly and then shook his head. "Apricot is fine."

Her heart clenched. It was the first time he'd told her what he preferred. He'd spent a lifetime bending, giving in to what was available, what was easy. She fought back tears.

"The good news is I have grape, too." She turned away so he wouldn't see how close she was to crying. "You will find I have jellies and jams of all kinds. Some of them I made myself. Every now and then we get invited to fruit farms and I get to come home with some truly amazing things."

"I can eat the apricot," he said quietly.

She put the grape in front of him. How often in his life had he settled because he thought he was still in a position where his wants and needs didn't matter? His selflessness was part of his charm, but it was also part of his problems. She put a hand on his head. "I know you can but I like giving you what you want. It makes me feel good, so would you please try my grape jelly?"

"All right." Again he sounded wary, as though her every word was a trap.

One thing down. "Now I need to cook the eggs. You always eat whatever I eat. I would like to know how you like your eggs, Bran. Please don't fight me. I want to know."

"I like them over medium."

She scrambled them most of the time but that was because she rarely cared. It was a simple switch to make in order to accommodate him. It seemed to her no one accommodated Bran, or rather they did it in all the wrong ways. Drew indulged Bran's dark side because he thought he was the reason for it. It was time to see if indulging his daily needs made him more willing to open up.

Or she was fooling herself if she thought that taking care of a man meant he would come to need her so much he would give up his determination to keep his secrets.

She cracked the eggs. Either way, they had a little time together.

"The jelly is good," he said, sitting back in his chair.

"I'm glad." Maybe she could show him it was okay to talk about it, to open himself up because she was the right woman.

At least she prayed she was. She intended to take the time to find out.

"What bothered you about Patricia? Specifically yesterday." She tiptoed around the subject, keeping her voice calm as though they were doing nothing more important than talking about the weather.

"She made it plain that I was welcome to spend some private time with her," he said, his voice tight.

Carly felt her whole body stiffen. Anger flared through her, but she fought to tamp it down. "I will make it very plain to the creepy bitch that she should keep her damn hands off you."

Yeah, she might not try hard. She walked toward her cellphone, ready to get Patricia on the phone and explain exactly how an Alabama redneck defended her man.

She found herself being pulled down onto Bran's lap as he chuckled.

"Whoa, there. You don't need to defend my honor. It's all right. I can handle her." For the first time since the incident the day before, he sounded like her Bran.

"Or I could punch her in her surgically perfected nose and take care of it."

He hugged her tight. "I think you would get fired and then I would be alone with her. Let's not do that."

She sighed and ran her hand through his hair. "She won't force you, not physically."

He was quiet for a moment. "It reminds me of something that happened in foster care. I wasn't molested or anything. One of the women made it plain I was welcome in her bed. I felt helpless and I don't like feeling helpless."

"You didn't . . ." She wasn't sure how to ask.

"I didn't, but it led to something worse. Can we have breakfast? I just want to have a nice morning with you."

She kissed his forehead and got up to finish the eggs.

It was a start.

*Chapter Fifteen*

One week later, Carly looked over at Bran and wished they were alone on the jet. They were almost alone, but the flight attendant smiled and asked if they would like a drink now that they'd reached their cruising altitude.

Bran smiled. "I wouldn't turn down a beer."

The flight attendant gave him a radiant smile, as though she knew Bran was one of those men who would always take care of a woman. That's what women tended to do around Bran. It was something she'd noticed in the last week since he'd become such a regular sight at Cain Corp. All women blushed around Bran. They smiled and then whispered to each other behind their hands as they watched him walk away.

She hated them all. And she definitely hated not having Bran to herself.

For a solid week Patricia had done everything she could to keep them apart. She would send Carly in one direction while she took Bran in another. Typically, Carly would be with the boss for much of her day, but Patricia now seemed to only need Bran around her.

She would send Carly home and keep Bran at the office until late at night, despite the fact that she had a nightshift guard.

Carly and Bran hadn't made love since that first day. She would wake up with his arms around her, but then he would get a call and they would be forced to head to the office.

She really hated her boss. They'd made absolutely no progress in the week since the incident and now it was almost over.

They were almost over.

"I'm fine," she told the flight attendant. Somehow the occasion didn't call for champagne.

"Bring her a glass of brandy, the good stuff," Bran instructed before turning back to Carly. "You're too tense. It's going to be all right."

She nodded and glanced out the window. They would be over Alabama soon. She wouldn't be able to see the small town she'd fled but she'd flown over it a hundred times in the last few years.

When he said it would be all right, he was talking about the plans for California. He wasn't talking about them. He'd seemed oddly calm the last week, as though he hadn't minded the distance between them. Maybe it was true. Maybe he'd been happy she hadn't been able to poke him and dissect him in the last week. He would kiss her from time to time, but she didn't feel the passion coming from him anymore.

It was like they were going through the motions until the inevitable end.

Somehow she'd thought he would try harder.

"Here you go," the flight attendant said, placing the drinks on the table in between them.

She left it there. She knew she should smile and play along, but she couldn't. It was easier to focus on work. As the flight attendant smiled brightly Bran's way before retreating, Carly popped open her laptop and started going through the menus again. It wasn't anything she hadn't seen a million times already, but it gave her something to focus on.

And seating charts. There were three dinners planned in the next week alone, and that didn't include the big party to celebrate the new season. Seating charts had become the bane of her existence. It was always difficult to figure out how to seat people with grudges against almost everyone in existence. If there was a nastier group of human beings than Patricia's LA crowd, Carly had yet to meet them.

So many egos. So many grudges.

"Hey, can't you do that later?" Bran asked.

"Is there something you need?" She didn't look up. It hurt too much to look at him these days.

"Yes, but I think I'm going to need some privacy to get it," he muttered before unbuckling his seat belt and standing up. "I'll be right back."

She wondered briefly what he was talking about and then went back to her dinner menus. Thursday night required a vegan option. One of Patricia's guests this season was an up-and-coming young actress who expounded on the health benefits of veganism, though she mostly drank her calories. Still, she would be angry if there wasn't an attempt made at gourmet veggies despite the fact that she would eat so little of it.

It seemed like feeding him was all Bran let her do these days. Oh, he was solicitous enough. He drove her to work every day, and then if he had to stay late, he made sure she had a ride or took a break and drove her himself. He held her hand. He acted like a boyfriend at the office and was kind to her at home.

But he didn't throw her down on the bed and find a way to get inside her.

Maybe he was bored. She didn't have a lot of experience. She'd tried to give him what he needed. It had seemed incredible to her, but what if it had been so-so for him? He had a ton of experience. Maybe he hadn't wanted to do it again. Maybe he was satisfied that they were going to do the job and then they would shake hands and say good-bye.

She'd thought he'd been genuinely relieved that she hadn't pushed him that morning a week before. She'd thought it was so they could continue their relationship, but apparently it was so they could continue the mission.

That was okay. It was fine. It had been foolish to think he would want her long-term anyway. He was all . . . well, he was Bran, and every female eye focused on him when he entered a room. She was her and that was that.

She felt him sit back down in his seat. She had to wonder if he was miffed that he'd had to come with her instead of flying out with the rest of the team. He seemed to have made friends with a couple of the guys. When she saw him he was always talking to someone, always joking around. He'd probably made more friends in the short time he'd been with the company than she had in all her years there. Patricia was flying out in the big, even more luxurious Jones Unlimited jet. It would have had even more pretty flight attendants for Bran to flirt with.

"Hey, you want to put away that computer?"

She didn't look up. She was fairly certain she was flushed and probably looked emotional. "I have a ton of work to do before we get to LA. If you like, I think there's a media system with movies. I'm sure they'll set you up."

"I don't want to watch a movie. I want to watch you. I'm going to watch you whether you like it or not, so you should decide if I'm watching the G-rated version of Carly or if I'm going to get some porn in. I personally vote for the pornographic Carly."

She looked up at him. "What?"

He was giving her that crazy, sexy smile of his. "Take off your clothes."

Now she was flushed for an entirely different reason. "Bran, I'm not doing that here, and why exactly are you asking me?"

His eyes narrowed slightly. "First, I didn't ask. And I want you to take your clothes off because it's difficult to fuck you while you're dressed. So take your clothes off."

She slammed the laptop shut. "You haven't touched me all week."

"What are you talking about? I kiss you all the time."

"That's nothing but cover."

He frowned. "Cover?"

"Yes, our cover story. You've kissed me when it was necessary. You've held my hand when other people were watching."

A long huff came out of his mouth, his frustration apparent. "I didn't think about the fact that people were watching." He shook his head. "Or maybe I did. I don't know. I took advantage where I could."

He hadn't taken advantage at all. "You don't have to pretend, Bran. I'm going through with it."

"Pretend?"

Was he obtuse? "Yes, pretend. We don't have to fake being lovers here. It's all right. You haven't touched me in a week. I get it. The physical part isn't something you want anymore. Maybe you never did."

"I wasn't sure you wanted me to. You've treated me like I'm fragile ever since that night. Or like you're scared of me. I was hoping it was mostly because you thought I needed time. I don't, by the way. My dick has been hard all fucking week, but she kept me at the office late enough that you were already in bed by the time I came home." He studied her for a moment. "I've been careful because I know I scared you that night. I don't want you to be scared of me."

Should she believe him? Or had he gotten a little horny? She was so confused. She wanted to believe him. He'd told her once that he wouldn't lie to her and he hadn't. He'd been honest about pretty much everything so far. With the singular exception of the night they'd fought, they got along spectacularly well.

The trouble was she didn't want to simply get along with the man.

He leaned forward. "Carly, you can't think I don't want you. This week has been hell on me. Do you think I wanted to be kept away from you? Do you think I wanted to stay close to her?"

His expression didn't change but there was something about the way he said it that made her soften. They'd lost a week to work and circumstance. Was she going to give up more time because she was stubborn?

"I missed you."

His hand came out, covering hers. "I missed you. You have no idea how much."

He tugged on her hand, drawing her out of her chair and into his lap. His arms went around her, his head on her shoulder.

For the first time in a week, she felt safe. She knew she shouldn't, but just being close to him felt so damn right. She leaned into him, giving up the fight. The truth was she didn't care why he hadn't touched her. It didn't matter as long as he did it now.

Her whole body had come to vibrant life the minute he touched her. She could feel her skin start to hum as though it knew soon it would be touched, caressed, and loved.

"I thought you didn't want me anymore." Somehow it didn't seem right to lie to him when she was in his lap, so close to him. It was easier to open up and let down the mask she wore. She didn't want to wear it with him. Not ever.

His lips found her jawline, kissing along the way. "Never. I want you every second of the day, baby. I've held back because I'm the one who fucked up. I wanted you to come to me, but you didn't, and then we weren't alone unless you were so tired you could barely keep your eyes open. Do you think I didn't want to wake you and roll you over and slide inside you? It's all I think about all day long. I'm supposed to be watching and observing the target and all I think about is how good it feels to fuck you."

His hand slid along her thigh, pushing her skirt up and finding naked flesh. Everywhere he touched turned aching hot and wanting. She could feel herself starting to get slick for him.

This was what she'd missed, the deep connection she felt the minute he laid a hand on her. She wasn't sure she could resist him even if he said all those horrible things again. He might be the weakness she couldn't overcome.

"I want it to be more than a fuck." If she was being honest she was going all the way.

He sighed against her. "It's more. Baby, that's just a word. I'll call it making love if you want. I can call it anything you want."

She didn't want to hear the word *love* out of his mouth unless he meant it. "Kiss me."

His hand moved up her thigh, inching closer to her core. "I used to hate going to sleep because I would have bad dreams. Do you know what I dream about now? I dream about you. I dream about you underneath me, you on top of me, you beside me. No one but you. All those dreams are filled with you. I hated the last week. I hated walking by your desk and not being able to haul you into an empty office somewhere and flip your skirt up and pound out all my frustration on your pretty ass. Every time you would look my way, my dick would get hard."

How did he do this to her? Two minutes before she was feeling sorry for herself and ready to declare their relationship dead, and now all she could think about was that hand cupping her over her undies. He slid a finger over her, brushing against her clit and making her shiver. She could feel the hard line of his erection underneath her backside and it made her mouth water.

His finger slipped over her clit again, a bit more pressure this time. She let her head fall back against his broad shoulder as he used his powerful legs to spread her wide, giving him complete access to her pussy.

Alarm bells rang but they were in the distance. Her mind came up with a million and one reasons why this was a bad idea, but she stuck on the only one she could validate.

"Bran, we're not alone."

His tongue traced the shell of her ear. "We're as alone as we need to be. Our nice flight attendant is currently flirting with the captain, and then she'll be in the kitchen for an hour. I let her know we wouldn't be needing anything from her for a good long while."

"Do you think she knows what we're doing?" She should get off his lap, but every time she thought to give it a try, his finger rubbed her again and her eyes unfocused.

His free hand moved up to cup a breast. "Does she know we're going to fuck? Yes, I think she's got a pretty good idea."

"But you didn't say anything, right? Just that we wanted some privacy. She could think we're having a business meeting."

"Sure. Except I told her we were going to fuck."

She gasped and tried to wiggle her way out of his arms, but they tightened and he pressed on the button of her clit. "Bran, you can't tell her that. It could get back to everyone."

"They know," he whispered. "They know we're practically living together and I bet they've figured out that I like to get my dick inside you as often as I can. I explained to the flight attendant that our boss is an evil bitch who's kept us apart for a week and that I couldn't go another second without getting my hands on you. See, that was discreet, right?"

He didn't understand the meaning of the word, but she couldn't bring herself to care. "It doesn't matter. I missed this so much. How can I miss something I never really had?"

He held her tight, working her clit in a rhythm guaranteed to send her flying. "We did have it and then I fucked it up. I won't do it again. You won't ever see that part of me again, Carly. I promise. I can handle it."

She doubted that. She knew it would come up again. He needed to handle it, but he seemed unwilling to do so and they had so little time left. She would have to decide soon what she was going to do. He would return to Austin and she would be left to figure out what she wanted.

She wanted Bran, but she wasn't sure it could work. She couldn't do what Drew did and ignore the fact that someday Bran's problems would land him dead or in jail.

She couldn't go through that again, but she also couldn't imagine life without him, without this.

"Let me show you." His dark voice whispered in her ear, erasing all the doubt and leaving nothing but desire in its place. "Do you know what this does to me?" His thumb kept up the pressure on her clit while his talented fingers slipped lower. "You respond so beautifully to me, like you were made for me. Tell me you didn't do this for him."

Him? Her arousal-muddled brain could barely process the words. "Are you talking about my ex? No. No one else, Bran. No one ever made me feel like this."

"No one else ever got you hot and wet and ready to fuck?"

"Not like you. Never so fast. All you have to do is touch me." She wanted to press up against him, to force him to work faster, but his arm caged her, his legs holding hers open. She was completely in his grip and she got the feeling that was exactly how he liked her.

"All I have to do is think about you and I'm ready to go," he murmured against her ear. "I want to make this last. Last a long time."

She wasn't sure whether he was talking about the sex or them, but it didn't matter because his fingers curled up inside her. She forgot about everything but what he was doing to her, how high he could take her. His long fingers fucked deep while his thumb circled and circled her clit until her body bowed. She shouted out as she came, forgetting that they could be heard.

"Yes, that's what I want. I want to hear you. They don't matter. No one matters but you and me. You're mine and those sounds you make are all mine. I want them." His pelvis pressed up as though he couldn't hold himself back a second longer. "And I want you."

She wanted something, too, but if she let him have his way, he would likely flip her over and start the process of making her come all over again. He seemed dedicated to proving he could do it. She wanted some control of her own.

"Please let me up." She could barely recognize the sound of her own voice. Was that sexy growl coming from her mouth?

Bran's hands tightened briefly. "I don't want to let you up."

She had to smile because sometimes he sounded like a kid who didn't want to give up his favorite toy. "I can't get undressed if you don't let me up."

"You'll get naked for me. Right here? Right now?"

He underestimated his own persuasion. The orgasm she'd just had was a baby one compared to what he'd given her in the past. She wanted it all. She had a whole week to make up for, and somehow when she was with him, the conventional Carly seemed to fade away and she became a woman who took what she wanted and damn the consequences.

And she wanted to put her mouth on him.

"Yes." The minute she felt his arms loosen, she got to her feet. Being so relaxed made her realize how uptight she felt most of the time. She knew there were always eyes on her, judging her, and that made it hard to be herself. But here with him, there was no place for self-consciousness. He offered her something she wanted even more than her pride. She wanted to be connected to him, and that meant throwing off her normal prim persona and being the Carly Bran brought out.

That Carly didn't mind being naked with him.

She turned to find him watching her. He sat back, his beer in one hand. He was the very picture of dreamy decadence as he tilted back the beer and then settled in.

And that was when she remembered that this man was a connoisseur of strippers.

His eyes hardened. "Don't. I don't know exactly what you're thinking, but don't. I want to see you naked. I don't want your insecurities to keep that from me. Look at my cock and tell me I'm thinking about anything but how pretty you are without those clothes on. Take them off. Show me."

He was a man who liked to watch.

She was going to give him a show.

His cock ached as he waited for her to decide. He'd seen the light in her eyes dim and he'd known there was no way she wasn't thinking about the vicious crap he'd thrown her way the night of their fight. If he could take it all back he would, even though some of it had been the truth. He had been with a lot of women, almost all of them with far more sexual experience than Carly. So why was she the one he craved? There had been many times in his life he'd needed a woman and found one to crawl into bed with.

That craving had turned and now when he needed a woman, she had a face. Carly's. She had Carly's smile and her curves and her sweet Southern accent.

He needed so much more from her than a fuck, but he wasn't sure he deserved it.

Her hands went to the buttons on her blouse and he knew it didn't matter. He would take her any way he could. He would plot and plan and do what he had to do to keep her after this was over.

The last week had been hell. He'd needed her so badly and he'd stayed away because he wasn't sure he would be in control. All day long he'd done that woman's bidding, smiling even when he knew damn well what she was doing. He'd shown up late at Carly's and his first instinct had been to wake her up, to brand himself on her and take out all the frustrations of the day on her body, making her cry out again and again so he could feel like the man he wanted to be.

But could he be the man she needed him to be? That was the question that had haunted him all week. Could he be the kind of man who could put the past behind him so he might have a future with her?

He was going to stop thinking about it. That was the key. He would think about her. She'd already taken over his dreams. There was zero reason she couldn't take over his waking thoughts, too. When it got bad, he would focus on her.

And he would stay in control. She didn't need to see that side of him ever again. No one did. He was going cold turkey on the violence and rage.

*Optimism.* That was his new code word.

*Lust* was another good one. He was feeling that word as she reached the fourth button on that prim shirt she was wearing, and he could see her breasts beginning to come into view. Pretty tits he could fill his hands with and pink-and-brown nipples that begged to be sucked and laved with affection.

They had hours before they touched down. How many times could he make her come? Would it be enough to keep her close when all of this was through? Would sex alone chain her to him?

For the first time he really thought about Drew's offer. His brother was ready to make an investment that could make Carly the new Patricia Cain, and he would put Bran in charge of all of it. He was bargaining, willing to hope that money and sex and the promise of power would get her to overlook the fact that he was a walking time bomb.

"Show me more." It didn't matter because he would find a way to take care of her. "Get rid of that bra."

He loved how she flushed. Her skin was still pink from her recent orgasm, her lips sultry and full, but she still managed to blush. He could take her a thousand times and she would still be so fucking innocent.

He wished suddenly that she'd been the only woman he'd ever known. What would his life have been like if he'd met her all those years ago? If his parents hadn't died and he'd grown up in some white-picket-fenced house and he'd managed to meet Carly and marry her?

He shoved the thought aside because that wasn't what had happened and it never would. He couldn't be innocent with her, so all he could do was protect her.

She tossed aside the shirt and before he could blink had managed to unhook her bra. Her eyes went to the spot behind him where the flight attendant had disappeared.

"She won't come in here."

Carly's lips curled up slightly. "And if we crash?"

"Then we should hurry because I'm going to be humping your leg on the way down." He wasn't going to hide how much he wanted her. Not from anyone. He'd told the flirty flight attendant that unless she wanted to see a whole lot of skin, she shouldn't show up again until they were about to descend.

Proving this wasn't her first rodeo, the woman had smiled and shown him where the condoms were stashed and then happily gone on her way.

And if this sexcapade made the rounds, he didn't mind that at all. He wanted every person at Cain Corp to understand that he belonged to Carly. No matter who paid his so-called salary.

"Those are some beautiful breasts," he said softly, arousal humming through him. "Why don't you touch them?"

She cupped her breasts, her pink-tipped nails contrasting with her skin. "Like this?"

"Is that how you want me to touch them?" He could definitely get into this game. A week's worth of stress and worry began to drain from his system.

Her hands tightened, thumbs running over her nipples.

Yes, she didn't like it when he was too gentle. She liked it when he took control. Even if it was only with commands at this point. When he put his hands on her again, she would want him to be a little rough.

His girl wasn't fragile. She was solid both emotionally and physically. She could handle him.

"Roll your nipples between your thumb and forefingers. Roll them. Tug on them."

She did as he asked, her breath fluttering when she tugged. Those nipples were flush and red from the pressure.

"Tell me something, Carly. Do you like it when I suck on your nipples?" He loved to hear her talk dirty. She wouldn't do it on her own, but she would respond in kind. If he gave her the chance, she would get lovingly nasty with him.

"Yes," she replied, her voice husky. "I love it when you suck my nipples, Bran."

That was what he wanted. "Take off your skirt now."

Her fingers skimmed down her torso and her thumbs slipped under the waistband of her skirt. It was a white filmy thing, a bit on the bohemian side. He liked it, but he liked her naked more. She slid the skirt down her legs. She'd kicked off her sandals the minute they'd sat down. He'd noticed that about her. If she didn't have to wear shoes she rarely ever did. When they got home, her shoes were off. Half the time if she was sitting at her desk, her shoes were sitting beside her. He would pull her feet into his lap and massage them at night, thereby turning her into a purring kitten.

Time. He needed more time to build rituals like nightly foot rubs and long sessions in bed and showers where he washed her hair. She was a sensual creature. She would become loyal to the man who gave her comfort and pleasure.

She stood in front of him wearing absolutely nothing but a pair of white cotton panties that were so fucking wet they hid nothing. She looked like a pretty girl whose man pleasured her and she expected more.

"Come here." He sat forward, spreading his legs so she could fit herself between them.

She crossed the space between them, bringing her body close to his. He let his hands find her hips, nearly sighing at the rightness he felt the minute they were skin to skin. He leaned forward and put his nose against her pussy, breathing deeply. Damn but he loved that scent. He wanted to keep it around him all the time. He dragged his tongue over the soaked material, happy when she shuddered and groaned.

"Please, Bran."

He loved it when she begged. "Yes. Take these off and sit in your chair. Spread your legs wide and I'll please you."

Her hands found his hair, sinking in. "No. I don't want that. I mean, I do, but I want something else first."

He would give her almost anything. He wanted to play with her, as his brother-in-law would say. Playing meant exploring the boundaries of their sexual relationship. Playing meant figuring out what pleased both of them. Play would draw them together, build intimacy between them. "What do you want, baby? What do you want more than my tongue on your pussy?"

"My tongue on your cock."

He had to take a deep breath. Yes, he fucking wanted that, too. He'd managed to do what he needed to do. "I have a clean bill of health, so I can fuck your mouth, baby. I can fuck it hard and come down your throat if I want to."

"I want to taste you. I want to run my tongue all over your cock and know I've pleased you."

"Then get on your knees." He sat back. He could definitely play this game. His cock tightened. "And open my slacks. Be careful. I'm really hard."

He could barely breathe he was so hard.

Carly sank to her knees, balancing herself against his legs as she eased into the position he wanted her in. Right where he wanted her. She stared up at him as her hands went to the button on his slacks. She eased the zipper down. "I can see that."

He held on to the arms of the chair, fingers sinking in so he wouldn't simply reach out and drag her down where he wanted her. This was her show. For now. "What are you going to do about it?"

She licked those plump lips of hers, the light shining in her eyes. "I think I'm going to have to kiss it."

She slipped her fingers under the waistband of his boxers, releasing his cock. It sprang out and he sighed with relief. Her fingertips brushed the flesh of his dick. His whole body tightened in pleasurable anticipation.

"Touch me first. Take me in hand. You can be rough. I won't break."

Her hand gripped him, heat enveloping his whole body. She pumped him over and over. Carly seemed to revel in being able to touch him. They still had so much to do together. So much exploration to be done. He never spent too much time with any one woman. Sex was about making himself feel good, giving to a woman so he felt like he had a place in the world.

Not so with her. He wanted to take, too. He wanted everything she had to give. Carly made him a little selfish. He wasn't sure that was a good thing, but it felt like it.

She leaned over and pressed a surprisingly chaste kiss on the head of his cock. He groaned at the sensation and then had to drag air into his lungs as the flat of her tongue ran over him.

Pure fire licked along his spine and forced him to grip the chair harder. He wanted to twist his fingers in her hair and force her to take him all. He wanted to fuck her mouth hard and come down her throat.

He forced himself to sit still as she explored him with her tongue. She dragged it over and around his cockhead, lightly sucking him between her lips. So good. It felt so damn good. He forced himself to relax back and watch the place where his dick disappeared into her mouth.

"That's what I want," he said, his voice low. "Your mouth feels perfect."

Her tongue whirled around and she worked her way down. Her head bobbed as she took more and more of him. He hissed when her teeth scraped lightly, but he enjoyed the sensation. It flared along his skin and brought him back to the moment.

He looked down at her, finally allowing himself to touch her hair. Soft and silky. Like the rest of her. Everything about Carly was soft, from her body to her heart. He let his fingers tangle in her hair, not guiding her precisely but showing her what he wanted. More. More of her mouth on his cock. More of her in his life. Just more of her.

Over and over she worked her mouth on his dick. She licked and sucked until she'd taken his whole cock deep. Wet and warm and soft, he let the sensation flow.

He felt the back of her throat and knew he couldn't take another second. There would be time later to be selfish. For now, he wanted her to come again, wanted to feel the tight clasp of her pussy around him.

More than that, he wanted to look at her.

"Stop." He tugged lightly on her hair. "Come up here and ride me."

She licked him one last time. He dragged her up, hungry to connect with her. He never felt more like himself than when he was deep inside Carly Fisher. When he was with her, he wasn't the lesser brother. He could make her happy.

She made him think he could be happy.

Her tongue tangled with his as they kissed. She could be shy at first, but when she decided she was in, his girl was all in. He adored her for how responsive and giving she was.

She stood and slid the soaked panties off her hips. "So the doctor gave you a clean bill of health?"

Fuck, the simple thought made him want to come. "Yes, and you're on birth control."

"No more strippers, Brandon," she said with a frown.

How could he explain that he wasn't tempted by anyone except her? How could he make her get it? "No more anyones. Only you. Only us."

He was committed to making it work. Somehow. Some way.

She settled herself on his lap, the heat from her pussy nearly scorching him. "For as long as we're together."

He intended for that to be a long time. He gripped her hips and thrust up, joining them in one long pass. He gritted his teeth against the desperate need to come. She was so tight around him. He held her close, feeling her gasp as he filled her up. He held himself still, looking up at her, wanting the moment to last. "For a long time, Carly. A long time. I've never wanted any woman the way I want you."

She kissed him again. Their tongues tangled up and rubbed and played while he gave her time to get used to his size. He held her still as he kissed her lips and then made his way down. He bent her back slightly, giving himself access to her nipples. This was what he'd wanted for a week, her open and ready for his pleasure, naked and welcoming him home.

"You didn't even get out of your clothes," she whispered as he licked her nipple.

He loved the way she squirmed. "I'll get out of them next time. I hear this thing has a nice bathroom with a shower and everything. We'll need to get cleaned up after all the filthy things I plan to do to you."

It was time to get started. They only had another five hours. He might be able to fit everything he wanted in. He could fuck her for hours but within a day he would be back on the job, and then if all went well, the job would be over sometime this week. He had to ensure when the job was over that she walked out with him.

He gripped her hips. "Come on. Take us where we need to go."

Carly rode him, bouncing up and down, taking every inch of him. He'd never in his life had sex without a condom. He wished there was absolutely nothing between them. It struck him that a baby would be a good way to make Carly stay with him. She would marry him. That would keep her by his side. A child could tie them together.

He had a sudden vision of Carly and a baby.

"Kiss me." He was getting emotional. She brought that out in him. No one in his life could bring that out in him the way she could. Anger, rage, those were always bubbling under his surface. But Carly made him feel more. Carly made him want more.

She leaned forward. She never let up on her rhythm even as she fused their mouths together.

They rode the tide, holding on to each other as they moved.

He felt her nails sinking in through the fabric of his shirt. He loved it when she went wild and left a mark. She shook in his arms as she came.

Her orgasm triggered his own. It started low, causing his balls to draw up, and then the sensation raced along his spine. Pure pleasure overwhelmed him and he forced his cock as deep as it could go.

Carly fell forward, her body wrapped around his. "So that was the mile high club?"

"That it was. I think we should become frequent fliers." He sighed and relaxed. His clothes were completely ruined and he didn't care. Nothing mattered except the woman in his arms. He kissed her and they both seemed content to not move, to try to make the moment last.

He needed it to last forever.

*Chapter Sixteen*

Carly took a look around the elegant ballroom. Not many people had a ballroom in their home, but this Pacific Palisades estate was Patricia's version of Versailles. Every single detail of the six-thousand-square-foot mansion overlooking the Pacific had been painstakingly selected, from the Italian marble floors to the crown molding to the swimming pool and fountain. Today the house was open to two hundred of Patricia's closest friends.

"Can you hear me all right?" a masculine voice asked in her ear.

And a few interlopers Patricia didn't know about. Carly wasn't used to all the spy stuff. Luckily she was definitely used to having a Bluetooth device in her ear. This one was simply on a different frequency. One of Drew Lawless's choosing. "I can hear you."

No one would think twice about her talking. She was constantly putting out fires and trying to make things go smoothly at a party like this.

"And I can see through the camera. It looks good for now." Drew's voice was steady in her ear.

She was wearing a small pin on her cocktail dress. It looked like a star with a diamond, but it was actually more spy stuff. It let Drew and the crew outside the house see what was going on from her perspective. Well, her left boob's perspective, to be more accurate.

She glanced down at the floor below. Guests were flowing in and out of the ballroom, the doors having been swept back and opened to the backyard and its spectacular view of the Pacific Ocean. Tuxedoed servers made their way through the crowd offering champagne and appetizers. There was a string quartet playing, and Carly had arranged for the Met's most popular soprano to sing later.

Carly had organized this party for the last five years and she'd never once been so nervous. Her hands had a fine tremble to them that wouldn't seem to go away.

This was it. If Bran found what they were looking for, they would be over. Well, she would have a decision to make. She got the feeling Bran wouldn't mind hanging out a bit longer. He'd even joked about the two of them taking a vacation. He'd offered to take her somewhere sunny for a few weeks.

She wondered if that was his way of saying good-bye. Or if it was his way of setting up their new relationship.

She'd slept with him every night for a week. He would come in late and make love to her. In the morning he would do it all over again. When he made love to her, she felt like she was necessary to him.

But when she tried to talk about anything serious, he found a way to make himself scarce.

What kind of future did she have with a man who wouldn't talk to her about his past? Who wouldn't even acknowledge he had a problem? She couldn't build a real life with him. She would always be waiting for him to explode and wreak havoc on everything they'd built.

She watched as he stepped inside. For now he was sticking close to Patricia's side, but in a few minutes there would be an emergency he had to attend to. It was all perfectly set up. They'd gone over and over the entire operation at least a hundred times.

The night before, Bran had managed to steal the keycard to Patricia's private office. He'd had Case standing by to duplicate the card and get it back to her before she knew it was gone. Drew had hacked into the house's smart functions. He would cover the code that would report that the door had been opened. Bran had a device in his pocket that would download all her computer systems and one that would connect Drew to the safe on the inside. It was electronic and therefore completely vulnerable to Drew's particular brand of evil genius. Bran would shuffle through her desk, the closet, and anything else in the inner sanctum.

As far as Carly knew, he would be the only person besides Patricia herself who had been in that room since the mansion had been built. She called it her sanctuary, her private haven. Carly had never even seen the inside.

"Is that who I think it is?" Drew's voice was a low growl over the headset.

Carly looked down and gasped slightly.

Shelby Gates strode into the ballroom like she owned the place. She was wearing a designer gown that showed off her killer curves, and she looked like a woman on a mission.

Her mission might derail theirs, and that would be a disaster.

"I'm going to head her off. Tell Case to wait until I'm in position before he starts the game. Again, keep the football out of play. Do you read me?" Carly started for the stairs.

"I hear you. I can't read you at all. I think you've watched far too many spy movies. You know, the term *football* typically refers to nuclear codes the president has." Drew was always so logical.

Sue her for sleeping through *Air Force One*. "You understand what I'm telling you?"

"Yes, Carly. I've already informed Case that we have a slight issue. If you don't get that woman out of here, I'm going to ensure she never bothers me again. I can have her shipped off to any number of deserted islands where she can't cause trouble. I own several."

She didn't doubt it. She'd learned Drew Lawless never joked about revenge. Of course, the man rarely joked about anything at all.

"What is she wearing?" Drew sounded even more irritated than before. "Is that even a skirt? It looks more like she wrapped a Band-Aid around her ass."

"It's a Herve Leger," she said irritably. Shelby looked gorgeous in the yellow dress. "It's perfectly respectable."

"Maybe it is on some supermodel who's never had a cheeseburger in her life. On that woman it should be a crime." He sounded awfully prim for a man who looked like sin when he took off his shirt.

She'd walked in on him and Bran and Case during one of their hot, sweaty workout things. There had been lots of high-tech equipment and all she'd seen were incredibly attractive male chests. While he wasn't as hot as Bran, Drew was definitely not a slouch in the muscle department. No man who spoke geek that well should look like that without his shirt on.

"I will be sure to tell her you disapprove."

"Yeah, tell her if I ever catch her trying to hack my personal system again, it won't be a desert island I send her to," Drew shot back. "It will be jail."

She had to smile at the outrage in his voice. It was nice to see that someone in the world could get Drew's goat. "She got on your personal system?"

"She got lucky."

Carly wished she'd been there. "I told you she was good. Now will you stop bitching long enough for me to find out why she's here?"

"She's here to cause trouble."

Carly worked her way through the crowd. She'd seen Patricia walking out toward the pool area, where several of her biggest financial backers had settled in around a station offering Scotch and bourbon tastings.

Shelby craned her neck trying to see over the crowd. Even in her sky-high heels she seemed to be struggling.

"She's going to fall in those heels." Drew was like Eeyore in her ear. "Like she needs to make her legs longer."

Carly managed to catch her friend. "What a surprise to see you!"

Shelby's eyes flared but she played along, leaning over for a hug. "I'm so happy to see you, too."

Carly embraced her, getting close to her ear. "What the hell are you doing here, you criminal?"

"That's the way to tell her," Drew said, approval making his voice rich.

Shelby frowned. "I'm not a criminal."

Carly took her by the elbow and started to lead her to a place where they could talk without drawing attention. "Trespassing is a crime and that's what you'll be charged with if Patricia catches you here. How did you get in?"

"My name was on the invitation list," she replied, still frowning as Carly forced her to the edge of the ballroom.

"I approved that list myself." She led Shelby down to the hall that took them to the residence section of the house. A security guard was standing close, but luckily he was a McKay-Taggart man and simply nodded them through. "You weren't on it."

She hauled Shelby into the nearest room. It happened to be a parlor. There were several throughout the estate. This particular one was Patricia's more personal parlor. The furnishings were fairly comfortable and the walls were decorated with artwork she'd collected and books she'd likely never once read.

The reality of what Shelby had to have done in order to get her name on that list hit Carly. "You hacked into my computer?"

Maybe Drew had a point.

Shelby turned, crossing her arms over her well-endowed chest.

"I'm going to confront her, Carly. I have real questions I want to ask her. I'm not going to let you talk me out of it this time."

Carly took a long breath. "Sweetie, I know you think this is a good idea, but it's a bad time. I need you to walk away."

She shook her head. "I can't. I can't prove that she killed my brother, but I can still bring her empire down. I want to know what she did with Francine Wells. The woman has fallen off the face of the earth and I think Patricia killed her."

"Does she know about Francine Wells?" Drew's voice had gone almost to a whisper.

It was still too much. She ignored him. There would be time later to deal with the mystery woman who had supposedly been Carly before Carly was Carly. "Do you have any proof at all?"

Shelby's jaw went tight. "I have a lot of coincidences. I need to stand in front of her and see how she reacts."

"She's going to react by throwing you in jail, Shelby. She's going to discredit you and tear you down. I need you to back off from this one."

"After everything she did to you? After what she threatened to do to your sister? You would deny me my one chance to look her straight in the eye and tell her I know what she did?"

She reached out and put her hand over Shelby's. "I know what she did. I promise when we can prove it, I'll let you go at her."

"Ask her about Francine Wells," Drew said.

For a person who'd told her to keep the mission secret, he was awfully chatty. How was she supposed to do that without explaining to Shelby that she had a Lawless in her ear?

"I'll never be able to prove what she did to my brother, but I might be able to do something more." Shelby leaned forward, whispering, "I think this is bigger than I imagined, Carly. When my brother started looking into her business practices, he found something else. Something that goes back twenty years. I'm worried about you. Someone's been working hard to ensure I can't investigate."

Ah, something finally went right. "Are you talking about Francine? Is she the thing that goes back twenty years?"

Shelby nodded. "It's weird, but ever since you told me about her, I haven't been able to stop thinking about it. She's a ghost, but she wasn't always. She was very visible up until about twenty years ago. Then she seems to have vanished off the face of the earth."

"Keep her talking," Drew ordered. "I want to know everything she knows about Francine Wells. I think I've missed something. Bran mentioned her before, but I've been thinking a lot about her lately. If she is who I think she is, she was close to my father."

"You think Patricia had something to do with her going missing? From what I understand, she was helping Patricia out up to a couple of years back. She was kind of the brains behind the business."

Shelby took a step back and started to pace. "But the records of her are so sketchy. She disappeared from Dallas the day after Benedict and Iris Lawless died. And she worked for the same company. I find it odd that she cleared out her apartment and left without any kind of notice. She didn't even contact any of her friends. Eighteen months later she shows up on the payroll of a start-up company called Strat-Cast. She disappeared from there and that's when it gets even weirder. Right about the time Patricia sold her shares of StratCast, Francine shows up in Florida, but there are no public records of her owning any property or leasing any space here. She wasn't employed by any company, but apparently Patricia gave her cash."

A chill went down her spine. No wonder Drew was interested in Francine. "I never met her, you understand. I've only heard some stories about her. She never came to the offices, but Patricia would go and visit her often. I got the impression Francine spent time wherever Patricia would go, so I would bet Patricia was paying for her house or apartment or wherever she was living. A lot of people who work for Cain Corp believe she was the creative brain behind the company. Patricia was the face and Francine was the woman with the ideas."

"Why did she leave? She disappeared completely around four years ago. And Patricia wasn't paying for her place. I found some correspondence between Francine and a lawyer. I looked up the address she used. It was owned by a woman named Leah Walker. Leah was killed in a car accident roughly the same time Francine disappeared."

Carly's stomach sank at the implications. How many deaths was Patricia responsible for? "I thought Francine had probably been an older lady. I thought maybe she'd passed on."

"She was the same age as my father. She worked for him," Drew said. "I didn't remember the name until Hatch jogged my memory. She worked directly under my father. She was quite intelligent and loved to write code. He taught her a lot. What she didn't do was cook. Hatch remembered the time she tried to bring a birthday cake for my dad up to the office. She'd mixed up salt and sugar. I find it difficult to believe that she was the brains behind *Patricia's Paradise.*"

How did he know that? He'd been fourteen at the time. She couldn't imagine he'd been very close with his father's coworkers, but then, he was Drew. He'd been serious about code at a young age. He'd also been obsessed with his parents' murders, so he'd likely done a lot of investigating on everyone around them.

"I've got a bunch of records on her," Shelby explained. "She was a year younger than Patricia herself and there's no death certificate on her. I've been looking into Jane Does in the St. Augustine and LA areas but it looks like a dead end. What I do know is she disappeared after the murders and it seems like she was given safety by Patricia Cain. I believe she's the woman who entered Steven Castalano's hospital room before he died. He must have had something on her or Patricia that they wanted to hide. So I want to find her, but I think they're onto me. When I get enough proof, I'm going to the one man they won't be able to buy off."

Oh God. *Don't say Drew Lawless. Don't say Drew Lawless.* "Who's that?"

Shelby's shoulders squared. "His name is Andrew Lawless. He's the son of Benedict and once I can prove that his parents were murdered, I'm going to him. He's out there and he believes what the police told him. He thinks his father killed his mother. He has no idea there was a conspiracy."

"Fuck," Drew said.

Carly turned away and muttered under her breath because it was good to be right about at least one damn thing. "I told you."

Shelby was busy talking about her plan. "I've been careful. I've talked to some people on the dark web about this, but I haven't told anyone what I'm trying to do. There's this man I'm working with. I'm going to tell him soon and I think he'll be able to help me, but I have to be sure. I need to look her in the eyes."

"I'm the man she's been talking to, damn it," Drew admitted. "Don't you tell her that. That's my confession to make. But we have to bring her in. You need to tell her who you're working for and then get your ass back out there. Patricia's on the move. If she calls for dinner early, we'll be fucked."

She breathed a sigh of relief. "Shelby, I'm working for Drew Lawless. He's actually an asshole and he won't stop talking in my ear and we're working this party in order to find something called a burn file that we believe will lead us to information on how Patricia, Steven Castalano, and Phillip Stratton conspired to kill Benedict and Iris Lawless. Believe me, he knows."

Shelby stopped, staring at her for a moment. "You're kidding, right?"

"Nope, he's also put a video camera on me so he's likely staring at your boobs right now," she confessed.

"Carly!"

She ignored him entirely.

"You are working for Andrew Lawless?" Shelby asked, her voice hopeful this time. "Don't fuck with me."

"I'm not messing with you. That's why I need you to not cause trouble today. We've got one real shot at finding the information we need and that's right now. After today, it will be at least a year before we have this kind of access. She throws one huge party like this a year."

Shelby nodded. "All right. I'll do whatever you want me to."

Drew's voice was a frustrated growl in her ear. "Tell her we'll contact her soon. Hatch wants to talk to her. He knew Francine pretty well. He's surprised she would be involved with Patricia at all. We want to see everything Shelby has. She can fly out to Austin with us tomorrow."

She was so going to be in on that meeting. If only to be able to say she told him so another million times. "Drew says you can go with us back to Austin in the morning."

Hope lit Shelby's eyes. "I'll do it. I'll bring everything I have. How can I help tonight?"

"Stay out of sight as you leave." Carly looked over at the clock. They were running late. She needed to get back to her place. This whole thing was a row of dominoes. It wouldn't work if the first one wasn't properly placed. "Just go back out and make sure Patricia doesn't see you."

Shelby hugged her. "I will. I promise. Good luck, Carly."

She hurried out the door.

"You are going to have to tell her you're the man she's been flirting with online," Carly said. It would go poorly if Shelby found out, and Shelby would find out. There was no question of that in her mind. Drew could save himself a lot of trouble if he just owned up. Shelby understood the need for undercover work.

Maybe they could talk about it over a nice dinner. She was going to enjoy playing matchmaker.

"Carly, I need you to walk toward the fireplace."

She rolled her eyes despite the fact that he couldn't see her. She pivoted and started for the door. "Drew, I don't have time for any more playing around."

"Stop and turn back toward the damn fireplace."

He was the most frustrating man. Now he was interested in art? She obediently turned and faced the wall. It was a beautifully done mantel reflecting the warm tone of the room. On either side of the fireplace was Patricia's collection of books. In this room she believed it was fiction. There was a whole other library dedicated to cookbooks and tomes on home décor and architecture.

"I need you to get close to that vase."

In the center of the mantel was a vase. It was pretty but oddly out of place since most of the pieces in the room would be considered true works of art. This, while done well, was obviously the work of an amateur. There were slight discolorations in the glaze. The ombré coloring went from light to pitch black on the bottom. It was large enough to hold a dozen flowers, but Carly couldn't remember ever seeing Patricia use it for flowers. It had always sat in the middle of the mantel. "It's been here since I've worked for Patricia. Are you a lover of pottery?"

"My mother made that."

Carly stopped. "Are you sure?"

"It sat above our fireplace until the day she died. I thought it had gotten destroyed in the fire. What's it doing here? She loved that piece. It was the first time she'd made one work. She told me all the others had folded inward, but this was the first time she'd gotten one to look like it was supposed to. She made cupcakes that day to celebrate and talked about becoming an artist."

She could hear the emotion in Drew's voice. "Do you want me to steal it?"

A knock on the door stopped that line of thought. Carly's heart jumped and she forced herself not to panic. As the door came open, she started talking.

"No, I don't want the sauce served on the chicken. It needs to be on the side, and I swear I will have someone's head if it isn't." She turned and saw the serving manager had found her.

Good. It looked like she'd stepped away to have words with the kitchen. Carly arched a brow. "How can I help you?"

Mr. Turner frowned apologetically. "I'm so sorry to disturb you but I need to go over how we're switching from cocktail to dinner service."

"Just go, Carly," Drew said, his voice hollow. "It doesn't matter. Getting into her office is the only thing we should worry about."

She felt her heart sink but knew he was right. "Let's take a look at it. I want to make the transition as smooth as possible."

She prayed she could make the mission go the same way.

Bran stepped forward, touching his earpiece. It was go time. Everything they'd prepped for, all the years of sacrifice, and it all came down to this. Patricia was the last person alive who could have the evidence they needed.

Patricia was laughing as some senator finished a joke. She was perfectly icy and cold and held such fascination for the people around her. He didn't get it at all. All he could think about was one woman wearing a black cocktail dress that hid her curves far too much for his liking.

He'd wanted to buy her a new dress, offered to take her to Rodeo Drive and find something properly bright and shiny. Carly had laughed it off. Apparently she attempted to blend into the background at events like this.

One day she would be the center of the parties she threw. She would be the center of his whole world.

She eagerly turned to him when he reached for her, so why did he feel like he was losing her?

He had to stop thinking about it. It made him edgy. She was coming with them to Austin in the morning. That had to be enough for now. He would ensure she was set up in a new place and he would slowly move his way completely into her life. She would be tied to him and he would do everything he could to make her happy.

He would forget about the past and concentrate on the future. That was all he had to do.

He glanced out and his replacement was on the way. Case strode through the crowd. Like the rest of the security team, Case was dressed in a tux that concealed the fact that he was carrying more than one weapon on his body.

"Ms. Cain, I'm afraid we have an issue I need to handle. Case is going to stay with you while I'm gone."

She frowned. "Well, fine. I suppose I can handle Mr. Taggart for a time, but hurry back." She straightened the lapels on his tux. "I've got you sitting next to me at dinner."

That was news to him. "I can protect you better from a distance."

"What fun would that be? Run along." She gave Case an icy smile. "Hello, Mr. Taggart."

The senator raised an eyebrow. "As in McKay-Taggart? My dear, you've moved up in the world if you're using them for your personal security."

Case gave Bran a nod as he walked by. In the background Bran could hear Case beginning to talk about how proud he was to work for a woman like Patricia Cain.

Yeah, he should have been an actor. His brother-in-law was far better at putting on a happy face than he was.

All he wanted to do was get the information and get the fuck out. He would finish the party and then tender his resignation in the morning. Patricia would still have McKay-Taggart security around her and they would have time to sort through the data and find what they needed.

And he and Carly would settle in. She would take the job at 4L and they would find their way. Oh, she hadn't agreed to take the job yet, hadn't even said she would actually move, but she was spending the next week in Austin with him and he would make her never want to leave.

What hope did they have if she refused to talk about the future and he wouldn't acknowledge the past?

He brushed the thought aside as he took the stairs two at a time. Carly was waiting for him up there and he intended to do his job and get them both out of danger as soon as possible.

She paced in front of the office. The mansion was quiet back here, having moved past the security guards and into what they all called the forbidden zone.

He took a deep breath and strode toward her. One more job and they would be free and clear. That was all it would take. This and they were done. He could hand over everything to Drew and get the fuck out.

If she wouldn't move to Austin with him, he would move to be with her. He wasn't ever going to leave her again.

Carly's eyes widened as he walked up. "Are you good to go? You can't be in there too long."

He walked right up to her and did what he'd needed to do all day long. He got his hands on her, covered her mouth with his. And the dark voices that seemed to whisper to him all his days quieted.

She was his peace.

He kissed her for a moment, needing the connection. When he pulled back, he was ready to go. "I'll be out in a minute. I love you, Carly."

He kind of liked the fact that her jaw dropped and he was in the office before she could say another word.

Let her think about that for a while.

He fumbled for a moment, his hand moving to his left to find the light switch.

"Did you actually just do that?"

Fuck. He'd forgotten for one glorious moment that his brother was in his ear and could hear and see pretty much everything. Drew was about a mile away, sitting in a rented apartment, probably looking like the world's biggest pervert because he was surrounded by monitors. He had cameras on the whole team.

"Could you wait until I find the light switch to bitch at me?"

"Once you find the switch and turn it on, you'll have a job to do, so right now is a great time to bitch at you. And I wasn't bitching. I was surprised that you would tell her something like that in the middle of a serious job. Move your hand up."

What did his brother think he was doing? "I'm looking. You know this would be way easier if you would shut up. And I told her because she should know."

"Are you sure you didn't tell her so she doesn't leave you at the end of this thing? I think she's going to require more than a declaration of love, Bran. I think you should maybe see someone when we get back to Austin."

Where the fuck was that light? He pulled out his phone and looked for the flashlight function. "I will be seeing someone. I'll be seeing Carly."

He managed to get the light on his phone to shine.

"I meant someone else," Drew said over the line. "Someone who can help you with your issues. Turn back to the wall, it has to be there."

His major issues right now had to do with his brother's deep and never-ending control freakiness. And he didn't want to think about that right now. "You're right. I need to concentrate on the job."

He turned the phone around and located a floor lamp. Thank God. He pulled on the cord and the room lit with soft waves of green and blue and yellow. It was one of those stained-glass lamps that looked like it was from another century. He was sure Carly would have a name for it but it did fuck all to light up the place.

"Case knows a guy in Dallas who deals with PTSD issues," Drew continued. "Hey, there's the desk."

"If you don't stop talking, I'll throw away this earpiece. Do you understand?"

A long sigh came over the line. "Set the drive I gave you to download and then get to work on the safe."

He could hear the disappointment in his brother's words.

He moved to the desk and located the PC, slipping the thumb drive in. The monitor immediately came up and requested a password, which the program on the drive began to find.

It was a specialty of Drew's, figuring out ingenious ways to get at information. If this particular computer had been connected to the Internet, they wouldn't have needed this act of breaking and entering. Drew would have done everything remotely.

The screen switched as the program located and used the password and moved on to pulling down files. A lot of files.

He sighed and flipped on the small lamp on the desk. It seemed to actually be more functional than decorative.

"I'm doing fine now," he said quietly as he began to look through the drawers of her desk. Apparently the woman liked stationery. There was a whole drawer filled with neatly stacked stationery and pens of all colors.

"You nearly killed that man. It didn't just scare Carly. It scared the fuck out of me, too."

"This is neither the time nor the place." He opened the drawer to his left and found some mail. He pulled the first one out when he recognized the mailing address of Steven Castalano's lawyer.

"There never seems to be one. I have to wonder if you're punishing yourself or me."

He ignored his brother because that line of thinking made him anxious. Antsy. He wasn't going there again. He was going to concentrate on the damn job. He opened the envelope, pulling out the letter. It was done on the law firm's stationery, typed out and official looking.

"I'm sorry, Bran. We'll talk about this later. You should probably move on to the safe."

But he was far more interested in the words on that paper.

We regret to inform you that despite the contents of his will and naming you as the benefactor to all contents found in his safety deposit box, we discovered the box was empty. According to bank records a woman with the key entered and was left alone with the box in question five days before the reading of Mr. Castalano's will. While we understand your anger at this turn of events, we are not responsible for the contents of that box. We will, of course, put you in touch with the bank manager, but he claims it was you who came in and collected the contents of the box. I've attached a copy of the sign-in sheets for the day.

"Are you reading this?" Bran asked, trying to get the camera at an angle where Drew could see.

"Five days before the reading of his will would have been the day of his death. I know it well," Drew replied. "That must have been where he'd hidden his file. There's zero reason for Patricia to write his lawyers and get bent out of shape if she'd gotten the file. So there were three burn files that we know of."

"Phillip Stratton destroyed his and replaced it with something that would help Ellie."

"Yes, and now Castalano's is gone," Drew mused.

"Who is Patricia Cain's beneficiary?" Bran looked through the rest of the desk, finding nothing of import beyond notes about ideas for her show. "Who would get her file if she died?"

"According to what Ellie believes, the last one standing was supposed to destroy them all. Stratton's files should have gone to the remaining members on his death. Castalano's would have gone to Cain at this point. Cain would then have everyone's file and it would have been up to her to destroy all the evidence."

"But there's a fourth party involved." He moved on to start looking for the safe. According to the records one had been delivered and installed in this room, but he wasn't sure where.

"Yes. I think I'm going to need to talk to your girlfriend. She's been holding out on us," Drew said quietly.

"Holding out?" Bran looked around and then stopped in his tracks. "Do you see what I see?"

Behind Patricia's desk was a large portrait of a woman with raven-colored hair. She was dressed in white, her hair up in an elegant bun. She stared out of the painting, her lips in a slight smile.

It was his mother.

"Okay, something freaky is going on here and I want to know what the fuck it is," Drew growled.

"Why does she have a portrait of our mother?" She looked so beautiful. He remembered how calm she was, how perfectly she did everything. When he dreamed at night it was of the house they'd lived in and how it always smelled good and dinner had been on the table. His mother liked to try new things and he'd been such a brat about it. He wouldn't eat anything. Night after night she'd been forced to make him grilled cheese so he would eat anything at all.

"I don't know, but I think you should check behind it for the safe. Patricia seems to have been very interested in our mother."

What did that mean? It turned his stomach to think about the implications. He touched the frame. It was gilded and when he pulled on it, the whole thing swung out and revealed the safe he'd been looking for. "It's here."

He forced himself to think about the task at hand.

"Do what we planned." Drew's voice had gone deep, calming. "Remember how to attach the device."

He focused, putting aside the thoughts that threatened to overtake him. His childhood pressed at the gates of his consciousness, rattling his peace. He had to hold it together because his blood was pounding through his system again. He managed to pull the panel off the front of the safe and found the wiring to attach the device that would override the safe's defense systems. He set it in motion and took a step back.

"I've got it."

"Good. Almost done," Drew said reassuringly.

"How is Carly?" She would be waiting outside for him. She wouldn't have walked away. The last thing he wanted was for some stray staff to come along and cause trouble for her.

"Your girl can handle herself. She's got a guest but she's managed to move him away from the office. You've got a few minutes, but we need to get moving."

The safe dinged and opened. Bran stepped forward and pulled on the handle.

The safe was completely empty.

"Damn it." Bran closed the safe again and detached the device, shoving it back in his pocket.

He turned to the computer. They wouldn't know if it led to anything at all until they went through the files.

It could all be for nothing. They could have worked all this time and failed. They could have absolutely nothing and he was taking Carly out of here before they knew. He couldn't leave her behind.

He would have failed.

It had to be on the computer. Why else would she have a solitary computer without any links to the Internet?

"Bran? I think it's time to move. The computer should have finished the download by now."

It had. He grabbed the thumb drive and moved through the room, turning the lights off once more. He had to keep his cool and get out of here.

It would all be over soon.

"Am I clear?" Bran asked. Drew would have a view of the hallway.

"Yes, but I need you to go out and turn to your left. Go down the back stairs."

That wasn't the route they'd planned, but he was game. He'd walked the house quite a bit in the last week and he could easily get to the kitchens through the servants' stairs. From there he would make his way back to Patricia and take over for the night. In the morning he and Carly would be gone.

He exited the room as quietly as possible and made sure the lock clicked behind him. The idea of Patricia Cain having that portrait of his mother weighed heavily on him. What had she done all these years? Had she sat in that office and smiled over her defeated enemy? Did she keep the portrait as a reminder of her sins? Or was it a trophy?

The trouble was he couldn't remember that portrait ever being in their house. His father had been a modern man. All the pictures they'd had had been photographs. They'd been taken by Benedict himself or a photographer their mother had hired to get shots of the whole family.

No one had ever sat for a painted portrait.

He was about to turn to the left when he heard it.

"Stop it. I need you to get your hands off me right now," Carly said in a low voice, as though she was trying not to make a scene.

He turned back.

"Bran, I've got another guard coming to her right now. You go the other way."

He wasn't listening to his brother. All he could hear was the fear in Carly's voice.

"I'm serious, Bran. I need you to keep your shit together."

But he couldn't. Not when he saw what was happening. Bran's world went red and he did the only thing he could do.

He attacked.

## Chapter Seventeen

Carly watched Bran slip inside the office and sighed with momentary relief.

It was rather nice to be alone with her thoughts. Drew would be guiding Bran through his portion of the job and she had a few moments to herself.

What the hell was she going to do? She wanted Bran but she wasn't sure how long they could last. Was she willing to move across the country for a relationship that seemed doomed to failure?

Perhaps it was time to think about her real future. If they took down Patricia tonight, she would have a decision to make.

If she took the job with Drew, she would be tied to Bran, and if the relationship didn't work, she would still have to be in his orbit. How would she handle watching him go back to his previous life? Would he find his way back to the strip clubs and easy sex of his old world?

Would he fight so often that one day she would have to wake up to a call telling her he'd taken one blow too many?

Maybe she should think about starting over somewhere completely new. Chicago or New York perhaps. Or maybe she should think about moving closer to Meri. Her sister had a few years left in school and then perhaps Carly could think about going back to college.

The idea of life without Bran seemed so dull. Like the world had been in black and white until he'd walked into her life, and it would be so hard to live without the color.

She glanced down the hallway. It was quiet up here. She could hear the low hum of the party going on downstairs. Would any one of those powerful people give her the time of day once she'd walked away from Patricia? Likely not. She would have to leave this industry and she wouldn't get a reference from her only employer for the last five years. She would be stuck with asking her old manager at the fabric store she worked at in Alabama. Yeah, that would go a long way.

If she didn't stay with Bran, would Drew help her? Or would he give her the choice of doing what he wanted or being left adrift?

She glanced down at her watch. Dinner would be served soon. She'd set everything up perfectly, but Patricia would expect her to be there to watch over the initial seating. Then she would fade into the background with Bran and they could talk about what he'd found.

A few more hours and she would be free.

Why didn't that seem more exciting?

"I thought I saw you walking up here."

Carly froze and turned. Kenny Jr. was walking down the hall from the left. He must have come up the back stairs. The upper level was supposed to be off-limits, but Kenny was "family" and knew all the ways in and out.

If he caught Bran coming out of that office, they would all be in trouble. They would have lost their shot and Patricia would destroy any evidence she had.

She had to get Kenny out of here and fast.

She plastered a smile on her face and prayed he couldn't hear how hard her heart was pounding. "Hey. I thought I'd have a quiet moment before the storm. You know how these dinners go."

He was dressed in a stylish tux, his hair swept back. He was an attractive man, if one liked his type. Lanky with a well-coiffed beard, he was the epitome of money and power. He joined her close to the railing and put a hand on hers.

His hands were soft. She'd never thought about it before, but his hand was warm and soft on hers. He didn't have Bran's calluses or masculine strength.

"I do know how these things go. Every one of those fuckers down there will have a complaint or a request. They'll want vegan this or Paleo that. They don't do it because they want the item they're requesting."

He did understand the crowd. She knew exactly what he was talking about. "They do it because it makes them feel special and powerful. It makes me feel crazy, but I think I've anticipated almost all the requests this time. I've become good at not only anticipating but also with timing."

"Of course. If you do it too quickly they'll think you're not specifically accommodating them."

It didn't work if they thought no one had gone to the trouble of making the item for them. So she had the five-minute rule. "While everything is already prepped and waiting, we wait five minutes before returning. I've got it built in to the dinner schedule. Speaking of the dinner schedule, it looks like my break is done. I should get back down there."

She turned and started toward the stairs that led back to the ballroom, praying he would follow after her.

"What is he doing here?" Drew asked in her ear.

Did he think she could stop and answer him? She turned back and sure enough there was Kenny. She gave him a smile. "Care to escort me down? I would take off these shoes but your stepmother would have a fit if she caught me."

Kenny gave her a warm smile and offered his arm. "Of course. And my stepmother should get on her knees and thank God you're here. She would be a mess."

"Very good, Carly," Drew said. "I'll have Bran take the back stairs down. We've run into a minor complication, but nothing we can't handle. Keep this asshole away from Bran. And be careful. He's flirting with you and I would say he's the type to get pissy when you turn him down."

That was ridiculous, but again, she couldn't explain their relationship to Drew right now. She moved toward the stairs. Her heels weren't that tall, but she could play the helpless damsel if it meant saving Bran from being caught.

"Somehow I think Patricia would say this is simply my job," Carly replied as they began down the stairs. They would take a left and be back in the ballroom in a few moments. She could already hear the quartet as they moved into a Brahms piece.

Kenny stopped suddenly, tugging on her hand. "I was actually looking for you. I wanted to talk to you away from all this mess. I think the time has come for us to discuss you leaving *Patricia's Paradise.*"

She glanced up the stairs. They were far enough down that he wouldn't be able to see when Bran slipped out of the office. Drew would make sure Bran knew which way to go. Still, she would feel better if they went down to the ballroom. "You know your father won't allow you to do a show that competes with hers."

"My father is in kidney failure. He won't last another month." He said it with all the emotion of a man talking about an insect on his windshield.

"And then you get to fight your stepmother for years over his will," Carly stated practically. "According to Patricia, she gets the network."

"I'm going to fight her on that. In her prenup, she wasn't supposed to cheat on my father, and we both know she's done it. I'm going to win this, Carly, and I'm going to build the whole new home network around you. Without you she's going to have nothing. She won't be able to find anyone who can do what you do."

She liked that he had such confidence in her, but she wasn't sure she had the same. "She'll be able to find someone else who can inspire her, as she would say."

"I think you should sit down and talk to me about this. We can go and get a drink and talk real numbers. Taking you away from my stepmother would be the shot on her bow, the opening salvo of our war, and I bet I've got more ammunition than she does. I'm willing to take this a long way, Carly, and I want you to be my partner."

She sighed and gave him what she hoped would buy her some time. If all went well, she wouldn't see him again. She wanted out of Patricia's orbit forever. She certainly wasn't going to set herself up as a challenger to the woman's crown. "I would love to talk to you. Maybe after the party. Like I said, dinner is going to be served soon."

He put a hand on the railing behind her, caging her in. "I think dinner is delayed a bit. From what I understand your boy got called away. She won't start dinner without him."

Anxiety started like a low thrum in the back of her spine. Something was off, but she couldn't exactly scream out at this point. And she couldn't have a fight with him now. "Why would she wait for Bran? I assure you she's got another bodyguard on her. She's got one around the clock right now."

He shook his head and didn't move an inch. "No, I happen to know she's changed your seating chart to include your boyfriend. She's got him sitting beside her all evening long. Have you thought about what that means?"

It meant that Patricia was trying once again to get her nasty hands on Carly's man. It wouldn't work and she wasn't jealous. She knew damn well Bran didn't want that woman. What bugged her about it was the fact that it would make Bran uncomfortable.

"I'll talk to her. It wouldn't look right to have a bodyguard sitting beside her." If they were sure they'd gotten what they needed, she would walk straight up to Patricia and give her a piece of her mind that had been a long time coming. Until Drew looked through the contents of that computer and whatever else Bran found, they needed to keep their jobs.

Kenny was uncomfortably close, invading her space. "I don't think that will work. Look, it's time for you to open your eyes and see what's going on. Everyone else knows she's going to take him from you. He won't stay with you. He'll go where the money is. He's nothing but a boy toy anyway. He can't give you what you need, but I've finally figured out where I went wrong with you."

"You are going wrong with me right now," she whispered. She could see people moving down the hall.

"No. I'm finally going to do this right. I didn't realize how physical a woman you are. You've always seemed so chilly, but I see it now. You need a man. Not that boy you've been playing with. You need someone who can take you where you need to go." He moved in, his head swooping down, and he covered her mouth with his.

"Carly, I've got Case on his way. He's going to deal with this. Do you understand? Stay calm and I'll get you out of this, and I swear to God that fucker isn't going to have a pair of balls when I get done with him." Drew's voice was a welcome presence.

She tried to pull away, but Kenny's hands held her tight. Too tight. She struggled in his arms, but he pressed her against the railing.

"Stop it," she said when he came up for air. She was oddly calm. Knowing Drew had seen what was happening and taken steps to deal with the situation gave her some peace of mind. "I need you to get your hands off me right now."

"I know you think because he's younger that he's a good thing, but I'm not going to let him fuck up everything I've planned," Kenny said harshly. "I've been planning this since the day I realized what you really do for that bitch. I'm going to ruin her and you're going to help me. We can do this the easy way, baby. You can join me and we'll even talk about making a relationship between us formal at some point. But I'm not allowing you to walk away."

She pushed against him because Case seemed to be taking his sweet time. "You don't have a choice."

That was when she noticed the photographer at the bottom of the steps.

Kenny dragged her against his body. "That's right. Those pictures will hit the scandal pages tomorrow morning and my stepmother will fire you. She'll rip you to shreds for being a gold digger and you won't have anywhere else to go. It's me or back to the trailer park."

She was so sick of this family. She pushed against him. All she needed was a couple of inches of space between them and she could get her knee up. She'd been taking self-defense lessons from Bran and Case. She was fairly certain with the right amount of force applied, she could kick the asshole's balls back into his body cavity.

One minute she was struggling to get out of his arms and the next he was falling away, tumbling down the final few stairs with two hundred pounds of pure rage on him.

"Damn it," Drew cursed. "Carly, are you all right? We have to get Bran off him. He could kill him."

She watched in horror as Bran started to pummel Kenny and the photographer got a good story.

She stumbled down the stairs. "Bran. Bran, please. Please, baby. I need you to stop."

It was too late. A crowd was gathering around the men, gossip already flowing.

Bran wasn't listening. His face had gone a florid red.

Case pushed his way through the crowd. "Everyone back!"

Case moved in behind Bran, careful not to slip in the blood that already marked the white marble. He wrapped a bulky arm around Bran's throat and dragged him off. Bran continued to fight, trying to put an elbow in Case's gut.

"I don't want to have to choke you out, Bran. Give it up," Case implored.

Bran was fighting imaginary demons, his eyes blank, and he struggled against Case's hold.

Carly stepped up to him, needing to bring him back.

"Get away from him, Carly. He's going to hurt you," Drew ordered.

She couldn't leave him like that. "Bran, please come back. Bran, I need you."

He stopped, his arms dropping and that blank look in his eyes fading. His jaw was tight with tension as Case backed away and he stood on his own.

Someone had helped Kenny up. He was bloody, but he looked up at Bran, his eyes lit with anger. "I will sue you. I'm going to make sure you do time for this."

Bran's eyes flared and Carly put a hand on his chest.

"What is going on here?" Patricia stepped through the crowd, a frown on her face. She looked up at Case. "Unless you want him in jail, you'll have him out of here in five minutes. Kenny, I want you gone as well. Carly, see to the dinner arrangements."

Bran's hand found her own. "She's coming with me."

But she couldn't. If what they needed wasn't on that computer, they had to have someone on the inside or everything they'd been through would be for nothing.

"Carly, if you want to leave, go with him," Drew said quietly. "If we don't have what we need, I'll find another way."

Somehow that made it even harder.

"Or I could call the police and have all of you arrested," Patricia said. "I would prefer to leave them out of this. You've already caused enough scandal for one night. And, Kenny, I'll let them take you, too. It's up to Carly."

That was clear. If Carly stayed Patricia wouldn't call the police. If she left, Bran could be brought up on assault charges. Yes, he'd been defending her, but that likely wouldn't matter since the photographer was obviously bought by Kenny.

Bran's hand tightened around hers. "Let's go."

She stepped back. "I'm staying."

Bran's eyes laser-focused on her. "Come with me. Right now."

Case stepped in between them. "Do I need to haul you out myself, Bran? She's made her decision and we need to let these nice people get back to their party. I'll take over for you and you should understand I'll have to write this whole incident up for the boss."

Tears pierced her eyes. Why couldn't Bran see that she needed to stay?

"And get out of my guesthouse as well," Patricia said. "You're obviously not going to continue on with my assistant. Not if she wants to remain here."

Bran shook his head. "I'll be out in a few minutes. I know when I'm not wanted. Good-bye, Carly. Have fun with this crowd. You obviously belong here."

He turned and walked out.

"Carly, dinner service in five minutes or you're fired."

Carly took a deep breath and with as much dignity as she could muster, turned and walked toward the kitchens.

"Carly, he didn't mean that," Drew said.

She calmly pulled the earpiece out.

She had a job to do and she intended to do it. There was no question now about the future with Bran. She had none.

But there was one last thing she could give to his family.


"What the hell were you thinking?" Drew growled as Bran walked in the door.

It had already been a shitty day and he still had more things he didn't want to do. The last thing he needed was his brother on his back. He tossed the thumb drive Drew's way. "There's your information. We're out of this. Do what you want, but don't ask me to be any part of it again, and if you ever put Carly in danger I will take you down myself. Do you understand me?"

Drew stopped, his expression shuttering. "I didn't put her in danger."

"You tried to keep me from her when she was being assaulted. She belongs to me. She's not a pawn in your game and you don't get to make decisions for us. We're out."

Hatch walked in from the kitchen. He took the drive from Drew's hands with a shake of his head. "Damn it, Bran. He sent Case to take care of her. He wasn't leaving her alone to fend for herself."

Bran was through with all of them. And he was also through playing games with himself.

He couldn't go on like this. Not and be the man Carly deserved. He'd hidden his secrets for so long that they'd been a part of his foundation. When he'd looked at her, when she'd put her hand on his heart and asked him to come back ... she hadn't been asking about a single moment. She'd asked him to leave the past behind and find a future with her. At least that was what he'd heard. In that moment he'd finally heard what she'd been saying all along.

He loved her. He had to choose her. He had to be honest with her even if she rejected him in the end.

But he suddenly understood that she wouldn't. She would open her arms wide and welcome him home. All he had to do was choose her.

"Bran, you need to go to her," Drew said as Hatch plugged the thumb drive in. "She wasn't choosing Patricia over you."

Bran shook his head. Was his brother high? "She was being faithful to the mission, Drew. I know that. Carly wouldn't choose Patricia over me. That's ridiculous. And of course I'm going to her, but I have to sneak back in. And I have to do something first."

"Why the hell did you say those things to her, then?" Drew asked with a huff.

Bran groaned. "What was I supposed to say? Should I have dropped to one knee and professed my love then and there? Carly knows that was all for show."

"I don't know about that," Hatch said with a shake of his head as the data files started to pull up. "She chucked her earpiece. She won't talk to us."

His heart clenched. She couldn't believe he meant what he'd said. "She's alone?"

Drew held a hand up. "Case is watching her and she hasn't gotten rid of her camera. I can see what's happening. She's working at this point. Dinner is almost done and she's been dealing with the catering staff. We have other problems, though. Someone's piggybacking our feed."

"What do you mean?"

Drew ran a hand through his hair. "It means someone piggybacked our feed and was listening in. I would shut everything down, but I don't want to lose sight of Carly. I've got a call in to Dallas. I think it might be one of McKay-Taggart's hackers. I know Ian wasn't thrilled about this job. He's likely keeping an eye on it, but it makes me nervous. Until he calls back and confirms, I'll be anxious. It's why I'm using a separate computer on the drive. I don't want anyone seeing that information."

So everyone had seen his issues. Everyone had watched him nearly ruin the mission and then dump Carly right there in front of a crowd. Did she believe he'd walked away cursing her? "I lost it again."

"Yeah, you did." Drew took a deep breath. "I think it's time to talk."

"I think I need to see that guy that Case talked about, but only if I can convince Carly to come with me. If not, then I'm going to need a referral to a therapist wherever we land." It might smooth things over between them. Carly would feel better if he was dealing with his problems.

Drew stared at him, his body still. "What are you saying?"

"I love Carly and that means I have to deal with all the shit I went through. I have to be the man she needs me to be. It means something else, too. I have to be honest with you. You left me there, Drew." He hated how emotional he was getting, but he had to get this out. He realized now that this was what sat between him and Carly. Even when they made love this anger inside him was a wall that kept them apart. He didn't want that. Not one second longer.

Drew's eyes closed and he nodded. "I know I did."

"Tell me why. I never asked because I thought I knew the answer."

Drew's eyes opened and Bran was surprised to see they weren't clear. There was a suspicious shine to them. "It was easier to leave you. I was busy building something and you were a teenage boy. I thought I would get you when you aged out of the system, like I did Riley. I want to tell you it was all about building something for us, but it wasn't. I wanted revenge and I chose it. I picked it over you, Bran, and I'm so sorry."

Bran took a deep breath. "Okay."

Hatch stood up, looking older than his years. "Don't think this is Drew's fault."

Drew held out a hand. "Don't, Hatch. This is between me and Bran."

"But it shouldn't be, damn it. He shouldn't be looking at you," Hatch said, his voice gravelly. He stepped in front of Drew and looked Bran in the eyes. "You should be looking at me. Drew was just a kid himself. I was a damn adult. I left all of you. Every single one of you. I left you behind and I feel it every day."

Oh, that felt good. Something opened inside Bran. "You were my father's best friend. He trusted you."

"I was your uncle," Hatch said. "Not by blood, but I was there when you were born. It was my responsibility and I chose a bottle over my best friend's children. I did that and I haven't known how to talk to you about it. We picked you up from the hospital after that terrible day and you didn't say anything. You never said anything, so I tried to be your friend."

Hatch was the one who took him to strip clubs after Bran had gotten kicked out of college for fighting. Hatch had set up another school for him and he'd shown up and taken him out that night with a fake ID.

In his own weird way, he'd been trying to teach him to cope, since Bran had threatened to run away if they sent him back to therapy. He was sure most people would say Hatch had been a terrible influence, but Bran had found a place there. He'd felt better there, more at home than he had in Drew's world.

They'd all been orphans. None of them had known how to cope. Drew had his revenge. Riley had women. Hatch had the bottle and then he'd watched over Bran.

It might be time to realize they'd all done the best they could.

Bran looked at his brother. "Would you do it again? Choose the same way?"

"No. I wouldn't. Ask me. Ask me what you want to ask me and let me choose again."

So his brother did understand. "Walk away. If you don't, we'll all drift apart. I loved them, too, but I don't want to lose any more family. Please let this be the last of it. Unless we find a name on that drive, hand all of this over to McKay-Taggart and let them handle it. Let us be a family again."

"All right." Drew put a hand on his shoulder. "I'll do it for you."

Something eased inside him. Something that had been tight for so long he'd forgotten what it felt like to be relaxed. He'd needed his brother to say it out loud, to admit what had happened. It made it oddly easy to say what he said next. "I forgive you, Drew. And you, Hatch."

He found himself in the middle of a mega man hug. It was weird. It was a little wonderful.

After a moment Hatch and Drew pulled away and Bran smiled, feeling lighter than he had in years.

"Are you ever going to tell us what happened that night?" Drew asked.

"Yes, but I have to tell her first." Carly was his main priority now. She deserved to hear his truths before anyone else. "And then I'm going to spend years in therapy because I apparently have anger issues."

Admitting it out loud wasn't so bad.

Hatch sniffled before turning back to the computer. "You're going to be lucky if that asshole doesn't sue you."

Drew had an answer for that. "I can assure you he won't. I happen to have footage of that fucker basically trying to rape Carly. I won't hesitate to ruin him with it if he comes after anyone in my family."

And that family now included Carly Fisher, who was going to find herself with a new last name soon if Bran had anything to say about it. Or maybe he'd find himself with one if she didn't want to take his. It didn't matter as long as they shared one.

"Holy shit." Hatch turned, his eyes wide. "We've got her."

"What?" Drew moved in behind Hatch. "On the murder?"

Hatch shook his head and pointed to the screen. "No. I can't find anything about the murder or any of the players. No mention of Castalano or Stratton or Francine. But this is a record of bribes she's made to certain officials to look the other way when she pays her workers slave wages. This one is proof that she hires children under the age of ten to work in her overseas factories. Well, this is why she had that system hidden and not connected to the Internet. She had to keep proof of the payments to the officials, but she couldn't let any of it get out. Holy hell. This will bring down her entire empire when we unleash this on the Web." He frowned Bran's way. "We are going to unleash this, right? You're not all angelic and shit now, right?"

Taking down the evil queen would be his pleasure. "Do it. But we do it the right way. We're going to need a reporter. I think Carly might know one. And hey, since we're no longer pursuing an investigation ourselves, Drew can finally admit to himself that he wants the hot reporter."

Drew turned a lovely shade of pink. "I don't . . . She is very attractive in a symmetrical way. I don't think she's the right reporter for this. Unless . . ."

His brother would never stop plotting. It was just his way. "I'm going to get my girl. Take down the security system in the guesthouse for me, brother. I have to go and set the scene. I have a lot to make up for. The good news is, I know how to make that woman happy."

It was something he intended to be an expert at.

# Chapter Eighteen

Carly walked into the guesthouse and sighed as she locked the door. Hours and hours had gone by and she could finally take a breath. And figure out what she was going to do with the rest of her life.

She'd gotten through the rest of the evening and managed to do the one thing she'd decided would be her parting gift to the Lawless clan. After Patricia had dismissed her with a disdainful sneer and told her to present herself in the morning to discuss how they would handle Carly's unprofessionalism, Carly had snuck into the parlor again and when she'd walked out it was with Iris Lawless's vase in her oversized handbag. She would present it to Drew as a good-bye gift to Bran.

She'd put her earpiece back in at the end of the night and Drew had been there. He'd explained that they had what they needed. She was free.

She was also alone.

Should she have walked out with him? Should she call him and talk to him? Or should she accept that they couldn't work?

Or she could fight. Fight for him. Fight for them.

She reached into her purse and grabbed her phone. His number was on speed dial. She heard it ring. Really ring. Like it-was-here-and-close-to-her ring.

"Hey," a familiar voice said. "You don't have to call. I'm here."

Bran stepped out of the kitchen, a glass of wine in his hand. He was wearing nothing but a pair of jeans that rode low on his hips. He'd likely ditched the tux as soon as he could. She had to admit that while she liked how he looked all dressed up, he was devastating like this.

"What are you doing here?"

He stepped forward and held out the wine. "I think you need this, baby. As to your question, where else would I be?"

She took the wine, but put it to the side. She might need it later because despite the fact that she was happy to see him, they couldn't ignore what had happened. Bran seemed to think he could blow up and then forget about it. They couldn't hide from it anymore. She loved him.

God, she loved him and she had to risk him walking out on her because her love was important. It was meaningful and she needed him to work with her.

"You said you were leaving."

He stepped in close, towering over her, but the look on his face was soft. "I knew I'd screwed up, Carly, and we had to make it look good for Patricia. I know I lost it and I apologize for how extreme it got, but you need to understand that I will not let anyone hurt you no matter what it costs me. I meant what I said. I love you."

The words warmed her, but they weren't enough. "We can't go on like this."

He cupped her face, tilting it up so she looked in his eyes. "I will see any therapist you want me to see. I will work on this. I'm going to do it with or without you. If you can't be with me now, I'll still go because I want to be the man you need me to be. I love you. You're it for me and I'm going to talk to you about something that's hard for me to talk about."

Hope filled her. "I want you to be able to say anything to me. I love you, too. If you'll work on it, I'll be with you. I'll be with you every step of the way."

He leaned over and kissed her forehead. "Don't say that until you've heard everything I have to say, baby. You might not feel the same way after you find out what I did. I was very selfish when I was younger."

She wrapped her arms around him, unable to think of a single thing he could have done that would cause her to walk away from the man he was now. "You told me your foster mom came on to you."

His hand smoothed down her back over and over, as though he found comfort in the contact. "She wasn't actually my foster mom. She was the girlfriend of the man who ran the home. It wasn't precisely a group home, but the man pretty much made his living off letting teenagers stay at his place. He was a bastard. Please don't think that every place I stayed at was like that. It wasn't. I put a lot of emphasis on it and I wonder if I shouldn't now. I had a few people who took amazing care of me, and circumstance led to them having to let me go. I was also difficult, to say the least."

She understood that his childhood had been chaotic, with the ground always shifting beneath him. He'd had no stable home, no people to grab onto when the storm hit. That crappy trailer park had been filled with women who would feed her and Meri when their mom didn't come home and men who would protect them. At the time it had seemed like such a terrible place to be, but she could see at least she'd had a family.

"I was there for three months and I'd learned when to hide," Bran continued. "If he brought home a bottle of Jack, I stayed out of his way. You followed his rules and he wasn't half bad, but when he got to drinking he could get nasty."

"You couldn't talk to your caseworker?" She didn't understand how all of it worked.

"I could have but by then I'd met Mandy and I didn't want to get separated from her."

She should have known there was a girl involved. "You loved her?"

"I did," he said quietly. "She was pretty and smart and she was nice to me. We had plans. We were sixteen and we made plans to go to college together when we aged out. She didn't have anyone on the outside so I decided she would come with me. Now that I look back at it, I think I was trying to change what had happened with me and Mia."

"Your sister?"

He nodded. "We ran away from our first home together. We were so little. I thought if we could find Drew and Riley everything would be all right. I damn near killed us both and they separated us shortly after. I think I was replaying that moment. I think I do it a lot. I want to hold on to something. I want something to be constant and I thought it would be Mandy."

"But you ran away again."

"Yes. The woman . . . she would get me alone and flirt with me. I was a big guy even back then. I probably looked older than sixteen."

"Don't. She knew how old you were, Bran. She was the adult. She was at fault." She was not going to allow him to complicate a very simple situation.

"She was at fault," he said with a sigh. "She did know how old I was and I never encouraged her. It made me uncomfortable. I didn't want to be in that position. She tried to kiss me one night and I pushed her away. She said she was going to tell her boyfriend I came on to her and he would take care of me."

"That's when you decided to run."

"No one would believe me. I was sick of being in a corner. Mandy wouldn't let me go alone. I guess we were stupid and thought it would be romantic. At that point I wasn't even thinking about going to Drew. I was going to leave everything behind. All of it. Just me and her on the road." A shudder went through him. "We didn't last a night."

She wasn't sure she wanted to hear the rest, but Bran needed to say it. "What happened?"

"We snuck out early in the evening. All we had between us was some stolen food and a couple of bottles of water and some money Drew managed to get to me. He would get me anything he could and at that point he didn't have much. He was starting his business and putting Riley through college. He worked two jobs and Riley worked as well and they passed me whatever cash they could. I had to hide it. Someone was always stealing, but at that point I had saved up about a hundred bucks."

How hard had that been for him to do? Even though she'd never had a lot of money, she'd spent what she had on candy and childish luxuries. Bran had none of those. "Where did you stay?"

"We walked for a long time. I thought I knew where the bus depot was, but I got turned around. I kept waiting for the police to show up. That's the difference between an eight-year-old and a six-year-old running away and two teenagers going missing. No one really cares about the teens. It's what you realize in the system. You seem to lose your value as you age. Every year puts more distance between you and the idea of a real home. That's why Mandy and I thought we could make it. Anyway, it got late and it was getting cold. I wanted to get a motel room, but they wouldn't rent to under-eighteens. So we ended up at an abandoned house on the edge of the city."

"Were you alone? Was it really abandoned?"

"We thought it was," he said. "We bunked down in one of the back rooms, but sometime in the middle of the night another group showed up. We didn't realize it was used for drug parties."

"It was a crack house?"

"Of sorts. I woke up in the middle of the night when someone crashed in. He was high as a kite. I don't know that he had any idea what he was doing. He started hitting me and then there were two of them. They beat the shit out of me and then Mandy tried to stop them. I didn't save her." He took in a ragged breath. "I laid there on the floor and one of them pushed her and she hit her head and she didn't get up."

Her heart ached for him. "Bran, that's not your fault."

"She was there because of me and I wasn't strong enough to save her. She was there because I couldn't suck it up and do what I needed to do to keep us both safe. Why couldn't I do it? Do you know how many boys at that age would have taken what that woman offered?"

How hard had the last few weeks been on him? To be placed in the same situation with a woman who had power over him had to have been torture for Bran. She looked up at him. "You had the right to say no."

He kissed her forehead. "It's more complicated than rights, baby. That world that I lived in, it was all about choices, and none of them good. Despite everything that had happened to me, I was still an idealist."

"Mandy died?"

His arms tightened a bit and she realized he was using her for comfort. It was a good thing to be used for. "I crawled to her after they were gone. I had a broken leg, both arms, and some fractured ribs. She hit her head and apparently died almost instantly. I was with her for two days before someone found us."

He'd lain there with evidence of his own failure. He'd probably wanted to die himself. He'd been so young and alone and in pain. "Baby, none of this was your fault. None of it. You were a child."

"We were all children. We all did what we thought was best to survive and there's no going back. I don't think I understood that until very recently. We've tried to re-create this home our parents built but we have to build something new. I want to build something with you." He looked down at her, tears in his eyes. "Tell me I have a chance. Tell me I didn't wait too long."

She realized one thing. She would never leave this man. "I love you. I'm going to marry you someday, Brandon."

He pressed his forehead to hers. "I'll go with you. If you want to go back to Florida, I'll be there."

She suddenly knew there would be no going back. Forward. She'd thought she wanted out, but now with Bran here the future seemed more open, the possibilities endless. Why should she settle? She didn't have to be tired of the fight anymore. She didn't have to be Patricia's good employee or keep her head down and try to get through.

It was time to figure out how tough she was.

"I'm going to Austin with you, but we're going to build something, Bran. You and me. We're going to build an empire."

A brilliant smile flashed on his face. "Your smarts. My support. I don't think we can go wrong. It doesn't hurt that we have a hundred million dollars in the bank."

No, it did not. She went up on her toes, pressing her lips to his. "Whatever happens, we're in this together, Bran. You and me. Nothing's going to take me away from you. Do you understand?"

He kissed her again, harder this time. His mouth pressed to hers and his hands found her hair, tugging her head back. "You and me."

His tongue plunged deep, taking her mouth in a pleasant show of dominance. She let him take over. He'd given so much of himself tonight that she wanted to give back to him, to give him anything he wanted from her. It was easy. She didn't have to be worried that Bran would take and not give. They were together and that meant something to him. He wasn't looking to move up in the world or to use her to get someplace.

She was Bran's destination. She could be his safe place.

She let her hands drift up his chest, warm skin under her palms. He kissed her over and over, letting her body heat up. Her weariness was gone and in its place was pure arousal.

"We can leave in the morning," he whispered. "I fully intend to fuck you on the plane. I like fucking you on private jets. The 4L jet makes Patricia's look like a bucket of bolts. We're going to have so much fun, baby."

He nipped her ear as he went to work on her dress. His hands found the zipper at her back and he dragged it down. He twisted the clasp of her bra until she was standing in front of him wearing nothing but her undies. Her skin tingled as he looked at her, almost anticipating the first touch of his hand.

Carly thought he was forgetting a few other differences between the two jets, though. They were important differences. "Yes, the 4L jet will also be full of your family."

Soon to be her family, so they probably didn't need to see her naked.

His hands found the flesh of her back and drifted down to cup her ass. He pulled her forward so the only thing between them was the denim of his jeans and the thin fabric of her underwear. "But they'll be plotting something. They're always plotting something. They won't even notice when we slip away to the bedroom and spend a few hours there."

"There's a bedroom?"

"Oh, baby, big brother travels in style," he assured her. "If the bedroom is too staid for you, I'll sneak you into the office and fuck you right on the desk. It doesn't matter to me as long as I get inside you as much as possible. You should get used to it. Now that I don't have to deal with that woman, I can be where I want to be. On top of you."

He lifted her up and she wrapped her legs around his waist as he kissed her again. Bran started moving back to the bedroom they'd shared while they'd been here in California.

"I want to get our own place," she said as he carried her to the bed. He lived with his brother and Hatch and she was certain it was a gorgeous place, but they needed to be by themselves. They needed to learn everything about each other, to bond and nest together.

"Then we'll have fun shopping for a place." He settled her on her feet again and stared down at her seriously. "Anything you want. I meant what I said, Carly. I love you. That means you come first. Above my family. Above myself."

Bran would put very little above his family, but that was what marriage would mean to him. He wouldn't treat it lightly. If he married her it would be because he wanted to be with her forever. God knew she wanted to be with him.

"You come first for me, too, Bran." For so long she'd put her sister's needs above her own, but Meri would not only understand, she would jump up and cheer and ask how many brothers Bran had when she met him.

"Take off the panties for me." He stepped back.

Well, she knew he liked to watch. As she intended to be the only stripper in his world from now on, she wanted to get good at it. Maybe she would take one of those stripper cardio classes. She felt like going a little wild. He brought that out in her.

And she brought him stability and peace. It was the perfect combination.

She turned around very slowly, bent over, and placed her hands flat on the mattress. "Do you want a show, Bran?"

He chuckled, the sound low and sexy. "I always like a show, baby."

Then she would give him one.

She flattened her back, spreading her legs wide. What Bran loved the most was watching her pleasure. She'd figured that out very quickly. Bran truly got off on giving her pleasure.

"You know, I think I understand why my brother-in-law is so obsessed with spanking my sister. Jeez, I just realized that sounded creepy. I'm only saying Case is into some kinky shit and I'm suddenly not averse to it." He moved in behind her and she felt his hand on her ass. He cupped her. "This is a damn work of art."

"I thought you wanted a show." She was willing to explore, but tonight she wasn't sure they would last too long. She needed him inside her too badly.

"Then show me." He stepped back, but not too far.

She let the world around her fall away. This was all about her and Bran and how they could make each other feel. Sensation. That was all that mattered now. It began with the emotion she felt for him, but it flowed out through her, making her skin sing. Her body was suddenly alive, more alive than it had ever been. She let her breasts brush against the soft cotton of the comforter. It made her nipples peak. Everywhere it touched felt like a caress. Carly moved up until she was standing again, cool air brushing her skin. She let her fingers skim down her torso to her hips. Very slowly, she pushed her undies down, revealing the cheeks of her ass. She thought her backside was too big, not anything sexy at all, but Bran made her think differently. When he touched her there, he took his time. He ran his hands across her curves and made her love them, too.

She kicked the undies out of the way and let her hands run up along her legs and to her hips and up to her hair. She'd put her hair up in a staid bun. That had to go. Pulling the pin that held her hair up, she sighed as it flowed down her back, completely wild. Like her.

She turned and leaned back against the bed. "You wanted my undies off. What do you think you're going to do now?"

His eyes flared. "I'm going to do anything I want."

She was okay with that because all he wanted to do was bring her pleasure. But not yet. "First, you're going to watch. You're going to watch me touch my breasts."

She ran her hands up and cupped her breasts, flicking her thumbs over her nipples. They hardened and she rolled them between her thumbs and forefingers. "I love it when you suck my nipples. When your tongue runs over me. I can feel it right now. The sensation starts in my breast and then it races through me. It makes my pussy warm and wet for you. Only for you."

His jeans were tenting nicely. "Then maybe you should let me have you."

Certainly he would, but she was having fun now. "Not until the show is over."

She backed up, her backside finding the edge of the bed. She eased up. There was a definite art to teasing her man. Bran was watching her, leaning back against the dresser where their clothes were neatly folded and side by side. She loved the fact that her underwear and bras were in a drawer next to Bran's.

Of course, she also loved the fact that he'd done the laundry because she'd been too busy with the caterers. He hadn't even been prompted. He'd thrown them all together and she'd caught him folding them hours later.

Yes, that man deserved a show.

"Do you know what else I love about you, Bran?" She backed up until she felt the headboard of the bed at her back. Very slowly, she let her legs fall apart. It left her pussy on display for Bran's attention. The fact that the air was cool didn't matter now. She was hot.

He stared at her, his hands going to the fly of his jeans. "Tell me."

She let her fingertips brush down her torso, skimming over her breast and the belly that always seemed too curved to be sexy. Not now. She felt her power. Bran had given this to her and she intended to revel in it. For the first time in her life she felt sexy and lovable. And she definitely felt like teasing her man. "You have the most talented tongue in the world, Brandon Lawless. You eat pussy like a god."

"Yes, when something tastes as good as you do, I think you'll find I never get tired of eating it," he growled her way. He shoved his jeans down, dragging his boxers with them and freeing his cock. That was the single most beautiful cock in the world. Long and thick. She loved to watch him, too. He strode to the edge of the bed, towering over her. "Maybe you should let me have a taste now."

"But the show's not over." She circled her clitoris with one well-manicured finger. "I haven't told you all the things I love about you."

"It's okay. I'm lovable. I get that. Now let's fuck."

She was in charge of this game for now. "Not yet. I think you need to hear these things, Bran. And I think you need to stroke yourself. I wouldn't want you to not be ready for me."

His hand gripped his already rock-hard dick. "I'm always ready for you, but please, continue. Tell me what you love about me, but understand, revenge could be very frustrating for you later on."

Carly was absolutely sure it would be. He liked to make it last and he was definitely good at making her beg. She envisioned long hours of being held on the edge before her husband finally relented and sent her over. So she wasn't passing this opportunity by. "I love your cock. I love how hard it is when I'm close and how good I feel when you fill me up."

She watched as he squeezed his own cock. Every line and plane of his body was pure perfection. So masculine and yet still beautiful. She rubbed her clit, imagining her finger was the flat of his tongue the whole time. When he kissed her there, he went all in. His mouth would cover her mound, engulfing her in pure heat and making her feel utterly devoured in the sweetest way possible.

She locked eyes with him and realized this was a race. The minute she came, he would be on her and there would be nothing she could do about it. Intent was right there in his eyes. He would have her over and over again tonight. He was letting her set the pace for now but the minute she went over the edge, he would be back in control again.

And that was where she wanted him to be.

She couldn't make it last. All the dirty talk and the heat in his eyes were sending her over the edge. She pressed down in just the right way and she couldn't help herself. The orgasm bloomed over her skin, making her flush and happy.

He was on her in an instant. Bran moved his big body with predatory grace, climbing on the bed and pressing her legs wide. Before she could take a deep breath, his mouth hovered above her pussy. "This is mine."

She was his and it was all right to belong to him because he damn straight belonged to her. "Yours."

He lowered his head and proved he was every bit as good as she'd said he was. He didn't hold back. He licked and sucked and loved every part of her feminine flesh. His tongue delved inside, fucking her as surely as his cock would. She reached up and held on to the headboard, fighting to stop herself from pushing against him. Every cell in her body was blossoming open, her whole being focused on the way he gave her pleasure. Bran gave her everything he had. He groaned against her, the sound vibrating into her skin.

He speared her with his tongue, his thumb running over her clit.

She shouldn't be feeling this. Not again. Not so soon. Somehow he dragged it out of her. She responded to this man in ways she couldn't imagine. It didn't matter that she'd come a few minutes before. She was right there on the verge again. It shimmered just out of her reach, teasing and taunting her.

When she thought she would go over the edge, he reared back.

"Not without me. Not this time. I'll let you come ten times before I give in tomorrow, but tonight I need you too much." He dragged himself up, showing off that amazingly cut body of his.

She could do nothing but watch him, enjoying the way he moved. Her Bran. He was fucking gorgeous and she couldn't blame other women for looking at him. As long as they didn't touch. He was hers. Only hers.

He settled himself against her core and she let her hands run along the muscles of his torso.

"I'm going to be a possessive girl, Bran," she vowed. He should know what he was getting into.

His eyes blazed with fire as he looked down at her. "I'm yours. I don't want anyone else and you should know I'm never going to want anyone else. You're everything to me. Everything I've been through,

I'm okay with it because it brought me to you. I wish I could have saved Mandy, but other than that, as long as I have you, it was worth it. Do you understand me?"

It was the deepest vow he could make. She definitely understood that. All the pain he'd suffered and he would take it again for her. She wouldn't change a thing. Everything she'd been through brought her to this moment and this man. The right man.

"I love you, Bran. I love everything about you. The good, the bad, the light, and the dark. I want you any way I can have you." She realized that now. She wouldn't have left him.

He kissed her forehead, the moment almost somber. "But I love you, so you get the best of me. I won't give you less. Take me."

He pressed in, his cock pushing inside and filling her in a way she'd never been filled before. Only Bran could do this to her. He was the only man who could make her feel like she was something more than herself when he was inside her.

He lowered himself down, giving her his full weight as he kissed her lips. He held himself still as though wanting more than anything to make the moment last. It didn't matter that they didn't have a piece of paper between them. They would be man and wife. The wedding was simply a celebration of the fact. They'd made the decision tonight.

She was his and he was hers and they would build a family. It was all she could ever want and yet it seemed so simple. She wrapped herself around him because there was nothing simple in the world. The world was harsh and filled with complexity, but if they always had this to come back to they would make it through.

Life was a series of choices that had led her to Bran and her final choice. Him. Always and forever it would be him.

He moved against her, his body making it plain that he was with her. His choice was the same as hers. He would be with her, growing with her, choosing her all of their lives.

His hips thrust, his cock going deep. She pressed up so he went as far as he could go. That was what she wanted. As much connection as possible, as deep as they could go.

He thrust in and pulled out, fighting her hold on him. It was a sweet struggle. She tightened her legs, wanting to keep him close as she pressed up. His pelvis rocked against her clit and her whole body responded, orgasm racing through her again.

She called out his name as he stiffened and came inside her. She loved the feeling as he came, the hot wash rushing through her. One day it would mean something different. It would mean more love for them, but for today, she was content that there was nothing between them.

She fell back, her whole body exhausted.

When he eased down on top of her, she knew the night was far from over.

Bran watched as Carly slipped out of bed. He was a little surprised she could move. He'd taken her three times and it was freaking late as hell. He couldn't help it. He needed to imprint himself on her. The urge was insane. Now that he knew she would stand beside him, he wanted all of the world to know. He wanted a ring on her finger and all the paperwork done.

He had to acknowledge that he might always be looking for a way to cage her in, to keep her.

She strode toward where he'd cast off his shirt long before she'd actually come home. Her backside was a thing of true perfection. He watched as she picked up his shirt and draped it around her.

"You know you don't need that," he said. He rather liked keeping her naked nearly all the time. She didn't need those clothes. She was pretty enough in her own skin. "You can stay the way you are. I don't mind."

Her lips curled up in the sweetest smile. "I didn't close the drapes in the living room."

What did that have to do with anything? "So? Do you think someone's roaming around outside Patricia's mansion at this time of night?"

She was so pretty when she thought he'd said something silly. He knew. She kind of half rolled her eyes and then sighed whenever he said something stupid. "She doesn't turn on the security during her parties, Bran. Too many people coming and going and they'll be doing it for another few hours. If she hadn't been so pissed at me, I would still be at the big house. She tends to use this time of the night to select someone to service her for the evening. I suspect she'd planned on that being you."

He'd been surprised he hadn't had to sneak back in. There was a gate, but it had been left open. Patricia had fought him on that. She'd claimed she didn't want her guests coming into an armed camp. Her laxity had been his salvation. He'd been able to walk right in and make himself at home in the guesthouse he and Carly had been sharing for the week.

"You know that was never going to happen, right?" All week he'd been on edge about how sexual Patricia was around him. It made him anxious and close to violence, and somehow now that he'd made the decision to deal with the situation, it seemed easier to handle. It was as if his whole soul had relaxed knowing he was going to find a way to cope. Not by ignoring the issues, but by dealing with them so he had a future.

That was the true gift his future wife had given him.

Her hands found his hair, smoothing it back. "I know. Are you okay?"

He groaned, but smiled. It would always be there. His past was marked with his vulnerability. Perhaps that was why he couldn't admit it until she'd come along. She made him strong. "I'm good, baby.

From now on any creepy chick who thinks she owns me has to deal with you. I'm sending her right to you."

Carly would always try to protect him.

"You better. I'll freaking take them out. Like I said. I'm a little possessive."

He believed her. He damn straight knew he was. No one was touching his salvation. He let his head rest in his hand. "I'm okay with your possessiveness. I think you'll find I match you, baby. Now, why are you getting out of this bed? There's zero reason to do that until the sun comes up. Drew's sending a car at a god-awful early hour. We've got to be at the airport at eight. We'll be back in Dallas before you know it. I'll have someone pack up your place in Florida and send us everything by next week. Until then, make a list of what you'll need and it will be waiting for us when we land. You don't need clothes for that."

She didn't need clothes for a good long while. Oh, she would say she needed them to get on the plane, but he would have them off her very quickly.

"I thought we were going to Austin."

He sat up. There were a few realities to face. "We should talk about that. The therapist I think I should see is in Dallas. He specializes in PTSD."

She moved toward him, reaching for him. "Then we'll stay in Dallas for a while. That sounds wonderful, Bran. We can find a place on our own and start to think about what we want to do."

He wanted to do her. Again and again. But he knew that eventually he was going to have to share her with the world. "You can start to plan how you want to roll out your show."

She smiled. "Our show."

That was his girl. She wouldn't leave him out. He was going to make a life out of working to make her dreams come true. It was easy since she was his dream. "Our show. Our network. Our brand. We can do anything."

The smile on her face made him believe his words. "As long as we're together."

"So come back to bed." They had a few hours. He would let her sleep. Eventually. When his dick couldn't stand up again, they would sleep.

She laughed, the sound filling the room as she pulled away from him with a broad smile. "No. I need a minute to recover. And I need to talk to you about something I might have done."

He sat up, letting the sheet drop around his waist. She'd thought he'd been leaving her. What had she done? They'd spent hours apart. He had to hope she hadn't done anything permanent. Not that anything was truly permanent. He'd learned that from Riley. He would get his brother on anything she'd signed. He would get her out of it. "What did you do, baby? Did Patricia make you sign a new contract?"

She rolled those pretty eyes of hers. "I didn't sign anything. I was always leaving Cain Corp unless Drew needed me to stay."

He was getting her off the battlefield of his brother's war. He wanted them all out. McKay-Taggart could figure out the issues and find the culprits and then they would all sit down and plan how to best bring justice about. They were out of the revenge business. "You're leaving tomorrow. You're quitting without notice. All obstacles have been hurdled. I won't leave you here."

Her nose wrinkled sweetly. Yeah, that was her you're-a-dumbass face. "As if I want to stay. No. I'm going home with you. But I might have committed a crime on my way out the door."

He frowned. "Crime?"

She nodded. "You know how I had to waylay Shelby? I don't know if you heard that or not."

His eyes widened. "Shelby was there? Like, scandal-book Shelby?"

He hadn't been in that loop. He'd only heard what Drew wanted him to hear, hence his violent confrontation with Kenny Jones Jr., who probably was going to sue him. They would deal with that, too.

"Yes," Carly replied. "She showed up and wanted to confront Patricia. I took her into the first room I could. It was the downstairs casual parlor. I've been in that room a hundred times, but Drew saw something I couldn't. Wait here. I'll be right back."

She turned and he watched as she sashayed away.

Damn, that girl was fine. He'd never seen a prettier one forward or backward.

He laid back, letting himself relax. She was his. She was going to stand beside him. He'd listened to her. Carly didn't blame him for what had happened to Mandy. He might always blame himself, but she didn't look at him differently. It gave him the strength to face it.

He'd actually faced a lot tonight when he thought about it. He'd stood up and finally told Drew and Hatch how they'd hurt him. For so long that had seemed like a pussy thing to do, but now he realized it took guts. It took a lot to stand in front of someone and not only speak the truth but be willing to hear theirs. Drew and Hatch had told him how they felt and now they were good.

Fuck. For the first time in so long, they were good.

He needed to see Mia. He needed to stand in front of her and apologize for taking her out into the cold. She wouldn't blame him. He didn't even know if she remembered, but there had been something freeing about saying what had happened. About asking for forgiveness and giving it in return.

Carly had given him that gift.

He'd spent so much time wondering if he was worthy of love. That wasn't the question that had freed him. He should have asked if he was capable of loving. That had been the point of his whole life. Loving Carly had made him a better man. Loving her had made him not alone. Even if she'd denied him tonight, loving her would have elevated him past the animal he'd allowed himself to become.

He'd accepted surviving without truly living.

Never again. He would honor her by honoring life. He would do what it took to heal. And that felt so fucking good.

He sighed and let it sink in. He was going back to Dallas. Where it all began. He'd been born there. In some ways he'd died there. Drew had relocated them all to Austin when he could, as though the city was tainted for them somehow.

But Mia had found Case in Dallas. Now Bran would find this new version of himself there.

Bran 2.0.

There was the sound of scuffling and Bran sat up.

He wasn't sure why, but something made him not call out. It was there on the tip of his tongue to say her name and ask her what the holdup was. He didn't because a chill went down his spine.

They weren't alone. Not anymore.

He wasn't sure how he knew because he didn't hear anything except something sliding along the tile, but he knew damn well someone else was out there with her. Maybe it was all his training with Case, but he rather thought it was years of having to know his surroundings. He'd never been safe. He'd always had to be on his guard.

He moved slowly, not wanting to give away his position. With great efficiency, he slid his legs into his jeans and got ready to move. Despite the fact that they were staying in a guesthouse, it was still a large property. It had three bedrooms and two living areas plus an office. He was fairly certain she'd gone back out to the main living space, the room that was the greatest distance from the master bedroom they shared.

He let his whole body go still, listening for anything, and then he heard it.

"Don't move."

That wasn't said by his Carly. The voice was deep and masculine. It was his cue to get his ass moving.

His heart nearly stopped and he could feel that red mist threaten to overtake him.

He took a deep breath. Carly needed more than a raging animal. She needed him to stay cool and calm if he was going to figure out what was going on.

He moved toward his bag where he'd left the SIG he'd been carrying for weeks. He'd spent a lot of time on the gun range lately. When he'd decided on his cover, he'd gone into training with Case. He'd become very proficient with the weapon.

It felt good in his hand. Somehow it calmed him and reminded him that this wasn't a fight. It was a mission.

"Go and take out the man," a deep voice said.

"If you hurt him I'm not giving you anything," Carly vowed. "You can find it yourself."

He moved down the hall and slipped into the small bathroom, leaving the light off. If this was about her mob debt he swore he was going to take the entire organization down. Carly was still talking, so she was alive. He needed to keep it that way.

"Fine, go and get him and then we'll see if she'll talk."

He waited, listening for the steps that would tell him someone was coming. The hardwoods creaked slightly and he watched through the crack in the door as the man strode toward the bedroom. He was dressed in black, his big body intimidating.

Bran slipped back out and followed their first attacker. He kept close to the wall. Shooting the man wasn't an option. It would be too loud and he wasn't sure how many men were out there. He'd only heard one voice so he hoped it was only two, but he couldn't count on it.

He glanced down at the man's hand. He'd come prepared. His gun had a suppressor attached.

Bran needed that gun. Maybe taking out a few of his men would make DiLuca think again. Of course after Bran was done, there would be no more DiLuca. He hadn't done what he'd needed to do before because they hadn't wanted the police involved. They'd been concentrating on taking down Cain and they'd needed all their focus there. This time around Bran would dedicate his life to ensuring this fucker never came after his wife again.

He moved in and attacked, bringing the grip of his SIG down as hard as he could. He had a good three inches of height on the man and Case had taught him right where to hit. There was a crack and then the asshole fell forward, the bed breaking his fall.

"Hey? Hurry it up," the man in the living room yelled.

"Got him." Bran deepened his voice as he reached down and grabbed the man's gun. Two guns were better than one. He thought briefly about shooting the man in the head and then realized he would have to explain to Carly why he'd shot a helpless man.

Besides, it would be good to have someone to answer a few questions.

"Well, bring him out here," the boss yelled. "This bitch is getting difficult."

Oh, that one wasn't going to survive. He only needed one person to question. He could kill the other one.

Bran moved more quickly now, readying himself to shoot the minute he got the chance. He stopped at the end of the hall. There was a mirror along the wall opposite him. He could see the reality of the situation reflected in it.

Carly was on her knees, a gun to the back of her head. The man who'd attacked her was alone.

"So here's the deal, sweetheart," he said. "You're going to give us what we came for or we'll kill your boyfriend. I assure you my associate already has him and it won't be pretty if you delay us in any way."

Carly took a deep breath and her voice was surprisingly calm when she spoke. "I want to see him first. Then I'll tell you where it is."

Where what was?

He didn't have time for that. The man had a gun to her head and the second asshole wasn't going to stay asleep forever. Luckily the mirror let him know where everyone was and all that training with Case made him confident.

He was in control. He could do this. He wasn't giving in to rage or letting his fear take over. Not when she was on the line. He could feel it threatening to bubble over but he held it together.

Breathe in. Step out. Pivot and aim.

He fired and before the man could turn and see him, there was a hole in his head and he was falling to the ground. A thud shook the floor.

Carly was up and in his arms before he could take another breath. She wrapped herself around him. "I thought they were going to kill you."

He held her for a moment. "We're okay. Get on your phone and call the police. The one in the back isn't dead. I'm going to tie him up and we'll figure out why DiLuca can't take no for an answer."

She stepped back, her hands shaking. "I don't think it was DiLuca. They didn't want money. They wanted something else. They wanted something I stole from Patricia's house."

Before he could say another thing, his shoulder slammed back and he suddenly couldn't breathe. He watched as a look of complete horror fell over Carly's face.

He touched his chest and it was wet. Blood.

His legs wouldn't hold him anymore and he felt Carly trying to put her hands on him.

But the world was getting dim.

The last sight he saw was Carly crying and then he was far away.

# Chapter Nineteen

Carly couldn't breathe. It felt like the world had slowed down, and she prayed she was dreaming because Bran was on the floor with a hole in his chest. He had a hole in his chest and there was blood. So much blood.

Pure panic rushed through her, bringing the world back to full-on raging speed.

She had to do something or Bran would die. He had a bullet in him. A bullet. Where had the bullet come from? It didn't matter because it was there and it had to come out. He was dying and she couldn't move.

She had to get the phone and call the police. An ambulance. He needed an ambulance.

"Don't touch the phone if you don't want to end up like him."

Carly looked up and there was a woman standing in the doorway. She was dressed in black but not like the men who had come before. This woman was stylish. She'd even worn killer heels for the crime spree. The hood to her jacket was up, but Carly could see her face.

She looked delicate, with high cheekbones and stark green eyes. Those eyes were icy cold as she looked down at Bran. "He looks a lot like his father. Not as much as Drew, but the resemblance is there."

She said it with all the emotion of a woman who'd just killed an insect.

Carly moved her body in front of his, trying to protect as much as she could. He was still breathing. It was shallow, but she could feel it. As long as he was alive, there was a chance. She couldn't let him take another bullet. "What do you want, Francine?"

There was only one explanation. The woman in front of her, the woman who had shot Bran was Francine Wells. And she definitely wasn't some elderly woman Patricia had victimized.

Her lips curled up in a slightly amused smile. "Figured that out, did you? You know I had an affair with his father? I'm sure he doesn't. Poor sainted Benedict and his pitiful wife. She was the most pathetic thing. I freed her."

How the hell was she going to get out of this? "What do you want?"

"I want the drive, of course. I want what all of the players in our little game want."

"I don't have it."

"Of course you do. I saw you take it. I assume you haven't had time to turn it over to Andrew yet. You know if his father had half his drive and focus, he could have been an amazing man. I actually admire Drew. He needs to stop poking uselessly into the past. There's nothing but pain for him there. Now, hand over the vase."

"The vase?" The words didn't quite make sense. What did the vase have to do with anything?

Francine sighed. "Why would you steal that piece-of-shit vase if you didn't know that's where Patty hid her burn folder? You know, the one in which we all make a pact to get rid of our problems and make a lot of money in the meantime. Obviously we wouldn't trust one another. We each had a copy of the file to ensure that no one would go to the police. It's not simply about Benedict and Iris. It's all of our sins laid bare. And that's the last one in existence. Once I have it, no one can stop me."

"You killed Steven Castalano," she said, her voice shaking.

"Of course. What no one knows is that I killed Phillip Stratton, too. A bit too much morphine in his IV after I was certain he had destroyed his copy of the file, and I sent him on to his just reward. He got sentimental in his old age. He destroyed it because he knew it would kill his daughter's chances to lead the company. I destroyed Castalano's. Now I'm taking Patty's and we'll be done. I want it now." She pointed the gun right at Carly's forehead.

"You're going to kill us both." She wasn't stupid.

"That's a chance you're going to have to take," she said with a careless shrug. "Or I can put another bullet in the runt there and end his suffering. It might be better for him in the long run."

"I'll tell you where it is." She could feel the cold metal of Bran's gun against her hand. She had to hope he'd taken the safety off because all she was going to be able to do was point and shoot if she got the chance.

"All right, why don't you do that?"

"It's in my purse. It's right behind you. You can see it there." She hadn't been trying to hide it. She'd breezed right out those doors and she hadn't cared at the time that Patricia might catch her. Patricia had been eyeing Case at the time. That wasn't going to happen. She trusted that the younger Taggart could handle her.

Francine backed up, never taking her eyes off Carly.

How long did Bran have?

"Why do you think Patricia kept that vase?" She would say anything to distract the woman, to put off the moment when she was absolutely sure Francine would get rid of all the witnesses.

Francine reached into Carly's bag and her gloved hand brought the vase up. "Patty thought she was in love with Iris Lawless. This is a memento of her lost love and one last bit of proof that stupid bitch ever existed."

She let the vase drop to the floor with a crash that resounded through the room. Carly saw what was left among the shards. A tiny thumb drive.

"We started with paper," Francine said. "When technology caught up, we moved to these, and now I have found all four and I can be free."

"I'm sure Patricia will have something to say about that."

"I killed Patty a few hours ago. She picked the wrong young man from her party, but then I always did know her tastes. I sent him in and he's done his job. One of the bodyguards will find her soon. So I win."

She bent down to grab the drive and Carly took advantage. She brought the gun around and fired, the sound shaking through the room.

"Stupid bitch." Francine fell back, but she was on her feet with one hand on the drive and the other holding her gun up.

Carly fired again, catching her in the arm.

Francine hissed but it didn't stop her. She pulled the trigger and Carly felt fire lick through her body as the bullet found her left arm.

She fell to her knees and then heard the most beautiful sound.

Sirens.

With shaking hands she forced the gun up again.

Francine was at the door. "Unfortunately, you're going to have to be a diversion. Damn it. Tell Lawless to stay away or I'll have to kill them all. Again."

The door slammed shut and Carly's whole body shook. She couldn't stop. Francine could come back. She could come back to kill Bran, and Carly was the only one protecting them.

So she forced her aching body to stay upright, to hold the gun.

When the door came open again, she nearly shot Case.

She slumped down in relief when she realized she wasn't alone anymore.

"We're going to need a bus. Two actually. We've got two down. Gunshot wounds," he was saying.

She reached out and found Bran's hand and hoped wherever they went that they would be together.

## Chapter Twenty

*Three days later*
CEDARS-SINAI MEDICAL CENTER, LOS ANGELES

Bran looked up at Carly and frowned. "I don't want any more Jell-O or liquid anything. I need meat. Get me a side of beef, baby. There's something in it for you."

She rolled those gorgeous eyes and shook her head. "Yes, I can imagine."

Hey, he hadn't gotten shot in the dick. That was working just fine. "Come on. We haven't done it in a hospital before. It could be fun."

His fiancée gave him that look he was coming to know so well. "When the doctor says you can have solid food, I'll be the first one to get it for you. Until then it's clear broth and Jell-O."

"You get to eat real food."

"I didn't have my spleen removed," she reminded him. "And no one had to resection a portion of my lung. I had a flesh wound."

It had been a little more than that. She'd taken a nasty shot to her left arm, but she was already up and moving. According to his brother, Bran had been in surgery for ten hours and they hadn't been sure he would make it.

Still, he was feeling remarkably well for an almost dead man, and it was all because of her.

"Fine, we'll make a deal. I will follow the doctor's every order, but the minute I'm cleared for physical exertion, you're all mine, baby. We're going to Vegas."

Her lips curled up. "No can do. I know what you're trying to do."

"Don't let him talk you into it," Mia said as she strode in the room with a bunch of cheerful-looking flowers. It looked like she wasn't alone. She'd brought her husband with her and Riley and Ellie trailed after them. "He'll say you're going for the sex and food and fun and then he'll get you tipsy and suddenly that white wedding with fifteen bridesmaids turns into you and him and a fake Elvis."

Case was grinning from ear to ear as he followed his wife. "Damn straight, brother. That is the way to do it."

He wasn't trying to be sneaky. He kind of wanted to get a ring on her finger as soon as possible. Especially since there was apparently some crazy chick out there from his father's past who wanted them all dead. "I thought we could pop in and get the deed done. If you would rather have a nice courthouse wedding, we can do that. Riley and Ellie's wedding was lovely."

Riley grimaced. "I wish you hadn't said that."

Ellie frowned. "My wedding was hasty and only to keep me out of jail. While I was happy to stay out of jail, it was not the wedding day I'd dreamed of."

"Yeah, well, it wasn't exactly the wedding night I'd dreamed of, either," Riley replied with a grin. "But we made up for that, and fast."

Ellie was practically glowing as she allowed Riley to haul her close. "Well, you did give me a hell of a honeymoon."

Bran looked up at Carly. "See, we should do that."

"No, someone in this family is having a big old wedding and I don't think it's going to be Drew, so it's gotta be you." She put the flowers with the rest. His whole room was filled with flowers and get-well presents, including one from Ian Taggart, who'd sent him a Kevlar vest with a card that said, *Wear this next time.*

Ellie looked over at Carly. "I agree. It's time this family had a gathering to celebrate something that doesn't end in a gunfight. Besides, I bet Carly's got one of those big books with all kinds of plans about her wedding."

She blushed. "It's not about me. I did a lot of spreads for the magazine on weddings and designs."

He wasn't going to Vegas. "Well, make it fast. Somehow I think when you put your heads together with Mia and Ellie, the three of you can make things happen."

He would take the white wedding in a church with hundreds of people, but he wasn't waiting too long. He was going to make that woman his wife.

There was a brief knock on the door and then Drew walked in, a grim look on his face. He attempted a smile when he saw Bran, but something was going on in his brother's head.

"How is the patient today?" Drew asked.

"Ornery," Carly replied with a smile. "So we're well on the road to recovery."

"My brother is never ornery," Drew disagreed with a shake of his head. "He's usually the easiest-going guy in the world, but he seems to get a little stubborn around you."

Because Carly wouldn't leave him. He knew now that his acceptance of what he was handed couldn't continue. He had to value himself. She'd taught him that. "Or maybe I spent too much time around my big brothers. Speaking of stubborn, how's it going with Shelby?"

Drew's expression went completely blank. "I've told her I changed my mind. She can do the story or not do the story. I won't stop her but I won't help her, either. She's on her own. I told you I would get out. I think it's for the best if what Carly said is right."

Carly had explained that Francine Wells had threatened them all.

Given that it had been Case finding Patricia's body that had led him to check in on Carly, Bran believed her.

She'd also told him that Francine had claimed to have had an affair with his father. He wasn't so sure he believed that.

"I spent a good portion of yesterday with LAPD." Carly settled in the chair beside his bed. "They're going to finish up the sketch I helped them with and then we can get an APB out on her. She won't get away with it and she's not going to be able to hurt us again."

"I've handed everything over to Ian and his crew," Drew explained. "They'll take it from here."

"We'll find her," Case promised.

They talked for a bit and then they left. Mia and Case were heading to dinner with Riley and Ellie, and Drew was heading back to the condo he'd rented for them.

Alone.

He had to hope his brother wouldn't always be alone.

Carly sat back down and put her hand in his. "You know, it might be fun to plan a wedding."

He brought her hand up and kissed it. "Tell me about your dream wedding."

He would be happy to make it come true.

Drew looked out over the gorgeous Pacific sunset. In the distance the pier was lit up, its lights and energy making him wish he was anywhere else. He didn't belong here. He didn't belong in the sun. Somehow in Austin he managed to avoid it altogether. He started his days before the sun came up and ended them long after it had set.

*I'm such a Cali girl. I can't help it. I love the feel of sunshine on my face.*

She'd written that to him not three hours before. He'd sent her an e-mail explaining that he wouldn't be working on the case, but he wouldn't stop her. He'd apologized for his actions. He'd told her if she was ever in Austin, they should have a drink. He'd made some joke about the heat in Texas. He'd been solicitous and explained all the crappy things he'd done to her in the name of protecting his family. He'd offered her dinner in exchange for siccing the feds on her.

She'd texted him back. She didn't mind the heat. Maybe they should get together.

Shit. He was blushing like a freaking fifteen-year-old and thinking about what he should text her next.

Nothing. He should damn well text her nothing. If she ever showed up in Austin, he could take her out, maybe take her to bed and that would be that. He wasn't the kind of guy who sent flirty texts to gorgeous troublesome sexy redheads.

Somewhere along the way she'd gotten to him. She'd made him feel. He didn't want to feel.

Now that Bran was good and Mia and Riley had their own lives, it was time to think about what he wanted to do.

The trouble was he had no fucking idea. Except seeing her. And that was a really bad idea.

The door behind him came open and Hatch stumbled in.

Drew sighed. "Long night?"

Hatch stared at him for a moment. "There are things you don't know. Things I don't want to have to tell you."

So that's why he'd been gone for two days? He'd disappeared after making sure Bran was going to come out of surgery all right. Drew had wondered, but Hatch could be mysterious at times. He'd kind of thought he'd made a breakthrough when he'd apologized to Bran for leaving them all, but it seemed to have sent Hatch right back to the bottom of a bottle.

"Then don't tell me." It was simple in his mind.

Hatch looked older than his years as he slid his body onto the sofa. "You serious about all of this being over?"

He wasn't sure how else to proceed. He'd promised Bran. He'd turned the Francine Wells issue over to McKay-Taggart. He needed to be out and there wasn't much he could do anyway. Patricia Cain had been found dead of a drug overdose. The police were looking for the man she'd been seen walking into her bedroom with, but Drew knew they wouldn't find him. Eventually they would conclude that Patricia had taken the drugs herself and it would be ruled an accident.

Francine apparently was good at hiding her tracks.

"I promised Bran I would be out. I turned everything over to McKay-Taggart yesterday," he explained. "Though I'm supposed to get the police sketch in. Also, I have Adam Miles running through the feed from Carly's camera. I don't think she knew it was still running."

"Did your brother know he made a porno?" Hatch sounded halfway amused.

Drew shook his head. "We're never telling him that. He would want to watch it but Carly would flip out. I haven't watched it for that reason alone. Miles is sending it back to me and deleting it off his system when he's through. Carly would die if she thought it was sitting in the archives at McKay-Taggart. I'll keep it on my system in case we need it. It's only got two angles. The dress was on the floor for a long time and then at some point in their never-ending sexcapades—Miles's words not mine—she hung it on a chair. He got a couple of images of Francine but he has to clean them up. He's sending them over later tonight."

Hatch went silent again.

"Is this about what Carly said? Or finding the portrait of my mother at Patricia's?" It was no secret that Hatch had been in love with his mother. He believed Hatch when he said nothing had ever happened between the two of them. He also thought Hatch mourned her to this day.

Hatch sat back with a sigh. "Things are more complex than they seem to a kid. You can mess up and still be a good dad."

Ah. "So he did have an affair with Francine."

"Yes," Hatch admitted. "It had been going on for about a year when he died. He told me your mother had turned cold on him. That they'd been fighting a lot and I didn't know everything. He talked about getting a divorce. Do you have any idea how I wish he had?"

Because that might have saved his mother's life. His phone vibrated in his pocket. "It doesn't matter anymore. I made a promise to Bran and I'm going to keep it. I told him I wouldn't go after Francine myself."

He glanced down at the screen. There it was. The police sketch. He couldn't look at it on his phone. He stood up and moved to his laptop.

"I can't get that portrait out of my head, Drew. There's something wrong with it," Hatch said.

"Well, you know Carly claims Francine said Patricia was in love with my mother." It had been a rough few days. He'd known no marriage was ideal. He was older than his siblings. He did remember some of the fights his parents had. He could remember his mother telling his father that being a wife and mother had taken everything from her.

It had been late one night and he hadn't been able to sleep. He could still remember how cold she'd sounded. So far from his mother. She'd talked about how she had a law degree but his father never listened to her.

Drew tried to push the thoughts out of his head. He didn't have the file and it had probably been trashed. McKay-Taggart was good but they couldn't fix what had been destroyed.

*So do what your brothers and sister did and move on. Be a man. Ask Shelby out. Ask her out and see where things go.*

"Then why kill her?" Hatch brought him back to the subject at hand. "If Patty loved her, why kill her?"

"The money, of course." It looked like Miles had come through, too. There was an e-mail from him with three attachments. He'd apparently managed to get three good shots of her.

While the police sketch was loading on his laptop, he used his tablet to pull up the pictures from Miles.

"I don't like Patricia having that portrait in her house. Iris never sat for a damn portrait. And she looks older than she did," Hatch complained. "It's like she aged her. Like she was still alive."

A cold chill ran down Drew's spine as the picture came up.

There was the woman who had attacked Carly and nearly killed Bran.

Again.

What was wrong with his eyes? The screen had blurred. He had to wipe his eyes to get it to come into focus and then his stomach turned.

He would know those eyes anywhere. Emerald green eyes and the camera caught a wisp of shiny, black hair. Like Bran's.

Hatch gasped behind him. "What the hell is that?"

He was pointing at the laptop screen. The composite sketch had come through. Carly had captured her perfectly, from her elegant nose to her high cheekbones. They'd joked that if she hadn't gone to law school she could have been a model.

"That's my mother."

Hatch shook his head. "No."

"That's Iris Lawless." He wouldn't call her mother again. Not after what she'd done.

Hatch fell to his knees.

But Drew stood taller, the betrayal hardening him in a way he hadn't been before.

He'd promised Bran he wouldn't go after Francine Wells. He'd said nothing about Iris Lawless.

It was time to teach his mother what he'd learned in her absence.

THE STORY CONTINUES
IN THE NEXT LAWLESS NOVEL

*Revenge*

COMING SOON FROM BERKLEY.
TURN THE PAGE FOR A SNEAK PEEK . . .

T his is a mistake."

Like he hadn't heard that before. Andrew Lawless turned to his business partner and tried to remember that Bill Hatchard was simply worried and rightly so. Drew was worried, too. It was precisely why he'd decided on the course of action he was about to take. He turned back to look out of his office windows. All of Austin was laid out before him, the lights of the buildings around him beginning to turn on as the sun set over the Colorado River. He could remember the first time he'd looked out these windows ten years before. It had been the first time he'd felt truly successful and he'd known everything he'd worked for would finally come to fruition. He'd known as he stared out that he would find the three people responsible for his parents' deaths.

If only there hadn't turned out to be a fourth . . .

"I explained all of this to you. I told you I wasn't sharing the information with anyone." He glanced at the clock. Only another half hour to wait. He'd set the meeting for after work in order to keep things quiet. Perhaps he should have set the meeting at his house, but he didn't want any gossip in case he got turned down. He also never knew when his brothers or sister and their spouses would show up. All of his siblings were getting ready to celebrate Riley and Ellie's marriage with a blowout reception he was hosting. It was still a few weeks away, but apparently receptions took as long to plan as a damn wedding. Nevertheless, he didn't want to tip off his siblings, until his plan was firmly in place.

He could hear Hatch moving, knew exactly where he would go. There was the sound of a cork popping open. Naturally Hatch went for the expensive Scotch. But then the man was a pro. "You're wrong about this."

"So you've said." About a million times since that terrible night when they'd discovered who the real villain was.

"Fine." Hatch's tone was short. "Explain this to me."

How did he get Hatch to understand? He turned and looked to the man who had been his mentor his entire adult life. "Mia's pregnant."

That should suffice. It made sense to Drew. Mia was pregnant and that meant he kept his mouth shut.

Hatch frowned. "What does that have to do with anything? That was inevitable the way she goes at it with that cowboy of hers. A pregnancy makes things worse. Now she's even more vulnerable."

Hatch wasn't a sunny-side-of-life person, but then neither was Drew.

"Yes, she is, but I suspect she'll be safe enough. She's going to try her hand at fiction instead of wandering the globe looking for trouble." His sister was a reporter and a ball of chaos. Rather like the woman he was about to meet. "Case and the rest of the Taggarts will look out for her."

"And the Taggarts would be invaluable in finding our target," Hatch insisted.

McKay-Taggart was the premiere security and investigative company in the country. Drew knew he wouldn't have taken down Steven Castalano and Patricia Cain without them. But he couldn't hire them for this job and Mia was the reason why. He couldn't ask family to put up walls, to risk relationships for his revenge.

"Do you know what Mia said to me when she told me she was having a baby?"

"Hopefully she said do everything in your power to ensure no one kills me or my baby because there's a psychotic bitch running around out there who wants to do just that," Hatch insisted. "If she didn't say that, then she missed the point."

"She told me she wished our mother was here. She told me she wished she could hold our mom's hand and ask for her advice. She cried because her mother is dead." It had ripped his heart out, watching his sister cry like that. He couldn't explain to her that the mother she longed for was alive and well and had killed at least five people.

The mother she missed had tried to kill them all.

Hatch took a place beside him, holding out one of two crystal tumblers with two fingers of the Scotch he'd paid dearly for. "You don't want Mia to know that Iris is alive and posing as Francine Wells. I get that. It's no reason to cut out Taggart."

"Ian Taggart would feel the need to tell his brother." It was why he hadn't already brought the man in. "He would tell Case and inevitably Case would tell his wife and Mia would find out. Once Mia knows, she'll start to research Iris herself."

He couldn't bring himself to call that woman *mother*. Not ever again.

"So tell her not to."

"Have you met my sister?"

Hatch knocked back his Scotch in one long swallow before turning dark eyes on Drew. "You can't allow Iris to walk around like nothing happened."

"I have no intention of doing that, but she was quite clear when it came to her instructions to Carly. She told us to back off or she would finish what she started all those years ago." When she'd murdered their father and his apparent mistress, then locked all the doors and set the house on fire with her four children inside.

Was it any wonder he didn't want to tell Mia the truth? She needed to think about her child. Riley and Bran needed to concentrate on the future and their partners. His family needed to move on.

It was his job and his alone to deal with their mother.

He'd promised them they would be free after they'd taken down Stratton, Castalano, and Cain. He meant to honor that promise. He would handle Iris Lawless on his own.

"Do you honestly believe she'll leave them alone?"

He had to. "She has for years. Twenty, to be precise. She could have murdered us at any time. We were in foster care. No one would have stepped up to protect us. If she didn't take us out when we were vulnerable, I don't see why she would bother now that we aren't. I believe she'll leave Mia alone for the simple fact that she married into a vengeful barbarian hoard."

That actually got a chuckle out of Hatch. "All right, I can buy that. I'm going to assume she's done her homework. If there was one thing Iris always was it was smart as hell."

Too bad she was also a sociopath. "She won't want to start a war with the Taggarts. She can't win that one."

"But you think she can beat you?"

"I don't intend to announce the fact that we're involved in a skirmish at all," he replied. "I've ensured that there are no records of that sketch in the police file. I've also investigated the police computer systems. There were no attempts to hack in before I scrubbed the file."

"But after?"

"I almost missed it," he admitted. "It was subtle, but someone downloaded the report made the night of Patricia Cain's overdose."

"She was murdered." Hatch could definitely state the obvious at times.

"I know that. You know that. The police in LA are calling it an accidental overdose."

Hatch shook his head. "Why won't they investigate?"

"Because I don't want them to. Because I wrote a large check to ensure that they don't." Oh, it wasn't anything so gauche as a bribe. It had been the offer of a man grateful to the police for keeping his brother out of the limelight surrounding America's most famous style maker's rather scandalous death. It wasn't something the Los Angeles PD didn't see often. Famous people overdosed. It happened. They'd been happy to ensure Bran's name had been kept out of the press and to quickly close the investigation. The tabloids had gone insane for a few days and then the reporters had moved on to different scandals.

All except one. And he intended to take care of her tonight.

Hatch swore under his breath. "I wondered about that. So if you're not going to allow her to get away with it and you're not going to use the police or your McKay-Taggart resources, I assume you're going to do this all by yourself."

"Not at all. I'm hiring an investigator, but one whom I can control." One whom he also wanted to get into bed with, but then that was all a part of his control plan.

"Another agency?"

"No, an individual." There was a reason he hadn't gone over this with Hatch, but if all went well in a few hours he would know anyway. There was zero chance of Hatch buying the story he was going to sell to his siblings. Riley and Bran and Mia looked at the world through the eyes of idiots in love. Drew was okay with that. He wanted them to stay that way. It was good for them, but it made them tend to see everything with rose-colored glasses.

The glass through which Hatch saw the world had turned pitch black a long time ago.

"So you hired a private investigator? I hope he's also a bodyguard."

"I intend to ensure that she's discreet."

Hatch went still beside him. "She? You hired a female PI?"

"She's actually a reporter, but she's a brilliant investigator." After all, Shelby had realized something was seriously wrong with his parents' case long before Drew had. She'd requested medical records, started digging in a way that led him to believe she knew something she wasn't telling her best friend, Carly. He'd stopped her at every turn, but only because he meant to control this investigation.

Shelby Gates would be allowed the keys to the kingdom, provided she was willing to sign the agreement he'd had drawn up.

Then he would have her and he would enjoy himself for as long as it lasted. Until the moment that she realized he was a manipulative asshole and walked away from him.

It was what women did.

"Tell me it isn't that redhead from LA. The one you got a hard-on around every time she walked in the damn room." Hatch didn't wait to sigh impatiently or for confirmation. "Damn it, Andrew, I thought I taught you not to think with your dick."

Hatch had taught him many things. And then there had been the lessons Drew hadn't needed. Like how to ruthlessly proceed forward, only protecting the things and people he held closest to his heart, the ones he'd been tasked to protect on that terrible night twenty years before. From the moment he'd felt the heat of the fire against his skin, seen his father's body and not been able to get to him, he'd known that he was responsible for his siblings. He'd done a piss-poor job at times, but this move was all about protecting them.

"Shelby can get into places I can't. She's also innocuous. Most people don't see past her chest and hips and all that hair to the ambitious woman inside." He intended to use that ambition against her. He would manipulate her with it. And reward her. She wouldn't get the prize she sought, but he intended to give her something conciliatory. He would give her what she wanted, not merely what he'd promised. "Once I teach her how to be perfectly discreet, she'll attract no attention to our family."

"So you're sending her out there like a sacrificial lamb," Hatch mused as though the idea didn't actually bother him. "She'll send you information, but if Iris comes after someone, it won't be our family."

He didn't correct Hatch about it being their family. Hatch was very much a member of the Lawless clan. The boozy, obnoxious, brilliant uncle who fucked up but was always loyal. Hatch had been loyal to Benedict and that fealty had switched to Drew when he'd come of age. Once Drew had sobered Hatch up, he'd proven to still have the business acumen he'd shown when he'd run his father's company. Hatch had applied it to 4L and they'd gone the distance. A few billion dollars later and they were still on top of the world.

And still had unfinished business.

"I don't intend to get the girl killed."

"But you're willing to put her in danger. You saw what happened to the last few people who even hinted at getting in Iris's way."

Yes, he'd heard what the woman had told Carly. As Bran had lain there bleeding, Carly had listened to a recitation of Francine Wells's crimes. Of course Carly hadn't realized she'd actually been talking to Iris Lawless, but she knew the woman who'd stood before her had poisoned Phillip Stratton before he could potentially tell all, killed Steven Castalano in his hospital bed the day before he was scheduled to talk to police, and sent someone in to murder Patricia Cain.

He was well aware of the risks his black widow mother posed. "Better her than my siblings, and she'll agree. She'll do whatever it takes."

"How can you be sure of that?"

"Because I've done a study on her. Because I've researched her." He knew all her data by heart, but he was intrigued at getting to know the real Shelby Gates. He wanted to see the woman inside the warrior goddess. She was so fierce and single-minded.

Did she fuck like she lived? Would she be a wildcat in bed, or sweet and soft after a man had given her everything he had? Would she curl up next to her lover and let him take care of her, let him adore her? Could he soften her with sex, with affection? Could he soften her so much that at the end she would consider forgiving him?

"So you think this woman is going to do your bidding because you offer her cash?"

"Cash is the last thing I would offer her."

"All right. What are you offering her?"

"I'm offering her the story of a lifetime."

Hatch frowned his way. "I'm confused, Drew. First you say you're going to hide everything so Mia and the others never have to know what Iris has done. Now you're turning it into a best seller."

"I'll give her the story. I'll even let her write it."

"But you won't let her publish it. You manipulative bastard. You're going to let her put her neck on the line and then take it all away from her. Damn, Drew. That's cold. And it could work. You have her quietly find what you need. No one ever has to know you're involved at all."

"I thought about playing it that way, but I can't. I need to be able to keep an eye on her until I'm sure I have all the research. I can't risk letting her tell this story. I'll stick close to her and when the time is right, I'll take her notes, her research, and everything else." He didn't like how tight his tie suddenly felt. "And I'll offer her something else. I'll get her any job in the world she could possibly want. She wants to work for the *New York Times*, I'll make it happen. She needs cash to set herself up as a freelance reporter, consider me her personal bankroll."

"And if all she wants is what you offered her in the first place?"

He shook his head. "She'll be reasonable in the end. She'll see that I can't allow my family secrets out in the open. It would hurt my siblings."

"So you're going to leave things the way they are? You're going to let everyone believe Benedict killed your mother and himself?"

"I don't know, damn it." He forced himself to calm down. He was never out of control. Cool. Calm. That was the only way he managed to get anything done. "Like I said, the situation is rather fluid at the moment. What I need to do is figure out exactly where Iris is and what she's been doing for twenty years. My brothers and sister know our father was a victim. That might have to be enough."

"And if she's living it up somewhere? What are you going to do? Are you going to ruin her life? You think that will solve your problem?"

"No. I will admit that I intended to make Castalano and Cain hurt. I have only one thing I want to do to Iris." He felt himself go infinitely cold. This was the real reason why he couldn't bring his siblings in. He knew how this ended. "I'm going to make sure she can never hurt us again. One way or another."

This was his burden. His responsibility. He had owed his father one last duty and then he would be done.

"All right. If you need anything, I'll stand by you," Hatch said, crossing the room and getting himself another drink. "How do you intend to keep an eye on her? Tell me you're not going to stalk her, because that can get nasty. Also, you would have to explain to your siblings why you've suddenly become fascinated with a woman who annoyed the hell out of you last month."

"I'm going to be her boyfriend."

Hatch sputtered. It was good to know his mentor could still be shocked. "What?"

"Part of the contract is that her cover for this assignment is as my girlfriend. It won't surprise anyone. Bran and Riley saw right through my reasonable annoyance to the illogical biological reaction I have around that woman. And Mia and Carly tried to set me up with her. I'll simply explain that the last time I was in Los Angeles, I asked her out to dinner and we began seeing each other. I'll be able to keep a close eye on her."

"I knew you were thinking with your dick."

Luckily his dick was a strategic thinker. He sat down and sipped the Scotch. It was oaky, with a hint of caramel and smoke. Would

Shelby like Scotch? Or would he have to stock his suite with frilly white wines and fruity drinks? His housekeeper was going to have fun with this assignment.

He sat back as Hatch went over all the ways Drew's penis would bring them down. Twenty more minutes and the game would begin.

One thing it definitely wouldn't be was boring.

**Lexi Blake** is the *New York Times* bestselling author of *Ruthless*, the debut novel in the Lawless series, as well as the Masters and Mercenaries series, including *Master No*, *You Only Love Twice*, and *A View to a Thrill*. She is also coauthor with Shayla Black of the Perfect Gentlemen series, including *Big Easy Temptation* and *Seduction in Session*, and the Masters of Ménage series, including *Their Virgin Mistress* and *Their Virgin Secretary*.